Dedication

For Anne & Barry K

"What's past is prologue"
Shakespeare *The Tempest* 2, 1

Palimpsest*: a manuscript or piece of writing material on which later writing has been superimposed on effaced earlier writing; something reused or altered but still bearing visible traces of its earlier form*

The Palimpsest Murders

Reed Stirling

Print ISBNs
Amazon print 9780228626268
Ingram Spark 9780228626275
Barnes & Noble 9780228626282

BWL Publishing Inc.

Books we love to write ...
Authors around the world.

http://bwlpublishing.ca

Copyright 2023 by Reed Stirling
Cover art by Michelle Lee

All rights reserved. Without limiting the rights under copyright reserved above, no part of this publication may be reproduced, stored in or introduced into a retrieval system, or transmitted, in any form, or by any means (electronic, mechanical, photocopying, recording, or otherwise) without the prior written permission of both the copyright owner and the publisher of this book.

Table of Contents

Prologue

Day one: check-in on the *Iphigenia,* our Boat & Bike home for the week, was at one PM.

Day seven: at seven-thirty AM, the body of one of our group was discovered floating in the oily turbidity between the stern of the boat and the concrete quay, hawser lines creating a contorted web of fixed lines above the macabre still-live. We were all taken aback, all shocked, incredulous, some decidedly reduced to tears.

A lot of water had passed under a lot of bridges between the two events and much consideration was required before definite links could be confirmed and conclusions arrived at with any certainty, the findings of Belgian police authorities on all accounts notwithstanding. We touring cyclists were all party to it, meeting on board, socializing in gabfests or biking along the scenic byways and stopping to comment on the windmills and historic sites, and, significantly, we all had our takes on everyone, the victim included.

"Fitting entrance to the portals of Styx," one erudite observer opined with an unobstructed view of the corpse, but by including that allusion here I'm definitely getting ahead of myself. Way ahead of myself. There was so much more.

Despite positive influences and up-beat attitudes acknowledged by crew and former bike-barge enthusiasts in their published reviews, it came as little surprise, really, given the circumstances – the close quarters, the social and physical dynamics of getting along with complete strangers given to peddling their own versions of truth, and the unavoidable witnessing of not-so-hidden intimacy. And, obviously, evident with the passing of the days, the not-so-hidden animosity. It was all so convivial at the start, festive and friendly, and for the most part that continued through the week. Conversing proved easy, one topic bouncing off another without restraint. Add into the equation, however, the thrust and parry of family conversation, dispute, dysfunction, and in particular the impassioned discourse of the enraged.

We were a very diverse group. I had to determine in each individual what was real and what was improvised, but more significantly what appeared to be rehearsed in order to influence those watching and listening. It all came down to interpretation. I had a sense of being in a drama involving a cast of thirty, including captain, crew, and chef, all playing the part asked of them and wearing the mask the part required. Seemingly, I was working with a soundtrack of varied voices always having to alter the tone of one to take in the other, and not coming to any definite understanding of what the script demanded of me. How did an initially easy-going group get drawn beyond their control into an appalling nightmare that began with a body bashed and then inexplicably trashed in the drink? And that, indeed, was just the beginning.

Many obvious questions were asked, but few answers truly satisfied collective curiosity. Why in the canal? Why two coins for the ferryman? Was the embossed jug, both admired and derided, merely symbolic? Who among the cyclists was hateful and motivated enough to kill? Observation invited contrarian points of view. Well dramatized in all of this was the implication that "blood will have blood," a theme, I confess, that my predetermined scheduling restricted me in understanding completely at first and therefore my apprehension of all that went down those last two days was unavoidably limited. My extended sojourn led me into an ancient world where sifting through the sands of time was as much an art form as a scientific discipline, bringing truth to light the objective of both. Given what was known and what inevitably was impossible to know, I'll present as complete a picture as time and place and imagination make plausible.

Amsterdam

The *Iphigenia,* a long, elegant lady clad in black proudly flying the Dutch flag, was formerly a costal freight-carrying vessel that had recently been converted to a touring barge suited for cruising inland waterways. I'd read all about it on the Boat & Bike website. She was moored at a busy quay no more than a convenient few blocks from my hotel in central Amsterdam. Across the waterway from the *Iphigenia* was the Nemo Science Museum, rising out of the depths like the hull of a great ship.

Joost Goossens at the reception desk welcomed me onboard. Other guests were signing in and being directed to their quarters. Sander Flinck led me down to my cabin, Starboard 8. With a sweeping hand over the twin beds, he said that accommodation on the *Iphigenia* was mostly double. I knew that, of course, and explained briefly why I was alone. Sander seemed interested in my story but not overly so, and with polite acknowledgement, he left me to settle in, having handed over a key. Sander had a nose like a Frans Hals character and broken veins in his ruddy face. There was ample history there, there had to be. He was a very large man with very large hands, the kind of imposing individual you would not want to disagree with, as some eventually would, about the paucity of hot water in your accommodation or how tired the towels seemed.

I set down my bag in a tidy little sitting area and accessed my private space: comfortable bed, en-suite with clean washroom facilities, a flat screen television, climate control equipment and a porthole offering a view of the outside world. What more? A safe for my innumerable worldly possessions. I locked up and headed out, secure in the knowledge I had nothing to lose except face when cycling in the company of strangers along the Lowland byways and when, if promises held true, my breath would be taken away.

A tall young woman laden with an impressive camera and wearing a colourful scarf came down the stairs as I turned to go up. I gave way, and thought it necessary, since we'd likely be neighbours, to introduce myself.

"Hello, Geoff Canter!" she responded, "Call me Vanessa. And this is my mate, Lucy, struggling with her professional wherewithal behind me."

"Canadian, eh?" Lucy said and grinned when I nodded agreement. Perceptive of her, I thought, and I hadn't doffed my cap or pardoned myself for no good reason as a lot of us do. She paused momentarily, securing her laptop and tote bag, let out a sigh, then followed Vanessa. Small earrings adorned her right ear like a miniscule silver chain of connections.

"It's along here, so it is," Vanessa called out, betraying an Irish accent. "Come through."

"Brilliant," Lucy said, disappearing like her mate into Starboard 10.

Frank Veridis spotted me on the upper deck before I spotted him. It must have been the Leafs ball cap I wore with more self-consciousness than pride, a suitable sun protector for my balding head, clement weather having been forecasted for most of the week. He beckoned me over to his table.

"Habs fan, ab initio," he said and then introduced himself. I reciprocated: name, place of birth with its obligated team allegiances, and then prolonged but unnecessary rationalizations for recent playoff losses. And so our friendship began by way of a home-spun historical hockey rivalry.

With less than an hour before the *Iphigenia* set out, signing-in was now in full-swing. More guests started appearing on the upper deck, some vying for favourable positions to take everything in. Among her companions, stylish in the light and colourful apparel that the excursion would suggest for their generation on such a sunny afternoon, one young woman stood out because she was dressed entirely in black, and that included black fingernails and black lips. Nouveau Gothic? I didn't really think so. Too sophisticated.

"And the cry is 'Still they come!'" Veridis said, and then raising his voice added for my benefit, "From *Macbeth*, you know, Shakespeare's drama about the murderous usurper who eventually had to pay the piper."

"Right," I said, vaguely remembering the plot, "the murderous usurper." I was beginning to wonder if the man sitting opposite me with a sardonic grin on his face was having me on. We continued conversing over the celebratory surround-sound building up, he occasionally sipping from a bottle of water and me without a drink but too lazy to get up and go get one. Eventually I would. For both of us, a cordial of renowned international respectability.

Frank Veridis had, it struck me initially, a Sigmund Freudish appearance and could have passed for that go-to guy you know, the most informed in your circle of acquaintances, the one you'd consult on any number of concerns and not just on what was required of you at this stage in your life to remain as slim as he. He wore a neatly trimmed grey beard, his ponytail was shoulder length, and he looked at you with intense, sparkling, grey-green eyes. What I eventually noticed about his casual attire, which included a faded denim bucket hat with a pinkish-red maple leaf centered over the brow, was the sensible shoes he had on. He certainly appeared to be in good physical shape for his age, which I judged to be somewhere in the seventies.

"Alone, are you?" he got around to asking.

"My wife Penny was unable to accompany me. Very unfortunate because she arranged everything for this holiday adventure, even going so far as to order online expensive cycling underwear for both of us, padded, as you may know, and two extremely portable travel bags in complementary colours."

Veridis' mouth curved into a smile that gave over to an amused sort of snort.

"Penny injured her leg cycling," I went on, "and hasn't quite recovered. An unleashed black brute was the culprit, a mongrel with blood in its eyes. Big confrontation with the dog's owner, a brute in his own right. It almost came to blows. A real bastard."

"I know the type. They're everywhere. They love to antagonize."

"Not only that, Penny's widowed mother, given to endless histrionic lament, is in need of care after taking a fall and sustaining serious head injury. She'd been played just prior to that by a telephone scammer who somehow had detailed knowledge of all her finances. She'd been victimized by dark forces. As to Penny and me, we'd definitely hoped to venture beyond cycling in the Lowlands. So, yes, I'm alone but determined to carry on as planned. After Bruges, it's Paris and then Greece where I hope to connect with my son David, an archaeology student."

"Excellent," Veridis said. "I'm a widower living alone in a townhouse on Île des Soeurs and coping well enough to proclaim that life is still good despite all the rot, including, of course, embarrassing internal gasses that spontaneously release. And, of course, the deflation of my beloved Habs."

Here, given the topic of conversation, I explained my intention to be on the Champs Élysées on the twenty-third of July to watch the finish of the Tour de France. Original family plans included several days in Paris and then time with David when his course work was completed. Penny coordinated dates, accommodations, every detail of travel.

"Unfortunate indeed, Geoff. The best laid plans, and all that. Did you know that a single family could reserve one of the many refurbished touring barges and have it all to themselves."

"A large, extended family, I expect."

"That would be logical enough, unless prestige is the motivation."

"To tell you the truth, Frank, I know of no such grand family."

At two PM precisely, the *Iphigenia* pushed out from the quay and headed south out of Amsterdam down the wide canal that connects marine traffic with the Lek River. We were on our way, launched by anticipation into who knew what. Veridis spoke of Amsterdam as a city of historical and economic significance, of its artistic and architectural achievements over the centuries, of its politic intrigues, and of how its citizens suffered immensely during World War II. Neighbours turned treacherous in the face of Nazis oppression. Blood was spilled. Families broke murderously apart. An uncle of his, injured here, was numbered among many Canadian heroes beloved of the Dutch population.

I referred to the city as an enchanting place. Still. Painted cumulous skies, seventeenth century galleons, and smiling cavaliers, these my childhood reveries perpetuated by reference material found among Penny's collection of art books and catalogues and most recently by a few hours spent in the Rijksmuseum. Fascination also lay in the fact there were so many bikes in the city, all sorts of bikes, delivery bikes, family bikes carrying three kids loaded down with gear, sturdier bikes with greater carrying capacity, electric bikes, and tricycles of every design and intent. Not to forget repurposed bikes collected out of murky canal waters by municipal workers.

"Victims of failed amphibian experimentation," Veridis opined and snorted again. Then he added, "Bikes and canals. Yes, that's it."

"Speaking of victimhood, Frank. On making my way over to enter Rembrandt House yesterday, I was knocked down by a veiled woman riding an Urban Dart, one of those elongated bikes with cargo capacity up front. She didn't stop. My fault, of course, due to the fact that I failed to look both ways before crossing the cycling lanes. Shaken I was, and somewhat ashamed because of my obvious inattention. A bystander helped me get up and get oriented. The upshot of the incident is knowing for certain that tumbling 'head over heels' can be taken literally, though the expression is usually understood as a metaphorical exaggeration."

"I take your point and can add to the certainty. My room in the Amsterdam hotel that I booked into was called the Chet Baker room. Chet Baker was a renowned jazz trumpeter whose rise and fall identify absolutely the vicissitudes of life. He was addicted to heroin and that may have been the reason why, in the spring of 1988, his body was found on the pavement by the entrance to the hotel. There is no definitive explanation for his fall from that second story window, a window I had occasion to look out often during my stay there. So, yes indeed, exaggeration will not necessarily render intelligible a man's fall from grace, fatal or not."

"Right, right. Tragic."

"Indeed, it was."

"Have you noticed, Frank, how Amsterdam edifices seem to have faces, some sad in aspect, some quizzical, some gay, some with lascivious curled lips puckered with expectation, some with features fading in the twilight?"

"Now you are exaggerating, Geoff," Veridis said, shaking his head slightly. "But I take your meaning. Adroit, if not over the top metaphorically."

"Factor into the architectural equation an immense cruise ship dumping thousands of visitors plodding along the streets and canals of the city."

"That too, my friend. It's Amsterdam."

At this juncture, Vanessa and Lucy appeared and greeted me by name as they made their way toward the bow of the *Iphigenia*. Vanessa's camera loomed large about her breast and Lucy had a cellphone in her hand. Animated discussion appeared to mark their activity.

"The young women of your acquaintance appear to be quite focused."

"That they are, Frank. Brits. Well one is. The tall one is Irish, I think."

Over the time before and after the departure of the *Iphigenia*, conversation between Frank Veridis and me ranged: other Amsterdam attractions including the red light district, Brexit, Covid-19 and the protocols authorities put in place, not all of them acceptable at home to all affected by them. We also got into film editing, electric versus traditional pedal bikes, the cost of new housing, Putin's invasion of Ukraine and its aftermath which would reflect greatly on the cost of new housing.

The canal we were cruising southward on seemed endlessly busy. It was treed on both banks for the longest stretch with occasional cyclists on adjacent pathways rolling along in pursuit of one another. We encountered a constant flow of barges and tankers heading northward washing up wakes that the *Iphigenia* plied through with the slightest of rolls. Trains along the east shore raced into or out of Amsterdam in seeming competition with freeway traffic that became increasingly apparent as we hummed through urban areas like Breukelen.

Other guests would appear on the deck, watch the passing scenery with fingers pointing hither and thither, engage with other passengers — I observed Vanessa and Lucy among them doing just that with the black clad young woman that I'd eventually get to know as Alexsis Troyes — then retreat to the interior lounge where the bar was open. I was thinking of heading there myself, which is exactly what I did, and then returned to the sun deck, hands full.

Veridis raised a sceptical eyebrow when we heard a short stocky man, smart phone in hand, say to the woman with him, "Over here, Babe, GPS says we're somewhere near Utrecht." Though he immediately reminded me of a French bulldog as far as stature goes, the most striking thing about the fellow's appearance other than the confusion of tattoos on his calves was the flocculent tonsure that highlighted a ruddy complexion. We'd get to know the couple as Mitchell Monk, who was brash and literally in your face, and Aimée Reeves, who was slender and bouncy and generally cheery, both of Milwaukee, Wisconsin, USA.

Two middle-aged women appeared and stood vacantly before us, cups of tea in their clutches. As smooth as good Vermouth, which we were now consuming in moderation, Veridis introduced me and then himself and then asked the women to join us, which they did, carefully placing their cups on the table and sliding in on the seats available. And so, sitting in a curious little circle we got to know about Olivia Nunn, English and fiftyish with short cropped grey hair and puffin cheeks, and Melinda Mancipal, about the same age, also English, with an engaging and encouraging smile, and about what motivated them to get onboard the bike-barge excursion. They both seemed physically capable, or at least as capable as I believed myself to be at the time.

"I was hesitant about coming on this adventure, wasn't I?" Olivia stated somewhat apologetically, looking from Veridis to me and then to Melinda, who was still smiling. I couldn't help but notice a blue tinge on the tips of Melinda's hair, which was short and visibly well managed. "But Mel, here, convinced me to join her, didn't she? The signs weren't right, you see. Nothing aligned. Portents were dark."

"You'll survive," Veridis assured her, tapping her hand gently. A silver patterned ring adorned her middle finger.

"Sorry?"

Olivia was hard of hearing, we discovered right away, hence the need to repeat or turn up the volume of a remark directed her way. Hearing aides were evident in stylish subtlety tucked in beneath her grey hair.

Melinda explained, "Mister Veridis said that you'd survive despite premonitions. Who dares, wins, remember."

"Spoken true to form, love," Olivia said in response. "Mel's an Aries and manifests all the traits typical of the species. I'm a Libra. And you, gentlemen?"

"I'm sure these nice blokes would willingly accommodate your immediate need to know, Liv, but why not just let observation serve your curiosity? Over the week, like. And then draw your own conclusions, yeah? Sound agreeable?"

"That idea portends well," Veridis said.

Right from the start, it struck me that Melinda Mancipal, whom the rest of us in time got to call Mel, was a very accommodating person, an endearing sort, solicitous of a friend's needs and well-being. That impression, revised somewhat, would last pretty much to the final leave-taking. Then again, when the bright exchanges and cheerful cordiality of the early going turned darker, I did on occasion question her motivation. Was she really as affable as she seemed? She had a way of saying things that cut right to the quick.

"Consider," Olivia began again after taking a sip of her tea, "that for several days we, virtual strangers all of us from all parts, will be connecting. Like right now. Or as we cycle along the bike paths sharing our impressions of this and that. Just imagine the sights and our reactions. Photo, anyone? Mind where you go there! Or engage each other of an evening in the different town venues that lie along our route. Or just watching the waters flow along the canals and rivers, under the stars even. All of us from different backgrounds and professions, and, as I take a quick glance around the deck, different nationalities, all linked by common interests, historical, cultural, and the like."

"But connected more palpably," Melinda added not in the least overriding the poetic rendering or accuracy of what had been described as a kind of cosy togetherness, "right, connected by an interest in cycling. Physical exertion of any kind, good for the head, yeah?"

Veridis commented without perceptible irony: "I appreciate your enthusiasm, Olivia. Grand expectations, good for the head as well."

That got an agreeable nod from a smiling Melinda.

"We cycle to work daily," Olivia said. "In Cambridge."

"Outstanding, ladies," I said, more than slightly impressed. I had to hold back from clapping my hands.

Olivia's face transformed itself into an unabashed expression of joy, which was most pleasing to see. Her eyes, watering slightly, sparkled. She seemed to have overcome her doubtful premonition about being on the *Iphigenia*. She reminded me of a grade school teacher I very much liked many years ago, whose dramatic affectation had students like me enthralled when she held forth on a topic like the glories of nature or how ancient Greek gods influenced human behaviour or, for that matter, the amazing dikes and windmills of the Netherlands.

Faces always intrigued me, and how they are all the same in general aspect — one forehead, smooth or wrinkled, two eyes, many colours, one nose, two nostrils, one mouth, two lips, one tongue, often forked, one chin, sometimes double, and so on — but so different on a personal level. It was all about how nature in its genetic manifestations arranged these individual parts that bespoke a family's or a society's definition of and response to perceived beauty or perceived wickedness. Naturally enough, twins, and their like, presented specific challenges. Growing up, I had personal experience of two identical sisters that delighted in confusing me. Innocent laughter at my expense, but laughter nonetheless, though fondly recalled later in life, motivated me, once pubescence had established itself convincingly on my behalf, to delve into the structure of the human head (about which my local barber had much to say regarding directions received from some clients for a certain hair style but because of the shape of the head in question, its odd-ball peculiarities in particular, he could not finesse his endeavour with anything like aesthetic assurance so he charged them what he called a cut rate). In time, I went on to explore eventual employment possibilities in psychology, biology, genetics, but settled on a career in filmmaking when I met my artsy-fartsy wife, Penny, who dissuaded me with good humour from continued attendance in a phrenology seminar. Cov-19 blunted my life-long fascination with faces somewhat, inadvertently directing my attention to the effectiveness, size, and style of the mask worn by any individual I might be dealing with face to face (so to speak). And a person's eyes, of course, their colour, their shape, their laughter or regret, but mostly what they refused to reveal. Voice was another matter of great interest.

As I watched and listened to Olivia speak, Melinda as well, I could not help but be intrigued by how they said what they had to say and the expressions they drew upon to articulate a serious thought or an off-the-cuff observation. Over the course of our time together, I would find them pleasing company, although Melinda Mancipal proved to be more of a mystery with her ever present, mostly pleasant smile, part Mona Lisa and part Cheshire Cat. It presented a challenge to my professional expertise.

By this point in the day, we had sailed past Breukelen. Gliding under bridges of assorted size and architectural design, the Lekkanaaldijk being one, we passed through Utrecht which was spread out on either side of the canal. Eventually we entered the Prinses Beatrixsluizen, a lock giving access to the Lek River and the town of Vianen. Here the *Iphigenia* docked, and bikes were offloaded.

An introduction and orientation meeting in the lounge had been called for 4:00 PM.

"Welcome on board the *Iphigenia*," Joost Goossens began. "Here we provide for guests an adventure that is Triple B. This means Boat, Bike, and Byways. This is the wording of a visitor in the reviews which we have accepted for ourselves. It is good. I am Joost Goossens."

Applause.

Joost then proceeded to introduce the crew that had filed in and formed a line in front of the bar. He began with Captain Diederik Vander Valk, in full uniform standing well over six feet tall. Ex-submariner and now engineer on the *Iphigenia* was Aldert De Vries, whose taciturnity would contrast greatly with the gregarious approach of other crew members. He was wearing a Greek fisherman's hat. Ruddy-faced Sander Flinck, mechanic, general deckhand, and dependable source for local information, was a physical specimen of Herculean proportions. Dirk Anders, from Haarlem, was chef and had served in that capacity on large cruise ships. His Serbian born wife Anna provided kitchen assistance as well as being responsible for housekeeping, and bar and table service. Lastly, Joost provided a bit of information about his experience as tour guide and his pursuits as a student of languages. He told us he was the go-to guy on board the

Iphigenia, "the procurer general." His craggy laugh bordered on a guffaw. Of all the crew, Joost would be the one we had most contact with.

Introductions completed, Joost discussed routes and procedures and the responsibilities of those cyclists riding independent of the group, which he referred to as the platoon (his term for the group of cyclists, a world of difference from the usual connotation of peloton as in the Tour de France). Guests were not required to cycle every day and could remain onboard should they wish. In the evenings, time permitting, guests were at liberty to visit the town or city where the barge was moored. We were all handed our own large overview map and advised that helmets (optional) and panniers would be found in room closets. Bike assignment out on the quay would immediately follow the meeting. Dinner at six PM.

I met Niels Visser, Beppie, his wife, and Pieter, their eight-year-old grandson, when bike fittings were being carried out. It appeared that Joost Goossens and Aldert De Vries knew Visser well and responded to his concerns with polite deference. I found Visser, who conversed with me in near perfect English, to be friendly and affable but in a decidedly reserved sort of way. He was a retired police officer from Amsterdam "now embarked with loved ones on an exotic holiday" as he put it with a noticeable touch of irony. Niels Visser was a very tall lookalike for the actor Henry Fonda, and when occasion caught him conversing with Captain Diederik, they were like two yammering giraffes, all angles and geometrical suggestiveness. The Visser family occupied one of the larger forward cabins.

Visser had his own bike as did Pieter, who entertained, I was informed, ambitions to be on the national cycling team when older. The boy, already all legs, had a crop of curly blond hair, a look of determination, and multiple scrapes on his knees. He'd come well equipped in his multi-coloured riding gear and held his bright orange helmet like a champion as he waited, impatient to be underway, with his road bike bouncing against his thigh. Not the usual scene these days, at home and abroad, kids of all ages with spiked hair, cheek studs, nose rings, and pins who knows where else, who appear in public decked out in get-ups that would horrify Goths and Visigoths. Young Pieter showed promise. He proved to be a quick study, given his limitations, in dealing with all the adults onboard. Sign language, that was how Opa Niels and Oma Beppie — they addressed each other in this familial way — communicated with their grandson. And later, when activity on the *Iphigenia* had become near ritual in terms of meals and outings, I would watch others, like Olivia, readily engage the boy. Along the way, I picked up a few meaningful gestures, most significantly those to do with hello and see you and how are things going.

As for Beppie, she had registered to rent an electric bike, but it would become obvious to me that she, like all the Dutch, was very capable on two wheels no matter the terrain nor the style of bicycle. She was open, gregarious, and would frequently give over to saying "Hè hè" which, I learned from Joost, was a Dutch expression meaning something like wow. She spoke excellent English, her accent less noticeable than that of her husband Niels or, for that matter, most of the crew.

The bike I attached myself to like a clown on a recumbent was quite unlike my road bike at home, yet it proved over the ensuing days to be serviceable enough: right size, sufficiently geared, comfortable seat, panniers for carrying all necessities or any totally unnecessary keepsakes accumulated along the way. The light, compact daypack I'd brought would prove useful much later on the trip.

Waiting to depart on our pre-dinner jaunt around Vianen, I quickly presented Frank Veridis to Lucy and Vanessa, both dressed appropriately for the cycling just like everyone else among us who had decided to get acquainted with our assigned bikes at this time. That included two Japanese fellows I had not yet greeted in any formal way.

"Holy hell, man, what's with *this* bike?"

And so, our attendant chitchat was stalled momentarily with Mitchell Monk's abrupt interruption to the easy formation of our little platoon, which I estimated to be about two thirds the total number on the *Iphigenia* guest list. He complained rather vociferously that the bike arranged for Aimée was totally inappropriate. It wasn't electric assist. As his concerns were made known to the bike handlers, he swung his arms about in wide arcs to indicate the company assembled now on the quay, all ready to set out. His voice was deliberate, emphatic, and slow paced. Then his arms gave over to exaggerated hand gestures intended to define the workings of the bike and how it was unfit for Aimée, his words voluminous but surprising polite at the same time. I would over the length of our week adventure see him employ similar antics, specifically hand and finger enhanced articulation like explanatory footnotes to a complicated text, while talking loudly to Beppie and Niels Visser, the Captain and crew (the cook specifically), and the Japanese, and, as would be expected, any one else encountered along the route who didn't speak English exactly as he did or who did not respond as expected.

"The guy's at least half-way to learning," Veridis pointed out with amused satisfaction as we waited and watched, "how to communicate with the young fellow. Very handy."

Ironically, I learned early in my dealings with young Pieter Visser the signing for BS, or more appropriately, total BS. Mitchell Monk struck me during the delay as the kind of guy at a golf tournament you hear shouting 'Get in the hole!' when some renowned competitor like Woody Lyons is teeing off on a par five. Total BS.

"We met that bloke earlier coming out of his cabin, bitching about something," Lucy said. With one hand on the handlebars and thumb and fingers of the other hand fluttering open and closed in imitation of blab-blab-blabbing, Lucy went on, "Going all yappy gob like that. Totally daft."

"Why is it," Vanessa added, "that some people behave as though all foreigners are either deaf or lack basic understanding of ordinary things? Gormless eejit, so he is."

Before setting out for the short excursion around Vianen to test the rightness of our bikes, Joost Goossens requested one of us ride as sweep. I volunteered for the job among the gathered assortment of the unwilling, but just for this once I vowed silently despite the cheers I received.

Riding single file was safest. That became apparent almost immediately. Chatting while cycling seemed like the social thing to do but it wasn't easy given the nature of some of the routes. Besides, pedaling and talking simultaneously with someone beside you didn't exactly make for traffic and road awareness. The combination just didn't come with the territory.

I had not cycled much in the previous months due to the big project I needed to complete before the hiatus, nor had I exercised much in preparation, Penny's predicament notwithstanding. So, an unexpected but acceptable surprise was that I laboured less than I anticipated to keep up from my position at the rear of the group. And so we proceeded in and around Vianen, keeping a slower pace through the central core. Ahead of me was Veridis and ahead of him Lucy and Vanessa. Lucy perky but steady and Vanessa in her casually elegant orange and pink scarf streaming behind her that I judge short enough not to get caught in the wheels. Veridis would express considerable interest in Lucy and Vanessa as "being totally with it for people of their generation" and I supposed they found his interest a compliment.

Up front and following along behind Joost was Mitchell Monk, Aimée Reeves on his rear wheel. By the sculpture of an immense dark horse on the main drag, Aimée slalomed awkwardly across the cobble stones but remained in control of her bike until a guy in a hoodie on a cargo bike loaded with wooden crates crossed swiftly ahead of her. She bailed in a mostly dignified fashion but hit the pavement with a series of yelps that was followed by a chorus of abuse from Monk who then had no choice but to circle back around those following and come to her aid. Aimée had sustained no visible injury as in scraped knees, bloodied elbows, or bumps to the head. She got back on her bike having retrieved her helmet, spinning ever so slightly, from the front hooves of the imposing horse.

"A narrow miss," I heard Vanessa say to Veridis, slowing down. Having pumped rhythmically to this point, she allowed herself an easy glide, her long legs at rest. She waved a hand out over her handlebars to indicate Aimée's predicament.

"Punning there, are you, Vanessa?" Veridis asked. "She's svelte to a fault, that young lady. And lucky."

Vanessa replied, "I can't abide that fellow's reaction. Disgusting." She grabbed her camera out of the pannier to take photos. One of Aimée quite recovered and cycling off around the square in pursuit of Monk, one of the horse, and one of Frank Veridis and me astride our bikes watching the goings-on.

Within an hour we had made it back to the *Iphigenia* without further incident. In other words, no broken bones, no blood on the cobblestones, and no additional impulse to call Mitchell Monk an asshole. Beyond the immediate activity around the barge, I noticed how the evening sky was setting up for a spectacular display of colour.

While washing up in my cabin, I decided how best to convey to my wife at home the events of the day and any observations worthy of note. Penny knew from all the research she'd done what the *Iphigenia* looked like so no need of a photograph there. My tablet and smart phone, both with functional cameras, would serve me well enough as far as pics of towns and windmills were concerned, waterways and tulip displays as well. On the other hand, right from the start Vanessa offered to forward to any who wanted them the photos she'd take. I did. It was something during our association that I came to rely on for my own records rather than my sloppy, off-the-cuff snapshots.

On the whole, what I hoped to establish was an accurate account of the week's activities to send home, not just one of beautiful scenes and well-served meals, but one with drama involving a variety of personalities that would shade in the human-interest side of things and contribute dynamically to the unfolding of scheduled events. The propensity to do so? Years of working with film scripts likely. In this regard, Mitchell Monk would serve as convincing antagonist or persona non grata amongst those whose acquaintances I had already made, with Aimée Reeves the perfect ingénue. As for a protagonist, Frank Veridis came immediately to mind, a persona grata for sure. On second thought, I decided he would be a very complex character to portray honestly or decisively or indeed convincingly. So, while towelling off and searching in the mirror for the blemishes that I knew were lurking there, I decided to protagonize myself. If you can antagonise, I theorized, why can't you protagonize?

Ironic, all that fanciful rumination in view of what would actually come to pass onboard the well-appointed, near-luxurious *Iphigenia*. How dark things emerge out of the shadows of one's past, both fascinating and horrifying at once.

The common space inside the *Iphigenia*, consisting of dining areas, bar, and lounge, was very warm and welcoming. Though narrow, it was spacious enough to seem airy. Light poured in through large windows (which I refrain from calling portholes). The bar, best described as horseshoe, with four accommodating high stools and a settee across from it, was located in the middle of the common area, the stairs to the cabins immediately adjacent. On both port and starboard sides of the room, tables had been elaborately set for the evening meal, one large enough to seat twelve, another suitable for eight or ten, the other table set for six. Against the bulkhead, aft, separating the galley from what was accessible to guests stood sideboards with bright silver bowls and coffee service paraphernalia. Towards the bow of the barge, a set of low tables with comfortable chairs served as lounge.

At six PM we assembled in the dining area. Seating at the various tables was assigned by room numbers or by family or group association. I was not the first of the returned cyclists to appear. Niels Visser and family already occupied one of the smaller tables in the company of the two Japanese guests I'd seen earlier. I learned from Joost that there was to have been a slightly larger Japanese contingent but the Putin invasion of Ukraine and concerns over Covid-19 and its legacy of complications limited the number actually showing up and signing on. The more outgoing of the two was Oshi Hashimoto and the other, who had even better English and knew how to sign, was Takashi Matsumoto. Both looked to be in good shape physically although Oshi was more muscular and had several ugly scars on his left forearm. The two men became known familiarly for the week as Kash and Hash. Lucy started with the monikers, which the fellows apparently got a laugh out of, and the rest of us carried on with the practice. Who knows what names they devised for any of us and there would be occasion enough to come up with pejorative tags no matter the language used. Kash was engaged with young Pieter. For some imaginative reason beyond the stereotype, Pieter was doing the Ninja warrior thing with Kash, who would complete the silent carving of the air and the chop-chop with "Hah!" Their comical little mime would carry on for the duration whenever the two met.

When Olivia and Melinda arrived on the scene and acknowledged all at the Visser table, Hash and Kash got up. The restrained head nodding rather than the more formal bowing led me to believe that they had met the women from Cambridge already. Then Vanessa and Lucy came up the stairs and offered a general hello to everyone, including members of the staff waiting in attendance. Frank Veridis appeared immediately after that and, looking about purposefully, suggested that those of us still standing about smiling expectantly at each other get seated. This we did, voicing vacuous comments while needlessly reintroducing ourselves. I was well on my way to collecting and filing names and personalities for my home-bound narrative of the Triple B adventure.

Mitchell Monk and Aimée Reeves appeared and hesitated about where to sit until Aimée pointed out the card on our table with their room number on it.

"Join us," I said, indicating two empty chairs.

"Reserved for you two," Melinda said somewhat agreeably and smiled.

Mitchell Monk and Aimée Reeves seated themselves, Aimée opposite Lucy, and Mitchell, his cellphone placed strategically next to the cutlery, opposite Vanessa. As they introduced themselves around the table, I detected weird looks passing between Vanessa and Lucy, frowns more than sneers. Ambivalent acceptance? Better with us than not, I figured, otherwise loud and gesticulated talk would likely have resulted had Monk been placed with Hash and Kash and the Vissers. On the other hand, Mitch could readily join in the Ninja warrior thing with Pieter and Kash but would obviously not be too silent about it. He would in effect add considerably to what Veridis would describe as muted din. Not to be endured.

Aimée asked, "What's with the name *Iphigenia* for a boat? Anyone? Mitch is clueless."

In point of fact, I'd thought to inquire of Joost about why the barge had been christened *Iphigenia*, but didn't, accepting the lazy possibility that it had been so named by the owner in memory of some wealthy dowager aunt who had bankrolled the conversion to a floating hotel. Frank Veridis thought it possibly connected with the mythological character whose tragic fate ensured that the Greek fleet could successfully sail to do battle in Troy. A blessing or a curse, he couldn't say. Lucy Hunter said she'd inquire, but we never heard back from her on that point.

When Melinda asked Lucy what she did for a living and why she was here, Lucy revealed that she was a London-based investigative reporter escaping for a fortnight the madding drive to uncover truth.

Lucy's real name, Vanessa then informed us, was Lois Lucille Hunter, but she liked calling her Lucy. Everyone called her Lucy. As for herself, she hailed from Galway. Her family name was O'Keefe but as a professional photographer she signed off as Vanessa De La Croix. She and Lucy often worked together and so periodically took time off together. "We're over the moon about this *Iphigenia* holiday," Lucy chimed in. "Very posh."

"Now tell us a bit about you, Frank," Lucy said. "We'll try to keep up."

"I've been retired for a number of years after a varied career. Developer, business entrepreneur, part-time academic, landlord, very diversified. Also involved myself in many fields of inquiry beyond the mundane. Remained physically active despite the depredations of aging that could plunge one into the morass of sedentary solitude if not challenged. Still an aspiring golfer finding it difficult now to shoot his age.”

“From what Frank’s told me earlier,” I added, “he’s still an avid cyclist. Makes sense, given where we all have chosen to be at this time.”

“Indeed, there are hundreds of kilometres of bikeways in and around Montreal,” Frank went on. “Well used, except in winter. But attitudes are changing. Cycling here under the circumstances described in the ads should be less challenging.”

“Unless there occurs an unforeseeable crash,” Lucy observed. “Like earlier, right? The law of unintended consequences, as the pundits like to say, despite all our good intentions. Commendable nonetheless, Frank, your efforts.”

“For an old man,” Frank said and grinned playfully.

“Very inspiring,” Lucy picked up again in response, “and I’m sure we all concur. Now you, Geoff, what about you?”

I contributed a little biographical info, more to do with my family and cycling interests than about my career in film editing. Then Olivia and Melinda briefly explained their work in Cambridge and how excited they were about cycling to Bruges.

More revealing, if not more inciting, was the arrival in the dining room of the guests that became known as the Conrad Steele Corps (Mitchell Monk’s term which we all adapted and shortened to Conrad Corps), a collected family unit, eight in number, with indisputably disparate parts. Their appearance became an immediate source of disparaging prattle at our table, idle speculation for the most part with the occasional fact thrown in by those purportedly in the know, like Melinda, or from someone like Mitchell Monk who’d had personal contact with Conrad Steele, the apparent overseer of the group. On my way to securing my bike earlier, I'd seen a middle-aged couple in the lounge having drinks, Virgil and Helen Troyes as it turned out, in the company of the three young women I'd observed earlier on deck, Alexsis and Isla, who were sisters, and Candace. Making the acquaintance of all in the Conrad Corps would take some time but I would definitely do so over the week given my natural curiosity about people and their personal stories. Troyes, I eventually learned, not Steele, was the surname of most of the family. All so intriguing their inclusion on the adventure — adding a totally unexpected human dimension with all its apprehensions to the beautiful landscapes and medieval towns I was daily passing through. It was like a double feature in a theatre, the gratuitously added feature having a complicated plot that you had trouble following. Thus, more names to take into account; more personalities to accommodate; more details to include in my nightly reports to Penny. Others at my table would certainly help fill in the blanks with all sorts of information, all supposedly legit. The Conrad Corps — even Olivia knew more about its members that first evening than I did, and so, surprisingly, did Frank Veridis.

"All toffed up, that lot," Melinda commented when they made their way past the bar to take possession of the long table that obviously had been reserved for them. Like a progression it was, rather than mere entrance and approach. Paying it forward on my part, so to say, and based on later introductions, they were in the order of their arrival at the table: Conrad Steele and on his arm wife Katrina who was called Kat; Virgil and Eleni Troyes, parents of Candace; Alexsis and Isla Troyes, Kat's daughters; and at the rear, Boyd Alexander Steele, who was Conrad's son. Whereas most of us, and that included the Vissers and the two Japanese gentlemen, were casually attired, those lining up at the long table for dinner were decked out in obvious finery, the exception being Alexsis who was still attired entirely in black — black tights, black skirt, black blouse, and as noted earlier, black lips and black fingernails.

Melinda said of Kat in a voice barely audible: "A well-preserved, middle-aged vixen. I can tell by how her eyebrows move. Agitated, yeah? And right now, she's agitated about something."

"Sorry," Olivia said, so Melinda repeated the comment in a manner that compensated for her friend's poor hearing. Olivia nodded and then added with ironic intent, "At least the girl with the brooding countenance is appropriately dressed for the occasion."

Low laughter from around our table.

Oddly, hesitation attended Alexsis and the others of her generation before Conrad Steele, evident head of the table, coaxed the woman on his arm into the chair next to the one he claimed for himself. I was not alone in getting the impression that the young ones were jostling for positions *away* from Conrad Steele, the most obvious one being his son, Boyd Alexander.

"How will they survive in the company of ordinary mortals peddling their arses off in leisurely comfort?" Vanessa asked but got no direct answer. A rhetorical question, surely. There would be many questions, rhetorical and otherwise, when it came to the Conrad Corps.

"Expensive bling," Mitchell Monk said, "like on royalty or football wives." He was referring to Kat's big ring catching the light as she picked up a knife and inspected it. An equally impressive set of rings on the other hand became evident when she pointed the girls to specific chairs across from hers.

At this point, Veridis tried to steer the conversation around to the agenda for the following day. He mentioned that Kinderdijk, a town on our cycling route and a world heritage site, boasted nineteen incredible windmills.

"Have your cameras ready," he advised all at our table, but all at our table would have none of it, or at least not yet.

"What about the head guy over there," Olivia said, "look at the size of *his* ring. Obscene, don't you think?"

By head guy Olivia intended Conrad Steele and a rather conspicuous ring riding high on the middle finger of his left hand. He was pointing to where his son Boyd Alexander, still standing back, should sit, which was right next to him on the left, and pulled back a chair for him as he had for Kat, now sitting on the right.

How large was the ring? Very large. Larger than a grad ring. More like what winners of the Super Bowl or Stanley Cup would receive, only larger and more ostentatious. The rings that Conrad and Kat wore with no obvious concern for comment just seemed to invite comment.

"Big rings, big symbolism, big deal," said Vanessa. "If he wears that when cycling, his bike will constantly be pulling to the left. He'll end up in a canal, so he will. As for *her* survival, well who knows."

Moderate laughter.

The first course was a salad concoction with a tangy sauce. On this occasion, our table was served first, then the Visser, then the Steele. The order would rotate as the week progressed.

"Schoonhoven is known as Silver City," Veridis said. "It's our first stop tomorrow. From what I understand..."

"Let me tell you about my dealings with that there dude," Mitchell Monk broke in impatiently. "Earlier, by the hot tub, when me and Aimée were checking things out. He was yapping to that tall, skinny kid with him and saying that tattoos on the calves of fat women are intended to distract from how unappealing they really are, how ugly. When the kid just shrugged his shoulders, he said — and I'm sure he wanted me and Aimée to hear — tattoos on thick men were even more ridiculous. Just attention seekers. All about insecurity. No way could he have meant Aimée. She has shapely legs and tiny tattoos. What got me was, what did he mean by thick? I felt demeaned, put down for no good reason. 'Want to take it outside?' I wanted to challenge him. And then I realized I was outside and so was he. I let it pass. And a good thing as, I recall, the man wears heavy aftershave. Bottom line, I've always wondered about men dousing themselves with the scent of rose buds."

"That ring of his might have done your face some damage, yeah?" Melinda pointed out. Aimée agreed in her quiet way and proceeded to rub affectionately Monk's tattooed right arm.

"I said to him before moving on that he didn't impress me at all, not at all. If you want to know the truth, that got to him."

"Whasaguytado, eh?" Veridis' slurred utterance came across humorously, an elision laced with sympathetic irony.

"An indelible first impression, yeah?" Melinda said more to Lucy than anyone else at the table, then she turned to me. "What do you think, Geoff?"

I could not offer an immediate response that would have sounded realistic let alone sincere. Had I'd got into it, my comments would probably have verged on caricature. I mumbled what appeared patently obvious about the group at the long table, something like "cosmopolitan" and then stumbled into the privacy of incoherent thought. I looked over to a grinning Veridis, who seemed to be getting a kick out of seeing me balk. He got back to reviewing the itinerary for the next day which involved taking our bikes on a fast ferry known as the waterbus from Alblasserdam to Dordrecht, where the barge would berth for the night. I was grateful for the diversion.

As to Conrad Steele specifically, I saw him on that first occasion as a kind of take-charge guy, an urbane master of ceremonies, so to say, a patriarchal figure totally at ease wearing extravagant duds. None of us, especially Olivia, could hear much of what passed for conversation across at their table. It was all hushed tones. As it was, we could hardly make out what was being said at the Visser table. Nothing but a lot of signing and an occasional "Hah!" from Hash.

I supposed there was an aristocratic element to be appreciated about Conrad Steele and his lady. Stately, perhaps. Or maybe just sophisticated. The same could be said of Eleni and Virgil Troyes. More cosmopolitan than aristocratic the lot of them, which is a fair distinction, although aristocrats need not be denied being sophisticated or cosmopolitan or, for that matter, behave in a quiet yet stately fashion.

On the other hand, my private estimation of Kat, brief though it had to be at the time of the first dinner, was that hers had been reduced to an austere beauty. There was an elegant insufficiency about her not clearly defined for me as yet, although she seemed formidable in more than subtle ways. How she moved, how she manoeuvred, how she motioned those with her to respond to her wishes. More imperious than stately would be the apt description. If anyone at our table had said she'd entered the scene somewhat faceless, I would likely not have disagreed. There certainly was an air of theatricality about her. I said, okay, yes, I see the resemblance when Melinda pointed out that Kat resembled Sophia Loren in her hay day but mirrored the virago. Asked for her opinion of Katrina Steele, Lucy provided a fairly pointed impression that a week on the *Iphigenia* would substantiate to some degree but not entirely; she called her "the bejewelled consort of a prince of commerce, employing all the stratagems of the distraught drama queen."

Our table neglected comment about the sons and daughters in the Conrad Steele cohort. But that would change. That evening they were just part of "an awesome appearance" as Aimée put. At this juncture, we all focused on the delicious pork tender loin that was served with small potatoes and legumes. Most appreciated by all about dinners on the *Iphigenia* was the variety. Portions were respectable and appropriate.

Over the course of the Triple B adventure, meals in common, the diners more than the randomness of breakfasts (where murmurings were heard of how poorly one slept and of indigestion suffered through the night on the part of the gourmands amongst us) would prove to be an invaluable source of information about those in our midst that could not be avoided. These sources were second only to the rides and the stops along the way for bag lunches packed carelessly and secured in panniers. Or in the lounge after the ride or on the deck in the afterglow of recovery from physical exertion. Or of an evening in the lounge or at cafés in any given town and the inevitable chatter that passed there for conversation. All part of what followed in the flow of every day.

But for information, read gossip. We all had our terms for it. Melinda and Olivia would say gossip and tittle-tattle. For Monk and Aimée it was scuttlebutt and dirt. On occasion Veridis would say *bavardage* with a Parisian accent. He would where others wouldn't, which was not surprising in the least. Not surprizing at all was his Dutch rending of *kletspratt*. And then he did surprise us when he came out with the German *kaffeeklatsch* and proceeded to explain at length its etymological relevance to the English equivalent.

On one occasion Veridis explained: "I'm given to delivering soliloquies of great import but only if I have an audience beyond myself. But I could never compete with the sardonic eloquence of Ron James."

I knew the reference but the others with us didn't, so I said Ron James was a gifted Canadian comedian with a penchant for stringing out long elaborate descriptions of a satirical nature. You listen and applaud the wit."

A good listener, that's how early in our relationship Penny described me to my future mother-in-law. Later she added, "when it suits him." As for the *Iphigenia* groups, I'd get to know a little about particular individuals by conversing directly with them, Aimée Reeves, for example, who informed how much into his music Boyd Alexander was — just good natured, friendly curiosity prompting me to do so if only on a superficial level. Others would inadvertently provide additional information: Olivia Nunn, for instance, or Melinda Mancipal who'd been talking to Vanessa De La Croix who'd overheard a conversation between so and so, or Lucy Hunter who had referred to Doctor Google to confirm some notion she was inspired to research.

One glorious evening relaxing with me on the deck — no, it was at Kaai22 in Temse, a café with a view of the Scheldt River where the platoon stopped for a half-hour break — at any rate, Veridis expressed the belief that in talking about others you reveal so much about yourself. True, no secret there. He also believed that so much more lies beyond the public persona, esoteric knowledge, possibly. I agreed again. I definitely kept quiet about certain things in my life, like I really wasn't into other people's dirt, not at all. And yet, what could I do when rubbing shoulders with a bevy of interesting personalities? Intriguing stories invited interest and, inevitably, intrigue. And so it went. Close quarters, close associations, open air, open ears and wagging tongues. Information overload.

"Stand not upon the order of your going, but go at once," Lucy quipped when dessert had been served and the meal was over, and staff were clearing tables and setting them for the morning.

And that's what we did. Frank Veridis and I headed out across the bridge and took a quick romp around the Vianen town square, studied the horse and decided it was modelled on the Belgian, returning to the *Iphigenia* with a nightcap in mind, something local. Sitting and nursing a drink at the bar, which was pretty well ours alone to enjoy, we continued discussing the anticipated highlights of the cruise and the historical sites to be explored, like Bruges, our final destination. In view of what he told me previously about his interest in existential philosophy, I suggested he might enjoy seeing *In Bruges,* a noir film involving two hit men living out life and death themes. He would make every effort to do so, he assured me, and then inquired about my background and involvement in film production. I related how I'd looked into courses offered at universities in the Toronto area but finally decided to pursue a fine arts degree with sound editing a major focus at Concordia in Montreal. Financial considerations, opportunity, and the life of the city itself figured in my decision to leave the home turf. Over the years back on home turf, I'd received a few nominations. It was rewarding, I professed as modestly as I could, to be recognized as professionally capable.

Our discussion of sound editing was petering out when the younger members of the Steele contingent, or rather the Conrad Corps, gathered in the lounge area, Alexsis first and then Isla shortly after that. A moment or two later, Candace appeared and positioned herself contrapposto at the top of the stairs, body weight on one foot, and stood like a classical Greek statue looking as though she were expecting to make contact with some Lowlands version of Pygmalion. Alexsis broke the spell and called her over. Then from out of the shadows of the forward deck, Boyd Alexander emerged. Even in his awkwardness he stood at least a head over Alexsis. They all gathered conspiratorially around one of the low tables, Boyd Alexander's knees sticking out like something only an out-of-sorts Salvador Dali could depict accurately. The women clutched their phones while Boyd Alexander was plugged into a MP3MP3 player or some such device like the one my son had and then abandoned when the girl he was seeing told him it resembled an infantile prosthesis.

"Some foreshadowing closing in on us," Veridis whispered when the group led by Alexsis started emoting. "This is where I take my exit, Geoff. I leave you to it."

Since Alexsis and the other three made no effort to mute their chatter, I made no effort not to eavesdrop. I'd more than likely get to know each one on a more personal level within the week, so my obvious listening in at this point was within the limits of acceptable social behaviour. So I reasoned. I might have reasoned incorrectly. I might even have been too conspicuous in my attempts to be discreet about the good listener I was thought to be. Nonetheless, how they appeared suddenly and stealthily in the lounge and the manner in which they did, single file, was more intriguing to me than what they had to say to each other.

What they had to say to each other left me without the larger context to fully comprehend their reasons for meeting this way. Curiosity sustained my need to remain at the bar and suck meaning out of the remnants of effervescence clinging to my pint jar. I had purpose even if all but Alexsis seemed not to. She was intense, her body language revealing. It was like being in my studio at home working on a sequence of film and trying to eliminate extraneous noises so that the dialogue in the final edit (of my mind) achieve perfect clarity, a purity of emotional outpouring, especially on Alexsis' part. My impression of her would fluctuate rapidly as I listened and watched; she was the lamentable heroine, her countenance one of constant disquiet, out of some dark melodrama where broken hearts prevail as tropes and memes and then it seemed I was observing a twit of a young woman, romantic and stupid, fast-talking and empty headed, and all in fashionable black. Time would prove me absolutely wrong in those simplistic, superficial estimations.

Alexsis faced toward the bar with the lanky Boyd Alexander next to her, which enabled me to see them and hear them clearly enough, especially Boyd Alexander with his very audible adenoidal utterances. Isla and Candace faced them, making what they said less distinguishable. The dialogue I heard, therefore, was much like a one-sided coin that I had to keep flicking with thumb and forefinger to get the head's up.

"Why this here and not the Bahamas?" Alexsis was saying. "Well might you ask that, Candace."

"The yacht is massive," Boyd Alexander said, "we'd all fit." Boyd Alexander had heavy large eyelids and he let them drop at this point as though in explanation. He struck me as somebody who had at one time owned a menagerie of exotic pets.

"I hated the confinement of the yacht and the phony visitations," Alexsis said. "The *Iphigenia* allows you to get about, see things of interest. Historical stuff, not just a bunch of beach hovels. However — "

Either Isla or Candace then made a comment about everybody getting along agreeably.

"So we will here, will we?" Alexsis replied, and then pulled the corners of her mouth down as much as to say, *are you kidding me?* For the first time I noticed plum-brown shadows under her eyes which she closed quickly and then opened again. It was like a sign of emphasis, a visual exclamation point. "I know this for sure," she went on, "this family fantasy was organized by Calvin Kinlaw at Conrad's behest. Kinlaw will be in Bruges when we get there. Chances are Archie Gallant will be with him."

"Who is Calvin Kinlaw?" Either Isla or Candace. Candace probably.

"Big time legal consultant. Been with the family for years."

"What?" from Boyd Alexander.

"He's your father's barrister, Boyd. You might have know that, at least."

"They tell me very little. Less than they do you."

"At least you and your mother get along."

"Sorta. She wasn't totally agreeable about me being on this trip."

"This will be different," Alexsis continued, "the planners thought, this family cycling thing. But it amounts to just another attempt to settle me down, to control me, to shut me up and bring me around. To accept the situation for what it is. Which is bogus, one hundred percent bogus."

"You do complain a lot, Alexsis."

"I've told you over and over again, Isla, it's all about control. You don't know the half of it. You forget how things used to be."

"So what do we do?" from Isla, I believe it was, in a voice tinged with exasperation.

Admittedly, my furtive monitoring of their little tête à tête did not go unnoticed by Alexsis. She had expressive, watchful eyes, no doubt about that. As I pulled myself up to leave — it was time — and nodded self-consciously towards the group in an awkward apology for my imposition on their scene, I noticed how her face had creased briefly into a wry smile which she definitely directed my way. Her knotted brow had relaxed noticeably. I'd have tossed them some bonbons to take the bite out of their discontent, but no, we weren't in Belgium yet and nothing was available on the counter. It struck me as I left the lounge that in dealing with those in her little circle, she was trapped in some desolate, lonely place between supplication and despair.

"So what do we do?" she repeated in mock tones. "What we've always done since, you know. Absolutely nothing. But that could change. Believe me, that could change."

Since *what*? I wondered as I headed down to my cabin.

As I attempted to write the first email to Penny from the *Iphigenia*, the lingering taste of the beer I'd developed a preference for served to remind me just where I was. The Netherlands. HollandPA, I decided, was a font of good taste that left the tongue tingling while fusing that spontaneous sense of wellbeing with an attitude full of gratitude and good intentions. Something like that. The traditional brew was likely to become habitual of an evening either at the lounge bar or under the stars. "Whatever floats your boat" as they said back in TO about one's choice of inspiration or for whatever gets you through the night.

As to tastes and sensations, there was also the dissolute side of being on the barge, a feeling best described as knowingly indulging in something completely new, something self-gratifying that extended beyond the cycling, the exploration, the physical proximity to others and the convivial delectability of shared meals. More, a nudging awareness brought on at that hour, I slowly realized, by the thrum of the diesel engine and its subtle reverberations in the quiet of my personal space, gentle undulations rendering the easy not-so-queasy floating sensation that continued to shimmer in me as the red streaks of twilight faded into the shades of night. During such moments of buoyant self-reliance — like being stoned on good grass — I was consumed by how light and wavelet played together bouncing spots of reflected luminescence across the ceiling of my cabin. Sufficiently into the moment, I took a deep breath, turned away again from the open porthole, and looked to the task at hand.

From me to Penny then, a six-hour difference in time between us: an accurate account in an email (and saved to Notes) so she'd have something to tell her mother about how, on my own by happenchance, I'd be misbehaving. Daily weather reports just to whet the old gal's appetite to be included. "Be accurate, but curb the enthusiasm," Penny cajoled me, a teasing reference about how I can wax poetic about particularly moving experiences. My capability to recall and propensity to expatiate, given the ability of others to be good listeners, were being lovingly mocked at the departure gate. The gift-wrapped journal she handed me I considered unnecessary, accounts of my euphoric trances to be transmitted electronically, if not ironically. Also rejected, on first arriving in Amsterdam, was the idea of using a recording app on my smart phone and downloading any sequence of conversation or talking points of a personal interest to my tablet.

"Take lots of pictures then," Penny called from the other side of the gate, "castles and windmills. But don't overdo the picaresque, dear." I was sure she meant picturesque.

And here, for the most part, I would allow Vanessa De La Croix's generosity to enter the picture. I attached the photo she'd forwarded to me of the group setting out earlier that evening on the Vianen ride: Joost Goossens as guide, the Vissers and the Japanese lads; Mitchell Monk and Aimée Miller; Olivia Nunn and Melinda Mancipal; Lucy Hunter and Vanessa De La Croix; Frank Veridis and me.

I typed in a quick profile of those with whom I had most contact, indicating their alignment in the photograph. I described Mitchell Monk as having great difficulty ingratiating himself to others, although Aimée Reeves was quiet and accepting. The Vissers had thick Dutch accents. Olivia Nunn and Melinda Mancipal were English and easy conversationalists. Lucy Hunter was a pleasant, articulate, informative young woman and the same applied to Vanessa De La Croix who was witty in an acerbic way. My closest ally was Frank Veridis from Montreal, a philosopher type who said that everybody comes aboard with baggage, many in light-weight portable carrier cases and packs, others burdened down with much heavier loads, both emotional and psychological. A rogues gallery, if ever there was one, I added in for humorous effect.

I made mention of the Conrad Corps that inspired the gabfest of questionable cordiality at our dinner table. Some mystique there. Some manifest discontent. Comments about the crew, the wonderful meal, and the excellent service followed next. I closed the account of Day One on the *Iphigenia* with the thought that she'd be missed by me as much as I'd be missed by her — poor me, really enjoying myself on this incredible adventure. I would in future emails layer in all the enthusiasm that my technician's mindfulness was capable of manipulating for her edification. And for the edification of her mother as well.

Covid-19 protocols in Amsterdam and on the *Iphigenia* were quite relaxed. Perhaps authorities here knew something those at home did not.

Vianen to Dordrecht

Breakfasts started at eight o'clock each morning, and ended with guests fixing their takeaway lunches as though engaged in a necessary life-preserving ritual. By eight fifteen all our group were present, coffee happy, and ready to engage.

"So, Vanessa," Veridis said, pulling a croissant into bite-size morsels, "yesterday you said you prefer to call your companion Lucy. Why is that?"

"Why Lucy, is it?" Vanessa responded, picking up a juice glass and holding it to the light. "Her name's Lois L. Hunter, so it is. Lucy, short for Lucille. Lucy sheds light on dark subjects. Her mind is white light. She's brilliant at figuring things out."

"That's quite the compliment, init?" Melinda said and Olivia nodded agreement once the comment was repeated for her. General affirmation followed around the table.

"Vanessa's photographs are brilliant," Lucy said in deferential response. "I depend on her eye to get what I'm after just perfect, don't I?"

"Like what?" Monk wanted to know. He wiped a smudge of butter off his phone and replaced the phone on the table.

"Like the London mansions of the Russian oligarchs, for example," Lucy replied. "I've often been accused of indulging in apophenia, but a lot of the time my hunches prove revealing."

"What does that mean exactly?" Monk again.

"Seeing patterns in unrelated events," Veridis put in, using fluttering fingers to illustrate his explanation. "We're all capable of apophenia if you think about it. Seeing God's visage in the clouds or Christ's in a bowl of hot porridge like in Geoff's there."

"Hardly," said Olivia, incensed. She began to fiddle with her hearing aid.

When Aimée asked how she got started in her particular line of work, Lucy explained that she learned her trade craft with Reporters Without Borders but was now associated with the Bureau of Investigative Journalism and claimed with pride the authorship of a recent report on the destructive results to the planet of the global shipping phenomenon (thousands of containers falling overboard in high seas, pollution in various ports, slave wages, and such like). She'd also published an article about the Russian influence on Brexit. Assignments varied: who, what, when, why. Where could be Stockholm, Chicago, Toronto, or Vienna. Brussels was mostly likely her next stop, or Paris.

"So, the London tabloids, yeah? Your area of expertise?" Melinda said and smiled at Lucy. The scepticism was evident.

"Not at all," Vanessa put in immediately. "It's more than hack work for the scandal sheets, so it is. Has nothing to do with invading personal accounts or eavesdropping on private phones just to get a story and grab the headlines."

"Work for the Bureau of," Lucy said calmly, "not the Murdoch organization. All legit pursuits. And no fabrications."

"From what I understand, serious professional journalism is what Lucy and Vanessa would be about," I interjected. "Human rights, corruption in high places, improving society, and such like."

"Got it," Monk said, playing with a knife as a point of focus. "Now let me tell you a thing or two about the lefties and their published lies. 'Woke rags' (air quotes included) is what we call them."

"Another time, perhaps, Mitch," Veridis said. "You don't mind if we call you Mitch?"

"Works for me," Mitchell Monk said agreeably, then leaned in towards Aimée. "Speaking of bringing things to light, this girl here got herself in the news just before we left. Tell them about it, Babe."

Aimée shook her head demurely.

"It was at a mall," Monk started in, putting his knife aside, "the usual kind of gun play in a mass shooting. Fortunately, there were few deaths. Fortunately, the shooter took it in the head. Aimée witnessed everything. Got interviewed for television and had her picture in the paper. Famous in the neighbourhood and across the nation."

"Fifteen minutes of fame, yeah?" from Melinda.

"Bingo. Me too. Fifteen minutes. I witnessed a hit-and-run incident. It was no accident, believe you me. And not suicide. Murder, in point of fact. An assassination police determined. I provided evidence. Was quoted in the media."

"Gang related?" I asked.

"Or family related as in a Mafioso power play?" Veridis asked.

"Not really determined as far as I know. It was awhile ago and I lost interest."

"In other words, Mitch, the 'hit' part of the hit and run equation is accurate (air quotes included)." Lucy's comment.

"You betcha. So you, Lucy, you famous too or what?"

"Infamous. My craven thoughts wander somewhere between what is absurd and what is obscene."

Vanessa, jokingly: "Lucy has a mentality as complex as a bong!"

"What's a bong?" Aimée asked.

"A device for smoking weed," Monk said, touching the side of his mouth with a finger and audibly sucking in air. "Like a water pipe, Babe. The kids use them."

"Taking the piss, is she?" Melinda jumped in, a knowing smile favouring her question.

"What do you mean, exactly?" Monk asked. "Taking the piss?"

"Having us on. Stringing us a line?"

"Got it. Pass the butter again, would you."

"Not famous," Lucy proceeded to explain. "Infamous, as I said, if the whole story be told. Don't mind my riffing on this one. You could exhaust the lexicon in any attempt to describe the extent of corruption evident in British high society vis à vis Russian oligarchs and their filthy lucre."

"Indeed," Olivia said, nodding her head and then fixing her hearing aide once more. A source of irritation for me but not beyond my ability to conceal.

As Lucy described the specifics of her work and circumstances surrounding the corruption, I noted how very expressive she was, how accurate Vanessa's descriptions fit. Perhaps Lucy's wire rim glasses, obscuring slightly a pretty face with rosy cheeks, were what contributed to the impression of lurking intelligence and attentiveness. She definitely had character. She represented herself exceptionally well.

"Authorities stonewalled real investigations," she continued, "as to who was involved and why. 'Political considerations' was the official retort. British attempts to appease Putin was like Chamberlain appeasing Hitler to attain peace in our time. Ukraine! You all know about that, I take it."

"So you do the research and get to publish what you find. That it?" Monk again, looking up from his phone that had got his attention. "They fight back, don't they, these oligarchs?"

"Naturally. Their usual method of retaliation is poison. A favourite recipe is called heartbreak grass. It's the choice of contracted Russian hit men. And that of other totalitarian state operatives."

"Serviceable as a remedy in domestic quarrels, yeah?" Melinda quipped. Monk guffawed.

As we began preparing our lunch bags from the breakfast offerings — breads, cheeses, cold cuts, fruit, and so on — Lucy went on to describe the flowers that produce the poison known as heartbreak grass, sources in the world, its use in homeopathic remedies, and the physical symptoms if ingested in error or by evil intention; she also related how Arthur Conan Doyle experimented with it. She'd obviously done her research on heartbreak grass.

"Case in point," Vanessa offered in support of Lucy, who was now folding the top of her lunch bag, "is Alexander Perepilichny. He was poisoned because of the assistance he provided Swiss authorities investigating a money laundering scheme by corrupt Russian officials."

"Let's just say I got blacklisted after I wrote up the story."

"Maybe you came down too strongly on the side of righteousness against moral flexibility," Melinda suggested with something less than a sneer. I detected an edge in how she was coming across with Lucy. Looks revealed a great deal.

"How do you know where to go and what to search for?" Olivia asked and received a tap on the arm from Melinda as if to say, good point.

"First, it's afflatus, let's say, then direction from those above me who decide on what matters, then plain hard work. Often, it's just chance."

"What Lucy means," Veridis said looking over to Aimée and then to Monk who were as nonplussed as the rest of us, "is she is subject to something like poetic inspiration or divine impulse and just as often she is the beneficiary of what chance delivers."

"Random luck provided from on high," Lucy added. "The thing is, I don't do sentimental tosh. Relevant shibboleths, often. And in so doing I try to eschew hot-button clichés or fashionable buzz words."

"Well played," Veridis said.

A bemused Monk shook his head and picked up his phone again. Another source of irritation, this addiction to phones, but in Monk's case I had no problem being unable to conceal it. I would wonder about Monk and Aimée and what their relationship was based on. None of my business, of course, and had nothing to do with preparing lunches for our cycling along the waterways really. Just part of the unfolding human drama. Yet, I'd often hear, as did others like Lucy and Melinda, reports of his grousing about Aimée's short comings. Veridis compared the complaints to a subtext for what was seemly social behaviour. In Vanessa's estimation, delivered that very morning as we loaded up our panniers in preparation for setting out from Vianen, Aimée was no more than his 'bint' on the side. Vanessa explained her take this way: "Mitchell Monk benefitted flagrantly from a good social bio in his Tinder Account."

Lucy and Vanessa were dressed in cycling shorts and jerseys of vibrant colours, their manes held sensibly in place with bright yellow scrunchies. Both young women appeared elegant in their high visibility gear but you could not but be amazed by Vanessa's long shapely legs that contrasted with Lucy's which were shorter and more muscular. Both were in high visibility good cheer. Manny of us opted to wear helmets, but not all. I had my Leafs ball cap for when we stopped and Veridis had his bucket hat. And like most, we both had gear suitable for cycling.

Before departing, Joost again requested one of us to volunteer as sweep. I got a lot of hopeful looks, so I relented. The yellow vest I got to wear, Veridis pointed out with some amusement, identified me as a guest cyclist of prestige and influence, even surpassing Conrad Steel in his amazingly colourful sportswear.

Through Vianen again, avoiding the menacing horse, and through the towered gate, slowing up as we manoeuvred across the overpass above De Lek, and then traversing the flats along the Lekdijk, the dike which follows the course of the river towards Schoonhoven, all the cyclists pedaling away between Joost at the front and me at the rear. Veridis was immediately ahead of me, and we exchanged comments when possible. Initial chit-chat picked up the rhythms that our movement on the bikes generated: the efficiency with which Joost organized the platoon that had such disparate elements in it, the promising weather, the physical condition of individuals, his age and mine. However, riding single file proved safer and less awkward all round. Otherwise, it was disparate thoughts and a desultory kind of conversation resulting from friendly patter and irregular pacing. Eventually Veridis pushed up to join Olivia and Melinda, leaving me to follow Lucy and Vanessa who were keeping a sort of gregarious rhythm.

After the better part of an hour, the group proceeded through the Veerpoort arch and after some right-angle turns into narrow streets, we came to a stop in the Schoonhoven central square where, red-faced all of us, we celebrated our first break. Service from the café was applauded because it was not only welcome it was also prompt. Veridis and I sat with Lucy and Vanessa, Monk and Aimée. Melinda and Olivia occupied an adjacent table. Joost had joined the Visser group behind us.

Looking over the scene of our collective respite and with no concern for any ironic undercutting of her own bright apparel, Lucy said, "That man's the godfather in gaudy, god-awful cycling shorts."

Vanessa put it this way: "Your man comes across like an idol of the marquee. Unjustifiably amplified, so he is."

The subject of their consideration, Conrad Steele. He was holding forth at the table some distance from ours. Notably, Kat was not numbered in his klatch of distracted listeners.

After finishing his coffee, Veridis excused himself. He wanted to get a little more information from Joost about the history behind Schoonhoven's title as Silver City.

"The gaffer's keeping up," Lucy said more as a question than a statement of fact.

"I have to work to keep pace with him."

"Not pushing him too hard, then," she continued. "A penetrating guy is Frank Veridis. I mean, he's the intellectual sort that cuts to the chase. Insight with a sharp edge. His observations are as relevant as they are amusing."

I nodded agreement.

"He makes a point rather decidedly, so he does," Vanessa added. "His eyes seem capable of scanning your private thoughts. Intense, sparkling, but not totally off-putting, if you see what I mean."

I saw exactly what she meant and again nodded agreement.

"We wondered, Vanessa and I, after dinner last night, if he were legit, if he were everything he appeared to be."

I'd speculated myself that there was more behind Frank's ironic smile and word play but not wanting to intrude with over-indulged curiosity, I decided to go only with what he revealed of himself. "And so?" I prompted Lucy.

"And so I did some research."

"Did you?" I said, wondering if she deigned to Goggle me for proof of authenticity as well. "It's in your DNA, I suppose, from what you said about your inquiring mind and what it leads you to do. What did you discover?"

Lucy said she'd discovered a great deal because there was a great deal to be discovered. Frank Veridis, her idea of a gaffer, had a PhD in physics and one in evolutionary biology. His real interest, apparently, was philosophy. He'd co-edited a humanist publication for a number of years. He offered criticism and editing assistance in his capacity as literary consultant. Gratis. He was the author of *The Great Unfolding,* a treatise on materialism, existential obligation, and the universal matrix which he called the Mother of all Matrices. Reviews called it a two-handed read, one hand on the book, the other on the dictionary. A YouTube article she'd uncovered, based on a piece originally published in his city paper, defined Veridis as an art collector of some repute; it provided a brief description of the historical mansion he co-owned with a longstanding business partner, one Tommy Scullion, where much of its statuary reflected characters out of the classical past, a pantheon of representative human excess and vindication. The most valued acquisition was an A.Y. Jackson from the Group of Seven, renowned Canadian artists. The refurbished mansion functioned as a venue for any number of events, receptions, conventions, school reunions and the like. When operating as such, it served as a good source of revenue for charitable works. As well as being frank and forthright, Veridis was a philanthropist and benefactor know for his generosity and his wit.

Before too long Joost started to round up the group. Everyone but Kat Steele and Beppie Visser were accounted for. Beppie appeared soon enough, exiting the café where WC facilities had been in constant use since our arrival in the square. But no Kat. Conrad grew more impatient and voiced angry imprecations within hearing distance of all preparing to depart. Impatient in her own right and all in black, Alexsis pedaled purposely down one side of the central commercial block, circled around at the bottom, then came up the other side in as determined a fashion as she could demonstrate, having halted more than once to look into storefront windows.

Still no Kat.

"Self-centered bitch," Melinda said, impatient to get going.

I could see where Melinda and Kat, like Conrad and Monk, would have to keep their distance from each other.

Virgil went searching on foot in one direction, Conrad in a second direction, and Joost in a third. Conrad returned empty-handed, as did Virgil. A smiling Joost eventually led Kat back to her bike and her husband's grim-faced but grand embrace. We could not but hear that she'd spent her time in a silver shop, and what she found there was absolutely delightful — so much choice, so hard to decide — but had trouble arranging for a deliver to the U.S. of an antique vase, embossed with silver. She just had to have it. Katrina Steele, Kat, rings all aglitter, held up the group by a good half hour.

The buzz surrounding Kat's dramatic return to the group was virtually tangible. Lucy said that the French tuck on her cycling jersey was absolutely de trop, over-the-top ridiculous. I didn't get the point and said so. Then Vanessa explained that the half-in, half-out arrangement of one's top, which was now in vogue, had nothing to do with haute couture coming out of Paris (or the recent craze for adopting French bulldogs) but was popularized on an American television series.

Got it. Not apropos.

We departed, finally, making our way back under the Veerpoort arch and along to the quay where we rolled bikes onto a ferry. As the ferry nudged forward, I entertained an impression of Schoonhoven: quaint. Veridis said that he wished he'd had more time to explore it more thoroughly, maybe make a purchase. Then he smiled enigmatically. Olivia asked Beppie how the name of the town was pronounced in Dutch. What we all heard in response was a confusion of scratchy sounds none of us could quite get our throats to cough up.

"Dutch pronunciation is not in the English vocal system," Veridis said authoritatively and got general assent.

Melinda Mancipal commented: "Too bad tour organizers didn't provide our lot with a sheet of subtitles, yeah?"

The ferry landed us on the nether shore of De Lek and here we reformed the platoon and headed south following the course of the river as far as Groot-Ammers. A stretch of four windmills saw the pace slow. Several stops occurred. Innumerable photos were taken.

At one such stop Lucy cycled up beside me. Then Vanessa, having finished with her camera, joined us. Looking over to where Frank Veridis was talking with Alexsis, Lucy said, "There's a darker side to the story we uncovered. It concerned a brutal court battle that sent mafia-associated construction bigwigs to prison. They vowed heavy reprisals against Frank and his business partner, Scullion, who was a developer and builder of some wealth and standing in the community. Opponents take offence regardless of locale. The Cosa Nostra operates everywhere."

"Right. As Frank himself said yesterday as we talked about everything under the sun except that particular issue: 'No matter the matter, there's always a deductible.'"

"I adduced," Lucy continued, "that some sort of corruption was a factor in the case and that the public did not get the goods they'd paid for, be it a government building, a highway overpass, or whatever."

"Exactly," I said, "Such abuse of public funds does happen. Whistleblowers take risks."

"A man as outspoken and direct as Frank Veridis could make enemies anywhere, even in a setting as genial as ours on the *Iphigenia*."

"Like fakery in the art world, so it is," Vanessa decided, "when cons and grifters cash in on forgeries of great works. Like a Rembrandt or a Vermeer."

"Crooks and shysters will always be with us," Lucy added, "that's a given. When it comes to art itself exposing corruption and social evil, Hogarth is your man. My favourite reformer and artist. Geoff, looks like we're heading off again. Saddle up."

We were indeed off again, travelling through lowland areas, passing corn fields and innumerable irrigation trenches. Somewhere near De Donk (I remember noting the road sign) we stopped an hour for lunch where Lucy and Vanessa, munching on sandwiches, picked up on their recent theme and rolled on from there. Visual art and its great practitioners — Caravaggio and the blood-soaked darkness of man's heart, the Renaissance and all its splendour, Leonardo and the brilliance of his artistic and scientific achievement, Rembrandt and the detailed expression of human emotion. I mentioned my wife had a fine arts degree and had made it her life's ambition to educate me in a number of significant areas, particularly in those everyday areas that had nothing at all do with the history of art. I explained why she had not accompanied me on this adventure, adding that we'd hoped to visit our son who was doing archaeological studies in Greece. This adventure, Vanessa opined as she extracted her camera from the pannier, would be like romping daily through history itself. She had a point.

I looked around the scene speculatively, trying to account for each member of our group. As sweep, keeping track of individuals was becoming habitual for me. Lucy followed my movement. Under Joost's encouraging direction we formed our platoon and the pedaling picked up again, cows to the left of us, ducks to the right, and waterways all around. At Edit's Droomijsje, thirty or so minutes later, we stopped for a short break. Some like Isla and Candace bought ice cream that was available from a vendor while most of the group refilled their water jugs. The scenery had not changed much since setting out. Rural. Flat. That was to be expected, of course. And the fine weather was a bonus. Warm and sunny. Like most, I appreciated a break here from the constant pedaling. I took a swig of water and looked about. Some in the group were lying against the grassy incline leading back to the cycling path. Overhead, small contentious clouds were ambling about against the brilliant blue of the afternoon sky.

Veridis nudged my arm and in a somewhat laboured breath observed the following: "Mitchell Monk, tattoos and all, is in need of air as much as I am. He resembles a baleen whale vacuuming in a cloud of krill. Saw him at lunch back there spitting like a hockey player horking his gastric acid on the ice as he skates reluctantly to the penalty box. Absurd, actually, Aimée Reeves on his tail, attempting to pass riders like Conrad Steele."

"Being sweep, I did notice his awkward efforts to overtake."

"Mitchell Monk. Miniature macho man, still competing, I fear, at least in his head, with the Steele paterfamilias. Testosterone in tandem with intemperance."

"Right, right."

"As I heard Joost say to Conrad, 'It's like Mister Monk has been hit by a windmill.'"

"Meaning?"

"Screwy. Nuts."

Veridis' mordant sense of humour became evident yet again when, falling in beside me, he described the Conrad Corps cycling along ahead of him as a rambling *cortège funèbre*. True enough, at one point their bunch in the line had looked like an entourage of sombre attitudes, Conrad and then Kat at the forefront, Alexsis at the rear with Boyd Alexander. I was sure they'd eventually break up into individual entities. Before long they did just that.

From Edit's Droomijsje we followed the well-travelled cycle path along the Groote of Achterwaterschap, all the way into Kinderdijk. Along the way through this popular recreational area with its renowned nineteen windmills, water to the left of us, water to the right, we encountered cyclists, hikers, pedestrians, family groups, tourists, all taking in the sites. I kept all our group ahead of me.

Joost gave us two hours to explore, enjoy the surroundings, have coffee, snack, and in some cases, like mine, recuperate from a hard few hours of cycling. After finding our feet on solid ground again, Vanessa took several group photos, the first of the nineteen windmills in the background. I asked her to forward me a copy. Others did as well before wandering off in pursuit of whatever the time allotted us allowed.

I began adjusting the tension on my front brake when Alexsis approached pushing her bike along like an introduction on wheels you couldn't refuse, kicked the stand into place, then set the lock, ready to engage me. She was decked out in black capris (the peddle pushers of an older generation in the guise of the contemporary) and a loose fitting, faded jersey with a familiar enough logo printed across the front.

"I'm Alexsis Troyes," she said with an emphasis on the surname Troyes. Pointing to her jersey she continued, "Like it says here, I just had to do it. Say hello, you know. You were very deliberate in your efforts not to hear what you were hearing. Amusing, really, but considerate of you."

"Ah, yes, last night. The magnificent yacht. The Caribbean. And... I'm Geoff Canter. Glad to make your acquaintance, Alexsis."

"And decent of you to leave when you did, Geoff, but there was nothing very cloak and dagger about what the four us were discussing."

"Understood. And that's comforting. Though motivated, you seemed overwhelmed by…"

"Family matters. Simply, family matters."

"And your apparent inability to muster… Well, obviously I couldn't say. I left wondering what you meant by 'since' which you left off saying."

"Since the death of our father, Victor Troyes. Conrad Steele over there, leading the family into the café where he will likely erroneously advance his theories to those willing to listen as to why Kinderdijk has been declared a World Heritage Site — that man is my step-father, nothing more."

I took in what she said, then gave a final twist to the break adjustment and tested its tension. I looked over the scene again and saw that the *Iphigenia* platoon had indeed dispersed. Veridis was leading Kash and Hash up to the viewpoint above the café. Still in sight but keeping a sensible pace were Olivia and Melinda in the company of the Vissers. The others in our group? I couldn't say. Here and there. Alexsis took my arm and led me over to the café entrance, offering to treat me to any beverage of my choice. I accepted, requesting a cold, lemon-flavoured Fuze Tea. She pointed me to a table as far away as possible from Conrad's and went to get the beverages.

Good to know that Alexsis Troyes bore no resentment for my having eavesdropped — unwittingly, I reminded myself. She presented the drinks with a sardonic grin. Without hesitation she then identified all the others in the laconic Conrad Corps slumped over drinks, inanimate for the most part, fatigue evident in their faces. Her understanding, probably, was that proximity would lead inevitably to eventual acquaintance if only on a by-name basis. Close quarters on the *Iphigenia*, not to be dismissed, nor group cycling and its breaks, such as the one we were all enjoying. With her finger-pointing and barely audible inflection — incantation, more like — it was as if she had suddenly awakened various characters in a Watteau tableau who had lain inactive in a prolonged state of arrested animation. Or in a state of speculative curiosity, given the collective interest of the *Iphigenia* guests I had already come to be engaged with. She identified her generation first: sister Isla was the brunette, her cousin Candace was the attractive blond, and Boyd Alexander was the longest version of a step-brother imaginable. The other three she identified briefly as mother, aunt and uncle, namely Kat, Virgil and Eleni.

"Very generous of your step-father then, this bike and barge adventure. Triple B, as the organizers call it. A real contrast to the usual family gatherings, I take it."

"Indeed it is. Conrad's largesse is less than you'd care to imagine, however, much less."

I did not pursue that point, not that there was any detectable invitation from Alexsis to do so.

She gave me a winsome smile, her cheeks rosy pink, the effects of recent physical exertion. And those dazzling, watchful, brown eyes of hers that held my interest right from the get-go. She had full, sensuous lips, unadorned by any early morning cosmetic application. Jet black hair hung in a ponytail — it was more of a coil — under a ball hat displaying a company logo that read AEP. She had opted out of wearing a helmet. When she saw me trying to determine what her tiny pendant earrings were all about, she said that they were replicas of the classical comedy and tragedy masks, in silver, and had been in her possession for years. I gave her a nod of appreciation.

"The world is two-faced, Geoff," she said in a raspy voice, the dulcet tones of her previous statements having hardened somewhat. "It's not what it presents itself as, especially where human interaction is involved. Deceit is the lingua franca of, you know, of day-to-day existence."

Alexsis glanced quickly over at the Conrad Corps stirring itself, the moue of annoyance on her face changing gradually to an expression of resentment: knotted brow, angry eyes, a brief curl of the lips.

Did she expect me to respond to or comment on what she had just come out with? Couldn't say. I had no idea how to interpret such an immediate and damning view of life, no matter how articulate. I had no certainty at all as to whether her words were simply a personal take on the symbolism attached to her earrings, comedy and tragedy, or just what? Which side of the stage was she standing on at this point I was at a loss to determine. I balked, amazed at such a dire declaration from a person who from all appearances was still in her twenties. My impression from the previous night, Alexsis Troyes as some romantic heroine full of doubt and disquiet, gave over to one where a mixture of almost palpable sadness and obdurate resistance spoke out from the core of her character, so young, so philosophically dark. In a very real sense, I was impressed with her but also dismayed by her. Can someone be impressed and dismayed at the same time? Then it struck me that she might be carrying on this way for the benefit of a much wider audience than me. An attentive audience she did have, and that definitely included Conrad Steele who was looking over to our little tête à tête as if to question her being where she was, conversing thus with a stranger, a complete unknown, and not where he intended her to be. Hard to read motivation, near or far.

In the pause my hesitation caused, Alexsis filled it with a long sigh of resignation. This she followed with a concerted series of taps on the bottle of Fuze Tea she'd brought over for herself, which may have echoed some tune she had in mind but to my ear it amounted to no more than a mindless distraction. For some crazy reason, the image of a barking pup at the half-open window of an empty car popped up in my imagination, then faded as quickly as it had appeared. I always disliked being a witness to another's unforced embarrassment, and at that point I believed she may have been a little chagrined at how presumptuous she'd been with me, yes, with a middle-aged guy of whom she knew not one iota. For a second or two, I focused on how light played on the rounded surface of the bottle she'd been tapping and then on the ring on her finger that caused the bottle to chime.

"It's a garnet," she said, holding her hand out. "Like the earrings, a gift from my father. Very ordinary, really, as such gems go except for, you know, for the associations."

"Lovely," I said. "Ruby red. Arresting." I noticed the geometric pattern in its silver setting.

"Lovely, yes, but the cruel complacency of what becomes an ordinary, everyday thing. Dad got it for me when we were all in Corfu, you know, the Greek island."

I waited for her to go on. Her voice, tense and tremulous moments before, grew softer, became more soothing in effect as fond remembering replaced what had sounded so negative. She did go on.

"Dad took us to Greece several times when we were young, Isla, my brother Forrest, and me. There was his business side to these get-away vacations, but that did not really interrupt the island hopping all of us enjoyed and the usual touristy things we did, even my mother, Kat. Forrest went mad for the sailing in the Aegean. I fell in love with ancient drama. We attended plays at Herod Atticus and at Epidaurus. Absolutely wonderful even for spoilt kids, the open-air theatres, sitting under the star-filled sky, even the fireflies seemed magical, you know. Didn't understand a word the actors were blurting out, but we knew the story that was unfolding in rather dramatic fashion because Dad always gave us the plot. I remember a play about what happened to legendary figures after the Trojan War. All about justice and revenge. And bloodshed.

"Back home, as a hobby, I enrolled in pottery classes after being totally enthralled with the ancient treasures and artifacts we saw in the various museums Dad had us visit. Produced a lot of ugly pots and jugs."

When she ended her reminiscence and looked at me expectantly, I felt it incumbent of me to tell her my son David had a fascination with all things ancient, particularly Greek mythology and the Homeric heroes.

"That's wonderful, isn't it?"

"I suppose it is. Yes, yes it is. In fact, David's in the Peloponnese right now attaining credits for his degree in archaeology. Fieldwork and all that. Real hands-on stuff in ancient soil. He does me proud. I'll be meeting him there before the month is out."

"A nice family connection. That's great. I'm envious. You know, we had an older sister, Jenny, but she's not with us these days."

"Why's that, Alexsis?"

"She disappeared. Completely."

"That's dramatic," I said, fumbling for the appropriate words to fit into the context that seemed bound to deviate from happy memories of happy families. "I mean, what...What about your brother, Forrest?"

"He disappeared, *got* disappeared, as they say, but not completely. We text each other, Forrest and I, and these days that's the extent of our communication."

At this juncture her phone chimed. It sounded like a bouzouki being plunked. She answered and then said she had to be off and that she'd enjoyed the conversation. She left me with the distinct impression that our conversation was anything but finished.

When Alexsis headed over to join the family, I wandered about taking in what info I could about this site, eventually connecting with Vanessa. She was manipulating something on her camera. I asked about angles and what she sought most in setting up her photographs.

"The right perspective," she explained, photographing the nearest windmill with her wide-angle lens. "I'm thinking of doing a travel article. Well, possibly. Part of the distraction from investigative work. Always need good visuals, so I do."

"Right."

"Geoff, you'll appreciate this recent take." She showed me a photo of Alexsis Troyes and me deep in conversation.

"Interesting perspective," I said, intending a joke.

"Good craic," she retorted.

We ambled over to where Lucy and the Vissers were sitting at a picnic table shaded by overhanging tree limbs. Visser added to the bits of information about the history of Kinderdijk I'd already gleaned from signs and tourist postings. Pieter was circling around, anxious to get going again. Within minutes we'd mounted up and were heading single file to a terminal on De Lek River. Here we loaded our bikes on the waterbus that would take us through the Alblasserdam area to Dordrecht where the *Iphigenia* would be moored and ready to take us onboard.

Alexsis sidled along to me standing by the bikes at the rear of the waterbus and picked up where we left off. She must have caught me studying her while she stood for a time among the women in her family circle. Under the afternoon sun, her olive complexion appeared highlighted in silver much like that of the others chatting with her. Alexsis definitely bore a resemblance to Kat, there was no mistaking them for anything but mother and daughter. The same could be said of Isla, only a little less so because of her upturned nose.

"You know, Geoff, this family adventure of ours does remind me in some ways of when I was younger."

"That would be good, then?"

"In some ways, especially right now, as we float along the waterway. It brings to mind a line I remember from long ago. 'Ferry me across the water, do boatman do!' Always thought it was mysterious. I was glad my eyes were brown, not blue as in what the boatman in the poem said. In high school, I learned it alluded to Charon and the River Styx. Isla, who knows all about literature — she's the poet in the family, always a book of poetry within reach — said it could be interpreted as passing on to the afterlife in Hades."

"On the other hand, Alexsis, from my limited understanding of how all that plays out, there is always the Elysian Fields to be wished for."

"If you're graced. You know, without grievance."

When she asked me if I was graced, I could answer only with a goofy smile and a shrug of the shoulders. As the ferry continued down the channel and we upon it, Alexsis revealed a little more of her story. I reckoned she had by then come to the understanding that I was a good listener, if not always open to contrarian views as in how "life sucks" as much as she thought it did. She must have thought me empathetic, nonetheless. She mentioned gaslighting and how effective it was in perverting truth and believed it led to the creation of a totally false narrative. She pulled out her phone, ran her finger across some aps, and showed me a black and white photograph of her younger self posing with arms akimbo.

"I lasted a week at finishing school in Switzerland," she said, and brushed her screen again. "That's my brother Forrest the day before he left us. Looks like a young Mark Wahlberg, don't you think?"

"Possibly, yes, I see a resemblance. Looks like you a bit. Same eyes, dark."

"We were close, the two of us. Things were, you know, so much simpler then."

Then she pulled up a picture of her father, Victor Troyes, whom she began talking about in very generous terms. In my eager and mostly accepting mind, Victor Troyes immediately took on the heroic proportions that she in a sudden fever of exuberance wished to convince me of. I remarked on family resemblance. Forrest, from the previous showing, was definitely his father's son, the brow, the broad smile, the curly locks. On the other hand, Virgil Troyes, her uncle, it struck me as I studied the photo more closely, was a slightly diminished version of his older brother though just as handsome in chiselled chin sort of way. Consanguinity applied equally to both Alexsis and Isla, specifically the olive skin tone.

Before landing and pulling out bikes from the stands, Alexsis mentioned that at different points and stops along the route this day she had connected with Lucy Hunter and Vanessa De La Croix, very interesting professional women, and then with Olivia Nunn and Melinda Mancipal, who were quite bike savvy, and then at one of the stops or wherever, she exchanged opinions about a lot of things with a very learned, older guy called Frank Veridis. She had to break away from the ordinary, by which she meant family and cousins who were "like a troupe of cubs and brownies following the leader, all wearing similar ball hats." Not her, though. She'd been convinced by Joost, who she thought pleasant and understanding, that the bike and barge holiday was to be as educationally rewarding as it was physically beneficial. Correct on both accounts. She'd make sure of that. Talking to people from different backgrounds was definitely educational. In fact, the whole adventure was starting to feel like a release, like an epiphany. She felt less cursed now than she did before.

Once the waterbus offloaded us, another long single file formed and meandered through scenic parts of Dordrecht. Joost had us stop on the

Nieuwbrug to take photos of the marina that provided shelter for some pretty snookum yachts. We bunched up, crowding the two-way bridge like a herd of sheep, with Joost issuing directions and waving us off to the right. Vanessa booed when Monk took several photographs with his cellphone of a bikini-clad woman down below sunbathing on the deck of her boat. We all clapped when the woman, surprisingly, dove into the somewhat murky water. From there, once the bridge cleared and everyone settled into line ahead of me, it was a quick run with a few sharp turns to the *Iphigenia.*

Sander and Joost set up to load the bikes back in their cradles on deck. Very efficient, it seemed to me, how they worked together. When all seemed right, it wasn't. Joost looked about, then at me with my sweeper's yellow vest in hand and called out that one electric bike was unaccounted for. They narrowed down the missing bike and the missing person to Boyd Alexander Steele. Being the sweep, I felt obligated to say something, but I didn't know what. All I could muster was that I'd check things out with the others. I had not anticipated Boyd Alexander not fitting in with the group, confusion on the bridge or not. Nor had I noticed his peeling off anywhere as the platoon, *Iphigenia* bound, stretched out after rounding tight street corners.

Joost told Conrad, who had come down from the deck more than a little put out by the situation, that Boyd Alexander had requested his own GPS and knew how to use it. He would know how to get back to the *Iphigenia.* All cyclists, Joost added with considerable emphasis, had a map and the day's itinerary sheet to consult if needed. Conrad nodded. I really could not read his reaction, but it looked like he was sufficiently assured by what Joost said, and he rejoined family members up on the deck.

I got very little out of the others when I asked around later about how Boyd Alexander might have slipped out of sight. Olivia's comment "that the young chap seemed in despair of keeping up" was of little comfort and did little to explain how I had failed in my responsibilities as sweep.

Aimée Reeves was signing with Pieter Visser when, with a long amber beer in my grip, I approached them by the hot tub. Her knowing how to communicate with him that way was both surprising and gratifying. It elevated her profile somehow. Pieter gave me a knuckle-to-knuckle greeting, then repeated the same with Melinda further along the deck. The boy laughed. I was sure he had seen Mitchell Monk do the knuckle-pump with those he'd met and felt comfortable with, and that probably included Opa Visser, now looking on with satisfaction at how easily his grandson had taken to mixing with adults. Melinda began to engage Pieter, their hand and finger motions like puppeteers practicing manoeuvres for a dress rehearsal of something ominous.

"Mitch is doing the rounds," Aimée Reeves said and flashed me a brief smile, an engaging smile normally, but mascara had run and smudged her upper cheeks, so she had a rather awesome facial appearance at that particular moment. I wondered if that ghoulish look had contributed to young Pieter's interest.

"Mitch is over there taking selfies with them," Aimée said, her chin raised quickly to indicate where he stood. By *them* she meant Isla and Candace, also looking a little played out after all the cycling. I certainly was a little played out after all the cycling and my apparent omission as sweep. So, it seemed, was Virgil Troyes standing near them in his steamy shorts and jersey, looking as though he was keeping an eye on things, the peak of his ball cap a means of eliminating unwanted detail. I knew how that worked.

"Mitch said I'm all sweaty. As if he isn't all sweaty. Them, too. All of them. Especially that Virgil guy but he was very nice when he spoke with me."

"You've a glow on, Aimée, that's all."

Hoping to downplay the source of her annoyance, I added for effect that a gentleman, like Virgil, would know the difference between sweating and perspiring. What I said had the desired effect. Her vexed mutterings ceased, and lightness began to grace her smudged countenance. Aimée had long, black eyelashes that seemed possible only on a rabbit or lemur. Very noticeable. Faintly perceptible grey roots marred her dirty blond hair which she held in place with a sporty headband.

During our brief conversation before Mitch came over, I learned that Aimée was on medical leave from her duties as a grade school teacher and had willingly accepted Mitch's offer of a novel getaway adventure in Holland and Belgium.

She'd loved cycling as a teenager and had never been to Europe. He was retired and looking for diversion. Also legally separated from his wife. When it came to her relationship with Mitchell Monk, I would get the impression over the course of the bike and barge adventure that she was more than merely an attractive mistress fulfilling his physical and social needs, but rather like a forgiving mother constantly placating his less than gracious behaviours, his insensitivities, and his invasions of personal space. Aimée Reeves, sufferance with a mid-west American accent.

"Funny, charming, spontaneous, but hollow," Aimée said before Mitch left off talking with Isla and Candace and came over to join us. The jungle of flowery tattoos on his muscled calves looked like it was steaming. The rose tattoo on his arm appeared to be bleeding. "It's been an adventure since the day we met," she added, "with lots of ups and downs."

As I was later to hear Virgil Troyes say of Mitch: "I imagine him stomping through the underbrush like a moose squelching anything underfoot and then bringing that force into the world of academe. Unimaginable."

Mitchell Monk knuckled me with more enthusiasm than the greeting required. Okay, that was expected. He took Aimée's water bottle and guzzled what remained in it which, I was pleased to note, wasn't much. I looked away for a moment to where Sander and Joost were securing the batteries of the electric bikes many were using. With a little nudge on her shoulder, Monk moved Aimée off to the side. Though a good listener, I heard nothing of the ensuing conversation. I was still hot and sweaty and more than a little miffed about Boyd Alexander's antics.

Later, I joined Veridis near the hot tub to enjoy another pint of HollandIP after the fetor of my physical exertion got washed down the drain through the miracle of copious hot water.

"So that string bean of a lad finally showed up," Veridis said, peeking out from under his bucket hat. "I witnessed the grand event. The unaccounted for American Boyd Alexander Steele, who was totally tuned-in, had not disappeared into any canal, had not got himself lost or waylaid, much to the relief of his father who, as far as I could determine while witnessing the reunion, expressed disproportionate concern for somebody out cycling on his own. Father threw son a look dripping with disdain, then headed down below. Evidently, Boyd Alexander was last seen on that little bridge across the canal. He was not sighted again until an hour ago."

"He's not a kid, is he? Knows how to make use of GPS and the junction network used by all cyclists. Routed himself back to the *Iphigenia* his way."

"Exactly," Olivia said, who had just joined us. "He just looked out of sorts trying to keep up. He did have an electric assist though. Maybe he had other reasons for going it alone or just plain breaking away."

"More power to him, I say."

Olivia added, "Melinda said she could not read the reactions of Alexsis and the other young women. But that Kat was a mixed bag of frustration and antagonism when he did show up. The other Troyes couple was not around. I'm off to the lounge to have a drink with Melinda. Join us, gentlemen."

I nodded appreciatively.

Olivia and Vanessa were sitting around one of the low tables in the lounge laughing over their drinks, spilling some, and, evidently, enjoying the craic when Veridis and I came in from the deck. He excused himself and headed immediately down to his cabin.

"Where's Melinda?" I asked.

"Over with the Vissers," Olivia replied. "She's ingratiating herself to young Pieter again and the Japanese lads."

"Right, right."

"We were just talking," Vanessa confessed, "about you and Frank."

"About how out of shape I am. And I am that, no doubt about it."

"Frank is doing well with the cycling, given his age," Olivia decided. "It's very encouraging."

"A great conversationalist, so he is," Vanessa said thoughtfully. Continuing that thoughtfulness, she added, "As are you, Geoff. You get along with everybody. And everybody gets along with you."

Coming up the stairs from below, Lucy chimed in: "Everybody, yes. Especially the sloe-eyed Alexsis Troyes. She's taken with you, Geoff. Everybody can see that."

"She has a story to tell. I listen well. And that's the sum of it, ladies. Alexsis is bright, well-read, informed. It's easy listening for the most part. Just like with all of you."

"Well, thank you, Geoff," Olivia said and gave me a big puffin cheek smile. "Gracious of you to say so."

"Got a college degree, so Alexsis told us," Vanessa said, "And then trained as a fashion designer. But you wouldn't think it, would you?"

Having manoeuvred over from the Visser table to join in our conversation, Melinda proclaimed, "Alexsis? That one fuses a come-hither look with a woe-is-me. Totally at odds, yeah?"

After a brief silence that none of us appeared willing to fill, Lucy observed somewhat playfully: "Alexsis Troyes could be the heroine in some Jane Austen novel, one with an obsession theme."

"Emily Bronte more like," countered Melinda, "a worthy companion for Heathcliff hiding in the shadows of the hedgerows or creeping through the tulips."

"Geoff, you're no Heathcliff, are you?"

"Not in this setting."

"The aggrieved Alexsis has made a pastime of enmity towards her mother and stepfather," Melinda said, eyes lifted upward with dismissive intent. She then affirmed what she'd said with an emphatic nod.

"Enmity?"

"Enmity, Olivia, absolutely," Lucy said. "Her discontent was almost palpable, even with the wind whistling through our wheels as we cycled along, and when stopped, sharing our complaints about what's wrong with the world."

"According to the mother, Kat, with whom I talked about raising daughters," Olivia offered, "Alexsis, more than her sister Isla, is still in a state of denial and bitter disbelief concerning the death of her father. Very sad."

"So mourning has evolved into a fulltime occupation to the detriment of the whole family," Melinda said. "You'd think Alexsis might have had it all out, including the cynical outlook, with some agony aunt by now. And I don't mean that stuck-up aunt of hers, Eleni."

I was beginning to detect an edge in the opinions of Melinda Mancipal, more in what she said than in the way she said it. She had a definite point of view on the character of Alexsis Troyes that did not quite measure up with the perceptions I entertained. As to the aunt, Eleni, I had not made her acquaintance as of that point, so I did not know if she were stuck-up or not. Admittedly, she was attractive as was her daughter, Candace. Just the same, hearing the various impressions of Alexsis Troyes from other women gave me pause. For the most part, however, she remained in the picture I had painted for her as the brown-eyed girl waiting for the ferryman to take her to where she was going. After all, in my own chronicle of the adventure, it was really all about the cycling, the sight-seeing, and the wonderful accommodations on the *Iphigenia*. Sharing the experience did not necessarily involve deep character analysis or indeed anything approaching character assassination. Appreciation of an individual's personality and his or her response to the historical world we were passing through together was sufficient.

"When we got around to discussing ideals and how they might apply to daily rituals," Lucy went on to explain, "Alexsis Troyes had this to offer: 'My dream kitchen comes well equipped with a chef and clean up crew.' Probably her way of saying ideals were impossible to achieve or if she had any she'd keep them to herself."

"That's perceptive of you, Lucy," Olivia said, and Vanessa agreed.

"But no one is that mysterious," Melinda decided. "Not even the headman of their tribe, Conrad Steele. I think I know him from somewhere. I just can't pull up the exact time and place. What do you say, Olivia? He seems familiar now that we've seen him out and about."

"Not familiar enough."

Monk arrived with Aimée as we moved towards our table and took up the seats we'd had the previous evening. The chairs were not marked with our names, of course, but it was as though we knew our places.

"Where's donnish know-it-all?" Monk asked and raised a few eyebrows. Aimée looked on patiently, holding the back of her chair. "Well, that's what you called him earlier, Olivia."

"I'm right behind you, Mitch," Veridis said, "stalking you and marking your every faux pas."

Monk went for a high-five with Veridis but the so-called donnish know-it-all eluded him by pulling out Aimée's chair for her. When we were all seated, Olivia clarified the donnish tag that Monk claimed originated with her: in her work she had dealings with Cambridge dons daily and the term was intended as a compliment to Mister . Veridis, not a put-down. She'd said knowledgeable, not know-it-all.

"That's brilliant, Olivia," Lucy said.

The Conrad Corps came into the dining area in much the same manner they had the evening before, the man himself in the lead role looking suave and masterful. There were a few gestures of recognition to those already seated, Conrad nodding at Visser, for instance, and Kat taking a quick look in Olivia's direction. All took up their former positions except for Boyd Alexander, who had not yet joined in. The women were dressed to the nines, but not Alexsis, who was wearing a black skirt and a loose-fitting black t-shirt with text on it that I could not make out from where I was seated. On her head, the by-now familiar ball cap.

"Like Hamlet, dealing with family betrayal," Lucy observed.

I wasn't sure what she meant by saying that, but it must have been appropriate judging from how Vanessa responded. Veridis smiled, as though knowing exactly what she meant.

"At least they're not *all* wearing those ridiculous hats at dinner," Monk said.

"What's AEP mean anyway?" Aimée asked.

Monk took up the question. "The logo is symbolic as far as I can tell. A globe with lines of longitude and latitude. Stylized letters overarching it all like a sexy leg. To do with business, I reckon."

"AEP stands for Advanced Electronic Processing," Lucy explained. "Alexsis told me about it and about the hats. Worth millions, not the hats, the company. The hat was Boyd Alexander's brainchild. For this family get-together, that is. Boyd Alexander will inherit a great deal if all goes according to plan. Which raises certain issues that she did not get into with me but hinted that they were dicey."

"I'm familiar with AEP," Veridis said. "The company is a leader in world-wide electronic components distribution. I own shares."

"Right, right. I've probably used some of their products in my sound editing."

"Wait a minute," Melinda said abruptly, the lorgnettes I'd seen her playing with previously dropping and hanging loose above her bosom. At the same time, Anna began serving the appetizer, starting with the Steele table. Baked salmon would follow as the main course.

"Yes, wait a minute," Melinda continued when she'd regained our attention. "Now I recall where I know Conrad Steele from. From home. From Cambridge. Of course. When he stepped out from under the shade tree, it started me wondering again."

"What tree?"

"At the lunch break we had today. Cycling. Near Donk. Olivia, think about it."

"What? Think about what exactly?"

"About AEP holding a conference at Christhill College."

"What's AEP?"

"It's his company, love. For heaven's sake, haven't you been listening?"

"Sorry."

"AEP is short for Advanced Electronic Processing," Veridis said, looking directly at Olivia.

"Christhill College Catering is where I work," Melinda continued.

"She's assistant to the executive chef," a more alert Olivia explained with some pride, "and is well respected for the job she does."

"That's grand," Vanessa said.

"I'm what you could call the chief provisioner. Ours is a prime location on Storey's Way. We have a reputation for being accommodating in a very pleasant and pleasing way and get many types of conferences. Olivia works for the B and B in the college and comes across when a big event is on. Like the AEP one."

"But I'm largely a server and chambermaid," Olivia clarified, blushing in a moment of modest protestation.

"So Mister Conrad Steele was there," Melinda continued in hushed tones. "A few years ago. He had a beard then, full, but well trimmed. Was thinner. That's why it took me awhile to recognise him. I had to deal with a complaint he registered, not about a dish that was served, but with *how* the dish was served. He mentioned something pretentious about *standards* in a cheerfully obnoxious way. It was sardonic condescension, nothing less. I was completely taken aback, knowing his going on like that was not in keeping with our reputation for excellent service. 'Inauspiciously' was the word he kept repeating. The dish had been served inauspiciously. Befuddling use of language, to say the least."

"Now I remember, Mel," Olivia said. "He complained to me first, but I didn't quite catch what he was saying and I broke out laughing, thinking he was just repeating a joke that he'd made before the assembly of company employees in attendance. I thought I was being polite, you see."

"That's brilliant," Lucy said.

"And so —"

And before anyone else could comment further, long, tall Boyd Alexander appeared. He walked slowly toward the Steele table where Conrad with an open hand indicated Boyd's place beside him. Conrad eased the chair out. As Boyd turned to slide in and seat himself, Conrad pulled the chair back further. Boyd landed on the floor in a heap of long arms and longer legs, cursing audibly. A momentary hush settled over the dining room, and then we heard Conrad say, "Sorry, son!" I could not decide if Conrad had inadvertently overextended his welcoming gesture or if the moving of the chair was a deliberate attempt to put Boyd Alexander Steele in his place and shame him at the same time. I gave Conrad the benefit of the doubt whereas others might not. Boyd Alexander got up holding his backside and sat down to the solicitous concerns of those around him, his father's not the least, but low-key and virtually muffled. Embarrassment registered on Kat's face. A restrained kind of anger registered on Boyd's.

"If looks could kill, we'd have a murder scene right here in the dining room," Lucy said.

Veridis responded with "A grand and inelegant coup de théâtre."

Pulling the chair out from behind someone — a slap-stick gag and unfortunately for Penny and me, a teenage stunt David once played on a friend. The friend ended up with a broken arm and the Canter family had hell to pay.

Conrad's ring. I noted it again when he pulled Adam's chair back, a big chunk of blinding bling in gold. Over the week, onboard the *Iphigenia*, occasionally along the cycling routes, or at cafés where circumstances pulled the platoon together as one, I would observe his habit of knocking the ring against a juice glass or his bike bell or a mug of beer. Was this action just unconscious nervousness or an attempt to draw attention to himself? I did wonder. Over all, though, he seemed like an okay guy with a lot of family to take care of. I kind of admired him. From a distance.

For his part, Mitchell Monk at the time of the chair incident had some scuttlebutt, as he called it, on the eminent Conrad Steele. It was vaguely business related, the upshot being that swanky dress and behaviour, even the generous gifts to needy foundations, really disguised vile brutishness, that Conrad Steele was not exactly what he appeared to be. "I had Aimée check him out on the internet," Monk declared with unbridled self-satisfaction. "The dude's got a tarnished halo and he's definitely no saint. Pulling the chair — go figure, right? Also, when I was chatting to the other daughter, not Alexsis, I overheard..."

"Isla," Vanessa said, "her name is Isla."

"Yeah, Isla, and the blond babe..."

"Candace. They call her Candace," Vanessa said insistently.

"Yeah, Candace. I heard Steele boasting to Virgil Troyes, who's his brother-in-law, I think, about visiting the red-light district of Amsterdam. Heard lots of goonish grunts designed, I reckon, to exaggerate performance."

"Interesting take, Mitch," Veridis said.

"That about sums it up," Lucy added, not hiding her ironic intent whatsoever.

A minor explosion of annoyance occurred among the Steele people when, at about the time that Anna started to bring the salmon plates to our table, Kat berated Alexsis for sitting with her legs crossed under her. "Smarten up!" Mother instructed daughter. "You're at the dinner table, not attending a yoga session!"

Muffled laughter all about.

Kat may have had a point, but I would not have made such a public scene about it because Alexsis so arranged was not as unseemly as her mother made it out to be. Nobody at our table deigned to comment. Snickers and raised eyebrows only as the salmon disappeared from our plates. But there was a loud "Ha!" from the Visser table when Alexsis got up and left the dining room clutching her phone like the only friend she had in the world. Conrad got up as though to call her back but turned and sat down again.

"It's him, alright, from the convention at Cambridge," Melinda said, and wiped her mouth with a napkin. There was no doubting her conviction.

"Ready to go?" Lucy asked Vanessa when dessert had been served and quickly consumed and the meal had pretty much run its course.

"We're going to take a stroll around Dordrecht," Vanessa said, rising.

Monk and Aimée had similar intentions and were pleased, Aimée in particular, when Lucy invited them to come along. The dining room emptied shortly after that, Eleni and Virgil Troyes, I noted in particular, making for the comfort of the lounge. Frank Veridis and I decided to pass what remained of the evening out on the upper deck. Kash and Hash were there writing in what looked to be journals. We saw Alexsis with phone in hand heading off alone. I may have been mistaken, but it looked like she was smiling. Her steps were brisk, purposeful. I wanted to think the best of her. I silently wished her well.

With twilight come and gone and my glass empty of reasonable possibility I, too, decided to call it a night. Veridis had retired. An awareness of darkness descending combining with an afterglow of a day well-spent had enveloped me. I wasn't tired to the extent that I'd crash immediately upon closing my cabin door, but a kind of fatigue had come over me by this hour influenced by the foreboding clouds that had built up to the west, casting doubt as to favourable weather conditions for the next group outing. I was definitely not the bundle of energy I'd been the night before, my spirits then uplifted in anticipation of so much. The day had not disappointed at all; in fact, I was both amused and elated by the dynamic created by people following people around bends in the road or people being with people in tight or restful shaded spaces where conversations gave rise to all kinds of opinions and impressions. You just had to listen politely and chime in when moved to do so.

The second email home to Penny needed to be completed. I resolved to do just that before punching the pillows. Her text to me was newsy enough — mother-in-law was doing well, son David exuded enthusiasm about what he was learning from professional archaeologists with a great deal of experience in Greece, and, alas, the tour de France was not being televised in Canada as it had been in the past. I'd left a reply half-finished after showering earlier, which I reread, amended where necessary, and then added to.

First and foremost I wanted to communicate a sense of the newness of place that I was experiencing (without her, unfortunately): the predominately low landscapes and the engrossing sights that surge there, briny waterways refulgent of the surrounding seas, places of age-old human habitation carved out of the centuries, church steeples rising above the quotidian flatness, the flora, the sultry winds, the benevolent sun and the cool shadows it created as you cycled through with bells ringing jubilantly above the susurration in your ears, all — and this Penny would appreciate the most — all bringing remembered masterpieces to life, nature imitating art imitating nature.

And of course, there were the voices, the many varied voices of those with whom you were experiencing it all. It was like being constantly attuned to some multi-level soundtrack until the quietude of your own private space was regained, as it was at different times during the day, as it was for the writing and sending of emails, and then you'd have the opportunity to sort everything out. I'd been dealing with voices and their modulations for years. If only I had the same insight into eyes, I might have proven myself more insightful, yes, even to the point of detecting if a fellow adventurer were having me on or as Melinda frequently expressed it, taking the piss. In a certain sense, I was coming up with new ways to appreciate people just met, frequently questioning in my private thoughts their motivation for saying what they did. Like with my work, where a character unbenounced to you, whose voice you were manipulating for maximum effect, turned out to be in terms of character nothing more than a cheat or charlatan or a murderous rogue, or an actress delivering lines in a B movie unconvincingly and not in keeping with the general tenor of the dialogue, or one wearing a period costume but not very suitably due to the distraction of rustling of fabric, rustling it was your job to eliminate. So maybe I meant *interpret* people just met rather than merely appreciate people just met. The corollary to these axioms: you'd think I'd be able to read lips, given what my life's works had been.

Send.

Dordrecht to Antwerp

Breakfast on the third day aboard the *Iphigenia* proved to be an extended affair in that we were barging out of Dordrecht. The cycling would commence once we'd disembarked in Willemstad, a small star-shaped community on Hollands Diep south of Rotterdam. The weather report for the day was promising.

Monk and Aimée joined us briefly, nibbled this and that with coffee, and after preparing their lunches left in silence. A rather unhurried and casually dressed Frank Veridis, draining his second cup of coffee, asked Melinda what she meant in saying that like many of us, Boris Johnson was a lot of things in a lot of places before becoming PM.

"A lot of things in a lot of places," Melinda explained, "simply means all the days of our lives lived wherever you might be at any given time. Days that reward us with well-deserved time off to enjoy a biking excursion in the Lowlands. That's what I mean."

"After retiring, Mel worked for my cousin's catering service in London," Olivia explained, "I put in a good word for her, of course. Then she got the appointment in Cambridge, and I joined her there. We're mates, going back to the sixties. We have a lot of history together, don't we? She's like an aunt to my two girls, isn't she?"

"After retiring from what?" Lucy asked.

"From the armed services," Melinda answered.

"Mel is ex-military," Olivia continued on behalf of her mate, "served occasionally as an operative in a covert surveillance unit, didn't she? Was very accomplished."

"That's brilliant," from Lucy, who went on to say, "So we'd better mind our ways on the *Iphigenia*, all of us, what, with all the goings-on."

"Who dares, wins, yeah?" Melinda said. "The motto of SAS. I dared but didn't win."

"Meaning?" Lucy again.

"Meaning I applied to SAS but did not make the cut."

"She was in excellent condition for her age," Olivia explained, "at the time she applied. Tell them, Mel. Tell them how you always keep your chin up, love."

"Even with my chin up I failed the preselection fitness test. I won't go into details, but The Hills challenge killed me. So, retirement, Cambridge and catering."

"Odd, how things go around, come around," Lucy said.

"Meaning?" Melinda said, echoing sharply Lucy's previous request for clarification. I was glad she did, having no clear understanding of the connection intended.

"Meaning how serving others you're now being served in what you call your well-deserved time off."

"Righto. And yet how you can still be required even from a distance to acknowledge sods like a Conrad Steele."

"And eejits like Mitchell Monk," Vanessa said.

"Sometimes he reminds me of a frog," Olivia said. "That affect with the tongue, if you see what I mean."

"More like a toad," Melinda countered and snickered.

Veridis said, "Perhaps behind those batrachian features of his there lies the promise of a prince."

"A prince of darkness, yeah?"

"A prince in disguise, Melinda, in need of release or at minimum in need of understanding about the reasons for his bumptiousness."

"You're not so fond of him yourself, Frank Veridis," Melinda challenged, then smiled apologetically.

"You'd think he'd be more cordial," Olivia said. "After all, he was a junior high school principal in America. That's what Vanessa found out, didn't you, love? She doesn't like the way he treats Aimée, doesn't like it at all. Isn't that right, love?"

"I can't abide that gobshite."

"Anyway," Lucy added, "we found out that Monk was dismissed from his position because of an extremely serious confrontation with a very influential parent. Got physical. In the gymnasium. Police authorities were called in, so reports on the internet go."

"That's the thing about all this electronic wizardry," Veridis said, "specific information literally at your fingertips. Instant gratification with a quick dance across the keypad."

"There was more," Vanessa said. "Lots of detail."

"Of course, there's more," Veridis said, dramatically pulling out his phone to inspect it critically. "There's always more. Details unlimited."

"What are you saying, Mister Veridis?" Olivia asked, fiddling with her hearing aid.

"Details available to the whole world upon request. That's what I'm saying. Social media and all that it entails. Not all the details, however, are dependable all of the time."

"A means for disinformation, yea?" Having said that, Melinda motioned us toward the exit and more or less herded us out on to the deck.

The weather continued promising although clouds had amassed to the west. There was two-way traffic on the waterway taking us to Willemstad, barges, tankers, the occasional pleasure craft. Veridis went to ready himself for the day's excursion. Some of the younger guests were positioned along the railing enjoying the passing views. Pieter Visser was fiddling with his bike at the end of the rack. Virgil and Eleni Troyes were sitting in deck chairs quietly into their own private world. No sign of Conrad Steele. And I wondered if someone like Conrad Steele actually remembered the incident and his part in it that the Cambridge ladies were at pains to recall.

I reintroduced the topic.

"I remember Steele's scoffing laugh beyond the glad-handing," Olivia said. "He wasn't exactly nasty all the time, but he wasn't exactly nice. I wasn't the only server he treated with disrespect though. There was also the incident with the fish soup. Remember that, Mel?"

"Our service at Cambridge Catering is beyond reproach, yeah? Just like on the barge here. So why the abuse of personnel? Why the suspicion when the lass ladled out the soup? What had he thought? That the staff decided to poison him just because we didn't like the look of his beard? To top it all off, there was no positive feedback from him or any of his lot, before, during, or after."

"Not a single *like*," Olivia said. "We do get them, you see, the likes. And the reviews."

"There's more than one way to grease the skid," Melinda said.

At this point Veridis reappeared in his cycling gear. Rubbing his hands together, he said he was anticipating the day's ride. Olivia said she shared his enthusiasm.

"A little while ago, Lucy," I began when concerns about physical readiness had been exhausted, "you suggested that knowing Melinda's past occupation we'd better all behave. You mentioned the goings-on. What goings-on?"

"Or were you just taking the piss?" asked Melinda. "Casting me in the role of super sleuth?"

"You do have a disarming smile, Melinda," Lucy replied, although she might have said alarming and I simply misheard. "Was just commenting on what we've all been aware of concerning the rest of the people onboard. You see things. But you also hear things not necessarily intended for your ears."

Lucy's observation that you hear things not necessarily intended for your ears struck me as quite accurate. Last night, for instance, I overheard a heated exchange in the corridor between Kat and Alexsis concerning the latter's solitary departure from and late return to the *Iphigenia*. It was well after midnight when my email to Penny got signed off on and I had not as yet hit the sack. I drew no conclusion about what I heard other than that the reprimand seemed disproportionate to the perceived delinquency, though I was fairly sure both had been drinking. Kat also reprimanded her daughter for constantly appearing in black.

"All part of the adventure, but intriguing nonetheless," Veridis concluded. All agreed.

Olivia said she heard I was keen on the Tour de France. So for the next while, in the interest of the cyclists sitting with me on the deck, I held forth, outlining the itinerary the race was scheduled to follow for the twenty-two cycling teams involved. By this date it was well under way and I was following it as best I could, after hours, so to speak. To begin with, the tour had three flat stages in Denmark, starting in Copenhagen, and then got into France in the main, with the Belgian city of Binche being the site of the start of one of the early stages. The mountain routes normally proved very challenging for all participants, including the favourites among the climbers who coveted the title of king of the mountain. The last stage, as per usual with the overall winner pretty well decided by that point, would end up on the Champs Élysées where I hoped to be in a position to view the final sprint. I held their attention for at least five minutes.

"So, Frank, you said you owned shares in AEP," I started anew, curious about why he'd invested with them. My success with the market had always been mixed.

"AEP provides outstanding and comprehensive supply chain solutions. It delivers products from Bosch to Zytronic. The company has a hundred sixty-nine locations in forty-four countries. In fact, in this area of Europe, one is just east of here. In Aalst. I could go on, as is my wont, but I won't lest I really bore you."

"What's the downside?

"The downside is what customers do with what AEP delivers. Russia, for example."

"But a good investment?"

"The company has been in operation since 1940. Tobias Troyes founded the company in Syracuse, New York. He died in 2005, leaving the reins to his son, Victor Troyes, under whose guidance the company came to be the giant in its field that it is today. I would not have invested without doing the research."

"Victor Troyes?" I jumped in. "He's Alexsis' father. And Isla's. Was, when alive, I mean."

"Alexsis still laments his passing from all that we've heard," Olivia said. "Especially from her mother. I can take or leave that one, if truth be told. So superior, like a head nun in starched wimple."

"You've heard correctly, Olivia." I did have an idea of how much Alexsis missed her father.

"So how does Conrad Steele fit in the picture?" Melinda asked.

"I can Google it if you like," Veridis offered, "but I would venture to guess that he fits in through family connection and not only because he married Victor Troyes' widow, Katrina. Kat."

"So he's nothing but a step-father to the two girls," Melinda said. "Problems, yeah?"

"There's a son out there called Forrest Troyes," I said with certainty. "And an older sister, Jenny, who is no longer in the picture. Alexsis confided that information to me."

"Usually, it's the wicked stepmother that causes all the conflict," Olivia said.

"That's clever, love," Melinda said, and gave her an appreciative look.

At this point in the conversation, I couldn't help myself from adding into the mix the most familial of hackneyed expressions: "You can choose your friends, but you can't choose your family."

Melinda smiled agreeably. Olivia nodded. Veridis winced.

"All very interesting, but let's move on," Veridis said. "We arrive today in Antwerp. Imagine, ladies, Antwerp. And all those diamonds."

Like me, those in our little ensemble seemed to drift off into private enjoyment of the passing scenery. We remained silent for a brief period watching a large tanker glide by on our port side. Massive. Where Vanessa took photos, Lucy would come out with an occasional comment with the word brilliant attached to it. Clouds that appeared ominous floated away.

Once the *Iphigenia* had gripped the dockside in the Willemstad basin, bikes were unloaded and sorted. A metal ramp, awkward in its angle and placement, led us up to an open area where we assembled for our day's outing. The ramp — not all were at ease in negotiating it and I feared someone like Olivia, carrying her pannier and helmet and stepping very gingerly ahead of me, might lose her balance and end up in the drink. I almost did, lose my balance and end up in the drink. I was grateful for Virgil Troyes' steadying hand behind me. Before beginning the ride, Joost did a head count, eighteen, excluding himself. I took note of all who were lining up in position: Joost in the lead, the Vissers three, then Monk, Aimée, Boyd Alexander, Alexsis, Olivia,

Melinda, Lucy, Vanessa, Candace, Isla, Hash and Kash, Veridis, Virgil and Eleni Troyes. I made sure to identify Boyd Alexander. Not present on the ride, Conrad and Kat.

Late morning was when the platoon really got going, first making its way through Willemstad, a tidy little city of historical significance that once featured a star-shaped fortification system of six bastions. Today a single, imposing windmill stands guard at one end of the peaceful harbour. From Willemstad we then ventured into rural areas with wide open, well-tended farms and domains. There were cornfields aplenty and, raising curious heads, countless horses in verdant pastures although less curious about our passing the ubiquitous cattle grazing at half speed. Of particular note, the topiary and manicured shrubbery of the more successful farms we'd passed.

Joost bought strawberries from a farm vending machine along our route (obviously he'd been here before) and took great delight in sharing them. A lot of friendly nods and pleasant exchanges. For the most part. Melinda, who had parked her bike near mine, complained to me about those with electric assist bikes not being in complete control of what they were doing, that when the pace slowed for one reason or other, they'd run up her back wheel. "I wish they'd use the bloody gears the way they were meant to be used," she said loud enough to be widely heard, and then knocked back her kickstand and readied herself to get going. She mentioned no names and I was not sure who among those with electric bikes she had in mind, but she'd been cycling ahead of Candace, Isla, and then Lucy at one point, the likely subjects of her scorn. I was under the impression that unpleasant words had been exchanged.

Before resuming, I did a cursory check and head count. All who had been ahead of me accounted for. After Boyd Alexander's late arrival on the *Iphigenia* yesterday I wasn't taking anything for granted.

East of the town of Halsteren an hour or so after the strawberries, Joost slowed the pace and had us halt at moated *Fort De Voovere*, an historical monument dating from the seventeenth century. Before opening the gate and giving us access to the grounds, he explained in some detail about the method formerly used to flood the moat and about the construction of the viewing tower called *Pompejus*. We had an hour to wander over the site, even climb the tower should we desire to do so. Some did have the desire. I didn't. I just wanted first to sit down and munch on the sandwiches I'd prepared earlier then maybe wander over the area taking in this and that. Before I could muster the energy to get off my duff, Isla and Candace joined me on the bench I had taken possession of.

Isla and Candace, indeed. They proved to be most agreeable and, surprisingly, open. They must have heard from Alexsis that I was a sympathetic listener. At times, however, I felt as though a mini competition had occurred between them to see who could hold my attention the longest. Male vanity be damned! I enjoyed an unearned ego boost even if I might have erred in determining their motivation. Penny would have been amused at the sight of it — two appealing young women chatting it up with a balding, avuncular middle-aged man. David would have been taken aback if not absolutely bemused, beguiled even in the way that fathers can sometimes negate long-established filial estimations of the old man's capabilities and even spark a little resentment. The opposite could also be proven true: sons surprising demanding fathers, sometimes in ways unimaginable. Boyd Alexander vis à vis Conrad Steele.

Candace first, or Candy, as she insisted I call her, but I could not bring myself to do so. Candy sounded belittling somehow, as in the expression *eye candy*. It struck me as undignified whereas Ace might have worked as a fit alternative to Candace. At any rate,

Candace Troyes was beautiful in the classic sense of the word, not cute or pretty or merely a lovely specimen of womanhood. I'd discussed the notion of beauty early in my career in editing with a co-worker several days running as we pieced together the sound track for a film that starred an exciting new actor on the scene who had begun her career in public as a cover girl. He said she was gorgeous. I asked him why he thought so, and that started what turned out to be more a debate than a simple exchange of opinions. We contested concepts such as voluptuousness, grace, glamour, allure, style, sensuality, charm; we got into symmetry, harmony, proportion, and the like, and in the process exhausted our understanding of aesthetic appreciation. We balked at the idea of including intellect as a prerequisite for being thought of as beautiful. We touched on cultural expectations and then on brain functions, zeroing in on what is beheld in the eye of the beholder. The only conclusion we reached in our male chauvinistic appraisal was that said budding young starlet was sexy.

When I provided Penny with the details of our discussion on the essence of beauty, she said with satisfaction, "You've been engaging in scopophellia, the pair of you."

Candace was as beautiful as her mother, Eleni, and just as shapely. Her long blond hair was tied today in a ponytail that hung down through the back adjustment of the black, crested ball cap common to all of the Conrad Corps when out on the cycling paths. She had full sensuous lips and a retroussé nose (displaying a tiny heart-shaped stud). Her complexion was olive-toned. Candace had startling green eyes that an aesthetically charged Botticelli might have fashioned; in fact, she struck me as one who could easily have glided off the center of a Botticelli canvass except for the fact she'd just been peddling along through a Lowlands grove and was presently involving me in conversation, conversation that went beyond the weather conditions and favourite colours. Previously she had struck me as quiet, demure, perhaps even sultry. On the contrary, she was absolutely engaging. And her beauty was spell binding.

When she asked how I was enjoying the bike and barge experience, I explained I found it both exhilarating and intriguing. When I asked her if she'd got the hang of handling an electric bike, she grimaced. She asked if I'd noticed how young Pieter Visser slurped form his water jug like a horse at a trough, then laughed. No, I had not, at least not yet. She'd learned I was a sound editor and asked about that. And then family dynamics came into the picture. She was studying to be a beautician but this gathering of the clan, as she put it, had interrupted her pursuits at least temporarily, and lifting her well-manicured left hand she allowed the fingers to quiver playfully. She let out a sort of giggle. I said she exemplified all that she aspired to, in spades, I emphasized, and she giggled again. Unlike Conrad and Kat, her parents had decided not to remain on the *Iphigenia* for the day. Put differently, Virgil and Eleni were getting more out of the boat and bike experience then she expected they would.

"That Mitchell Monk guy," she said, "you know him, don't you? He's at your table. And his companion."

"I've made their acquaintance, yes, but I couldn't claim to know either of them."

"He's been coming on to me, the creep. And that poor woman, she's been giving me the eye. Like it's my fault that he's coming on to me."

"You have nothing to fear from her, Candace. I'm sure of it. Him? Well, I couldn't say."

"He reminds me of this guy at the college who assailed me. A stalker type. Phone calls. Emails. Texts. Unwanted close encounters."

"A stalker, you say. Were you in danger at any time? What happened?"

"My father, you know, Virgil, took care of the problem in a very convincing manner."

"So no more stalking."

"Definitely no more stalking."

Candace did not go into any details about how Virgil Troyes handled the problem, and I did not push for any. All she added was that her father "knew people" but provided no details as to who they might have been. She drew silent for a moment, looked at Isla who was listening with interest, then picked up again when I mentioned that Monk was a bit of a character. I did not go into any details as to why I thought that. Candace did not ask for any; she probably had her own details to sort through regarding Monk's character.

"Did you know he just about got into a fist fight with my uncle Conrad that first afternoon on the *Iphigenia*. You know who I mean."

"Right, right, your uncle. Monk can be rambunctious. He's very familiar with the old *Why I oughta...*"

"Conrad would have given him the old *Why I oughta* back. With interest. My dad's capable of the same. In spades, to use your words."

"Your father appears to be very solid. Physically, I mean."

"He's that alright. So's Conrad. Conrad's not really my uncle, I just call him that. Kat's my real aunt, though. Calling Conrad uncle bugs Alexsis, so I just call him by his first name when I'm with her. She's climbing the tower with Boyd Alexander who, as far as all this family stuff goes, is not my cousin. But Forrest Troyes, who is not here with us, is my cousin."

"Alexsis told me a little about Forrest."

And with mention of Forrest, Isla decided to pipe in. She said that she missed her brother just as much as Alexsis did, only she wasn't as vocal about it, and that Forrest as a subject of discussion in the Steele household was limited although she was sure Kat and Conrad argued about him constantly. After all, Kat was his mother even though he'd made threats against her life, or so Kat, turning on the tears, had claimed on the occasion of his birthday a few years back, a celebration the birthday boy did not or could not attend. It was determined that Forrest suffered severely from a personality disorder and was analysed as capable of violence. Outbursts of rage were not uncommon. Conrad claimed Forrest was mad and banished him in the sense that he had him institutionalized for an extended period of time. In many ways he was still banished.

"If it had not been for the intervention of my father," Candace said, "who knows what might have happened to Forrest. Kat and my father also get into it about Forrest. Her exasperation over the issue of a recalcitrant son is diminished considerably, I'd venture to say, by my father's understanding and his more nuanced response to a delicate family problem. He's supported Forrest over the intervening years in a lot of different ways."

"True," Isla said, "so true. Your father's been great."

"Do either of you foresee a positive outcome?" I asked, totally absorbed by the fact that both young women were willing to reveal so much about the dynamics of their family.

Candace hesitated to answer, then before nibbling on a croissant pulled from her lunch sac, she said speculatively, "A positive outcome, Geoff? Not in the immediate future."

"Probably not at all," Isla said, getting up and looking over to the tower. She waved at Alexsis at the top, Boyd Alexander beside her looking like a turret. Isla encouraged Candace and me to do the same, which we did, and then she sat down again.

"Things were much better for all of us when my father was around," Isla continued, "especially for Forrest who, I admit, did have his issues. But who doesn't have issues? My father was killed in a car crash, you understand. Tragic. Mother rallied and continued strong in her resolve to carry on although Forrest became virtually impossible to deal with after that. Enter Conrad Steele, stage right. He took control of the situation and eventually married our mother. Neither Alexsis nor Forrest thought much of that arrangement and blamed mother for encouraging the union. Conrad's more conservative in his views than our father was. He's overprotective, domineering in fact, but I get along with him well enough. I have to. Alexsis calls him tyrannical, a gas lighter of the first order. She also insists Mother is in on the scam that's been like a curse on us. I can't really complain except for the fact I have little money and little independence."

"That's absolutely not the case with Alexsis," Candace said, looking for affirmation from Isla which she received through a series of nods. "As far as I can see, she never stops complaining about how things have turned out. Misery personified is Alexsis."

I got the implication. Alexsis' grieving was no mere pastime but a fulltime occupation. Mourning had metamorphosed into raw emotional repugnance.

"She's uninhibited in her rebellious resistance, you understand," Isla continued where Candace left off, "and not only to Conrad. Says we're getting ripped off by Conrad with Kat's consent. With Alexsis it's more than just passive-aggressive behaviour toward them, it's more like out and out attack mode. While I sometimes raise my eyebrows in disappointment about how decisions are made and how they affect me personally, what Alexsis does raises alarms. She behaves very badly. Manifestly so. Resentment motivates her every action, her every utterance. In truth, she revels in something like an ecstasy of hate for both Conrad and Kat."

"You couldn't miss the dark clothing she wears," Candace observed. "In my view, it's like she's out to make a mockery of bereavement. Know what I mean, Geoff?"

"I do," I responded. "And I have thought that what she wears is a little out of keeping with the generally colourful tone of participants and guests on the *Iphigenia*. A little odd, maybe, given the passage of time since your father's death which, I believe, goes back a few years. In my limited conversations with her, Alexsis hinted at some of the points you've both made about your family circumstances. She also mentioned an older sister."

There was a momentary pause in our conversation. We watched Joost in the company of Kash and Hash cross a short distance in front of us to where most of the bikes had been parked.

"It appears our departure is imminent," I said, gathering up the wrappings I had let fall under the bench.

"We still have some time," Candace said, "before the hour is up."

"Geoff, my memories of Jenny are vague at best," Isla stated without hesitation. "I was quite young when she was around, you understand. I would write poems about a missing older sister, like a princess locked away in some mythical tower of yore waiting for a handsome hero returning from the wars to rescue her and bring her back to the family. Enter Archie Gallant, stage right. But then Jenny disappeared, stage left. As far as I know, Jenny and Archie were engaged. Alexsis knows more about all that than I do. She contends that because Calvin Kinlaw, the lawyer, failed in his efforts to save Jenny, we were cursed somehow by fate. She sees a beautiful world suffused with light as designed to torment us. If the colour of the evening sky is crimson and the firmament beyond tinged with scarlet, she would see it as edged in blood. I don't get that thinking at all. I just romanticize what might have been."

"Isla is a published poet, Geoff," Candace explained. "She turns her dreams into sonnets and the like. This morning she read me a first draft of what she called 'Grand Piano.' Very curious."

"In my dream, I was frustrated by the maestro who would not let me discover why the piano played in such a muted fashion. Translation: Conrad Steele frustrates me in dream as he much as he does in real life. I sublimate. An Emily Dickinson wannabe is what I am."

Isla's voice trailed off.

Before our adventure on the *Iphigenia* concluded, Olivia Nunn would comment: "A mob cap is the only detail missing to complete the picture of the demure Isla Troyes." The image, Olivia would continue, originated with the costume and antics of a fellow worker at a Cambridge dress-up party she helped cater under Melinda's supervision. The height of incongruity, Isla in a mob cap as she peddled at a would-be conversational pace along the cycle path leading to Bergen Op Zoom.

Isla Troyes was in her early twenties, twenty-two maybe, but I didn't ask. She was not striking, like Candace was or, for that matter, Alexsis, whom she resembled in subtle ways. Isla was plain in her appearance (dowdy is too critical a term — objective description has its limits) and, it seemed to me over the time I observed her, she made little attempt to change that appearance. She wore no makeup: her face often looked blurred, her features obscured by lack of cosmetic definition of any sort, so unlike Candace. No pink blush in evidence at any time, morning or evening. She obviously demurred when it came to facials. A brunette with a saddle of faint freckles over her upturned nose, she possessed washed-out blue eyes that led one to suspect her absented minded gaze was permanent.

On the whole, I found Isla to be well-spoken, imaginative, and very subjectively insightful; she appeared to be more given to the interior life of the spirit than the world of push and shove where her sister Alexsis operated. She was patient and accepting but not, as was reported by Lucy who observed so much about everyone onboard, without a stiffer side that was bolstered, surprisingly, by a streak of self-assertiveness. She had her opinions, certainly, and voiced them when coaxed to do so. As Lucy pronounced in the context of the Alexsis-Isla rivalry: "One's reservation about voicing an opinion does not equate to not having one." And within the same conversation about the same, she went on to say: "I witnessed Isla, from all appearances quiet, reserved, and retiring, strike out at Alexsis over some comment she made about Boyd Alexander. Virtually hysterical, it was as if she had completely lost it and would physically do harm to Alexsis, the more physical and assertive of the two sisters."

I was taken aback when I heard that about Isla Troyes. Also a party to that conversation, Veridis had smiled agreeably, that is to say, knowingly, as was usual with him.

Those who had chosen to climb the *Pompejus* tower were beginning to head back to the bikes, individuals like Virgil Troyes and Frank Veridis, God bless Frank's pumping heart. It was interesting to see how all individuals in our Triple B adventure were intermingling at this stage, Monk and Oma Visser, for instance, Aimée and Vanessa. Alexsis and Lucy had definitely bonded. Eleni had been sitting with Olivia and Melinda for the longest time under a shade umbrella on the café terrasse adjoining De Schaft, the tourist information centre. Joost eventually called us together and announced we would now be heading along a connection of well-shaded tracks through a popular recreational area known for its nature trails, forest groves, and sand dunes. He was unsure if dunes was the correct word. We would get to stop for another break in a convenient location with access to a café and its WC facilities.

When up and cycling again, Candace and Isla nudged themselves into the line just ahead of me and made every effort to delve deeper into the topics they'd already broached. It proved difficult, of course. When cycling in the company of others, you could get parallel and exchange a few words, no problem, repeat them by shouting, but you could not sustain anything like real conversation.

"When we take our next break," I encouraged them, then repeated what I said in a much larger voice.

Our next break came some time later in the middle of a forested area when Joost led us to a sandy area to park our bikes. Locking bikes had become habitual by this point just like lifting the pannier off the rack and taking it with you. We were at a crossroads in what was indeed a recreational wonderland, a kind of green intersection with access to a café with shaded, outdoor tables. I was sweaty and thirsty and grateful for the respite. Likely others were feeling the same. How could they not be?

"Time for another iced tea," I heard myself declare and ambled across searching for the nearest vacant seat.

"We got this," said Isla, who was following right behind me. She gave the order for three iced teas to a waitress who was heading into the café, where upon she and Candace sat down with me. I was grateful for their simple gesture of generosity. Veridis was about to join us but thought the better of it and made for the table where Monk and Aimée had settled along with Joost. The rest of the group had scattered comfortably and conveniently here and there about the café compound. Joining Lucy and Vanessa were Virgil and

Eleni, the latter two periodically casting furtive glances our way.

Candace said: "You know, Geoff, that creepy bastard Mitchell Monk"— she pointed over to where Monk appeared to be giving an earful to another waitress, a rather tall one that he had to look up to — "he also made a play for my shy little cousin here. You don't like to talk about it, do you, Isla?"

"Not much."

"When did this occur?" I asked. I could just picture it. Monk perceiving Isla to be passive, and with her vague looks, receptive to any facsimile of male attention afforded her. I've often been proven wrong in making similar assertions about what motivates individuals of the gentler sex. In other words, Penny had my number in that regard and called me on it. Often.

"Last night," Isla said. "The guy's pathetic, you understand. He's a user. I mean loser. Attempted to take liberties with me. Boyd Alexander was watching and got angry. He confronted him. Sort of. He just towered over him more or less. Boyd Alexander need not have bothered, though. I turned the guy off myself when I asked him if he ever read Phillip Larkin."

"Phillip?"

"Larkin," Isla said, demurely, batting her eye lids and giving her head a little shake. "You know, the poet. Don't you just love his work? I do."

And again I could visualize the encounter between Monk and Isla. Part of the allure for Monk must surely have been Isla's drawing on her anthology of flirtatious insecurity and allowing innocence to invite unintended sexual attention.

"He hadn't a clue what I was talking about. Then his lady friend appeared. Boyd Alexander whispered a few words in her ear and then, quite angry, she disappeared. 'Cunt' was the last word I heard Monk say. I hate that word with a passion and resent anyone who uses it to put you down no matter your sex."

"If Conrad had been around," Candace added, "I'm sure sparks would have lit up the night sky."

"Precisely. Exit Mitchell Monk, stage left. Hurriedly. Boyd Alexander in pursuit, shaking a fist. It's my way of describing the end of totally despicable scene."

"As of yet," I started in again," I have not had the pleasure of meeting and talking with Boyd Alexander. A tall fellow, indeed."

"Six-six, I believe," Candace said. "He can lift me three feet off the ground when he has a mind to. He dropped me over the side of the yacht into the Caribbean once. It wasn't premeditated. He meant me no harm. He was just showboating. Has an odd-ball sense of humour. Likes video games. He's plugged into his MP3MP3 player constantly. Music is Boyd's passion, also his escape. A simple guy, really."

"So not cut from the same cloth as his father."

"You got that right, Geoff." Isla said. "And yet he can be aggressive. You wouldn't think it though."

"Right, right. Not to be underestimated."

"Not in the least," Isla continued. "Alexsis and I argue about Boyd Alexander. She claims he will inherit everything that's ours. I shrug my shoulders. Boyd Alexander's not at all materialistic. He couldn't care less, you understand. He doesn't even drive. Truth be told, he hates Conrad as much as he hates Kat. How would I know that? I get inside his head. We talk. We're not really close though, Boyd Alexander and I, but sometimes I think we're closer than I am with my sister Alexsis, which shouldn't be. She and I disagree on just about everything. Even poetry. Emily Dickinson's beyond her. But she knows what cerements are. I explained all that to her. She just shook her head and laughed begrudgingly."

When the break was over and all the in group were mulling about the bikes, Joost said that we had time enough to visit the Canadian, British, and Commonwealth War Cemetery if enough people were interested. If so, we'd have to pick up the pace over the final kilometres in our approach to the Kreekraksluizen where the *Iphigenia* would be waiting for us.

I walked with Veridis through the rows of headstones marking the ages and origins of the fallen, young men indeed, some still in their teens, some barely out of them. Impressions: the slaughter of innocence, the absurdity of war, the futility of unbridled ambition to dominate when it's really death that calls all the shots. I cursed again Putin's invasion of the Ukraine and followed Veridis out of the cemetery, head bent.

"If Putin's people followed the example set by Boris Johnson's people," I said to Veridis when we got back to our bikes, "the world would soon be in a better place."

"From what I understand," Veridis responded, "Boris Johnson pulled the PM plug after a host of officials resigned from his government. Regime change in Russia is in order."

Led by a time-conscious Joost, the group made an energetic last push south and west to home base on the *Iphigenia* along well used two-way cycle paths that skirted Bergen Op Zoom. Riding along like a spectre inside my helmet was a troubling sense of the dark side of history and how it repeated itself in new and improved ways, destruction the purpose of research and innovation. I supposed the atomic energy plant on the horizon, its hyperboloid cooling towers like monstrous egg cups spewing out vapours into the blue sky, yes, I supposed viewing that distant site might have had something to do with the fretful and disturbing thoughts I was entertaining about humanity's collective survival, let alone wide-spread murder of civilians prompted by revenge and other dark emotions boiling up as though out of a witch's cauldron. I had to pick up speed to reach Olivia, pedaling along determinedly way ahead of me.

Arriving on the quay along the Kreekrak Lock and sighting the *Iphigenia* was like a homecoming.

"All accounted for," I informed Joost and handed him the walkie–talkie and yellow vest.

Virgil and Eleni had joined Conrad and Kat standing on the deck where they welcomed — with measured enthusiasm, it seemed to me — Isla and Candace back into the fold. From Conrad I got a nod of recognition if not of dubious acceptance. I could not be avoided, could I? A smile from Eleni Troyes was greatly appreciated, just like the last one at the stop in the forest café. A lovely acknowledgement indeed. On the other hand, Kat remained aloof. When Boyd Alexander and Alexsis joined them, my mind went back to what I'd learned earlier about family dynamics, or as someone like Alexsis might put it, clan conflicts. Nothing was clear, not by a long shot. Wasn't this holidaying all about cycling and enjoying the historical domains? Even for them? The only verifiable certainty I could come up with as I looked on was that Boyd Alexander towered over his father, a father who gave him an unexpected (judging by Boyd Alexander's abrupt reaction) paternal pat on the back. They subsequently exchanged a few words. The give and take between them reminded me of the dialogue a ventriloquist engages with his left hand (and / or right), leaving viewers uncertain as to who the real dummy was, who the straight man was, and who got the laugh. Boyd Alexander was not laughing. He wasn't even smiling. While the older generation remained on deck, Boyd Alexander, Alexsis, Isla, and Candace quickly disappeared below.

In no big hurry to refresh, I remained on deck to watch the quayside proceedings. All aboard and bikes secured, the *Iphigenia* motored out, heading into the channel. Niels Visser joined me, and we shared a few observations about the canal system and the importance of Antwerp as a shipping centre and port of entry. When he left to see to Beppie and Pieter, I carried on watching in a sort of restful reverie, enchanted all the while in the here and now of the passing moment. The long HollandIP helped. Periodically I'd look over to the Conrad Corps still milling about and, like me, taking in the surrounding views. I thought back to Candace's quip about her parents' expectations and how they were exceeded. In one visualization of some duration, Conrad and Virgil stood big and tall and looked intimidating against the overhanging sky; as though from a warrior class in another epoch, all they needed to complete the picture developing in my imagination were breastplates and plumed helmets. Kat and Eleni were fashionably attired courtesans, of course, grace and beauty personified, and perfectly complementary, even if they lacked the required braided locks and silver amulets. When Kat produced a compact mirror and inspected her face, the spell was broken. She's had all day to look attractive, which she was, severely so, but always with a touch of the licentiousness about her. On the other hand, Eleni, poised, self-possessed, and lovely in so many ways, struck me as perfectly statuesque. And I wondered, my furtive glances prompting further imaginings, was competition a factor in the relationship between the two women. And along similar lines of dubious reconnoitring, were Virgil Troyes and Conrad Steele rivals in any way? I had the feeling they were.

As the afternoon passed into early evening, the wind picked up and storm clouds began to amass in the west. I retreated inside and observed the river traffic from the comfort of the lounge as the *Iphigenia* meandered its way up the Scheldt River, steady as she goes. Its berth for the night was in a basin reserved for tourist barges south of the busiest part of the port. It allowed easy access to the old city and all the noted attractions. However, rain pelting down on the decks dampened any enthusiasm for excursion beyond the lounge. Lightning flashes provided a dramatic background to our arrival in Antwerp.

Before heading down to wash up and prepare for dinner, I revisited Veridis' contention that so much more lay beyond the public persona of any individuals you might encounter, no matter the circumstance, and that in considering them, even talking about them in an attempt to size them up, you revealed a lot about yourself. And yet, to be honest, I'd learned so much about my bike and barge fellows, Steele and his contemporaries, in particular, and even those like Boyd Alexander I had not yet met directly and conversed with in any significant way. No doubt about it, personal revelation minced together with opinion and hearsay invited curiosity and I'd had copious amounts of all to ingest by this point in the adventure. I'd have to sort through much before getting back to Penny once the information received settled on the right side of the *Iphigenia* truth ledger.

Others had taken note of just who had been my companions for the day, I was sure of it. I, too, was subject to friendly scrutiny, the attempt to see beyond what I was willing to reveal of myself, open guy that I was and always had been. Curiosity had gossipy neighbours and a range of big-eared hangers-on. It also had a voice frequently evincing a touch of malice. Reading faces in close quarters, I determined, was not only amusing, it was also challenging.

Prior to the beginning of the evening meal, Joost announced that according to the schedule set for the next day, we would have two hours in the morning to visit historical Antwerp. As to present decisions, though still windy, the rain had let up, so those intending to leave the *Iphigenia* to take in the city by night should feel free to do so. His announcement got mixed reviews.

Seating at our table in the dining room continued as it had been previously, more or less. As per usual, meals were efficiently and graciously brought to us by staff, all three courses consumed with hurried delight. Cursory commentaries regarding the day's cycling and the sights seen served as aperitifs, much tastefully presented, some less so. Talk of developing muscle aches and fatigue were not to be endured with anything more than a grunt of sympathetic understanding followed by a bite of bread, a swallow of wine or gulp of water, and an occasional upturned eyebrow or head shake. Hunger assumed many faces. Overall, there was general agreement about the benefits of organized companionship.

"One for all, and all for one," Vanessa said. "Isn't that how it goes? Like with Covid, we're all in this together."

"Not entirely, matey," Melinda countered. "Mitchell Monk and Aimée Reeves, conspicuously absent from the table, yeah? You'd have to be blind not to understand why. Too much unsolicited togetherness, yeah? A little wandering off the prescribed paths of acceptable behaviour."

That said, Melinda directed our attention with a raised dessert fork to the Steele table across the way. There, it was the same assembly of bums in the same order of seats as decided upon previously.

"Righto," Lucy said. "The mixes and matches in the game of happy families."

"Speaking of which," Melinda added, "don't you think our beloved Olivia Nunn is a spit for Mrs. Baker?"

"Which Mrs. Baker?" Vanessa asked.

"The original Mrs. Baker," Melinda said and smiled, and then added for effect, "from 1880 edition."

"I've no idea what you two are talking about," I said, completely at a loss as to what they were talking about.

Melinda provided me with a quick explanation. "A card game. A bit like Go Fish, yeah? The right cards bring the right family members together. The Steele family exemplifies themes relevant to the designs of the game. Very ironic."

"Got it," I said, still a little miffed. "Had you said they were like the Borgias, I might have understood sooner."

Then Veridis chimed in: "Geoff here is not as obtuse as he sometimes appears to be. He knows what's going on in their happy family. Got the inside track, haven't you?"

"I listen with an open mind to what others say to me. I can piece together relevant info into workable dialogue. It's been a vocation, actually. A calling to the altar of cinematic art."

And then Vanessa quipped: "And those two young ladies who bent you ear this afternoon, acolytes of yours now?"

"Acolytes? Why not? But only in the sense that they are physically and conversationally capable of keeping up."

"Brilliant," Lucy said.

"So who's doing what this evening?" I asked, more as a distraction than a point of genuine interest. The look of eager curiosity on Melinda Mancipal's face was the primary motivation for my attempt to shift focus. I felt as though I were facing down a grinning pit-bull. The answers to "who's doing what?" proved to be as scattered as it was misleading. Personally, I decided to leave Antwerp's city hall and its historical surroundings until the morning.

Veridis agreed with me in calling off the sightseeing that night. After strolling around the quays in the immediate area of where the *Iphigenia* was docked, commenting on the tall ships we came across and the tall buildings rising above and beyond them, we sat down at an estaminet, a small café serving alcoholic drinks. Veridis was like an encyclopaedia of information, some of it useful in appreciating the architecture, some of it intended to add to my general vocabulary, most of it serving both functions at once. The diachronic, Veridis explained, was concerned with the study of changes occurring over a period of time, be it in languages, mores, or other cultural phenomenon (vs. synchronic with its more immediate focus). I also learned that a fenestella was a niche in a wall, which was pretty much where we were sitting discussing everything under the stars, from the evolution of sailing ships to medieval cathedral construction, topics about which Veridis knew a great deal. As to modern film techniques, I knew more than he. We touched briefly on the fact that Japanese PM Shinzo Abe had been assassinated. Inevitably we got around to life on the *Iphigenia*. It was as though we'd tacitly agreed to observe the goings on and then later in surroundings conducive to our intentions (like over a beer at a bar) compare notes. He'd dubbed our little conspiracy the "wry sanction file." In that context I mentioned that Isla Troyes' reticence and second-fiddle silence disguised her more authentic self, that she was deeper than her awkward appearance would suggest.

"Ah, yes, her concentrated look of respectful vacancy," Veridis said. "Totally misleading, of course. As Mitchell Monk no doubt discovered."

"Apparently, Monk is not popular with Candace either. Nor with her father, the imposing one."

I was taken aback when Veridis gave me the low-down on Virgil Troyes. On top of the *Pompejus* tower he and Virgil had spoken about forts, defenses, moats, medieval warfare, conflict and combat generally, and, naturally enough, contemporary theatres of conflict including Putin's indefensible war on the Ukraine. Virgil Troyes proved to be quite informed. According to Veridis, he was a well-rounded, by the book straight shooter who had served in the US Marines and had been deployed to Afghanistan. Though related by marriage, he didn't see eye to eye with Conrad nor for that matter with Kat who was first married to his brother Victor. How Veridis pulled all that together I hadn't a clue.

"An open book, was he?" I asked when he paused for a breath.

"Not entirely, as would be normal. Didn't get his shoe size."

"But his animosity towards Monk, yes?"

"Indeed. Protective of his daughter. As far as my conversations and observations go, Monk's really not very popular with Vanessa. Not at all. Her animosity towards him is palpable. I surmise, of course, but my sources are impeccable. Lucy, for one. She is a font of information. Our dependable go-to gal."

"She's developed a firm friendship with Alexsis. Which is good for Alexsis who likes to emote."

"I've come to the same conclusion."

And so in the context of his French *bavardage,* Dutch *kletspratt,* German *kaffeeklatsch,* or in plain English, scuttlebutt, Frank Veridis with his usual humour and wry objectivity continued his account. He expanded on Vanessa's loathing of Monk reporting that she resented his treatment of women as commodities. More to the point, she suspected with good reason he was capable of more than emotional or verbal abuse: she'd casually photographed Aimee's bruised upper arm and had much to say about what she called physical evidence. She knew of what she spoke, and hinted at similar abuse in her background; her step-father was abusive in the extreme in all ways, her younger brother suffering several broken limbs as a fifteen-year-old. The oppression Vanessa'd experienced growing up continued when she was induced to marry a man given to bouts of excessive drinking that inevitably led to bouts of indiscriminate rage. Lucy confided that Vanessa's alcoholic ex lost his life in a bloody Dublin street fight.

Keeping company with Vanessa and Lucy, Veridis assured me, also provided him with info about Melinda. At some point since starting out on the bike and barge adventure, an exchange of ideas about what the media expected of women in high office developed into a source of friction between Lucy and Melinda. By the time opinion had overrun suggestion and vaunting ego superseded personal pride, Melinda said the skin of Lucy's hands was like crepe paper which led to Lucy, whose rough hands are exactly that, rough, making uncomplimentary comments about the tattoos on Melinda's fat legs, basically calling them ugly and unbecoming. Hence as a matter of course, Lucy joked, some background research on Melinda, her military service, her covert operations (so-called), and even her brief employment as a mercenary before retiring to Cambridge. Fact: Melinda Mancipal was capable of physically roughing you up should you get on her wrong side. Surprizing then, given the catering story we'd been given earlier by both ladies from Cambridge, that Conrad Steele and other company representatives escaped from the AEP conference unscathed, having virtually insulted a woman who was well armed with an agile mind and a knowledge, allegedly, of what it took to get the upper hand or to get even for having been put down.

Heading back to the *Iphigenia*, Veridis and I caught up with Lucy and Vanessa dawdling along, holding themselves together against the wind. A short distance ahead of them were Mitchell Monk and Aimée keeping an even slower pace as they leaned into each other looking as though they had bonded in something like complete togetherness.

"We saw the two of them in the Grote Markt," Lucy said, "rummaging through the bibelot in some souvenir shop not far from the cathedral."

"Folderol in both behaviour and purchase," Vanessa added, "like a couple of teens, so they were, looking for something of value among the trinkets."

"Make-up after the break-up."

"Monk's a guy with a wandering eye," Veridis said, knocking his fist against my shoulder, "victimized by reaching beyond his presumptuous but friendly fist-bumps.”

Vanessa stopped and said with absolute conviction: “I’d fist-bump the little gobshite right in the yap if he presumed to try it on with me, so I would.”

“The proverbial knuckle sandwich,” Veridis said dryly. “You’d be punching above your weight class, of course.”

“And below the belt as well,” Lucy added.

“That would be grand,” Vanessa concluded and began walking again. The fist pump she effected was not only unexpected, it was also very amusing.

Commotion reigned in the lounge of the *Iphigenia*, a distraught Kat Steele holding centre stage. She tottered on the edge of a lounge chair surrounded by an ever-expanding group of guests concerned with, if not actually overwhelmed by, her emotional effusion. They resembled a Greek chorus full of tragic presentiment, curious about what was unfolding and yet holding back ironic observation — so Veridis insinuated as I stood with him by the entrance.

Crouched down awkwardly, Isla attempted to soothe Kat with murmurings of comfort while rubbing her shoulder — affectionately, maybe, but I wasn’t sure about that. Other family members formed an inner circle while the rest of us collected about the periphery where innuendo passed among us as fair comment. Joost Goossens was the last of the crew to put in an appearance. He shook his head repeatedly. Not present at this point, Kash and Hash, Beppie, and young Pieter. Neither was Conrad Steele present and that according to Olivia, sidling up to me and pulling my sleeve, was the reason for the display of amplified distress unfolding before us.

“Katina Steele, the drama queen, agitated beyond reason,” Melinda whispered in my other ear echoing Lucy’s epithet for Kat from earlier.

A very concerned Captain Vander Valk stood tall before said drama queen. Niels Visser stood tall as well but seemed less concerned when he lowered himself to say in a voice loud enough for all of us to hear, "My dear lady, the hour is not so late."

"Oh, but it is," Kat said, waving a finger. One could not miss the diamond light her hand gave off, incongruous somehow, given the situation, just like the cluster of rings on her other hand. She pulled away from Isla impatiently and rambled on about dangerous and seedy local attractions.

Then cutting to the chase with his typical directness, Visser asked, "Going off alone, is unusual for your husband?"

Seemingly, all the breath of her daily existence, it struck me oddly, had been in preparation for the deep gulp of air that accompanied her answer to Visser's question.

"No!" she shouted, impatience and exasperation increasing.

"Not so, ja?"

"Well maybe. Yes, he's done so before. In Amsterdam, what?"

Coherence in her response was sadly lacking and she knew it. Her eyes flicked here, there, everywhere. It was as though she had just become aware of an audience.

"And this night?" Visser continued. "You talk about local attractions."

"Some place he wanted to visit. What he called the hundred windows."

Virgil Troyes stepped forward then and said, "Conrad referred to it a couple of times as Villa Tinto and talked about the blocks of red-light windows one finds there."

"Schippersstraat, ja?" Visser said. His words came across like an incantation, indecipherable but somehow meaningful.

"Ja, Schipperskwatier," Vander Valk added.

"Conrad wanted Boyd Alexander to accompany him," Kat broke out, her voice tremulous and rising, "to get educated, as he put it, to become a man. Finally. To be a man. Boyd Alexander refused his father's request. You said no, didn't you, Boyd?"

Boyd Alexander, standing next to Alexsis, bowed his head as Kat's voice intensified, filled as it obviously was with angry accusation. One could not misinterpret Kat's snide ruefulness, her focused blame.

"Pathetic, what?" she said, somewhat rhetorically, her implication being that the obvious villain of the piece was standing right there for all her audience to bear witness to. Sad to behold such a glaring specimen of male reticence. Kat struck me as being rather pathetic herself. Her plucked thin eyebrows seemed to possess a will of their own, arching and falling independent of each other.

If I remembered accurately, Kat had been overly upset, antagonistic actually, when Boyd Alexander, erroneously believed to be missing, arrived late to dinner. Boyd Alexander's animosity towards his father had to be playing into her present histrionics. So, another over the top reaction to her loss of control, just like her angry accusations when an inebriated Alexsis returned to the *Iphigenia* much later than would have seemed appropriate for a single woman alone in a strange environment.

Since setting out on the *Iphigenia*, this was the first time I had a real close-up of the woman. She was definitely formidable, no doubt about that, imperious even, possessed of an elegant yet hardened beauty. Vanessa's earlier estimation of Kat as a well-preserved, middle-aged vixen came to mind as I watched and listened to her, but any imagined resemblance to Sophia Loren was fading quickly. She was striking in her grandiose posing, seeming as though she'd slid well down the reverse side of an ancient Greek vase intent on focusing our interest on her and her misery, the one-time exemplar of easy command and sensuous self-indulgence. I was considering the possibility that Kat Steele was living up to the character she had invented for herself in view of the performance the role of forlorn wife and rejected mother presently required of her. We'd all noted the air of theatricality about her, Lucy in particular. As to what I actually observed of her face that night in the lounge as she entertained us with her anxious but less than sober self-absorption and resentment, whatever the detail, I could not avoid considering her likely dependence on Botox and all the meretricious beauty resulting from its application. Kat had brown eyes that appeared to be anything but lustrous on this occasion because of the smeared mascara shadowing them. Patches of darker pigment crested her high cheeks. The woman could boast having perfect teeth, the better to bite you with, I suppose, and an aquiline nose sloped perfectly for looking down its length at you. I was intrigued particularly with how she worked her lips, which were full and nicely shaped, and how she slid words into statements with iambic stops and starts designed to smite verbal opposition.

Veridis in muted tones said Kat's well supported and abundantly exposed fleshy bosom served to distract more than not. I silently agreed. Had Penny been party to my observations and argued the décolletage of Kat's evening wear was evidence of breast enhancement, I'd likely have agreed. She wore a fashionable silver perm, a bob of sorts, that might have been described as very peri, like her recalcitrant eye shadow, but I really couldn't say that with any authority. When Melinda whispered that Kat looked a lot like Betty Boop, I thought the comment unwarranted and unjust. I shook my head in disagreement.

Stepping forward, Joost spoke a few words in Dutch directly to Visser. The meaning of what he said was lost on me until Visser, directing his attention to specific members of the Steele group starting with Kat, asked if Conrad had intended visiting the diamond district of Antwerp. Did anyone know if he made any purchases? Kat shook her head as did Alexsis, Boyd Alexander, and the others. Virgil said that Conrad had expressed some interest in buying diamonds, but he didn't know for sure if he'd followed up on the idea.

Joost spoke again. In Dutch. I got the impression judging by Visser's reaction that the purchase of diamonds figured significantly in the developing drama. In response to Visser's follow-up questions, Kat emphatically stated she did not believe buying diamonds was the reason for Conrad's absence at this hour.

"Do you think all this kerfuffle has to do with diamonds then?" Olivia asked.

"Meaning, do I think Conrad Steele got rolled for them," I responded as effectively as I could, mindful of how she was hearing impaired. "Can't really say, Olivia."

"Things will get sorted," she assured me. "They usually do. Though I really don't like her, I pity the poor woman, her not knowing."

"Agreed," I answered, turning my attention back to the poor woman who had from all indications dismissed the idea of diamonds figuring in her dilemma. She was now pondering the space immediately before her eyes in a blank sort of way, an indication, possibly, of fatigue, of inherent wariness. Then again it may have been she'd paused in order to recall accurately lines from some well-rehearsed script. She arose from her seat knocking Isla and then sat down again. She stared across at Boyd Alexander and then pointed her diamond mounted finger at Alexsis who all along appeared to be quite unfazed by her mother's antics.

"And you're no help at all, Alexsis," Kat said, "in this hour of need."

"You're getting hysterical again, Mother," Alexsis said. "You know very well what motivates Conrad on certain occasions."

"We did not embark on this adventure so that you could announce to the world your discontent nor your dislocation, Alexsis. But to join in a family expedition amicably and not be so wilfully impudent, so disdainful of Conrad."

"Disagreement does not automatically imply impudence, Mother dearest. Nor does disdain."

"Parental direction should be less an affront to you personally than you've always made it out to be. Particularly where Conrad fits in. It's all about family unity, what?"

"That wave broke on the rocks ages ago."

I heard Mitchell Monk, who was in my immediate vicinity, say to Aimée, "That there, Babe, what's going on now, is nothing but melodramatic. I don't like the guy they're all upset about, but he probably went to get some gratification unavailable from her."

"I wouldn't know about that," Aimée replied.

"As to the fancy bitch and her rings, maybe she says she's devoted to family, but she seems more devoted to herself. We've heard enough."

It was getting to the point where I, too, had heard enough, and so, apparently, had Veridis who was no longer holding up the doorpost behind me. Most of us in the spectator ring seemed to be in agreement with Monk, who took his exit, Aimée following. Lucy, however, stayed on. The situation had obviously evolved beyond concern regarding the return of Conrad Steele. Before heading down the stairs, I heard Visser assure Kat there was nothing to be worried about. As it turned out, he proved to be correct.

In the corridor before I managed to close my door, Olivia asked, "What's that saying? The woman pretends too much, I think."

"The lady doth protest too much, me thinks," Vanessa said, punctuating the quote with a slight shaking of her head. She carried on past Melinda and Olivia towards her cabin. "Comes from Shakespeare's *Hamlet*. Fits the present context, so it does."

"Kat and Conrad Steele are at odds with each other despite the spectacle we just watched in the lounge," Melinda said in an argumentative voice. "I heard them disagreeing most vehemently about the daughters' behaviour, especially that of Alexsis. And that of Boyd Alexander, of course. Adjacent rooms, yeah?"

Yeah.

In my dispatch to Penny, I outlined in point form the highlights of the third day that saw us delivered to Antwerp. I tried to be as inclusive as I could without weighing down my comments with too much detail. I started by writing that Antwerp was known for its nightlife, considered the implications, then deleted that sentence, taking a less strident approach. Tact was essential, something more prosaic, and so I began again with measured steps, included scenic highlights, and closed off mentioning plans for sightseeing in the morning.

However, I could not but help come back to a familiar theme: the interplay of characters on board the *Iphigenia*, from good old Frank Veridis to Joost Goossens, from the barbs of Melinda Mancipal to the fact-based revelations of Lucy Hunter, with particular focus on Conrad Steele and his claims on the rest of his unobliging clan. What struck me as both surprising and significant was the willingness of the younger adults like Alexsis to say so much about their positions in the family and the conflicts arising therefrom. Somewhat astounding was the public display this night of dissension that verged on personal attack. Speculation sprang up, naturally enough, along with conjecture and surmise, all bolstered by information provided by others with observations to share, realistic or not, but engaging, nonetheless. For someone like Alexsis this bike and barge adventure was educational, purportedly, and provided perspective on a number of things unavailable under normal circumstances, and that included relationships within the family and without.

In the service of truth and authenticity, I typed in an additional bit of info: I was of the opinion that Frank Veridis was as good listener as I was.

Antwerp to Dendermonde

I had a restless night, falling in and out of startling dreams dramatizing darkened landscapes, undulating waterways, and moats flooding with debris. Had Kat's performance in the lounge affected me in some way, subconsciously, let's say, or had simple overindulgence provided both the context and content of my fitful sleep? As a rule, I put no faith in anything like a medium's interpretation of the unusual or the out-of-the-ordinary strange as phenomenologically meaningful for, or psychologically relevant to, one's mental state, but such a night as I passed instilled in me what only could be described as a premonition. A premonition of what exactly? I couldn't say. The best I might come up with was that these nightmarish sequences were disturbing, peopled as they were in obscure ways with individuals from the *Iphigenia* taking the shape of shadows. When half-awake at some point, I thought I heard whispering voices in the corridor outside my berth. I checked and discovered nobody. When completely awake, I put the night behind me, performed the usual functions of the new morning, and prepared myself mentally for another demanding Triple B experience, allowing concern over the dreams to fade.

Trust Lucy Hunter to have gathered all the relevant facts and then present them to us during breakfast about what actually transpired to incite Kat's unwarranted hysteria. She pieced together the sequence of events with helpful information from those most connected in time and place with the doings of Conrad Steele, most notably his son, Boyd Alexander. Unsubstantiated speculation was minimized due to subsequent conversations with Virgil Troyes and Joost Goossens who, with a nod from both Niels Visser and Captain Vander Kamp and grateful encouragement from Kat, offered to go look for Conrad. They found him on his way back to the *Iphigenia* sauntering along the quay, grinning to himself, cock-a-hoop happy for having spent a unique few hours visiting the local attractions in Schipperskwatier. Although there might have been hell to pay for causing such a public exhibition of family discord, the mystery of his late coming was solved. Also not a mystery, as he proclaimed while being helped to board the barge, "The whores are on horseback in this town."

Before setting out for the Villa Tinto, Lucy reported, Conrad Steele sat with Kat, Isla, and Boyd Alexander in a rhythm and blues bar in the Grote Markt. Alexsis was decidedly not with them. He expected Boyd Alexander to accompany him deeper into the inner city to view the sites by night and enhance his knowledge of the world. Boyd Alexander protested. Conrad insisted he was offering him a unique father-son experience. When son refused father absolutely, Conrad set off alone intent on a unique experience of his own.

Lucy further explained the diamond connection: shortly after arriving in Antwerp, Conrad got into a minivan arranged by Sander Flinck and headed into the diamond quarter to keep an appointment, also arranged by Flinck, with a high-ranking representative of the Antwerp Diamond Exchange. Details of that meeting were not revealed but the suspicion was that nothing came of it, as Kat had insisted.

In conclusion, Lucy posed a salient question to us as she packed herself a convincing lunch. "Were Kat's antics really a reflection of her concern for Conrad's welfare or staged to curb Alexsis' intransigence? I overheard her say to Eleni, 'That little bitch of a daughter, I'll strangle her one of these days. What?'"

All agreed it was a well-put, provocative question.

At about nine-thirty we cycled single-file to a site by Het Steen Castle where Joost would watch over our parked and locked bikes. This arrangement allowed us free access as tourists to the Grote Markt and surrounding attractions. We were left, as they say, to our own devices for two hours. Unexpectedly, Niels Visser offered to accompany Veridis and me and answer any questions we might have about the history of the old city. Beppie and Pieter? Pieter would be dragging Oma to a couple of bike shops he'd long wanted to visit. I'd hoped to spend the allotted time visiting *Rubenshuis* much as I had visited Rembrandt's house in Amsterdam — Penny would be pleased about that since it had been on her to-do list. Veridis and I accepted Visser's offer and spent a good hour in the Cathedral of Our Lady, Antwerp. An acceptable and rewarding compromise. Veridis was moved by the Gothic architecture and held forth with Visser while I wandered about consumed by the ubiquitous art and the many works of Rubens on display that otherwise would have been missed. I mused before two large triptych altars, Baroque to the core.

As scheduled, we boarded a waterbus near Het Steen, bikes and all, and coursed down the Scheldt River to a landing twenty minutes upriver and here the cycling would begin. While Sander handled the tickets and oversaw the secure arrangement of bikes, the rest of us sat in a comfortable lounge blabbing about the day's itinerary.

Olivia expressed her estimation of the bike and barge experience this way: "If you're on a pilgrimage, and let's face it, that's sort of what we're on, a pilgrimage, what is revealed in the long run is who you are as a person, affable or spiteful or something in between. Consider our destination, Bruges, a city of mystical significance. How could it be otherwise?" Interesting angle, most agreed, especially in light of all the recent tensions.

From Veridis' point of view, what was unfolding was a comedy of manners minus what 2022 understood as manners, with the witty, satirical put-downs of convention-bound higher society morphing into an abstract of the family farce you might have seen in the early 70's with a ditsy wife and *woke* kids attempting to placate a mean control freak who was nothing but a throwback to primitive opinions and prejudices. A stretch, to say the least, but convoluted enough to be entertaining.

My estimation: having to some degree figured out group dynamics, long established friendships, and curious family alignments among the *Iphigenia* guests, I still remained dismayed by the staging of an unavoidable bit of social realism being enacted onboard and along the byways. Why the Conrad Corps resistance to the bon vivant feeling of the group as a whole? Why come all this way to cycle through historic domains, to participate in social activities, to sit down at wonderful communal meals, why all this just to bicker? Granted, I was not working on a film, noting timbre of voice and clarity of delivery, concerned with synchronization and the elimination of extraneous noises that distract from the clear articulation of thought. I'd obviously become more deliberate in my assessment and understanding of the total persona. How much did you take at face value? Were individuals not really what they appeared to be at first blush? How much was said or done to impress or deceive? In effect, additional questions that prodded the curious mind. Mine.

We meandered through areas of Flanders roughly following the Scheldt River. At one point we pulled off the main cycle path, circled the outskirts of a small community, and entered the grounds of Kasteel

Wisserkerke, which was situated in a very imposing manner in what appeared to be the middle of a small lake. Joost assured us the reason for the digression was for viewing what he remembered as a world-renowned landmark. He was disappointed, however, that the famous castle was undergoing upgrades and renovations and did not make for great picture taking with scaffolding and plastic sheeting enclosing the ancient edifice like a cocoon.

Heading back along the country lane to the main bike track on the dike, Boyd Alexander shouted out that he had a flat tire. We all stopped immediately, dismounted, and began milling about voicing opinions about the road surface. Of all the cyclists in our group to get a flat and delay setting out, it had to be Boyd Alexander. I feared he would once again be the victim of Conrad's scorn and he was, in the form of a subtle kind of belittling made evident when father completely disregarded son's profuse and profane apologizing by walking away from the scene, his head shaking as though in excruciating pain, to lie alone on the grassy verge of the lane. Kat looked heavenward then away towards the distant dike. Suggesting the incident would prove to be no more than a minor inconvenience, Alexsis still had a job in assuaging Boyd Alexander's embarrassment and hurt feelings. She appeared to be in an up-beat frame of mind, however, and laughed when he inadvertently dropped his helmet on her foot.

Boyd Alexander wore this day a cherry-coloured sweatshirt and beige pants with tight, elasticized bottoms. My son had a pair of these joggers for no more than a week then made shorts out of them. Knocking my arm, Melinda passed the following comment: "In that get-up, the poor young sod looks like an elongated ice cream cone."

I nodded half-heartedly.

"With a major meltdown coming on, yeah?" That smile again.

"It won't take long," I assured her. "Fixing the flat, I mean. Not any imagined meltdown."

Joost saw to the repair of the inner tube, Visser acting as second, with Pieter looking on and giving grandfather encouraging nudges and occasionally slurping from his water bottle. According to Monk, anxious to be off and quietly cursing events, the interruption lasted thirty-five minutes. During most of this interlude, I conversed with Kash and Hash and expressed my regrets concerning the death of Shinzo Abe, their former prime minister. I found it a chore to determine what their real response to the assassination was, though they responded in a polite and respectful manner. Were they in favour of it or not? Difficult to ascertain.

At our table under shade awnings in The Wharf, a café in the town of Temse overlooking the river where we stopped as scheduled for coffee, Veridis noted that Alexsis' mood seemed to have changed and mentioned the fact to her as she slid past us to join Boyd Alexander, Isla, and Candace at a corner table.

"Sometimes life delivers you a surprise that you welcome wholeheartedly," she said, and left it at that. Though still decked out in black right down to the ribbon in her hair, she smiled a smile I had not seen before, not exactly Mona Lisa and not exactly Sphinx, maybe a combination of both.

"And yet, I don't expect to see the dark lady do a caper," Veridis said, once she joined the others, "here or anywhere else. It's not in her."

"Who's doing a caper?" Melinda wanted to know as she and Olivia approached our table carrying icy beverages.

"Nobody we know," Veridis answered. He pulled out a couple of chairs as best he could and then swigged from his own icy beverage. Judging from her edgy reaction, pursed lips, insouciant shrug, his response did not satisfy Melinda at all. Begrudgingly, she repeated the foregoing q and a for Olivia who sat down in a heap and nodded what looked like approval, the kind of nodding approval that thirsty gulps declare unreservedly.

Lucy and Vanessa sat down at an adjacent table, the latter asking if everybody saw that cosy little campsite by that cosy little lake we'd passed. All did, except Olivia. Conversation turned on the fine weather and on how well the ride was going until Conrad, standing by the bikes with Kat, called Boyd Alexander over. Reluctantly, he answered the call.

"He's shy, but far from humble," Olivia said. "He has a mean little laugh if you happen to be in his vicinity when he... I dare say, you know what I mean. And he's easily piqued."

"We know what you mean, love," Melinda agreed.

"What's he do when not here on this trip constantly being crushed by his da?" Vanessa wanted to know. "Like, is he a student, got a job, or what?"

Veridis answered promptly: "He works in the New York home office of the company, truculently, mind you, and from everything else his ersatz cousins were at pains to tell me, he frustrates as best he can all his father's expectations."

"Thereby using up all the available bandwidth within his capabilities," Melinda said. "He seems nonplussed most of the time."

"I try to picture Boyd Alexander," Veridis said, "as more than a costive and disenchanted young man caught in a tough relationship. His situation is not unusual, where son wilfully alienates father because isolation is preferable to the unrealistic demands imposed on him."

"Passive resistance, yeah?" Melinda said.

"The opposite may also be true," Veridis continued, "where son expects too much. Not the case here. Boyd Alexander, it seems to me, enjoys the bonhomie of self-imposed solitude."

"Perhaps he has a fear of crowds," Olivia offered.

"A crowd of one, yeah?" Melinda added. "Or maybe two. An overbearing father and saucy stepmother."

At this point Lucy contributed her two cents worth of admissible hearsay. "I overheard a frustrated Conrad on the q. t. say to Kat that he told Boyd Alexander he often reminded him of an inflatable floppy tube. They're called air dancers, I believe, these tubes. You see them in used car lots waving arms about to grab attention. His father riffing on him like that, imagine."

"Imagine the resentment," Vanessa said.

Mitchell Monk in a near stentorian roar told us that Joost was getting the group ready to depart, that we had some distance to cover before calling it quits for the day, so we best be up and at it quickly. I was the last to leave the table, having checked for what might have been forgotten, a reflex action now, this habit of the sweep. The last to leave the corner table was Alexsis, just ahead of me. It was soon apparent that she'd picked up on the scuttlebutt at our table because she stopped and turned to deliver this puzzling assessment of Boyd Alexander Steele: "He's mostly Boyd and slow on the uptake but sometimes he can be Alexander, a fact not registered yet with Conrad Steele."

Shortly after leaving The Wharf, we crossed a bridge called Temsebrug (a logical enough name) and followed paths along the eastern shore of the Scheldt as far as Sint-Amands. Within an hour, Joost led us into a small enclave housing the oddest building I had ever seen, an atelier called the *Kunst Woestijn*. Before introducing the artist-host, who had come out to greet and show us around, Joost gave a brief description of where exactly we were and joked that the exterior of the establishment — he pointed to a car on the vertical against a wall and then to a large stone rendering of a sort of prehistoric fish, grotesque but bizarrely welcoming — that the exterior was as much an artistic attraction as the interior where we would see and appreciate a varied exhibition, the work of local artists and craftspeople.

After hearing the story of how things evolved to enhance the exterior of the structure — particularly fascinating among the many curiosities attached to the walls were stones with fossils embedded into the intricate brick work — I separated myself from the group and retreated to a stone bench where I nursed the shin that I'd just bashed on a solid piece of sculpture near the stairs as I walked and gawked at all the eclectic artifacts on display. No, what I hit, or what hit me, was a solid rectangular mass of stone set on a pedestal.

Chomping down on a chocolate bar he didn't seem to be enjoying, his brow bent, Boyd Alexander sat completely alone on one of the parking area chairs plugged into his MP3MP3MP3 player, the picture of sullen indignation. He lifted his chin in a vague form of greeting when I gave him the hi-sign, and then looked away. I wondered what he wondered about when not in defensive mode or completely tuned out, or in this instance, tuned in. He unplugged, out of deference I wanted to believe, and gave me a little bit of a smile.

"Not interested in any of this?" I asked, sweeping one hand about while rubbing my shin with the other. "I was thinking you might find it all sort of intriguing."

"Why's that?" he countered, after swallowing. He had an exaggerated, active Adam's apple.

"It's kind of exotic, don't you think? Far flung? Incongruous?"

"I really haven't given it much thought, one way or the other," he answered and allowed his heavy eyelids to drop as though to articulate complete disinterest.

Boyd Alexander could grow to look like an aging Clark Gable, I thought at that moment, a very long one, but the face had to be rounder and have darker eyebrows and a stash that was more than soft buff fuzz. On the other hand, the ears were perfect. To be fair, I envied him his wavy dark hair, shocks of it, despite its having been moulded under the influence of his bike helmet into a modified brioche shape. The adenoidal voice would have to go.

"I noticed that Alexsis and the others seem to be getting something out of it," I continued. "And the older folks."

"Their prerogative."

"How are you enjoying the biking?"

"No problem, except for flats."

"That wasn't so bad, really. Could happen to anyone."

"Sure. What's wrong with your leg? You're Geoff, right?"

"I am. And you're Boyd Alexander. To answer your question, I bashed my shin on a very solid display of stone, over there."

"Could happen to anyone. Someone like me, for instance."

"Right, right. You ride an electric assist, I noted."

"I do. By choice despite..."

"Despite?"

"Despite my old man hacking on me about it. Called me a perfect specimen of the snowflake generation and regretted having to do so. Like, he said riding an electric bike was taking the easy way out. Like, even Alexsis rode a regular bike. Lucy Hunter rode a regular bike. And the woman with the fancy camera. Like, electric bikes were for girls such as Candace and Isla and someone older, that English woman, Olivia. The irony is after the first day, he replaced his regular bike for an electric one. Sander arranged it."

"An electric bike," I mused, "go figure." Conrad Steele on the kind of bike he mocked his son for riding blew the impression my imagination had projected of

Conrad as a mythical stalwart. It diminished him somehow.

"He didn't say why he got one, Geoff, but I know why he got one, to keep up with Virgil."

Given that Boyd Alexander had resisted saying too much, I was surprized that he launched so readily when the bike issue came up. It was like a catalyst for the twenty or so minutes we had together, me nursing my sore shin, and he nursing his many resentments. Once started, it was if he couldn't hold back. Just as Alexsis, Isla, and Candace had not held back. He related how Conrad rooked him into a scheme designed to disarm Alexsis, meaning that he was to engage her in a very sincere and meaningful way, converse with her amicably and hint that she should drop the animosity routine for the good of the whole family. That was his special job while on the *Iphigenia*. Yeah right, he scoffed, and then coughed up what Olivia had described as a mean little laugh. Mitigate acrimony and outrage, yeah right. Be subtle, yeah right. He confessed how Alexsis saw right through him. Immediately. She understood the reason for his own misery and called him on it. She teased him mercilessly but with a kind of compassion. She was clever and manipulative and understanding all at the same time. She told him he was incapable of subversion. He had to agree, at least where she was the intended target.

I let Boyd Alexander know that I understood perfectly the bind he was in, that dealing with conflicting allegiances was emotionally draining, and that I truly sympathized with him in his difficult situation. He gave me a thankful look, and then swallowed, as though gorged on the kindly words I had just spoken to him. He kept going. He confessed that he loved Alexsis. I could see why he would say that and told him so. He was glad to see that maybe today she seemed to be undergoing a change of heart, but if so, it had nothing to do with anything he might have said to her. He admitted a willingness to do anything for her. Unconditionally. Then he got into how love could pull a guy in opposite directions, all kinds of directions, this way and that, that way and this. He resented how his father had treated his mother before the divorce, an ugly, painful divorce, and found it very difficult to accept, let alone love, his stepmother Kat, the usurper. In dealing with that hard bitch, he sided with Alexsis. He had reason enough not to love his father at all but could not find the words to describe for me the pull their relationship had on him, although he figured he did love him in a way despite everything. Getting to that point in his personal revelations must have cost Boyd Alexander a great deal. I was quite moved by this sincere, this spontaneous outpouring of self. He suddenly stopped, it dawning on him, perhaps, that I was no more than a stranger he'd just met, that all he knew about me was my first name, and that he'd gushed forth without reserve the many pent-up frustrations his young life had delivered him.

Niels Visser and Joost were coming down the *Kunst Woestijn* steps, others following, and that drew Boyd Alexander's attention away from me and my interest in his story. Soon most of the group had exited the atelier and were preparing to depart. I did a cursory head count. Two missing. That co-related with the unattended bikes where Conrad and Virgil stood shaking their heads and mumbling things incomprehensible to the now cultured ears surrounding them. On the upside, Mitchell Monk used the edge of a coin to tighten some screw on Olivia's bike when she mentioned to him she kept hearing a rattling noise when traveling over cobbled sections of our route. Decent of him. More time passed with many a comment made about how good that first gulp of beer would taste when back on the *Iphigenia*, if only what was obvious could get sorted.

Joost kept looking at his watch and yammering away to Visser in Dutch. And still no Kat nor Eleni.

"So what do you think of this place?" I asked Veridis in an effort to make time wasted be of some benefit. He was getting antsy. He kept manipulating his hand brakes, depressing and releasing them so that his bike moved back and forth in controlled fits and starts.

"My off-the-cuff take on this place? Something Gaudi on a northern holiday might have inspired, part show room, part museum, part ménagerie à la carte, with free entry into the labyrinth of creative minds."

"I didn't get inside."

"Inside?" Lucy put in, pushing her bike between Veridis and me. "It's intimate and varied. Neatly arranged displays of paintings, sculptures, pottery, exotic photographs, and an extensive array of jewellery. Jugs. A lot of weird jugs. Very interesting. The polished stone carvings are brilliant. Caught my attention and, unfortunately for the rest of us, that of Kat and Eleni, who engaged each other in a competition, verging on bitchy, as to who could hold the host's attention the most. For example, Eleni, drawing her hand slowly across a burnished horse head sculpture: '...out of the sands of the Sahara, you say?' Kat, her ringed hands cupping a carved cat's head, 'You deliver across the pond, what?' Why we're still waiting out here is because the two of them are probably still at it in there. Bullocks to their self-absorption, I say for all."

Melinda burst out with, "Sod this catering to fakery, yeah?" She stood near Joost, her fingers wrapped around the handlebars of her bike, one foot on a peddle.

Then Olivia chimed in: "I dare say, a bit like a bake-off in there."

"Finally," Virgil said for all of us to hear as Kat and Eleni emerged from the building and started down the stairs in the guise of princesses, middle-aged ones at that. Kat stuffed some paperwork into her pannier, smiled at Conrad, and then gave the bell on her bike a little victorious ring.

"Be on the boat by midnight, yeah?" Melinda said and grinned at Joost who must have by this point developed an appreciation for her sarcasm.

As the line that formed behind Joost eased across the cobbles and into the lane, I did another headcount. Two were missing. Boyd Alexander, who had positioned himself just ahead of me, said he saw Isla and Candace take off down the lane just as their mothers appeared on the steps. I conveyed the information walkie-talkie to Joost who replied that time required the platoon to keep going. I'd obviously lost focus in my responsibilities as sweep, too occupied like everyone else, with Eleni and Kat's competition.

Isla and Candace appeared an hour after the group had settled in on the *Iphigenia* and eventually, we got to hear their story. They admitted getting lost leaving the *Kunst Woestijn*, setting out in what they thought was the right direction, which was absolutely, Joost emphasized, the wrong direction. For the group to access the riverside route into Dendermonde, backtracking for some hundred metres or so was necessary. Isla and Candace headed straight out convinced that they would be overtaken within a few minutes. They ended up riding around in circles, then advanced determinedly down a country lane into a watery cul de sac, and then somehow got back to "downtown Sint-Amends" and the atelier. When questioned about how they were successful in reaching the boat, they said a guy parked on the atelier premises asked if they were lost and could he help. He had an Urban Dart full of camping equipment. He was travelling around. His English was pretty good, but with a heavy accent, and knew some French, so no problem. He wore a grey hoodie. Dolf, Dolf Van Handelaar — that was his name although he didn't mind their calling him Mr. Van Hoodie — had a scar on his cheek and tattoos on his arms and a death's head ring on a finger of both hands. It was almost as if he knew who Candace and Isla were and where they needed to be. He guided them as far as a Macdonald's outlet in Dendermonde, pointing out how to get to the barge, which was moored a short distance away. They offered him some payment for his help, and he took it willingly. He offered them some marijuana to smoke, for which they were grateful, but they declined his offer. Asked it heroin were of interest to them. No. They were happy nobody panicked and reported them missing, they were resourceful after all, and would have got to the *Iphigenia* eventually.

Dendermonde. Road construction impeded our platoon's access to where the *Iphigenia* was located. The obstruction and delay brought on disagreement between Conrad Steele and Virgil Troyes about how to proceed, a virtual shouting match in the midst of all the heavy and slow-moving traffic that surrounded us. Exhaust fumes from vehicles vying for position added another unpleasant dimension to our sudden and unanticipated distress, as did the cacophony of klaxons blaring in surround sound. Most disconcerting, especially for someone like Olivia who began messing with her hearing aides.

"Leave to Joost, the directions!" Niels Visser called out, obviously put off by the Conrad versus Virgil take-charge rivalry that was more distraction to all of us than anything like helpful guidance, well-intentioned though it might have been initially.

"Sod it!" I heard Melinda shout. She was near Conrad, and he looked to be leading Kat in a direction he had chosen for her. Totally wrong, as it turned out.

By this point we'd bunched up and had to merge with another troupe of cyclists from some other touring boat and barge entity coming from another direction and heading who knew where. Despite the confusion, and the silent fuming that ensued, we reached the *Iphigenia* safely. It was moored in a quiet location along the Scheldt outside the city centre, with a beautiful bike path right there to follow come the next day.

I slipped into my off-the-hanger duds after showering and headed up to the lounge to enjoy a long glass of HollandIP. No one else was about except Anna who was working casually behind the bar and with whom I exchanged a few casual remarks until kitchen duties called her away. In the contented, mindless zone that ensued, I followed my thoughts as they drifted back across the doings of the day, not all of them completely satisfying. Periodically, and no doubt mindlessly, I'd hold up my glass and study the amber liquid against the ambient light.

"I'll join you, if that meets with your approval."

Conrad Steele stood towering over me which explained, I quickly realized, why the amber liquid I'd been so intrigued by had suddenly changed its tone. He wore white chinos trousers, a silky, pale blue shirt, and around his neck a paisley cravat. Leather sandals. The scent of eau de cologne that hung about him was pleasant, if not a little overpowering. Conrad Steele was given to the sumptuous life alright. He called for Anna who came and brought him the specific brew he ordered and then he sat down opposite me. He had what I'd previously not detected, a slight English accent that fully blown would have had Melinda Mancipal deride as plummy or posh. How about cultivated English accent? Could a guy bark out an order for a pint in a plummy, posh, or cultivated accent? Lucy would have said yes and Veridis would have agreed. Conrad knew my name and I knew his, so no cursory introductions were necessary. He studied me as I reached down and massaged my shin, more out of habit now than the need to feel the abrasion that inattention saw fit to fix upon my left leg. He looked to be in fine fettle, recently shaved and thus eloquently effulgent, poised and eager to engage, so instead of asking how his cycling tour was going and how he was faring, I asked after his wife.

"Kat is in our cabin delighting in an extravaganza of self-pity somewhat like how her daughter reacts when taken to task," he said, then smiled, showing teeth in a way that put me in mind of a discontented terrier.

I didn't pursue the issue of self-pity but supposed Kat had overheard some of the snide comments from other guests about the delay she caused at the *Kunst Woestijn* atelier.

"I refer to Alexsis Troyes, of course," Conrad continued, "her older daughter. I understand you've met and conversed with her. So with Isla. And so with my son, Boyd Alexander."

"I have. Very charming, all three, and also Candace Steele. Lovely young people."

"Candy is a knock-out," he said, his effort at being affable striking me as artificial, if not inadvertently suspect. "If you don't mind my asking," he went on, "what's wrong with your leg?

"Got into a scrape with a stone, earlier, during the *Kunst Woestijn* stop. I started bounding about like a peg-leg-pirate. A bit of an abrasion, but it's settling down. Joost provided me with some ointment, and I've attended to it. Cycling back to the *Iphigenia* was a bit of a strain, but I got over it."

"If I recall correctly, at the time of your 'scrape with a stone' as you term it, you did not enter the atelier like everybody else. You spent time with Boyd Alexander, is that not the case?"

"That's exactly the case," I replied defensively. His question came at me like a bit of cross-examination that Perry Mason of television lore might have brought forth with amicable detachment against a villainous character being charged with cold-blooded murder. I reached down and began rubbing my shin again in an effort, subconsciously, no doubt, to disabuse Conrad Steele of his not-so-subtle accusation of —. I hadn't quite figured out what yet. A bit too melodramatic, nonetheless, for real life encounter on a Dutch barge.

"Chemistry," he blurted out. "You understand chemistry, I take it. Of course you do. They say certain athletes have chemistry, a quarterback and a tight end, a centre in hockey and his winger. The same can be assumed about ordinary people, a mother and daughter, a father and son, friends, and new acquaintances. My point is, you seem to have chemistry with the 'lovely young people,' as you describe them, that you met and talked with along the byways and canals. Is that not the case?"

"That's exactly the case." Implied in Conrad's analogy of people having chemistry, I determined, was that I'd trespassed onto his turf. I tried to take into account his point of view, his role as father, and for that matter, as step-father to Alexsis and Isla, but hearing the derisive rasp in his voice didn't make it easy. He'd turned slightly sinister. I sensed a friendly-faced threat.

"Yes, that's exactly the case," he said, sounding like me and sounding like he'd got me. He started tapping his big ring against the side of his pint jar not because he was nervous, or giving play to some symbolic gesture, but because he intended, I couldn't help but consider, to annoy me. And I recalled Melinda's chiding of Mitchell Monk about his confrontation with Conrad when she said that the oversized ring could have done his face some damage.

"Connections and meeting people no matter what age," I said, "that's what this boat and bike experience not only advertises but provides in spades. It's like we've all signed a contract of willing participation. We all roll along in very tight social settings, don't we? I've embraced other new friendships as well as those you're most concerned about. Can't help but be friendly and open."

He took a long draught of his beer, then looked over my head at something that may or may not have been there to distract him, then at his sandals, then over to the bar and the array of bottles behind it. Then he puffed up is cravat with a deft movement of his ringed hand and nodded. It was as though my rejoinder was of little relevance regarding what he had challenged me with, and yet somehow it was incumbent upon him, with the slightest inclination of his head, to appear to care. I grew increasingly aware of the perfumed airiness enveloping our little interview, our little give and take. What had been Monk's description when facing Conrad down? The scent of roses?

A nod to me, such as it was, and then he blinked, his brow knotted the way I'd seen Boyd Alexander register perplexity or apprehension. Conrad had intense, watchful dark eyes, and he was watching me with them in a manner that I could only interpret as an effort to intimidate. Eagle-eyed, I thought to myself, that was what he was like. Raptor-like, with a narrow nose on the point of which a small specimen of dried shaving cream had staked a claim.

"We're a family, the Steeles," he said, "a well-integrated, totally together, successful family, and I want to keep it so. I take it you understand that?"

"Of course, I do," I answered, remembering a guy I worked with once on a television project who threw out banalities to see if he could get a rise out of anyone listening and, if listening, take offense. Then he'd go all vexatious if challenged, or act hurt, betrayed.

"Of course you do, Geoff, and that's fantastic. This holiday was undertaken by all of us to solidify *all* our relationships. Besides — "

"Right, right," I interjected, "got that, to solidify all. As to my easy connection with Alexsis, Isla, and Boyd Alexander, it must be my avuncular appearance that drew them into conversation with me, or my willingness to listen without censure, or my sense of social grace or sense of humour." I then added with emphasis, "Or the scent of my deodorant."

It took some effort on his part, I was certain, to offer up a modicum of a smile after hearing me say all that. A sort of smile actually broke upon his face. He was a handsome man and, despite his menacing approach to a pre-dinner conversation with a co-passenger, I admired the way a shock of his longish, gray hair hung over the right ear like something a *GQ* reader might stare at in one of magazine's ads for the latest coif in vogue for the sophisticated gentleman of wealth and position. An accidental arrangement, surely, for a man of Conrad's years, just like that dab of dried shaving cream carelessly overlooked.

All very contradictory, the basis of Conrad's reproof — I certainly considered it a reproof, a rebuke of what Penny always referred to as my open and genial personality, and I rarely, if ever, contradicted Penny. Absolutely incongruous, his less-than-friendly stance, given what I'd learned previously from Isla and Alexsis on our stops, and in the *Kunst Woestijn* parking lot from Boyd Alexander. It just didn't jive. I had already modified my earlier, somewhat generous view of the man as a well-meaning, take-charge kind of guy who was without doubt urbane, sophisticated, and masterful, but also a domineering *paterfamilias*, to borrow from Veridis' vocabulary. Unlike others who witnessed the incident, I'd given him the benefit of the doubt when he'd pulled back the chair for Boyd Alexander too far from the table, whether intentionally or not, and Boyd Alexander landed on his ass in a heap of arms, legs, and shame-faced curses. "Sorry, son!" was no more than a facile, public display of fatherly concern that in retrospect was arguably quite insincere. And so, of necessity, my re-evaluation of any benefit of the doubt I extended Conrad at that time. It was evident, at least now it was even more evident, that a large gap existed between father and son. As to Alexsis and Isla, if they were to be believed, and I did believe them more than I did Conrad, they had absolutely no power, no real income, no independence, and their presence on the *Iphigenia* was effected by coercion and not necessarily by choice.

On the other hand, in his defense, Conrad was not a big, truculent, nasty, loud-mouthed and impatient man, which depiction would have reduced him to mere caricature, a Charlton Heston character, for example, all brow and bravado and deep-throated exhortation. No doubt, somewhere behind the persona, behind the public presentation of the successful chief executive officer of a large corporation, an authentic self was capable of enjoying a species of peaceful co-existence with family even as he pedaled though the lowland byways of Holland and Belgium on an electric assist bicycle, the kind he denied his son. Did he love his son? Probably. After his fashion. For who could reject one's own flesh and blood outright? But Boyd Alexander, the apple of Conrad Steele's eye? Possibly, but an apple with too many soft spots and too many bruises to take into account. An apple that hadn't fallen close enough to the tree.

"In the name of your good faith, Geoff, let me get you another beer — us another beer," Conrad offered, converting his irritating splurge of grievance to a facsimile of grace. "HollandIP is it?"

I agreed and he immediately called for service. Apparent flexibility on his part, I had no objection to that at all, although I didn't expect him to come out with a jocular "Hey, man, I was just messing with you." I didn't think him capable of jocularity.

Once Anna drew us second pints and brought them over, he launched into a modified *apologia pro vita sua* starting with "Geoff, you must understand..." The family adventure on the *Iphigenia* was not all pleasure for him. He had business dealings in

Amsterdam before embarking and in London prior to that. Hard bargaining, he guaranteed me and explained why. Moreover, the business end of things would continue while en route to Bruges and end up in Brussels.

"I understand completely," I said agreeably, and then took a swig of beer.

"We'd hoped that this rather novel kind of holiday," he continued, "would benefit all in the family, Alexsis in particular. You may have noted in talking with her that she is very high strung. Very independent. Singularly rebellious against our good intentions."

"She seemed in a happy mood today." When I said that, Conrad grimaced, then took a drink, a long one, and then went on.

"Let's hope it continues, this happy mood. Seeing her smile makes for smiles all around. Kat especially. Unlike Isla, who is more passive and accepting, Alexsis has found it difficult to deal realistically with the death of her father."

"Who, I believe, was Victor Troyes."

"Precisely, Victor Troyes," Conrad said, tapping the side of his pint jar again. "He was my cousin and I loved him dearly. But life has us move on, doesn't it?"

"And death."

"Precisely. Alexsis resists that fundamental understanding. I can appreciate her sentiments, soft sentiments, if I may call them that, but she is anything but soft. You must understand, her memory is faulty. She conceives of Victor as princely, of royal bearing, as in when she was just a child and she was his little princess with a tiara riding on her curly locks. Truth be told, Victor was a decent man, a good father, and had a terrific head for business. I suppose what Alexsis means, in the real world of today, is that her father was dignified, honourable, and well respected. That is definitely how I saw Victor as did all who entered his world. And, of course, Kat loved him dearly and suffered his loss with a great deal of emotional strain."

Nothing new there except for Conrad's point of view, one that he shared with Kat no doubt, and the pint of HollandIP he stood me. No more than a logical enough rational from the other side of the family divide. In the back of my mind, the words Alexsis hurled at her mother the previous night about Conrad's propensity to stray from the warmth of a familiar bed. It seemed to me that she had his number on the subject of fidelity. I refrained from asking about Forrest, Kat's son, no longer in the family portrait according to Alexsis. Father and sons, difficult enough. Fathers and step-sons, who knew?

"As to my son Boyd Alexander, I have heard Isla arguing with Alexis about him. The contention is that he hates me as much as he hates Kat. I doubt that very much. Ah... please don't misread how I phrased that."

"Right."

"I know Boyd Alexander well enough to say emphatically that he hates no one."

"That would be comforting for both you and Kat."

"Comforting indeed. Boyd Alexander is a fine young man. He might strike you as indigent and apathetic, uncommunicative for the most part, but that's far from the truth. Despite appearances he has character."

I read bumbling awkwardness and reticent behaviour in what Conrad meant by appearances. The most fitting thing I could come up with in response was that his son was very tall.

"He gets his height from his mother's side."

"Got it," I said, thinking Conrad was working towards some kind of conclusion in his effort to knock what he perceived to be the scales from my eyes. That's how I saw it then. Here, Virgil Troyes entered the conversation, voicing his growing concern that Candace and Isla had not yet returned. Eleni was very worried and had gone to consult with Joost whose response was that they had maps and the itinerary of the day and would safely make their way to the *Iphigenia* with time to spare before supper. He'd seen this kind of "group deviation" before. Not to worry. Boyd Alexander had returned when believed lost, hadn't he?

Joost proved himself prophetic, if accurate assessment of a familiar situation could be called prophetic. A moment or two after Virgil had brought the matter to our attention — I was the sweep, after all — Candace and Isla rushed into the lounge, red-faced and glowing, looking for something to snack on. Alexsis followed them in. Settled, calmed, they told their story, which settled and calmed all concerned, especially Virgil who said he would immediately inform Eleni and Kat of their safe return. Before Alexsis led Candace and Isla down to their cabins, she approached Conrad in a kind of jerking movement. He recoiled, his head pulling back awkwardly.

"Don't be such a bubblehead," she said, and swiped with a delicate finger the dried spot of shaving cream off his nose. Comic relief of a sort. To save face, as it were, Conrad had no recourse but to drain his mug of beer. And having done so, he conveyed the impression that what had just happened really left a bad taste in his mouth. When Melinda appeared smiling in her usual gap-toothed way, Conrad looked at her with a disparaging eye, puckered his lips, and departed. Among other things about her person that would be off-putting to him, she revealed in her contorted kind of curtsey just a little too much leg, her robust tattoos to the forefront in a show of prideful disregard.

Setup for dinner that evening followed the usual pattern. Everyone was present and accounted for at our table. Hash and Kash arrived late at the Visser table, offering more than ample apology. At the Steele table all was as would be expected except for the absence of Alexsis which, in light of previous doings, might have been expected. Olivia offered me sympathy when I mentioned my sore shin and how it came to be sore. Veridis offered me sympathy when I mentioned having been seriously engaged with Conrad Steele over a couple of beers. Then Vanessa contributed her account of Conrad's account of his altercation with Virgil at the Dendermonde intersection, "in that way he has of half-whispering something behind his hand in a pseudo show of confidentiality. Virgil may have rationalized his route through the traffic build-up, he said, but he hadn't given it much thought. Then Conrad asked if I understood his meaning. I did. I positively understood his meaning. It was *his* rationalization for losing it, for being so loud and aggressive. I told him that, so I did. He was not at all receptive to my version of what happened. In fact, well, you can imagine — "

Monk said he was sorry to hear that Vanessa had been subjected to Conrad's nastiness. He knew how vulgar he could be. Aimée was equally sympathetic. In appreciation of all the sympathy that was going around our table, I gave a summary of how Candace and Isla had been lost and found and how they managed through the sympathy of a guy in a grey hoodie to get back to the *Iphigenia*. Lucy added to my account by saying that she'd seen the hoodie fellow earlier that day at one of the crossroads we cycled through. Melinda said that she also saw the fellow but that the hoodie was blue, not grey.

When the appetizer appeared on table, the chatter stopped, but not for very long.

Melinda asked me what I thought about the lorries that had parked in the middle of downtown Ottawa. "During the winter carnival season was it? The incident gained worldwide attention. Called the freedom convoy, yeah?"

"Please refrain from calling it that," I answered. "It was more of a right-wing protest against government protocols to deal with Covid-19."

"Freedom convoy, my ass," Veridis broke in. "A joke of a protest supported by extremists, anarchists, nihilists, anti-vaxers, conspiracy theorists, and a good representation of malcontents and social misfits driving eighteen wheelers. And, not surprisingly, Conservatives."

"The symbolism of the Canadian flag has been damaged," I argued, "defaced in sundry ways, worn mockingly as capes, presented upside down on trucks and jackets. All that was bad enough but juxtaposed with confederate flags and Trump banners was over the top."

"Vile impulses," Veridis said, "from south of the boarder kept it going. Destructive. Dangerous."

"Better served to have used the Ukrainian flag in protest against Putin's illegal invasion of the Ukraine," Lucy suggested.

"My sentiments, exactly," I said.

Apparently following up on an earlier discussion, Veridis asked Monk, "Are you still of the opinion that Covid-19 is a hoax? If it is a hoax, who benefits?"

"The chemical and drug companies," Monk asserted. "That's who. They've been called a cabal of profiteers."

"Called that by whom?"

"It's on the internet. On some news channels."

"Sources. Sources matter," Veridis said. "It is absolutely irresponsible of those at the controls of social media and the disinformation networks who foist false ideas upon a population all too wiling to believe the bullshit."

"Confirmation bias," Lucy said, "comfortable armchair for the unthinking, for those incapable of critical analysis."

"Can work both ways," Monk interjected, "your confirmation bias."

"You're right, Mitch," Veridis went on, "but what Covid-19 has reassured me of is the crass stupidity of the human race."

"What's that?"

"Not the whole species, Mitch, but a good percentage of it who believe they are informed and therefore they possess superior knowledge to those really in the know, the scientists, the researchers, the medical professional, and those in position of authority informed by the facts, not some point of view proposed by a well-know athlete, television personality, or popular actor."

Olivia said, "My orthodontist's receptionist theorized that its all been a big conspiracy. Just to keep people in line."

"They're the one who upset me the most," Vanessa said, "those shites loosely attached to the medical profession. Add into the equation religious nuts who believe, sincerely it must be, in light of the inane statements and objections they come out with as to why they object to vaccination, that if it is God's will, then this, that, and the other, and so on ad absurdum."

Lucy said: "Call conspiracy advocates or anti-vaxers misguided or indeed totally out of touch with the reality around them where the death count continues to mount, then they call you fascist and pedophile and agents of the state and threaten you physically."

"Not exactly snowflakes," I added, "these Ottawa truckers and their supporters with their obscenities and slogans of hate. And definitely not in the woke camp."

It was as if with my reference to the woke phenomenon I triggered Frank Veridis. "Our CBC," he launched, "the equivalent in some ways of your BBC, recently came out with outrageously ridiculous directives, eighteen words you can't use lest you offend someone, anyone. For example, black sheep, black mail, blind spot, gypped, tone deaf. Nothing more than an attempt to bowdlerize our very existence until we're reduced to nothing but emaciated spirits or gutless wonders."

"Sounds lame," Lucy said.

"Sod it," Melinda said with emphasis. "Let's eat."

Our table was first to be served again and Anna began delivering the main course, *Confit de Canard* she called it, but before Melinda or anyone else managed to tuck into the duck dinner, Joost standing in the light from the bar announced the arrival of a new guest onboard the *Iphigenia*. At this juncture Alexsis entered the scene smiling. More noticeable than the smile, she'd thrown off her dark attire for an aqua blue, long flowing shift.

"Love her chiton," Vanessa said enthusiastically. "Classic Greek, so it is."

"Everybody," Alexis said in a voice clarion clear, "this is Fletcher Christian. He is better known as Flex. Please welcome him into our ranks."

Initiated by Joost, a round of applause followed. Easily explained, at least in my mind, was the change we'd noted that day in Alexsis' demeanour. She led Flex, who proceeded with the aid of a cane, over to the Steele table where Anna was finishing up her quick preparation of an additional place setting. Cushioned in the crook of Flex's left arm was a large jug that Aimée said looked like one that drew her attention at the *Kunst Woestijn* atelier. With little difficulty in manoeuvring, Flex presented the jug to Kat. Indeterminate murmurs arose around their table.

"Looks like a cinerary urn!" Conrad declared in a loud, mocking voice. He replaced the jug back on the table in front of Kat. He lifted both hands, palms up, his meaning clearly that he had no explanation to offer to Kat as to what was happening. She seemed as miffed as Conrad and equally unreceptive to Fletcher's being there, jug or no jug. Conrad pulled in air through his nose impatiently, then directed a reproving frown at Virgil. I could see where Kat and Conrad would not be cycling along amicably with Flex no matter how much Alexsis seemed to have lightened up.

Alexsis had this to say about the jug: "Don't make more of it than what it is, a decorative vessel offered as a gift. It's a replica, apparently, of an ancient Greek specimen. Empty, which makes Flex less complicated than you'd like him to be." I had no idea what she meant by that, but I was sure she delivered her retort as though aware she had an attentive audience, which, of course, she did. That audience? Everyone in the dining area at the time. She and Flex seated themselves. His chair faced into the room and provided the rest of us a clear line of sight. In contrast to his poor reception from Conrad Steele, Flex received a bracing handshake from Virgil and one from Boyd Alexander. Other than Kat, the women appeared to be equally receptive to having Flex join them.

Kat pushed the jug into the centre of the table and picked up a knife and fork. Others followed suit and hailed Anna now serving them the *Confit de Canard* with as much flourish as she did when serving us. As to us eavesdroppers, we saw fit to focus, at least temporarily, on what lay on the table before us. Furtive glances and raised eyebrows and occasional comments spiced our relishing of the duck.

What was he like, this Flex?

Flex looked to be in his mid twenties. Though of lighter complexion, he bore a marked resemblance to Woody Lyons. His build was comparable to that of the famous golfer who had recently suffered a career ending accident. Flex had short blond hair in a brush cut. Quick head movements marked how he responded when this one and that one at the table drew his attention. He'd pulled his eyebrows into a concerned V-shape over his eyes when Conrad put him on the spot, but then he let out a bark of a laugh that set some at the table giggling. He had a winning smile. Attire? Jogging suit, yes. Ball cap in rear pocket that, I suspected, he'd wear front to back. And cross trainers to die for if you were twelve years old. I'd noted his footwear as he drew himself across the floor behind Alexsis: the elaborate shoes looked to have been the creation of Japanese or Korean auto designers, all angles, bumps, indents, and protrusions with platforms by Platypus Corp.

Before dessert was presented to our table, Lucy was able to fill in a few more details on who exactly Flex was other than an apparent acquaintance of Alexsis Troyes. Among other mundane factors like place of birth, age, and social status (single, unattached romantically), not a lot was overwhelmingly intriguing as far as I was concerned. At present he was studying economics at Western Washington University but was considering dropping out of the program. He had become a bitcoin enthusiast. He'd played college football and two NFL teams had interviewed him. Other interests: theatre, cycling, spelunking, mountain climbing, skiing, and (occasionally) slash-dashing. Most revealing — I expressed my wonderment with a string of aha grunts — was that among his friends was one Forrest Troyes, a close associate since boarding school.

I asked Lucy how she got her info so quickly. She tapped her iPhone and said Facebook, and LinkedIn. Two photos, which she flashed about, supported the assertion that the friendship was of long duration. She also said that accommodation on the *Iphigenia* was no problem for a late comer like Flex. There had been cancellations leaving at lest two cabins vacant.

When Aimée asked me why Flex's friendship with Forrest Troyes was such a big deal, I explained that Forrest Troyes was Alexsis and Isla's brother, who lived outside the family circle ever since Conrad Steele became head of the household. That explained why he was not part of the Conrad Corps sitting across from us.

"Exiled," Lucy said knowingly.

"In a manner of speaking," I said, not really as much in the know as I might have liked.

"Slash-dashing?" Melinda said, raising her eyebrows. "Anyone?"

Even Veridis never heard of the term. He was determined to find out.

Dessert was delicious apple crumble, topped off with a dollop of custard, and sprinkled over with crusty flakes of chatter. The post dinner scramble for seats in the lounge came about as usual, the difference this evening being that Flex had became the centre of attention for many, including Olivia and Melinda and others from our group like Mitchell Monk who was curious about what NFL teams had shown interest in Flex and Aimée who had a question about the jug (that Kat abandoned and eventually found a place on the sideboard). Eventually I roused myself from the table and headed down to my quarters, the dulcet tones of Flex's immediate reply echoing as I descended.

At the appointed time, I'd settled in comfortably on deck. Overhead, beyond ambient city light, a receding blue sky with lavender undertones. A slight wind, undulations, minor movement of the barge, its diesel engine providing only the hint of a hum.

Veridis joined me carrying two mugs of HollandIP. His first utterance was a definition of slash-dashing which Flex had given him: from position A, participants follow the logging road up to the appropriate height and then from position B, determined by mutual agreement, scramble down the slope through the slash, that messy web of branches and other debris left hither and thither among the stumps after logging operations had moved on. First back to position A wins. Last down buys the beer. A group activity. The challenge tests agility, balance, perception. Perfect for training. In his latest outing, Flex fell and injured his left leg and that, he said, was why he had to rely on a cane for support. Fortunately, it was not a permanent setback as far as future athletic endeavours were concerned.

"Never heard of it, Frank, I've never heard of slash dashing."

"Very inventive."

Veridis and I then considered Conrad's reaction to the arrival of Flex, agreeing that the reason for such a blatant rejection of the young man ran much deeper than his audacity in presenting Kat with a singularly ugly piece of pottery. In light of what we knew of the triangle of strained relationships — Conrad and Kat, Flex and Forrest Troyes, Alexsis — was the jug a peace offering? But why such overt disapproval?

"You'd think Flex would be easy to read, but he isn't."

"Meaning?"

"Meaning maybe he's more than he appears to be. I mean not just a kooky college kid. I mean informed. Before grabbing these jars at the bar, I encountered him in the hallway where, just between him and me, I expressed disappointment that Conrad had not been receptive to his joining the party. Flex's response was surprising and direct. He insisted that Conrad was a grafter by nature, no matter the family connections and the wealth. As a so-called parent to Alexsis, Isla, and Forrest, old Conrad could give Cinderella's stepmother a run for her money. A lot of resentment built up over the years on Forrest's part. He'd been cut out absolutely. And as his closest friend, Flex shared in that resentment. They schemed together on how to take revenge, all for naught, of course."

"Alexsis tells much the same story. About Forest being ostracized."

"With Flex here, she seems more determined to challenge Conrad."

"Agreed."

At this point I felt motivated to reveal a little more of what I was feeling about my earlier dealings with Conrad, and how since the confrontation I'd come up with innumerable terse and crafty responses that might have served my pride better.

Veridis snorted. "The old *ésprit de l'éscalier* trope," he said, "perfect put-downs in twenty-twenty hindsight. Sweetmeats for the muttering brain."

"Right. I get that."

"From what I've heard and observed, Conrad Steele interprets animated verbal resistance as respect or, better, as a species of reverential high regard, and then he treats the adversary so engaged to his amused denigration. He is eristic in his approach to argument, more interested in being thought right than determining truth. That was evident when he engaged Mitchell Monk and me in discussing the Covid-19 pandemic. Mitch kept a respectable distance from an antagonist he previously opposed so vehemently."

Our attention was diverted when Alexsis and Flex appeared below. They were exiting the *Iphigenia* using the gang plank that gave access the bike path. They could not help but be aware that we were observing them. They walked on together, (perhaps hand in hand, it was hard to determine,) he using his cane with rhythmic manipulation, she with her cellphone in one hand which she dropped and then retrieved. We followed their progress into the shadows.

"Before wishing us a good night," Veridis continued, "Melinda had this to say about Flex: she detected a certain shiftiness in his responses about his so-called dearest friend Forrest Troyes, as though he were guilty in some way of causing him harm. This was especially evident with Alexsis and Isla listening in. Alone, she contended, he filled your ear with his athletic exploits, blah, blah, blah. Slash dashing, yeah?"

I laughed at Veridis' Melinda-like conclusion. He went on in the same vein.

"Melinda also said she overheard Monk telling Virgil that the prophet put pussy in jihadi paradise as a reward for service. Virgil took offense, threatening to knock his head off, believing the remark to be no more than prurient suggestiveness about his daughter, Candace. 'He told Virgil to sod off in familiar American slang' is the way Melinda put it. The confrontation occurred at one of the café stops when they were discussing religion. Virgil has faith."

We got on to discussing other characters and the best way to respond to them when misunderstanding might result from things said. Then the route to Ghent tomorrow occupied our thoughts. Half an hour later, Flex and Alexsis reappeared. She seemed to be bounding out of the shadows. As for Flex, he must have thrown off his spavined gait the way a horse throws off a shoe. He appeared to walk normally. Veridis remarked how the cane seemed more of a prop than a brace.

We took our empty jars back to the bar and called it a night.

In my dispatch to Penny, I began with a note on Boyd Alexander. While some of our table klatch had a rather low opinion of Boyd Alexander, I explained how, after watching and listening, I was developing a sympathetic affection for him and so provided details that would give Penny as complete a portrait of the young man as seemed relevant at the time of the writing. Monk called him a gomer. Aimée thought he was a sad sack. Melinda and Olivia referred to him on more than one occasion as a prat with unearned privileges. For the record, these silver-tipped sibyls had the habit of referring to Conrad Steele as a tosser and Mitchell Monk as a knob and wanker. I provided Penny with no equivalents for what she might consider obscure appellations. Colloquialisms, I wrote by way of explanation. Vanessa was kinder when she dubbed Boyd Alexander the mook who moved like a mountain.

I related seeing a parallel in the behaviour of our son David, who for a time in his adolescence seemed to have withdrawn into self-imposed isolation; this was the case, seemingly, with Boyd Alexander. The Oedipus factor? Possibly, but resolved. David proved resourceful and resolute. I saw no reason to deny Boyd Alexander similar inner strengths. Hadn't Isla warned against underestimating him because, if pushed, he could shove back with surprising force most aggressively? That notion was seconded by Alexsis who claimed his *Alexander* didn't always play second fiddle to his *Boyd*, by which she implied, I reasoned, that he was like Alexander the Great when push indeed came to shove. If her understanding of him was correct, he was emotionally, mentally, and physically capable of striking out against oppression in whatever form it presented itself.

Penny knew I was an inveterate listener. She needed no detailed explanation of my modus operandi among the guests on the *Iphigenia*. She was already cognizant of certain areas of misunderstanding and conflict among them. I explained how I was tempted to intervene, to interpose myself between this one and that one, which was by and large uncharacteristic of me, my normal course of action being to fall back into the shadows or slide to the periphery and merely observe. I'd hear what others intended me hearing, offered understanding, and that would be the extent of it. In effect, I'd be looking on from the shelter of anonymity, from the computer screen of my mind where a script was being enacted beyond a sound editor's ability to influence it in any meaningful way. I was okay with that. In contrast, Frank Veridis inserted himself right into the mix to make a relevant comment or cast doubt on the argument on one side or the other. Lucy Hunter would contribute some droll observation while Melinda Mancipal would come out with something cynical but insightful. Objectivity, right? I concluded the point by suggesting that had Penny been with me and party to the same influences, we would in the after hours be indulging in *bavardage* and *kaffeeklatsch* and expanding our very own version of the wry sanction file.

Knight errant? Not this guy. I added that bit in for effect.

The role of knight errant, I hypothesized for Penny's benefit, suited Flex, a new arrival on the barge and friend to Alexsis. I described how I imagined him rescuing her from physical and emotional captivity, metaphorically brandishing his sword (in reality a cane) and shielding her in protective friendship and amicability. Such action would be an affront to those who would deny her and her sister their freedom. Knight errant, for sure, but not in terms of derring-do or valiant but dangerous endeavour, just as a solid shoulder to lean on, a shoulder her long-lost brother Forrest purportedly fist-pumped over an extended period of time in pursuit of common interests.

Larger than Mitchell Monk as general antagonist who could really piss people off in his own right, and that included cook and crew, the real ogre of the piece continued to be Conrad Steele in concert with his wife, Kat. Opposed, Alexsis, for the most part. And to some degree, Boyd Alexander. My position as an outsider, who'd heard tales from all sides of their family conflict, was liminal. Nonetheless, dealing with Conrad was challenging. Not challenging at all was reconciling the impressions others had of him with my own. For Alexsis, Conrad was ruthless and manipulative. For Flex, a big-time grifter. Olivia thought him arrogant and overbearing, but very good with Visser's grandson, Pieter, even attempting to sign with him. I might have extended the list, but decided, as I had previously, to throw in a few random out-takes.

Vanessa: Heard Conrad refer to Flex as "that upstart parvenu."

Melinda: "Virgil engages Conrad in argumentative jocularity which increase the latter's ire."

Lucy quoting Melinda: "Frank Veridis and Geoff Canter suck one into dialogues only dilettantes are capable of."

Ouch!

Being completely into what I was typing, I did not check back to see if I'd actually identified clearly all the individuals referenced, confident that my first email to Penny would have seen to that. She would definitely know who Frank Veridis was. Being quick, she'd catch on quickly. Then I recanted, reiterating who was who and where whoever sat at mealtime. Mitchell Monk and Aimée Reeves were the couple from the American mid-west; Olivia Nunn and Melinda Mancipal were from Cambridge; also English, Lucy Hunter was an investigative reporter while her associate Vanessa De La Croix, Irish, was a professional photographer; all at the same table with Frank Veridis and me. Olivia commented that those at our table would make an excellent substitute panel for the television show she watched faithfully called *Mock the Week*.

The Dutch threesome, Niels Visser, Beppie, Pieter, and the Japanese lads, Hash and Kash, occupied table two.

Table three included Conrad Steele, Boyd Alexander, and Kat with her daughters, Alexsis and Isla; Virgil and Eleni Troyes, and their daughter, Candace; and now Fletcher Christian, aka, Flex.

I attached a couple of photos that Vanessa had sent me identifying Joost Goossens, our MC and cycling guide, in one; and Isla and Candace in the other, a wall of the *Kunst Woestijn* atelier in the background.

Before signing off, I described for Penny my impressions standing before the magnificent Rubens in the cathedral in Antwerp. In her email to me, she'd asked about what the cathedral offered in terms of great works. I answered her query about my ability to sustain the pace of the cycling. No problem. And was I following the Tour de France? As best I could. I mentioned having scraped my shin but that the injury was minor and would not restrict me in any way. Yes, I was indeed sleeping well.

Send.

Dendermonde to Ghent

During breakfast, conversation centered again on the surprise arrival of Flex onboard the *Iphigenia*. That made sense, I supposed, new face, new personality, new relationships in the Conrad Corps to align. Cracking the shell of a hardboiled egg, Lucy said that she found no definition of slash dashing in all her internet searches. What did we think about that? Veridis provided for all at the table, most of whom were shaking their heads in ignorance, the description of slash dashing he laid on me the night before. From Flex himself, he assured everyone. The least confused by his description was Lucy, who remained sceptical about its being an activity young men at university, even Americans, would indulge in.

"Taking the piss, yeah?" concluded Melinda.

"Flex seemed genuine," Veridis said. "But you're right, Melinda, he might just have been jerking an old man around. Pass the jam, would you, please, Aimée."

"Did you get a look at the sweatshirt the lad's pulled over his head this morning?" Olivia asked. "Has a big curious face on the front."

"So it has," Vanessa agreed.

"Like those faces on portraits or whatever by Renaissance masters," Olivia went on. "They look like they're following you around the room. Their eyes, right? You can't help but keep looking back at them. Makes you feel guilty sometimes. Spooky."

"Winks and nods and silent curses. Faces on blokes capable, when alive, of speaking out of both sides of the mouth. Get a grip, love, yeah?"

"Right," I said. "It's just a contemporary sweatshirt favoured by the generation. My son had a similar one for a time. Its only threat was its very identifiable stench. Teenage boys can produce odours that slap you in the face."

With a nod to Melinda after consuming the last corner of his toast and jam, Veridis said he hoped no fata morgana would arise that morning out of Flanders' misty landscapes or, for that matter, off anyone's sporting apparel.

The jokes puzzled Aimée. She just wanted to know about the jug Flex put on the table. Since then, it had been placed by an unknown hand on a bar shelf between the Advocaat and Blue Curaçao. She'd take it home, if permitted.

Vanessa asked her what she was planning, to take her partner's ashes back to America in it? Mitchell Monk, finishing up his coffee, coughed. He was not amused. He started packing his takeaway lunch, making no effort to disguise his anger.

Melinda said Aimée would probably be welcome to the jug, then bagged the ham and cheese sandwich she'd prepared. And so with all of us, lunch preparation for the cycling to follow.

I thanked Vanessa for the photos she'd sent me. I was curious about Vanessa's camera. She talked briefly about her wide-angle lens and what it allowed her to include in her shots. What lens did she use when on the job? It depended on the subject of investigation, which was determined by Lucy and her superiors.

Did investigative reporting affect their personal lives, I wanted to know. The question definitely hit a nerve with Lucy. She said she was exhausted by the endless pursuit of truth regarding assassinations and official British responses to Putin's kleptocratic clan and corruption in the UK generally. She described Britain's echelons of the self-serving as playing Jeeves to a corrupt Vlad the Impaler Woosterov, but more like the butler servicing his vices than the valet dressing them up in socially acceptable attire. The allusion delighted Veridis.

"Stitched me up," Lucy continued, "the authorities did, or those toffs in a position to thwart my efforts to speak truth to power. Got fobbed off on lesser issues, not that rescuing the environment is not important. Played it low-key for a stint after the threats."

"Threats? What kind of threats?"

"Threats that upset my equilibrium, verbal, written, social media trolling, and the like. Got questioned by coppers in rumpled suits down at the nick. Have a record on form available to authorities influenced by corrupt politicians. Civil cases raised their ugly profiles and so did the scar-face of organized crime."

Vanessa, in relief, summarized their findings in regard to criminal activities on the home front: England, a silent and generously rewarded partner, was allowing oligarchs to infiltrate political, economic, and legal systems; the country was open to plutocratic criminals and crooked elites; basically the corruption originated with money laundering and what one of their associates and critic of what's been going on since the fall of the Soviet Empire called "financial dissimulation" through shell companies, tax shelters, and offshore trusts. The essential aspects of the problem were bent accountants, a morally flexible legal representation, greedy politicians, and those rewarded by seats on the board of companies.

"In other words," Vanessa concluded, "the structures in place that reward the wicked and exploit the weak."

"So shut the fuck up if you know what's good for you," Lucy said, her voice full of passionate intensity. "In other words, I got death threats."

"Death threats? Really?"

"Really! Consider the assassinations of whistle blowers by the Russian mafia, hit squads, or secret police — deaths egregiously termed suicides by British authorities. Only the strong remain unfazed by threats of retaliation. That's us when we're not here on bikes in technicolour outfits. Though the National Crime Agency was over a long period of time virtually stymied, decades, in fact, now with Putin's invasion of Ukraine a lot is getting sorted."

"Since you've made enemies of people in high places, as you've claimed, any fear of real physical harm coming your way? Even here?"

"As in being taken out by a contract killer?" Lucy said. "In Holland and Belgium on holiday? Haven't given that idea any thought really. Shadowy figures are just figures emerging out of the shadows and from under the cover of shade trees. Hadn't thought to look over my shoulder since boarding the *Iphigenia*. No fear here, Geoff."

"Let's hope not," I said.

"Bring some good news to Ghent today, shall we then?" Veridis said before getting up and heading down to his cabin.

By nine-thirty, *Iphigenia* guests and their lunches were out on the dike path following the meandering Scheldt heading to Ghent. No doubt about it, the role of sweep appealed to me. As far as group cycling went, a time-tested, sixties' cliché seemed apropos regarding the cycling styles I observed ahead of me: different strokes for different folks. When Virgil Troyes pumped the pedals, his knees protruded out to the side, left, then right, then left again. Olivia pedaled madly, then eased into coasting over a distance that eventually widened on her to the point where she had to pedal madly again. From all appearances, Lucy knew how to slipstream behind someone like Niels Visser, whose long legs appeared to punch the air under his extended arms. Never less than feisty was Beppie, who personified matronly competence.

Those on electric assist bikes looked like they had it easy, but Kat constantly bobbed up and down and when alongside Conrad, he frequently had to give her a push or a pull. His legs operated like pounding pistons. Monk rode his bike as though he were training an uncooperative pony. None of the younger ones swayed from side to side, as was definitely the case with Aimée, although on occasion Isla's left foot would slip off the pedal. Same with Veridis, who mostly rode ahead of me. Plugged in always to his MP3 player was long, tall Boyd Alexander. He required little effort to keep up despite what had been said of him previously; his riding style was smooth despite the fact his feet looked like they rendered the pedals invisible. Smoothest of all was Vanessa. I'm pigeon toed, but no one commented on that fact.

By this point in my duties as sweep, it was easy to identify who was where in our single file moving along in unison, though at times it seemed we were functioning like a concertina adorned with bells and red panniers, tight in corners and then stretched out along a straight run by the side of a canal. Lucy and Vanessa in their customary high visibility attire were easy to keep track of. The same with Olivia and Melinda in their yellow helmets. Young Pieter Visser's cycling club jersey always placed grandfather ahead and grandmother behind. And so on, each in a position established at the outset, Joost in company colours leading, but over the course of the day's outing, with coffee and lunch breaks and extended stops at attractions, where you started in the morning was not necessarily where you finished up in the afternoon, except for the lead and the sweep. I got a kick out of the rotations even though I was teased as being nothing but a line monitor. This day, a new combination appeared ahead of Veridis who was again immediately ahead of me: Alexsis in her dark garb and Flex in his fanciful sweatshirt. Any slash dashing injury he might have sustained did not in any way hamper his ability to ride a bike. His cane with a knobby handle stuck out of his pannier like an aberration. Conrad Steele was not participating in the day's trek to Ghent, but Kat definitely was. She started out just ahead of Flex and Alexsis and seemed determined to keep them near.

By ten o'clock we'd reached a point where we had to get from the east bank of the Scheldt River to the west. A small ferry provided the crossing. Joost collected small change from each of us to tip the operator, who welcomed us aboard with a wide grin. When all the bikes had been stashed at the stern of the vessel and all the tips had been handed over, we moved out. The crossing took no more than a minute, if that. Alexsis tapped me on the shoulder and repeated the line from her childhood rhyme that had once mystified her.

"'Ferry me across the water, do boatman do!' Remember our conversation from the other day, Geoff?"

"I do. Not quite the River Styx here, so not as mysterious as all that, true?"

"True."

"Elysian Fields on the other side? Or Hades?"

"Either way, it depends on the ferryman. If you remember, Geoff, to ensure passage to the other side, two coins were needed. They were placed on the eyes or in the mouth of the deceased. Traditions vary."

"I have only a vague memory of such a *rite de passage,* if I may call it that."

"Our Charon favours a wide but ambiguous smile, doesn't he?"

As we bumped into the landing slip, all I could muster as an answer to her question — she was just joshing me as Flex listened in and Kat watched with a keen eye, a mother bear on the alert — was a goofy smile and a shrug of the shoulders. My default response when words failed. To expedite procedures, Joost directed us to grab any bike and run it up the ramp. They'd get sorted before we set off again.

Between the ferry crossing and Donkmeer, a beautiful resort-oriented lake, we encountered a herd of obstinate sheep that provided us with entertainment of a sort lasting ten minutes or so. Disagreements as to time-honoured shepherding rituals and the best dogs bred for herding occurred immediately upon our being stopped, Mitchell Monk offering his expertise, which by and large went unappreciated. He argued with Olivia like a zealot on a crusade, which induced Melinda to challenge him with, "Such loud, nasty, insane talk will have you sectioned, mate."

"What do you mean sanctioned?" he asked, reining in his grand gesticulations.

"I said sectioned, not sanctioned. Institutionalized, yeah?"

"Loony bin," Vanessa explained.

At a café called *Spijskaart* situated on the western shore of Donkmeer, we took our scheduled coffee break. An excellent location for a respite, Veridis opined, with its garden tables and large umbrellas and WC facilities. The group broke up and settled at various tables in more or less predictable groups, the exception being that Mitchell Monk and Aimée joined Virgil and Eleni. I wondered about that decision. I recalled the story Candace told about how Virgil handled the stalker who had pursued her. In saying only that her father "knew people," she left much to my imagination. It remained active in that regard, especially now with Monk's unlikely move. Was it a subtle kind of provocation or a gesture of reconciliation? Whatever it was, it seemed likely that Monk thought twice about subjecting Virgil to a fist pump. Under the same umbrella, Kat had placed herself between Virgil and Eleni and within earshot of her daughters who were sitting close by with Flex, Candace, and Boyd Alexander. Joost had his coffee with the Visser group.

Coffee at this point in the day was most welcome, Cappuccino apparently the popular choice at my table, one shared comfortably with Lucy, Vanessa, Melinda,

Olivia, and Veridis. Nothing unexpected by that arrangement.

Olivia munched on the cheese sandwich she'd prepared for lunch but confessed being unable resist enjoying it with the coffee that Melinda brought over to the table for her.

"Cheese, yeah?" Melinda said, and then out of the blue added, "Chalk and cheese."

"Apples and oranges," Vanessa immediately said, pulling the orange peels she'd been amassing into a pile next to her cup.

"Sixes and sevens," Olivia said, and then took another bite of her sandwich.

"Ups and downs, ins and outs," Lucy said, looking to Veridis and then to me. I thought to say "meat and potatoes" but didn't. I pulled out a hardboiled egg from the lunch bag in my pannier, and gave it a gentle crack against the tabletop.

"Six and two threes," said Olivia, indulging her evident fetish for numbers.

"Maybe tomorrow," Veridis offered, "it'll rain cats and dogs. Let's hope not."

"Off the cuff, yeah?"

"Spur of the moment, Melinda," Veridis answered, lifting his cup at her in a gesture of recognition, "no question about it. I'm all for folksy parlance."

"These sayings are like tools in the toolbox, yeah?" Melinda continued. "A means of ready communication."

"In instances," Lucy countered, "when we dare not venture outside the box."

"I've a lovely sandwich, too," Vanessa said to Olivia, "ham and cheese, so it is. But I'm saving it till later. That way I can both have and eat it."

Our round table give and take regarding colloquial expressions might have continued had it occurred anywhere else, at our lunch stop, for example, with more time for us to relax and babble on, or on the deck of the *Iphigenia*, the cycling completed for the day. It struck me as I ate my egg that the banter was just an easy way of asserting your presence among peers after having cycled hard for a couple of hours, a way of saying, "I'm still here and willing to continue with you." Detectable, though, was a rivalry between Melinda and Lucy.

"Because of e-talk and the likes of BFF and LOL," Lucy said, "much of the wisdom contained in age-old aphorisms is now lost on the younger generation, as in those amongst us like Isla, Candace Troyes, and Boyd Alexander Steele."

"No Conrad Steele with us today," Olivia noted, her cheese sandwich but a memory now.

Lucy gave us the lowdown as to why Conrad remained with the *Iphigenia*, as to why he was "conspicuous by his absence," as she phrased it. The barge would see him in Ghent long before the arrival of the cycling group. He had to attend a business meeting with the AEP plant manager from Aalst who would be driving into the city. According to Virgil, Lucy's avowed source, the meeting concerned innovative approaches for distribution of bundled hardware. Virgil was not invited to the meeting.

How Lucy Hunter never failed to provide us with bits of information about this one or that one never ceased to startle me. Having said her piece, she was the first to get up from the table, and of course we followed suit, but not into the WC where she all but vanished.

A very short ride from *Spijskaart* umbrellas, Joost had us stop at what he called "the butterfly garden" for those with photos in mind. A few took snap shots but what struck me as significant was the show of what could only be described as fabricated interest. Pungent smell, crepitation of insects, and the jerky flight of a single butterfly, that was it as far as I was concerned. Melinda was of a similar mind and spoke it. We soon gathered our collective wits about us, and pedaled on, despite Kat's insistence she be given more time to enjoy the ambiance.

"Flat tire!" I yelled into the walkie-talkie I pulled awkwardly from its holster. "Flat tire, Joost. The group's breaking apart."

We were exiting the Kalken area along a paved road, when the problem occurred. Our single file arrangement was stretched out and was now in two definable groups, those ahead of the bike with the flat and those behind it. Joost who was way ahead and now out of sight responded. He'd turn around, get back, and sort things out. The group behind included Veridis, who had been riding right ahead of me, then Candace, Isla, Virgil, Eleni, Monk, Aimée, and Boyd Alexander. Alexsis and Flex marked the separation. The front group had disappeared around a corner.

Whose bike? I could not establish that immediately. Not Boyd Alexander's again, I hoped. If it were, at least he would not have to endure the wrath of Conrad nor the disdain of Kat. She was out of sight, in the "break-away group" as Veridis wryly observed, referencing tactics used in races like the Tour de France. In his backtracking, Joost stopped and got off his bike where Alexsis now stood arms akimbo by the side of the road. I moved up the line to observe, as did Virgil. The flat? The back tire of Flex's bike, which he was struggling to turn upside down, having removed the pannier from the carrier. Boyd Alexander moved into give him a hand and then turned to assist Joost by handing him the tools required to get on with the job. Joost set about cutting the culprit inner tube out from the tire housing through the wheel spokes, an easy extraction given the complexity of the rear wheel with its chain and gears and cables. He replaced it with a two-ended inner tube that made the effort required to fix things look rather easy. While this was taking place, Flex looked on, supporting his right side with the cane he'd obviously pulled out of his pannier.

I stood with Virgil and watched the proceedings. We exchanged opinions about the use of two-ended inner tubes, also the benefits and short-comings of e-bikes. He said Kat had the habit, especially when stopping or negotiating a slight incline, of letting the bike control her momentum which resulted in running into the bike ahead of her. Eleni had a similar problem, he noted, as did the tattooed woman from Cambridge, Melinda, despite all her complaining about the short comings of other cyclists. He described her as having a mercurial character and a crooked smile. I asked him what he knew about our new arrival, Flex.

"Solid," he said, "the real deal, a trusted friend of my neglected nephew, Forrest Troyes. A sad case, that arrangement. Beyond my understanding, really. I help where I can."

"Too bad about Flex's limp. A great athlete, from what I've heard."

"Injured himself slash dashing with Forrest," Virgil said and then gave his head a little tilt to the right. "Beyond my understanding as well."

"So, your nephew Forrest couldn't make it, I mean, join the family on the boat and bike experience."

"Conrad had his lawyer Calvin Kinlaw organize the holiday for the family. Though I've had some dealings with Forrest myself, as an uncle like, I had no real influence in Conrad and Kat's decision to leave him out it. Flex, his good buddy, complicates things for them."

Virgil was being friendly and informative, but he wasn't giving too much away. He seemed relieved when Candace moseyed over from where she'd been chatting with Eleni, both in bright vermillion shorts and tops. She pushed her bike ahead of her with just a little struggle, then kicked the stand into place. She asked Virgil if he'd given any further thought as to what song he was contemplating for the karaoke event scheduled this evening on the *Iphigenia*.

"Something patriotic, Candy, like 'Stars and Stripes Forever'."

I didn't think Virgil Troyes capable of such a tongue-in-cheek riposte. I must have snickered.

"And you, dear, still set on that Venus ditty."

"Alexsis thinks I should. And Flex. Boyd Alexander, too, and you know him and his tunes. It was a great hit once upon a time, a favourite among the golden oldies I prefer listening to. Music from your era, Dad."

Candace turned to me and asked how I might contribute musically to the evening's entertainment. No doubt she was disappointed when I shrugged my shoulders and offered her a silly grin, then fumbled with the walkie-talkie getting it back in its holster. The karaoke party, so-called on the *Iphigenia* events calendar, must not have registered in my addled brain as something significant to look forward to. Such shindigs were not normally what appealed to me, nor, thankfully, to Penny.

"Joost told me they had a good repertoire of hits," Candace said, more to me than to her father. "A wide selection from across the decades. You'll find something, Geoff, I'm sure."

How could I deny such positivity, such well-meaning encouragement? I'd probably find a way.

"Looks like we're ready to roll again," Veridis called out. "Joost just gave us the signal."

By twelve-thirty we reached Laarne and dispersed ourselves around the square by the Kirk Van Laarne that was situated towards the east end of the centre. My left shin ached a little — a reminder to watch where I walked when gawking at local sites like castles and old churches. I did a cursory head check. All accounted for, all sitting around and munching on lunches.

The main drag of Laarne was busy — cars and the usual flow of locals on assorted bikes. It seemed that the favourite mode of transportation in this pretty little town for a mother with small children was the elongated Urban Dart. Such bikes were ubiquitous in the Lowlands. Even the camper in the hoodie who rescued Isla and Candace and directed them to Dendermonde last night operated one.

Lucy was sitting on a low stone wall nearby eating a chocolate bar. She picked up her phone when it rattled and did a lot of head nodding for approximately two minutes. When the call was completed, she turned to Vanessa who looked on quizzically.

"My next assignment. The International Conference on Human Rights in Brussels," she said, "if I'm up to it. I am. Definitely, although it might cut into our extra days in Bruges."

Our half-hour up, Joost marshalled us into a tight, safe line. We pursued him down the main street only to stop again, this time outside the gates of Kasteel Van Larrne, a restored medieval castle with moat. On this particular date, it was closed to the public, so those inclined to take photos had to do so through the portal of the grand entrance way. Joost answered whatever question he could about its history. Within five minutes most of us were prepared to get going because getting to Ghent was really what the day's adventuring was all about. Nonetheless, Kat persisted in asking seemingly pointless question about the castle which Joost felt obliged to answer. Mitchell Monk began rocking on his bike. I wanted to do the same but couldn't quite manage it. Bike bells began to ring impatiently. Then we were off again. Thankfully.

Windy conditions prevailed for the run into Ghent from Laarne. A short stint along a wooded path came as a relief from the intermittent gusts we faced in the open farmland our route led through. We met up with the Scheldt River again, and followed the well-used, riverside path in a wide, westerly arc through the outskirts of Ghent into the city center. Busy streets, cars, vans, constant noise, and ubiquitous exhaust fumes. I had concern for my own safety let alone those ahead me, all with different abilities and little experience in negotiating stops and starts through crowded intersections. Lucy and Olivia were confident urban cyclists; however, this was not familiar Cambridge but a foreign city with unknown traffic patterns requiring I keep a vigilant eye on them.

However, I worried more about individuals like Kat and Eleni getting through to our planned stop without incident, no matter how idiosyncratic their decisions about proceeding. Joost led us along a high-density commercial avenue, past city hall and other memorable buildings we dared not fully take a look at. We circled through a rather busy touristy area and entered the Fietsenparking with its extensive arrangement of stanchions, an underground installation for bikes. Overhead was a busy thoroughfare giving access to Sint-Michielsbrug, a stone arch bridge of historical significance across the Leie canal. Dismounted, bikes locked, panniers in hand, we took on what Gothic Ghent had to offer, as Olivia said, "safe and sound." We had three hours to follow our interests, whimsical and otherwise.

Gathering us in a pack outside the bike garage, Joost said he had received a request — he did not specify who made the request — to lead a group of those interested in visiting religious centres of great import in what he called "old town Ghent." In the immediate vicinity were two churches that fit the description, Sint-Niklaaskerk and Sint-Michielskerk. He'd oblige and try to provide any relevant information where he could about the history of these renowned structures and the artwork, sculptures, and statues they housed. He warned that he was no expert and that he was not particularly religious. Olivia was the first of several who signed on.

I opted out, as did Veridis. My idea was simply to wander about and take it all in. It had occurred to me that Ghent was a city Penny and I would enjoy touring around on some future trip. I made a mental note to include the point in my email to her before calling it a night. Exactly that, wander about the Gothic inner city where the streets reeked of history. Aware of Veridis' knowledge of architecture and his propensity to hold forth, I asked what he thought of my plan which, I surmised, would also take us, should he accompany me, into the university area. After all, Ghent was a university town with a putative seventy thousand students stationed throughout its precincts.

Great idea, Veridis conceded, he loved to go on about fenestration, but he had something different to propose and I was sure he knew I'd defer. Join him in visiting Gravensteen, Castle of the Counts, from what he believed to be the eleventh century. It boasted a moat, he stated with certainty, and other fascinating features like a donjon and a hall displaying the full array of medieval weaponry. Veridis claimed he had a morbid fascination about torture chambers and oubliettes (an aspect of his character not yet revealed), and needed to indulge it in such an inviting and intriguing site which was, according to the sources online he consulted, of major historical importance in the evolution of the city of Ghent.

"I'll be disciplined," he said when I agreed to accompany him. He allowed himself a quirky smile, then added, "I'll even pay for your entrance fee."

We spent approximately two hours touring around the ghastly site, Veridis adding details of his own to what the audio guides gave us. He was in an expansive mood. I was in need of a drink. The most rewarding part of our tour was the panoramic view of Ghent you got from the high, crenelated walls.

Before walking over to Gravensteen with Veridis, I happened to notice an Irish bar in the vicinity of Sint-Michielsbrug. Across the way was where all our bikes had been stashed. Easy. Accessible. I told Veridis I'd pay for his stout or whatever brew he set his heart on as we hoofed it back to the central area and the pub. He didn't take too much convincing.

"So, Geoff, any lasting impressions?" Veridis asked after the waiter brought us our drinks. We sat at an outside table, one of a series facing the busy street where trams and tourist buses created a constant flow of momentary distractions, with pedestrians and cyclists, many cyclists, adding in local colour.

"Baroque over barbarism," I answered after a moment's hesitation, the image of gruesome instruments of torture revived in my imagination. "My choice any day of the week."

Veridis snorted, then quaffed back a good measure of stout. We got around to discussing history and what defined civilization and what motivated human behaviour for good or for ill. We seemed to focus on the latter, touching on such human motivators as fear, ignorance, greed, and desire for power and dominance. I suggested that desire for revenge could turn unbridled, raw emotion into murderous action. Abounding records verified the fact in historical accounts, literature, and drama extending back to the ancient Greeks. Veridis maintained that despite advancement in many spheres, science, medicine, philosophy, industry, human beings were still very capable of inflicting pain and suffering on each other. Ego, indomitable ego. We waded into positive territory and what a motivated ego could produce — beauty, creativity, intellectual advancement. Eventually our talk picked up on the individuals we thought were creative and the stories they were willing to tell.

"Believer it or not, Frank," I started in, "I've inadvertently become a kind of chronicler of other people's affairs. Nothing as queer as folk, right? Riding along pulling together tales from the *Iphigenia*. Snippets of record from lives being lived, to be credited or not. In other words, given the nature of this trip, biking and barging as a group endeavour, I somehow get to play the part of interlocutor. Talk begets talk, I suppose. It's only natural to be conversing with people. As Alexsis Troyes claimed, talking to others can be educational. It certainly is revealing."

"I know exactly what you mean, Geoff," Veridis said. "Like being a post-modern Chaucer. Substitute the medieval city of Bruges for Canterbury, and we're well on our way."

"Chaucer. Chaucer. Right, *The Canterbury Tales*."

"So you know Chaucer?"

"More or less. The gang of pilgrims riding along on horseback to the cathedral, the miller, the knight, the monk, the reeve, the nun, and many more. Each had a tale to tell."

"Some of the tales were edifying from a Christian point of view, if you remember, some not edifying at all. Entertaining, yes, and rather ribald."

"Wouldn't necessarily lose your soul listening to the Wife of Bath."

"Indeed, *Amor vincit omnia*. Not likely to be the case here on the *Iphigenia*, but a lot of laughs regardless."

Mitchell Monk and Aimée Reeves sauntered by, stopped, and intimated they wouldn't mind taking a load off their feet. Touring the churches had proven exhausting.

"Please sit," Veridis said, swinging a chair out in a welcoming manoeuvre. He inadvertently set our panniers tumbling to the sidewalk. "Have whatever you like. Geoff's buying."

They ordered and then got around to answering our queries about how they spent their time. Aimée did most of the talking. Mitch listened patiently while consuming the fancy bottle of Belgian beer, a large one, that I'd be paying for.

"Fascinating city," Aimée said, more or less concluding her remarks, "although Mitchell does not quite share my enthusiasm for what has endured for centuries."

At this point, Aimée pointed across the street at a hooded individual riding a cargo bike loaded down with what looked to be camping gear. He was advancing slowly up the slight incline leading to the Sint-Michielsbrug, now populated with tourists on the bridge taking photos of the Leie.

"That's the second time I've seen that guy today," she said as though excited by such a possibility in a city with multiple versions of a passing cyclist, wearing a hoodie, in this case dark blue, riding what Veridis defined again as an Urban Dart. "What do you say, Mitch? Same guy?"

"They all look alike here," Mitch said. "So many students about."

Aimee persisted, claiming she'd seen Flex talking with "the hoodie guy" down in the bike parkade just before Joost gathered the group together to decide on sites to visit. Vanessa was close by. She could verify. Maybe. Then Aimée let it rest when Veridis announced it was time to rejoin the group.

"Flex may have siphoned off from the group to go to the WC down there," Vanessa confided to me when I pursued the point once we gathered on the Pakhuisstraat. "But a bogeyman in blue coveralls? Not a bit of it."

Neither Candace nor Isla were able to confirm the sighting and thus identify the guy Aimée described, if indeed it was the same guy they had met previously.

We had a good half-hour's ride before arriving at the *Iphigenia* moored this evening in the general vicinity of Evergem on the Ringvaart north of Ghent proper. Before starting out, I did a head count, determining that all were present and accounted for. Ironic somehow when we arrived, Conrad standing on the sundeck waving each of us aboard like long lost friends. And I thought, maybe I could like that guy given half a chance. Possibly. Well, maybe not. I looked forward to my post-cycling, pre-dinner rituals and the downtime they allowed me in the solitude of my own headspace. We'd all assemble for dinner soon enough.

"How they brought the good news from Ghent to Aix," mused Veridis, the last to seat himself down at our table.

"How did they?" Olivia wanted to know.

"By horseback!"

"These days it would be on a bike," Melinda quickly put in. "On e-bikes, yeah?"

Veridis conceded the point.

"So, Geoff, you're a film editor," Lucy said, "and according to Mister Frank Veridis here you've won some awards." She too had cottoned on to HollandIP. She placed two tall glasses on the table, one for her, one for Vanessa. I would not have been surprised had she Goggled me and my work out of pure curiosity.

"Few nominations, even fewer awards," I answered. "Shared them with other professionals in the field. One for sound design. Another for best sound in a dramatic series. Also, the Atlantic Film Festival Award of Merit."

"That's brilliant," she said.

"Do you do the music for a film?" Vanessa wanted to know.

"No music, just dialogue and effects. I take the source dialogue and improve it, to eliminate interference from other sources of sound on the set. Several soundtracks have to be integrated into a consistent, flawless pattern."

"How do you do that?"

"An involved process that requires channelling, synchronizing, mixing, and so on. But I don't want to overwhelm you with jargon or, for that matter, bore you." I let my voice trail off, sipped some beer, and then looked beyond Vanessa's countenance that shone with expectation and interest. The jug that Flex presented Kat, I observed with a now wandering eye, still remained on the bar shelf. It intrigued me for a passing few seconds. What else might it have been called? A vessel? A vase? Ewer? Crock? Conrad had referred to it as a funeral urn.

"No, go on, Geoff," Lucy said, bringing me back to the table and my work in sound editing. "We do something similar in getting our articles ready for publication."

"Okay. Well, I attempt to refine dialogue, or enhance it to achieve the desired intensity or, in some cases, tone it down. I have a digital audio workstation and while doing my effects I operate three computer screens."

"Do you fiddle with the dialogue?" Olivia asked. "Can you change it?"

"The object is to render it pure. It's all about clarity."

"Rather like perfect pitch," Vanessa said thoughtfully.

Before I could comment further, Joost Goossens, standing by the bar and seeing that all guests were accounted for, requested our attention. He advised us about the weather forecast for the following day. Heavy showers likely in the afternoon. Rain gear advisable. He then handed out the itinerary sheets for the trek into Bruges, adding a few historical facts about the city. The karaoke entertainment was on for the evening, as promised. He finished with the hope that we enjoy the salmon steaks prepared so delicately by our chef Dirk Anders and his sous chef Anna who had begun serving. He retreated to his station, then turned back to ask if anyone found a phone. The one belonging to Mitchell Monk had gone missing. No one had, but that didn't matter, because Mitch jerked up from the table to say he'd retrieved it in the bottom of his pannier.

Interest in my sound editing work continued after the laughter subsided, Vanessa and Lucy leading and others following. Aimée looked enthralled. I did not want to disappoint her.

"A lot of what is heard in a film," I explained in answer to her question about final product, "gets added after the fact. There are sound libraries. And software for specific effects. For a winter animation project, Aimée, I relied on a collection of serviceable sounds that depicted walking in snow. There were many."

"Like aesthetic or thematic layering," Vanessa said rather appreciatively.

"Pretty much. Like right now, if our conversation were being recorded for a film about the *Iphigenia* and its guests, editing would require elimination of extraneous and distracting ambient sounds. What Conrad and Virgil are arguing about over there at their table, for instance. Or, as the case might be, if we were cycling along, we'd have to deal with bike squeaks, rolling of wheels, rattling chains, voices in the background, chirping birds, barges, and boats."

"Fascinating, so it is," Vanessa said.

"Like with cooking, yeah?" Melinda interjected. "You get your ingredients out on the table, then the real work begins as you mess about mixing them all together to present the perfect plate. It's all about presentation, yeah?"

"Exactly."

"Compliments to chef Dirk Anders," Vanessa exclaimed, dabbing her mouth with a napkin and taking a drink.

"Absolutely brilliant," Lucy agreed, forking up from her plate a morsel of her salmon steak.

"An inspiration, so it is."

"No argument about that, ladies. We're all of the same opinion, I'd venture to say. Now tell me, Geoff, what about CGI, how does it factor in, or does it, where your editing work is concerned?" I thought

Veridis might have been up on that cinematic innovation but, apparently, he wasn't.

"It's new, CGI, computer generated imagery. Doesn't apply directly to what I do. Interesting, however. *The Irishman* is a recent film that exemplifies its application. The main character's older face had been technically enhanced to give the impression of a more youthful version. Tough to get it right, I thought. The film's about Jimmy Hoffa's disappearance back when, a still unsolved mystery. Hit squad or what?"

"A continuing conundrum, yeah? Concrete being a heavy medium."

"Have you done work on socially relevant films?" Olivia asked.

"Some, I suppose, but nothing that corresponds in depth to the work that Vanessa and Lucy have done."

"How about mysteries?" Mitch asked.

"My last project, a major one lasting three seasons, was a detective series for television. The leads were a husband and wife who were well equipped to gather clues, reveal in the process the workings of the human soul, and thus solve crimes. No nominations for that work but it did help pay the bills."

"Intriguing," Vanessa said.

"Brilliant."

"I see what I do as a puzzle requiring, despite all the software available to me, a great deal of concentration. Sometimes it's like trying to solve an enigma cloaked in a variety of subtle possibilities. One with a lot of characters to decipher in terms of motivation. Like who murdered whom and why. Also to be determined are when, where, and how."

"Geoff, you're becoming a fabulist," Lucy said and laughed. "Keep it up and you'll be writing your own script for your own film where you manufacture all the voices and sounds."

"Mind how you go, yeah?" Melinda said, tapping Mitchell Monk on his arm.

"Indeed. Treat Geoff with respect," Veridis warned, "or he'll write you into the plot and maybe not in a good way."

Laughter.

"So the war in Ukraine?" Lucy asked. "Anybody?"

I welcomed the new topic as I was beginning to find it tedious going on and on about my work as sound editor.

"Russian aggression of the usual kind," Veridis suggested.

"Bloody, treacherous, unconscionable," Olivia said shaking her head. "Those poor children. Homeless."

"Putin's invasion of the Ukraine," I said, "is the only way to describe it. I've long entertained more than antipathy for the Russian president. It's more like hatred, but impossible to articulate let alone act upon in any useful way."

"It's a war of self-aggrandizement," Veridis said. "For Putin, who has, as you implied, Olivia, no conscience at all."

"He's all about his legacy, isn't he?" Monk offered. "Like with Trump. Only difference is, Trump's not a murderer."

"Let's not go there, Mitch," Aimée said. "Please. No this and that about Trump."

"Works for me, Babe."

"And we don't want to go on about Boris Johnson," Belinda chimed in. "Let's just hold him in aspic if not in contempt, yeah?"

"His eccentric English persona got him a long way," Lucy said decidedly. "I've had to research him on more than one occasion."

"Boris Johnson is a party animal," Melinda said. "Both ways."

"He was Mayor of London before becoming Prime Minister," I said, feeling a need to contribute something about the man, limited though my knowledge of him was, "and educated down your way at Cambridge. Or am I mistaken?"

"Mistaken," Vanessa piped in. "Educated at Oxford, so he was."

"As I've said before, he was a lot of things in a lot of places before becoming Prime Minister," Melinda said. And then smiling, she added, "Contentious like the rest of the nits in Westminster."

"About Boris I can say very little," Veridis said. "I believe Mitch is right about Putin, however, but not about Trump, whom I will abstain from commenting on though I could go on ad infinitum. As to legacy, you will have zero legacy if your country is obliterated with the rest of the world."

"That is bleak" Lucy said, "but I follow the logic."

"Did you know that a restaurant in Paris," Veridis went on, "after receiving threats, had to clarify the difference between the French-Canadian comfort food called poutine and Vladimir Putin. In French, his name is pronounced like poutine. Putin has, as we all know, esurient appetites when it comes to expansion."

"You mean, his greedy need exceeds his grasp," Lucy put in. "And his eyes are bigger than his belly?"

"Seems to be the case after how many months of inflicting hell on an innocent population."

"Those poor children," Olivia declared once again. "He has blood on his hands."

While dessert was being served, engineer Aldert De Vries, whom some at our table, including me, thought of as standoffish and somewhat bumptious surprised us in a couple of ways. One, it was he, not Joost, setting up the karaoke machine. He was smiling widely as he did so. And two, he was the first to take the microphone in hand and deliver the goods. Still wearing his Greek fisherman's hat, he unleashed the soundtrack and gave a very convincing rendition of Neil Diamond's "Sweet Caroline." As far as I could determine, there was no better way to get *Iphigenia* guests, who were sipping Captain Vander Valk's complimentary flutes of champagne, even more psyched up to participate: *dun, dun, dun* repeated and then extended as long as Aldert repeated the sweet Caroline chorus, a decrescendo of single syllables but echoing with increased intensity until he raised his hands, enough.

"Brilliant," Lucy said.

"He's got things going, alright," Veridis said when the applause died down, "he's done the introductory come-on before, I'm sure."

"Not his first rodeo," Mitch piped in.

"Who is the next one?" Aldert De Vries asked, looking around. "We have every song music available."

He focused his attention on Isla and then on Candace, holding out the microphone at arm's length. I saw Boyd Alexander nudge Alexsis' shoulder, but she shrugged the encouragement off. Surprisingly, Aimée Reeves got up from our table, approached Aldert, spoke quietly to him, and took the microphone. While he messed about with the karaoke machine, she addressed herself, looked at the ceiling for a moment, then took a series of deep breaths. When the music revved up, she launched herself into a song I'd not heard in years, "These Boots Are Made For Walking." Begun with a catchy diminuendo, the music and the lyrics Aimée delivered had her bopping from side to side as though she'd popped out of a video of caged go-go girls from the sixties. Penny and I enjoyed watching such retrospectives the networks occasionally programmed for late night viewing. My memory could reach back only so far, therefore in the present context I was grateful for the rewinds. Monk was getting a real kick out of the performance. When Aimée finished, she sashayed sassily back to the table, where he greeted her with a hug and kiss. Much applause, especially from our table.

"Brilliant," Lucy said. "Brilliant."

Aimée's effort seemed to inspire others. First was Candace who got up, talked briefly to Aldert, and then prepped herself. After a driving introductory riff, she got into the lyrics of "Venus" and could easily have passed for the goddess herself, so evocative of fire and desire that the words in the lyric avowed. Loudest cheers for Candace came from Virgil and Boyd Alexander who stood up and clapped their hands madly.

Not to be outdone by any young upstart, Beppie Visser arose and approached Aldert. In a moment or two, she was in the middle of the Beatles' "With A Little Help From My Friends" rendered in English with just a hint of a Dutch accent, particularly on the word "somebody" as in "somebody to love." She got loud cheers when she took the mike, even louder when she handed it back to Aldert. Difficult to determine what young Pieter Visser got out of his grandmother's rather startling performance.

Flex was next up. He ambled over to the bar without his cane for support and got Aldert to pull up "Mack the Knife" and at the appropriate time, he flashed his pearly white teeth, which caused an outbreak of agreeable laughter all around. In crooning how scarlet billows were starting to spread, he threw out his arms in a sweeping gesture, hands uplifted, as much as to say, we're all in this together as witnesses to MacHeath's bloody treachery. Though Flex's voice lacked the smoothness of the professional jazz crooner — what did I really expect for an ad lib interpretation of MacHeath by an amateur? — with fingers snapping rhythmically, Flex dramatized exceedingly well the intriguing imagery of that old classic.

"I recall hearing Bobby Darrin do that song on television back in the day," Veridis said when Flex returned to his seat and the clapping dwindled out. I couldn't compete with Veridis on that point, although I did know the song from listening to classic rock and golden oldies on radio, particularly when my son was a teenager and learning to play guitar.

"Who?" Olivia asked, adjusting her hearing aids.

"Bobby Darin," Veridis replied, "Song comes from Bertolt Brecht's "Three Penny Opera," so my memory tells me."

"My research," Lucy said, placing her phone back on the table, "tells me that MacHeath originates from John Gay's "The Beggar's Opera" and that Brecht and his associate adapted the character to suit their dramatic purposes."

"Who's John Gay?" Olivia asked. "And who's that other guy?"

"Don't worry about them," Vanessa said. "They have no bearing on our enjoyment of what we just heard."

I had not expected during a karaoke session intended for entertainment of *Iphigenia* guests that an outbreak of duelling points of view would ensue. In the aftermath of an electronic simulation of a once renowned artist and his or her hit, remembrance versus research would compete for the last word. Just as entertaining as the music itself.

"My turn," Melinda said, tapping Olivia's arm resolutely.

I was all for that, and so, apparently was Veridis and everyone else at our table. Once into it, Melinda gave us an acceptable but somewhat scratchy version of "Summertime" that netted her more plaudits than I thought she deserved. She did not possess a sufficiently bluesy voice. Her bow upon concluding the final dragged-out note seemed superfluous. When she returned to the table, Olivia reminded her that she'd promised to sing "You'll Never Walk Alone." After all, Olivia explained, the song came from Liverpool.

"Did it?" Veridis.

"No, it didn't," fact-checker Lucy said. The song, adopted by Liverpool supporters as an anthem, originated in an American musical called "Carousel."

Olivia wanted to know how Aldert could pull so many old songs out of his karaoke box. While waiting for the next volunteer to step up, Veridis provided an answer that seemed to satisfy her curiosity. Quite likely Aldert's unit was state-of-the-art, equipped with all the latest filters and mechanisms for unlimited music downloads. Everything, anything was accessible these days. He mentioned a couple of name programs that would facilitate the gathering of songs, break them into component tracks, and deliver enhanced sound quality. I acknowledged Veridis explanation with a "well-done" nod of the head. No sooner had I done so when Melinda, having willingly played her part, challenged me, further dispelling my belief that karaoke as primetime pastime appealed mostly to the young.

"Surely, Geoff, with all your experience as an expert in sound manipulation, you could do a little lip sync and voice over for the benefit of the whole company. We're all in this together, yeah?"

In truth, I had considered for a fleeting few seconds doing Leonard Cohen's "Hallelujah," which was Penny's favourite. I backed down from the possibility, believing the song didn't quite fit the gregarious tone of the moment, but I did get to do it, later, without karaoke assist, in my own head in the privacy of my own musical world. As to the gregarious mood of the room, some who took the mike saw fit to alter it by changing, as they say, the tune.

"Right," I said. "I see your point, Melinda. I'll give it some thought. What about you, Lucy?"

"I'm considering Ed Sheeran's "The Castle On The Hill" but all in good time."

"Be grand," Vanessa encouraged. Likely she had a good reason for saying that, but I had no idea of the song or the artist Lucy mentioned.

"And you, Vanessa?" Aimée asked.

"Van Morrison, likely one of his best loved."

I recalled Aimée describing Boyd Alexander as an encyclopaedia of musical history, able to talk tunes as far back as the big band era. Few of us could go back that far. The sixties were hard enough. The fifties? Forget it. Well, maybe Veridis could stretch himself across the decades to Elvis.

Boyd Alexander took the floor and spoke to Aldert. Then he addressed the room.

"This rarity is from The Band's *Big Pink* album, circa 1968. "I Shall Be Released" composed by Bob Dylan."

The lyrics of the song — I was not familiar with them at all — were extremely moving and Boyd Alexander sang them as though he were living them right there in front of us all. Erie, uncanny, the sound of his voice, so like that of the poet who in recent years won the Nobel prize for literature. In terms of what the future held, Boyd Alexander's choice of that particular song among the many that Dylan produced was so very, very ironic.

I hung around for Vanessa's rendition of "Brown Eyed Girl." I remembered the song with its up-beat lyricism. It got my foot tapping. I watched Vanessa's lips to see how well they matched the words. Perfect, from a technical perspective. Then Virgil Troyes got up and started in on "The Eve of Destruction." Chances were that he had Putin's invasion of the Ukraine and the vicious slaughter of its citizens in mind. Struck me as related. At this point I figured it was time to leave and made it obvious for anyone who might have noticed that my shin was bothering me, so absolute was my effort to rub it that I nearly convinced myself it was still actually aching. Excusing myself when applause for Virgil started, I slunk off to my cabin.

In my post-karaoke email to Penny, I asked for her indulgence, given the truncated account of the day' doings I was composing. I described what I could of Ghent, emphasizing the appeal of visiting this fascinating city with her in the future. I referenced touring around Gravensteen castle with Veridis but avoided including any ghastly points of interest. Details of the evening's karaoke entertainment that I survived, however, took up two lengthy paragraphs that I had to amend in several spots. No mention of Cohen's "Hallelujah." On the other hand, I explained why Flex's version of "Mac The Knife" impressed me the way it did. Boyd Alexander was, in Lucy talk, absolutely brilliant. Like an omen.

Food on the *Iphigenia* next: no matter the dish, meals were always beautifully prepared and served. Melinda Mancipal, who ran a well-recognized catering business in Cambridge, never failed to stamp each presentation with her seal of approval. A real character was Melinda Mancipal.

With so much going on at all times of the day, I was losing track of events in the Tour de France. I needed to be kept up to date.

Random observations included in the email:

The chatter and exchanges of fellow barge and bikers continue to reveal enthusiasm. The general mood is positive. Impressions verge on the wondrous, for example, at Kinderdijk, but rarely reach ecstatic expression.

Accents vary, be they Dutch, American, British, or Irish; Japanese second only to the Dutch in deciphering difficulty.

Frank Veridis whistles while cycling if not engaged in conversation which is difficult while riding, so a lot of whistling.

Interesting how voices differ in conversation and in song. Also Interesting, how different women use their hands when posing, holding a glass of wine, reacting to or making a point, which has nothing to do with accent. Vanessa De La Croix leads with an index finger. Lucy Hunter fiddles with her earrings as though beating out a tattoo but one only she can hear. Olivia adjusts her hearing aid. Aimée Reeves frequently interweaves her fingers. Despite the many rings, Kat rubs her hands frequently enough for Veridis to drop with humorous intent another line he admitted borrowing from the bard: "What, will these hands ne're be clean?"

The Conrad Corps continues to summon speculation, not all of it complimentary, but definitely not dark, or noir, as Veridis likes to say when discussing fiction. So far, most talk involves Conrad Steele and his stepdaughter Alexsis who, it is thought by many, has morphed grief of loss into a bitter, full-time occupation. Mourning becomes Alexsis, as Veridis said. But with the arrival of a friend called Flex, she's allowed a little more light into her life.

"And so it goes," I typed into my conclusion, "enhanced by songs, rumblings in the passageway, giggles, harrumphs, complaints of sore muscles, coughs, and thumps in the night that have nothing to do with the running of the diesel engine that ensures all's well that ends well onboard the *Iphigenia*."

Send.

It was very late. I took a deep breath, closed things down, and turned to the porthole for one last look at the night before crashing. What I saw surprised me, Flex alone walking determinedly along the cycling path towards Dendermonde.

Ghent to To Bruges

My first cup of coffee saw me sitting alone for a short spell contemplating our arrival that afternoon in Bruges and why that city enjoyed the reputation as being Venice of the North. A canal excursion was in order and I would induce Veridis to accompany me. He'd pay his own way, of course. A couple of touring reprobates, the two of us. I thought again of *In Bruges*, the dark comedy film I'd recommended to him, given his philosophical bent, that dramatized the life and death struggles of two Irish hit men hiding not so inconspicuously in the medieval city.

Lucy was the first to join me. She gave me the highlights of Act II from last night's karaoke entertainment. She didn't hesitate, just started right away, correctly assuming that I'd be interested. I was. Kat and Eleni demurred as might have been expected. So did Frank Veridis, as might also have been expected, although he gave some thought to doing, had he worked up the gumption, the Rolling Stones' "You Can't Always Get What You Want." Sadly, no gumption evident and none forthcoming. Niels Visser and Joost Goossens did a drinking song together in Dutch or maybe it was in German, she wasn't sure. Mitchell Monk sang a Johnny Cash song, all twang in the best country and western tradition that, to Lucy's ear, verged on rural Baroque. Alexsis and Isla both chose songs of recent popularity, contemporary numbers about which Lucy was absolutely clueless, but she clapped approval for the girls anyway. Olivia got around to hearing "You'll Never Walk Alone" — in her own wavering voice. Conrad Steele in a deep, boozy baritone did a number where through his warbling, winks, and overt gesturing he played one woman off against the other, Kat and Eleni being the women in question. Lucy couldn't remember the name of the song Conrad sang but remembered well Melinda's comment when he finished and took a bow: "Narcissistic twat!" He thought he was a stylist flashing that big ring as he pointed here and there. Imagine! However, when the karaoke session was over, Melinda, a few glasses of wine to the good, started playing up to Conrad, agreeing with everything he advanced, even talking about his company's successes. And how did the meeting go that day? And did he remember a conference in Cambridge? He did not remember specifics of the conference in Cambridge, just that the service was A-1 okay. Like a minstrel of misdirection, he was.

"Right, right," I said. "Chemistry. Or some version of it."

"Be that as it may, embarrassment prevailed in many a 'good night!'" she concluded, getting her coffee ready.

I thanked Lucy profusely for her summary, replete with asides, and passed the sugar over when she asked for it. Then Veridis joined us and with the inspiration that morning coffee provides he started in on the social benefits of karaoke and how last night it brought the generations together. Lucy pretty much agreed with him while I had a slightly different opinion which I pretty much kept to myself.

"Gen X leading and ahead of Gen Y by millions," Veridis said and grinned mischievously.

"Where does that put us, Frank?" I asked.

"Keeping pace, Geoff, keeping pace," he answered, and then took a long drink from his coffee. "But you know, Millennials will be running the show."

"Known also as Gen Me." Lucy said.

"Known also as Echo Boomers," Veridis said, "with their easy access phones and gadgets, plugged in constantly to all their electronically generated friends when solitude grips them. Though confident and tolerant and not totally oblivious to the passing world, they're narcissistic and believe themselves entitled. Witness Alexsis in her direst moments."

"Vanessa and I..."

"You and Vanessa pass as totally savvy millennials exhibiting the many strengths of your generation. Admirable."

"What's next, Frank?" I asked.

"Gen Z. Followed by Gen Alpha, aka the glass generation."

"Enlighten us, Frank."

"Reality for them asserts itself only through a device with a glass face, tiny technology known pretty much since day one, their infantile curiosity enhanced by pablum smears on all shiny surfaces within reach. For obvious reasons, the youngster Pieter Visser provides the exception or so it would seem. My business interests deal with all ages and generations."

Our conversation then turned to the difference between progeny and prodigy, to fathers and sons and parental expectations vis à vis filial successes: his son was a marvel, a big success on Bay Street. "Owns half of downtown Toronto," Veridis asserted with a self-conscious grimace. "He's Gen X and in total control of himself. What about your guy?"

I said that David, no doubt about his being a Millennial, was totally involved in an archaeological dig at Mycenae on the Peloponnesus. He'd been a fan of Greek mythology since childhood and as a kid loved digging things up in the garden, the dog's buried bones, for example, or spoons and tools he himself had put there. His achievements lay ahead.

"And someone like Boyd Alexander?" Lucy asked.

"Plugged in absolutely," Veridis answered without hesitation.

"What generation are the Japanese fellows?"

"They're ageless, Geoff, wouldn't you agree?"

Vanessa appeared, then shortly after that, the rest of our group. Breakfast rituals proceeded as usual at all three tables. Talk amongst us centered on just how successful the karaoke party proved to be. During the exchange of opinions, I got a few inquisitive looks that motivated me to explain my early retirement. No doubt the thinking was that if old Frank Veridis could hold out, why not old Geoff Canter. After all, he had more than a couple of years on me. Melinda's ambiguous smile was disconcerting and put me off my scrambled eggs. Veridis regarded me sympathetically. I figured he knew what I was thinking.

"Vanessa," I said, "Your *Brown Eyed Girl* rendition got my foot tapping. A favourite from back when. And I like what you did, Aimée. And your *Summertime* was pretty good too, Melinda."

Sensing my stumbling attempts to avoid the obvious, Veridis asked me, "Do you think Aldert's karaoke unit is equipped with personal recording ability?"

"Quite likely," I answered immediately, "if it's the latest and greatest. I never thought to look it over."

"That being the case, folks," Veridis said, "had any of you asked, you could have had Aldert De Vries record you doing your number and present you with a CD to take home as a memento."

"Endless summer, yeah?" Melinda said, nodding at Olivia.

Mitchell Monk posed what I took to be a rhetorical question. "Have Aimée walk her boots all over me again?"

"And again and again," Vanessa added. She seemed pleased to be getting a dig in.

"No bloody way!" Monk snarled.

Olivia offered the following opinion. "Though Flex was convincing in his interpretation, even comical, *Mac The Knife* is a spooky song. It was as if the lad knew MacHeath personally. I never liked that song. It's ominous, I dare say. Poor Suky Tawdry."

"I see where you're coming from, Olivia," Lucy said, "MacHeath's a dangerous character who wears threat like a new jacket. On the other hand, I have nothing but praise for Boyd Alexander and how he held his audience completely spellbound."

"Did anyone notice Conrad's reaction," I asked, "when Boyd Alexander was doing his number?"

"Conrad seemed miffed," Lucy answered. "No, riled, vexed. Tapped his ring on the side of his glass. More an unconscious reaction, I think, than a deliberate effort to distract from his son's performance."

"Pathetic, yeah?"

Joost appeared and asked for our attention. We'd be setting out at nine o'clock. He gave us a cursory weather report — wind, and rain showers in the afternoon. Dress accordingly. Rain gear advisable. Then he asked to meet with Hash and Kash and also with Flex and Alexsis to get specific GPS information.

"Satnav," Melinda said, getting up from the table. "Left to their own devices, can they be trusted?"

Another rhetorical question. It seemed likely Flex and Alexsis would be cycling to Bruges independent of the larger group and, even more likely, independent of Hash and Kash.

The sky above the Flemish countryside was smoky-grey and saturated with threat. Unanticipated roadwork forced Joost to guide all eighteen of us along a route reaching the outskirts of Lovendegen. Here we circumnavigated the town, Joost at the head of the group, me at the tail, as usual now, and soon picked up again on a track leading us to the north bank of the Kanaal Gent-Brugge which we followed in a westerly direction. Along the way we came very close to a paddock where a pair of Belgian horses stood head to tail like granite statues.

"Halt, Joost, halt," I called into my walkie-talkie once I'd wrestled it out of the holster. "The horses here, somebody stopped."

That somebody was Kat, judging by the gap that had opened between her and Conrad. Niels Visser had been riding immediately behind her, followed by at least half, if not more, of the group, which now got bunched up into a cacophony of awe and uncertainty. Joost brought the smaller, forward group back.

"Brilliant," said Lucy who had moved in closer to me. "It's like the brutes are posing for us."

"Belgian draft horses," I heard Visser explain to Kat, "are typically blonde. Also chestnut, I think this is the correct word. These two specimens are special. Grey is not typical. Grey is very rare."

"Straight from the horse's mouth," Melinda said, and showed her teeth with humorous intent.

Steamy droppings enhanced the earthy odours of the enclosure but did not dampen the enthusiasm of the shutter bugs. Out came the phones. I could never understand the propensity to take selfies at the drop of a hat but having these incredible equine beauties as backdrop somehow passed as acceptable. Comic, however, the vying for position and the need to gain the best perspective. The horses were dark, the skies were darker, some of the looks exchanged even darker yet.

"Where exactly are we?" Aimée asked when a half-hour later we pulled off the narrow, bank side thoroughfare we'd been following for a good distance since leaving the Belgians. "And how much farther?"

"At the Café Vaart-Noord, yeah?" Melinda said, indicating the sign above the entrance way. We parked the bikes, the gang of us taking over all the outdoor seating, and engaged, table by table, a very patient young server who spoke excellent English.

"I know exactly where we are," Monk said, accessing phone and GPS app. He also pulled out his map. After a moment's calculation he declared that we were exactly twenty-five point eight kilometres from the market square in Bruges. He and Aimée now sat with Visser and me, Candace and Isla. Young Pieter was fist-pumping with Boyd Alexander at an adjacent table. Visser said he believed Beppie called "this one" accurately. He pointed to the sky. Wise that she'd opted to remain with the *Iphigenia* on such a threatening day.

In full view from the Café Vaart-Noord terrace was the Kanaal Gent-Brugge. Visser pointed out that we would be following it all the way into Bruges. Consulting his map, Monk agreed and showed the proof to Aimée. Boats, barges, and pleasure craft worked their way up and down the channel. Difference in size and speed left different kinds of wakes. I was content just sitting with my Cappuccino and watching their progress, sharing a comment or two with Visser and listening in on what Candace and Isla were saying about Alexsis and Flex. Conversation turned from the brooding clouds overhead, to the imposing size of the Belgian draft horses, to the fun had by all at the karaoke event last night. I complemented Candace on her "Venus" and added that my wife and I once danced to that song at a wedding we were invited to. Memorable because of the driving beat and the sensual lyrics and the fact that I pulled a muscle that kept me virtually inactive for a week.

"Thanks, Geoff."

"I'm sorry to have missed your song, Isla."

"You didn't miss much."

"No, it was fabulous," Aimée insisted.

"It was a very nice song, what she did," Visser said, nodding pleasantly at Isla. "So with the sister, Alexsis."

"Speaking of Alexsis," Isla said, "and therefore Flex. He was showboating a bit doing his *Mack the Knife* routine. But you know what, his joining us here is the best thing for Alexsis. He's made her smile. Made her drop the antic disposition so upsetting to both Conrad and Kat. They're as thick as thieves. Flex and Alexsis, I mean."

"True enough," I said, "she seems more settled now."

"She can be so over the top in her resistance, constantly exaggerating about how hard done by she is. You can't always take everything she says at face value. She's capable of outright lying. Believe me, I know."

"Right. I suppose that applies to all of us, being capable of lying, I mean."

"So, for your sister, Flex is good medicine, ja?" Visser said.

"A perfect fit. Off together today. I hope they get back to the *Iphigenia* safely."

"You girls got back after getting side tracked, didn't you?" Monk said. "Even without GPS."

"We had help," Candace pointed out. She turned to Isla and then added in a sing-song voice, "We got by with a little help from our — " She hesitated. "I don't remember the guy's name. Rolf?"

"Dolf. Dolf Van Handelaar," Isla said.

"Anyway, we called him Mr. Van Hoodie," Candace concluded, and indulged herself in a little laugh.

After a moment's silence Isla said, "You know, as far as the karaoke went, I thought Hash or Kash might have tried to do some song but neither did, even though it looked like one or the other might take up the challenge."

"It's not like they would be giving away state secrets," Monk said. "They don't say much, do they?"

Hash and Kash, inscrutable to some degree for most of us. As for Monk, I'd observed how he proved unable to break through the veneer of polite rebuff try as he might with the hail-fellow, well-met shoulder knocks he directed their way.

He shifted position at the table in order to take a selfie, making it obvious that he wanted Candace in the frame. Aimée frowned. Had she been able to growl, she would have then. And if a menacing stare had more edge, we'd have had a corpse to drag into Bruges.

When Joost indicated it was time to go, Visser pointed to the sky again and said, "Not so good omen."

"An ill wind as well," Isla said and then drained the dregs from her coffee mug.

Having crossed to the south side of Kanaal Gent-Brugge, we spent the better part of an hour facing into a headwind. More rich farmland, and cows, sheep, an occasional horse or two — if you dared looked beyond the back wheel of whoever rode ahead of you, Candace and then Isla in my case. Given all the golden oldies that had recent play in my head, it was no wonder that I kept singing the refrain in Bob Seger's *Against the Wind*. It became a mantra that sustained my willingness to keep pumping the pedals. Were the karaoke invitations on again, this evening, for instance, I would definitely volunteer to do *Against the Wind* and do so with a lot less humming. Meanwhile, we skirted the town of Beernem, making our slow way along the south bank cycling path and came to rest in a small picnic area that provided some protection from the elements. Benches, several of them and a long anticipated lunch break. Small mercies.

Situated down below the bike path on the shore of the waterway was an establishment called *Jachthaven,* a bistro cum marina. Joost advised us that we had sufficient time to go down to enjoy the amenities, by which he meant, basically, the washroom facilities. I eventually followed on, having wolfed down my lunch sitting on one of the picnic benches with Joost. He looked a little worn out. I must have looked the same because he asked if I could still handle being the sweep. If not, Mitchell Monk said he could do the job. Mitchell Monk? Usurp my position? I wasn't having any of that. It struck me that Conrad or Virgil would be more interested and capable of taking over, more in their character.

"I'll survive," I told Joost.

Yachts secured along several *Jachthaven* jetties bobbed unevenly. Ragged-edged blue tarps flapped insolently against the ties that bound them. Canopies and umbrellas on the deck of the bistro beat out an unsettling rhythm as the wind asserted its nasty will. Other rattling noises. What had Isla intimated back there, that an ill wind blows no good? She'd got that right, alright. Feeling at ease or even comfortably warm seemed an impossible luxury and I knew I'd have to dig deep into my pannier to retrieve anything like the energy required to continue in a positive frame of mind. Mitchel Monk be damned!

"Queue for the loo," Olivia told me before she headed up to the picnic area.

"Right, right."

The rain that had been forecast started to fall by the time we all got back to the bikes. Most sensible cyclist in the group had already donned their raingear. I unravelled my portable plastic poncho from the pannier, grateful that Penny insisted I pack one. I'd need it. Doing a headcount proved awkward but I managed. Before we got going at a reasonable speed, the heavens opened like a giant sluice gate and the rain met us full on, whipped into our faces by the relentless wind. After a few minutes on the path, we reached an overpass and stopped under it. Despite the overhead protection, small puddles of water pooled around where we stood together dripping. No need for another head count. We were all there, huddled together, it struck me, like a herd of sheep, Joost as shepherd, me as sheepdog with a toothy attitude and a willingness to more than bark.

Decision time. Remain under the overpass till the downpour let up no matter how long that would take or cycle on like professionals through the storm, outrace it in effect? Soldier on despite the hardship was the majority wish: after all, the day was about reaching Bruges and besides, the nasty weather came as no surprise to anyone, and raingear was declared to be required. I was coming to understand, much to my chagrin, that there really was no way of knowing how people reach the decisions they do, no way to assess their judgements accurately. I was already pretty much drenched, wet on top and down my ears and wet with sweat on the inside. "Suck it up," I told myself, wiping sunglasses clean again — now there was an odd bit of irony — but I knew for certain I'd have to endure a miserable hour's tough slogging to reach Bruges, our imagined Mecca, the would-be promised land. But then, so would everyone else. In preparation for the forthcoming assault, I shook myself like a soaked, long-haired mutt and straddled my bike, anticipating that only mad peddling on my part would keep Candace and Isla in sight. I licked the salt from my lips.

The South Flanders Bistro, located at the lower end of the Kanaaleiland, a virtual island at the junction of waterway and motorway, was where we congregated once we'd reached Bruges. Our approach to the city required a series of traverses, crossing by bike bridge to the north side of the Kanaal, then crossing back to the south side, and then following along the Bargeweg road to where we came to a halt in an extensive, zoned area that accommodated tourist busses, campers, and parking for the marina. By this point in the afternoon, the rain and wind had petered out. I could swear all of us were being subjected to a sunburst of whimsical optimism as we stood around an elongated, outdoor drinking table entertaining each other with snappy narratives of personal performance vis à vis the lousy weather. Some talked briefly of the energy that determination provided while some gave over to praising individuals for effort shown, and a few notables succumbed to self-adulation. I could not decide where I fit in, but I really appreciated the cold beer. And so it went, exuberance in different guises prevailed outside the South Flanders Bistro while we waited for the *Iphigenia* to pull up along the Kanaaleiland bank. Yappy crows congregating in nearby trees looked on with what sounded like avian amusement.

Conrad said he was certain we'd passed the *Iphigenia* before we crossed over to the north side of the waterway. How could I have missed it? Well, I must have.

"Taking on a supply of water," Joost explained. "Thirty minutes, guaranteed, it arrives here."

"It can't get here soon enough," Kat said. Her body language indicated that she was exhausted, her extended arms lying limp on the countertop. Her hair reminded me of a rag mop, a very wet one. Eleni's hair looked like it had been coiffed by a stylist with a penchant for circles, spirals, and onion rings. Amusing, the effects that exertion at odds with the elements produced in human form and make-up.

"My body was trying to kill me," Olivia proclaimed in a vaguely triumphant way.

"I'm knackered," Lucy admitted.

"Ditto," Veridis said, his voice dripping sympathy. "But we hung in there pretty well. And you, too. Lucy."

"Got soaked," Aimée said. "But Mitchell was very encouraging."

"Bingo, Babe! You're right, I did well."

By this point in day six of the Triple B adventure, everyone was pretty much familiar with everyone else, or at least able to exchange anecdotes while rubbing shoulders, wet ones in iffy raingear. Chatter came easy. It was a form of relief, some of it a bit on the edgy side.

"Had a couple attempts to wipe me out," Monk said, pointing his chin at Veridis and then grinning spitefully. "Running your bike up the back of mine, not cool."

"Inadvertent, surely," Virgil suggested, "riding conditions being what they were. Eleni had the same problem. Same with Conrad."

"Exactly," Conrad agreed and rubbed Kat's arm.

"No need to complain, yeah?" Melinda said and gave us all a wide smile. "Cheers."

"So, Bruges, finally," Lucy said. "Who's doing what?" She looked expectantly up and down the table. "Tomorrow's the last day."

"What are your plans, Lucy, for when it's all over?" Eleni seemed genuinely interested. "Back to work or — ?"

"An extra day in Bruges in Vanessa's company and then it's on to my next assignment."

"Where would that be?" Eleni asked.

"Brussels. International Conference on Human Rights."

"You're not one of these despicable social justice warriors, are you?" Monk asked.

"Whatever my beliefs, Mitch, when on assignment I just do my job to the best of my abilities."

"Well played," Virgil Troyes said.

Vanessa had taken a seat at a table by the entrance to the Bistro. With her were Candace, Boyd Alexander, Isla, and young Pieter Visser. They were involved in flipping through their phones and commenting on photos. Much laughter. They all appeared as though they'd been put through the proverbial ringer, presumably the ringer of an old-fashioned washer. Very noticeable, long legs in shorts glistening in intermittent bursts of sunlight. Boyd Alexander's seemed to outdistance Vanessa's by a couple of feet. It then occurred to me — apropos in terms of our recent activity — that they'd just come out of the spin cycle rather than squeezed through the ringer.

"We also have extra time in Bruges," Eleni confided. "After that, Lille, where we take the Chunnel train to London."

"As for our contingent," Conrad said, "I meet this evening with my solicitor at the Magnifique. He is here on a short stay before accompanying me to Brussels on business matters. Kat and family have an extra two days in Bruges after which they will join me in the capital. Then back to the USA for all of us."

"We do need the downtime," Kat said. "But then there's Flex to consider, what?"

"Sweetheart, there's no need to concern yourself about Flex or his influence on Alexsis. Kinlaw and I will deal with all that." Having made such a public declaration, Conrad tapped his glass. I had the sense that he was trying to suggest he really was the take-charge type and that he had arranged things perfectly for the benefit of all concerned. He provided details about the wonders of the Magnifique, in fact, too many details.

"Sounds intriguing, Conrad," said Veridis, who had been quiet for the longest time, happy just to be listening while pulling on his beer.

"No worries, Conrad," Melinda said affably. "After day seven, Olivia and I head back to Cambridge. Back to work, yeah?"

"Are you going to take the jug with you?" Aimée asked Kat, whose posture was now a little more upright. "You know, the one Flex presented to you that's on the shelf in the bar of the *Iphigenia.*"

"Don't be ridiculous, girl!"

Joost smoothly worked in the fact that once we were all off the *Iphigenia,* preparation for the return to Amsterdam would begin for him and the crew. A new group, a new adventure. Niels Visser said he would go back to being retired and maybe write his memoires or a series of murder mysteries based on his career as a detective. Veridis said he was heading back to Montreal, and I said I'd be continuing my interest in the Tour De France in Paris and meeting my son in Greece after that.

Within an hour since our arriving at the bistro, Joost heard from Captain Vander Valk. The *Iphigenia* had landed and was ready to receive us onboard again. At this point, Conrad raised his empty glass and expressed his thanks to all the good people, all the fine fellow cyclists and passengers, that had made this adventure for his family and him the success it continued to be. Great group chemistry, he emphasized, in concert with a most accommodating crew. Continued success to all. Yeah, Conrad Steele could be an okay guy when he wanted to be. What followed after his masterful little speech and the collective cheer it raised was a mad dash to the *Iphigenia* by most of the group, some of their glasses left half-full. Shower time. Hot water. What could be more motivating?

Thinking of a possible future bike-barge adventure with Penny, I asked Virgil and Eleni about the hotel accommodation they'd booked in Bruges. We were pushing our bikes along at a casual pace — it was a short distance from bistro to barge and hardly merited mounting up Virgil said rubbing his posterior. Candace had joined us. Veridis and Visser kept pace behind.

"Hotel Burg," Eleni said, "overlooking a canal. Very reasonable."

Virgil added, "We couldn't possibly compete with the suite of rooms that Conrad has reserved at the Magnifique. Truth be known, Geoff, by comparison, this family here, though connected, we're just small change."

Hearing that, Candace broke out laughing, then explained. "Remember the other day when Isla and I got side tracked and how that hoodie guy on a long black bike helped us get back to the *Iphigenia*. Like, he tried to rip us off for thirty euros which we didn't exactly have on us at the time. American dollars? Yeah, he preferred American dollars. We handed him over about twenty bucks American in one-dollar bills and bits of small change."

"You didn't?" Eleni said in a pseudo-surprized tone of voice. She gave Candace an endearing look that broke into a beautiful smile. Their mother-daughter relationship, it struck me at that moment, contrasted so very greatly with that of Kat and Alexsis, but then I had a little more insight into the dynamics of the latter.

As we approached the *Iphigenia,* we met Hash and Kash releasing their bikes to the crew. We followed suit, panniers in hand. Hash explained that he'd had a flat but managed to get it sorted. Conrad met them half-way up the gangplank, virtually blocking their passing, and ours. He wanted to know if they had come across Alexsis and Flex, who had not yet made it to the barge. I took note of Conrad's intense blue eyes, so watchful, so suspicious. Hash and Kash had not seen Flex and Alexsis since starting out that morning. Virgil behind me told Conrad to relax, the kids would be here all in good time.

Sufficient hot water remained for my shower and by three-thirty or so I felt revived enough to approach Veridis about taking a short canal tour through Bruges before supper at six. He willingly agreed, in fact, thought it an excellent idea, but he let me know that he'd be calling it an early night because of a need to conserve energy for the following day. I was of the same mind. And body. Happily, Melinda and Olivia invited themselves along. Their helmet-pressed hair had been seen to, Olivia's worked into a sort of natural perm. Nice. Less so their scent. It was as though they did a slow dance around the perfume counters of a reputable department store. My under-arm salve refused to compete.

Melinda said she'd registered a complaint with Anna down in the passageway, telling her that the towels in their room were very tired towels indeed. Anna was inclined to replace them. Sander was in the vicinity working on a door handle, a loose screw, and came to Anna's defense. In his usual grumpy way, he barked out that the towels were tired because "you women give them a hard workout every day. You show them no mercy, ja?" Melinda and Olivia got a laugh out of Sander's cajoling. And they got new towels.

Leaving the *Iphigenia*, we crossed the bright red Bargebrug and walked through the treed Minnewaterpark to a more vibrant area of the city. Within ten minutes we had boarded a very accessible and comfortable touring launch, Veridis in a forward seat behind the pilot/guide, the rest of us on the port side. A group of American tourists sat behind us full of excited opinion. The launch was half full.

"This will do nicely," Veridis said. "On the other hand, there's an interesting torture museum that has piqued my innate interest in the evolution of execution devices, but I'll save that for tomorrow, should we have time enough after the cycling."

"Taking the piss again, are you, Frank?" Melinda said, saving me the trouble of commenting. "As for me and my piqued interest, I must do chocolate here despite the Gothic packaging. My sweet tooth insists."

We'd all agreed that taking the half-hour canal tour was a relaxing way to get an impression of the city from a different but revealing perspective, to get a sense of why it was described as the Venice of the North. Visiting the sites of historical significance like the famous Belfry of Bruges would wait till tomorrow afternoon, at least in my plans it would. The celebrated Bruges Beer Experience had a definite appeal and would fit in nicely after the cycling. Possibly. On Olivia's must-see list was the Basilica of the Holy Blood.

As we motored slowly along, the guide provided salient info about the history of various structures. Filling in the momentary silences, Veridis began and continued lecturing the three of us on fenestration through the ages, emphasizing the beauty and symbolism of the Gothic lancet window, examples of which were many along the waterways we were meandering through. Then he joked about defenestration, the venerable art of throwing someone out a window. How about out of a boat, Melinda quipped. When I said the bridges were particularly interesting and explained why, he said I was becoming a pontist, which Olivia, tapping me on the arm, thought a great compliment. I wasn't sure, given Veridis' bent for intellectual fun, frequently esoteric in content. Approaching what the guide called the Gruuthusebrug, we saw Mitchell Monk and Aimée Reeves poised on it, preparing to take photos. They waved to us and we to them. Even the Americans behind us waved. Swans surveyed the water in the vicinity of the bridge looking to get their pictures taken.

"Funny about Aimée liking that jug so much," Olivia said distractedly. "She's a lovely young woman. Him, well, I wonder. Very cocksure. Aggressive."

"You mean her liking the jug despite its inherent ugliness, yeah?"

"Not really that ugly," Olivia contended. "It's a nice shade of pink, isn't it?

"Pink it is for sure," I said supporting Olivia who often had to contend with her friend's contrariness. "Odd shape, yes, but not really distorted."

"In the few words I managed to exchange with Flex, without Alexsis shuffling her feet, that is," Melinda went on, "he said he thought of it as the symbol for a new start. He had not seen Kat in a long time, not since before her marriage to Conrad. It was meant as a simple gift. An acknowledgement."

"Flex must have meant the image of the phoenix on its side," I said, visualizing the jug. "The phoenix is symbolic of new life, of regeneration, is it not?"

"It is that," Veridis said. "But remember, folks, the phoenix is reborn out of ashes. I think Conrad had it right when he called it a funeral urn. Fits the symbolism just like the cork lid fits the top."

"No ashes, no new life, yeah?"

"Precisely."

Before we landed on terra firma, Veridis explained excrescence when it came to the expansion of existing buildings. He was not competing with the guide, he was just being Frank Veridis. His observations were intermittent. He lamented the superfluous addition of unattractive elements frequently found on otherwise beautiful structures, but provided no examples of what he had in mind regarding what we passed. He termed the aberrations a form of usurpation but was vague about what he meant. Maybe tomorrow he'd be more forthcoming. As for our little canal tour through historic Bruges, it proved worthwhile in more than one way, Frank Veridis at his whimsical best.

Dinner, day six. Before Anna began serving the appetizer, Joost Goossens gave us the lowdown on the route planned for the last day of what he like to call our Triple B adventure. He would be leading the group out beyond the city through polder landscapes, which he described as low-lying land protected by dikes, eventually getting to the shore of the North Sea. Dunes, sandy beaches, and assorted cafés all awaited our arrival. When returning to Bruges, we would have sufficient time in the city centre to visit important attractions. Lock bikes and take panniers. Those wishing to cycle independently were welcome to do so. He ended his spiel with the invitation to congratulate our "hard working and dedicated chef" for what would be another delicious meal. Implied in his words was a hint that all members of the crew would welcome any tip our gratitude and generosity might deliver. Much clapping. Then the meal got under way as usual.

Arriving late in the dining area were Flex and Alexsis, both receiving stern looks from Kat when they took their seats. Had Conrad been present, I surmised, stern looks would probably have erupted into stern words, words with blunt-force impact. Flex said something which must have been funny because all at the table broke into laughter, including Kat. Having stretched her ear, so to speak, Lucy said it sounded like he and Alexsis got side tracked searching for another jug, one more acceptable to Kat's tastes and sensibilities.

"Jug's gone," Aimée said in a short, sharp utterance. It was more of a yelp. Visibly distraught, she grabbed Mitchell's arm in a firm grip and shook it several times. I thought her concern disproportionate to the situation she forced us all into. But her observation was correct, no ugly jug on the bar shelf.

"There was never any guarantee, Babe," Mitch said, lifting her fingers from his arm one at a time. "It's not like you were going to rip it off."

"No, I wasn't. But Kat hates it, doesn't she? I just thought, you know — "

"No mystery about its not being where we last saw it," Veridis said. "It will show up, Aimée, and it still could be yours to take back. Everyone here knows how fond of it you are."

"Right, right," I said as agreeably as I could, and then focused my attention on the saltshaker in the centre of the table where it lined up with the butter dish, not the pepper. No doubt I was attempting unconsciously to avoid being a witness to a useless bit of embarrassment from a person I'd grown fond of.

"Ask Anna about it," Vanessa suggested.

"Later," Mitch said. "After we've all eaten."

"Brilliant," Lucy said.

"By the way, where's Conrad in all this jug talk?" Vanessa asked.

"To jug or juggernaut?" Veridis said and winced. He raised a protective elbow against sceptical frowns.

"That is the question," Aimée chimed in happily.

"Conrad's definitely not going to be having dinner here," I said.

"Won't he be missed?" Olivia asked.

"Not by Boyd Alexander," Lucy said. "And not by Alexsis, or for that matter, Flex."

Veridis then held forth on the matter of Conrad's absence. "He's not here, launching darts across the table at Flex and Alexsis, because he's taking a meeting with his lawyer in town, a fellow called Calvin Kinlaw, at the Magnifique. He let us know in no uncertain terms that the Magnifique is a five-star hotel with superb amenities."

"He certainly described the bar in superlatives," Melinda said.

When Vanessa declared that Bruges had some pretty impressive hotels, that the lodgings she and Lucy had reservations for was modest and within their means as working stiffs, a heated discussion of price points for accommodations followed. Verbal exchanges, based for the most part on previous travel experiences, took us through the appetizer and into the main course. Who was doing what after the meal came next and led to me declaring that I'd had a demanding day and planned only for some downtime before retiring early. Early to bed, early to rise, wasn't that the old aphorism? Tomorrow would present new challenges. Olivia agreed whole heartedly. Lucy and Vanessa would amble through the streets of Bruges to take in all things Gothic. After a few vague notions about sites worth visiting, Veridis said he had some reading to do. Mitch and Aimée were noncommittal.

"Go looking for the pink jug, yeah?"

In truth, the day had drained my enthusiasm for social intercourse. I sought solitude on the upper deck in need of no company but my glass of HollandIP while a cacophony of cawing crows added a plangent dimension to the ambience of the evening. But, not surprisingly, company eventually came to me. Grey evening light gave over to louring skies that evoked an ill-omened presentiment of what cannot be defined or counted. I was at a loss to explain the feeling. Though in my private space on the *Iphigenia*, I inadvertently allowed other guests to invade my thoughts and their presence there helped dissipate the disquiet I had begun to experience. I'd seen Boyd Alexander, Isla, and Candace head off past the campsite in the direction of the red bridge. Good, tour the town!

Alexis and Flex followed on at their own pace, he evincing less of a limp than previously. She kind of skipped about the way I'd often observed little girls as old as six or seven toss themselves from foot to foot, like hopping sparrows as they followed parents down the isle of a department store or along a path or across the parking lot to their SUV— nature's imperative, DNA programmed, universal in its application. I imagined Alexsis would have bopped about this way when as a kid she held her father's hand. The Vissers had probably gone down to their quarters. Not unexpected. Like with Veridis. I saw Virgil, Eleni, and Kat saunter over to the lounge after dinner and plop themselves down. I couldn't account for Hash and Kash, their movements often furtive as Veridis pointed out. No idea about Mitch and Aimée. As for Conrad, he was probably well into his meeting with Calvin Kinlaw.

I suddenly got put off with myself, letting my duties as sweep enter into time completely unconnected to doing a head count and now a head count was doing me. I was just getting over my little bout of self-recrimination when Melinda appeared and asked did I mind if she joined me. Her smile was less disconcerting than usual. In fact, it was ingratiating in a pleading sort of way. She was welcome, of course.

Before she sat down with her drink, she sniffed the air. A trail of smoke curled about overhead having drifted over from where some camper was barbequing meat, in essence a miniscule flaw of wafting flavours.

"You just can't avoid the aroma of ...What is it?"

"Pork," she declared. "Probably sausage."

"You've an exquisitely trained nose, Melinda."

"Comes with the territory. I do have all kinds of training."

"Your catering, and so forth. With Olivia in Cambridge. What's she up to at this hour?"

"Knackered, so retired early. And wounded."

"Wounded? In what sense?"

"Wounded emotionally. Hurt feelings. Belittled. Before going down, she had a few words with Kat who was still in the lounge with Virgil and Eleni. I accompanied her. Put it this way, Geoff, I've had a very informative day. Exhausting, like yours, but filled with greater understanding of those with whom we share so much. The Conrad Corps particularly."

"When are they not the centre of our attention?"

"You know Olivia and her social niceties. She rattled on abut how interesting all the guests were, how diverse they were in so many ways, and how the experience on the *Iphigenia* brought us all closer together. Shared interests, yeah? Kat said she shared interests with next to nobody on the barge, least of all Olivia."

"Ouch!"

"Dear Olivia, she was broadsided. She is quite sensitive, as you probably know. I could see her trying to rise above the insult, to challenge Kat, but she could not overcome the emotion welling up within. 'Why say that?' That's all the defense she could muster. Kat delivered on why she said that, showing the poor woman no mercy, just her teeth. Virgil and Eleni were totally taken aback."

"Understandably."

"I got angry, very angry, told Kat she'd rue the day she offended my closest friend. I could have murdered the bitch! Ripped her face off with all its bogus cosmetic enhancements right there and then. I told her to piss off, and then took Olivia's arm and led her away."

"I would not have thought Kat capable of such despicable behaviour."

"She was. She is. But there's so much more, Geoff, so much. The cabin walls are thin, at night in particular. The passageway only so wide, but so revealing if you have a mind to listen."

It was like Melinda had just hooked into a QR Code that granted her unlimited insight into the ways of Conrad Steele, Kat and her kittens. Admittedly, I was not averse to hearing all she had to say especially when she informed me how I was implicated, how my relationships with members of the Conrad Corps had come under unfavourable scrutiny. I thought back to the occasions when I chin wagged with Alexsis and with Isla. Then there was the little one-on-one with Boyd Alexander that Conrad challenged me over, chemistry and all that. And that was Melinda's next point of contention.

"Conrad was really worked up about his son having a heart to heart with you, Geoff, back at the *Kunst Woestijn* atelier the other day. He was irate, seething with unabashed fury. 'I could kill that kid!' I heard him say exactly that to Kat, didn't I? He was raging."

"And to think I was just being friendly to a young fellow who reminded me in some ways of my son. It's really disturbing that an innocent conversation could engender such a venomous reaction against one's own flesh and blood. When Conrad broached the subject with me, he was insistent but definitely had control of his anger. I gave him his due, reluctantly. I tried to appreciate a father's point of view."

"What's more — despite the lovey-dovey act at the South Flanders Bistro that we witnessed earlier today, Conrad and Kat are frequently at odds with each other. She gave him shit about being stinking drunk after the business meeting he had in Ghent, which was not the only time he overindulged in sampling Belgian beer. Remember the night in Antwerp? Nothing for a son to model his behaviour on. By the by, Conrad was pissed last night by the time the karaoke wound up. But so was I. Sadly."

"So I understand."

"Olivia and I heard them disagreeing most vehemently about Alexsis now that Flex is on the scene. Not very edifying, what they had to say about the two of them."

"Flex does present a new influence in their family alignment. I haven't figured out his role just yet. But he seems to have brought Alexsis out of her blue funk and dark threads."

"Kat and Conrad say bullocks to that. They say bullocks to a lot of things, so I've gleaned from talking to others like Lucy and Vanessa, bullocks to how Alexsis exaggerates about her sad and repressed lot in life, bullocks to the fact she lies about the restrictions Conrad put upon her and Isla, bullocks to her unending grief over the death of her father."

"For my part, I've listened to what both Isla and Alexsis have to say. They're very convincing."

"I share that opinion, Geoff. They are indeed convincing. You know, in my little chats with Eleni, who is both astute and shrewd and anything but longsuffering, she complained to me about how Conrad disrespects Isla. In his view, she behaves like a prepubescent teenager, and he berates her over always having a book in her hand."

"That's cheap. Demeaning. Isla's quite an intelligent young woman able to express herself extremely well. She understands what her life is and accepts it. On the other hand, Alexsis is fighting for her complete independence. I have the feeling she will achieve it one way or another. She's very clever, very resourceful."

"As you said earlier, Geoff, tomorrow's another day."

"Right, I did say that. A bit off a cliché."

"Also, have you ever noticed the friction between Eleni and Kat when fixing their morning coffee? Jostling as muscle toning, yeah?"

"No, I haven't but I can visualize the scene."

"Well, there you have it. My tittle-tattle, a week's worth. Thanks for putting up with me, Geoff. I know you were seeking peace and quiet. So, I'll be off now, love."

And wishing me a good night, Melinda disappeared. Melinda Mancipal, always candid, rarely kind, came across in a version of herself I had not thought her capable of. Gossipy, yes, but not with her usual irascible sarcasm. In the privacy of the upper deck that the night arranged for us, she found no need to be abrasive as was her wont when she had a larger audience, one in which Veridis' witty turns held sway. As she unwound the threads of her observation, her tone actually grew gentle, unassuming, evocative of sympathetic understanding even — other than when she voiced anger at Kat's attack on Olivia. In one instance, she seemed uncharacteristically vulnerable, betraying that hard-nosed attitude and instinct for dire action I earlier attributed to her. And yet, the information she relayed as delicately as she could substantiated much that had troubled me about situations I found myself involved in. I shared her concerns and her antipathies. Nonetheless, she remained a character with lethal potential and one I would not want to get on the wrong side of.

Before starting on my email to Penny, I checked the photos Vanessa said she'd forward to me depicting the day's activities: the long table at the South Flanders Bistro with all of us lifting glasses in a salute to Joost; one of the group huddled under the overpass while the torrential rain impeded our cycling progress; a candid shot of me at the picnic table above the *Jachthaven* jetties looking anything but enthusiastic. I was undecided about including that one in my attachments. Only two made the cut. As to the text, it developed mostly as an extension of previous comments about the varied personalities on the *Iphigenia* and how despite the general affability of all, as in the karaoke entertainment, for example, friction and disagreement could and did engender dynamic scenes of conflict. I did not mention my conversation with Conrad Steele nor provide extensive detail of the dissentions Melinda recently described. After all, I did not want to paint a negative picture of the kind of bike-boat holiday I wanted Penny to enjoy with me in the future. In order to be more relevant, I referenced the John S Sargent portraits that she showed me when I struggled with the varied characters delivering dialogue in the last television series I worked on. I forget her actual design in having me do so, but I remembered it helped. To get a clearer picture of what I was on about here, I encouraged her to envisage me at my desk at home surrounded by computer screens and totally involved with the editing process. As to present considerations, specifically the individuals on the *Iphigenia*, "think profiles," I typed in, "batting eyelashes, noses dripping with rainwater, eager mouths gulping beer, forked tongues, and lips tightly compressed into patterns of insistence and resistance. All so intriguing."

No doubt about it, I had deceived myself with regards to how well my physical conditioning had prepared me for the daily cycling demands. I confessed not being keen to participate in the route projected for the last day, tomorrow, day seven. A good night's sleep would determine my decision. Ironically, I dozed off before addressing other concerns Penny had expressed in her latest text to me. What aroused me out of my haphazard slumber was a thump on the passageway wall, followed by laughter that could not be supressed. Opening the door slowly, I discovered Isla, Candace, and Boyd Alexander leaning on each other, trying to muffle their drunken merriment and only half succeeding.

"Don't plan, Geoff, to cycle much tomorrow," Isla managed to say. Then she slid over to sit on the bottom stair. I took her words in two ways: as an apology for disturbing me so late and as a

premonition, no, a certainty, of her forthcoming hang-
over.

I smiled knowingly. Candace sniggered then sat
down beside her. Boyd Alexander guffawed. He took
to leaning against the wall like a flying buttress, then,
after a moment of head bending, righted himself. No,
he wasn't going to be sick. Again, small mercies. In a
matter of moments, all three were sitting on the stairs
facing me like kids on a bleacher being interrogated
by the coach. Candace had wanted to check out the
Magnifique to see what a five-star hotel had over a
three-star. One thing for sure was its opulent bar. And
that's where they met Archie Gallant who had arrived
with Calvin Kinlaw, Conrad's barrister. Archie
Gallant, Isla remembered, was once engaged to Jenny,
her long departed older sister. And that's where they
spent much of their evening in Bruges, in the
grandiose Magnifique bar although Boyd Alexander,
not surprisingly, went off on his own for an hour "to
explore about" as he put it. They thought they might
have run into Conrad in the hotel, but he was nowhere
in sight. No real difficulty getting back to the
Iphigenia once they figured out which way was south.

I wished them all pleasant dreams as they toddled
off to their rooms. For me in my own room it was
definitely time to Send.

Bruges

Breakfast on the seventh morning of the Triple B adventure — fruit and yogurt, coffee and croissants, and the regular servings of nourishing comestibles. Present at my table as usual were Lucy, Vanessa, Olivia, and Veridis, but conspicuous by her absence, Melinda. Also missing, Mitchell Monk and Aimée Reeves, who always arrived eager for their first crack at the coffee bean, and their absence left me wondering about what they had got up to.

At the Visser table, Niels, Beppie, and Pieter; missing, Hash and Kash, who were often on the scene before I arrived.

Present at the Steele table were Virgil and Eleni, Flex and Alexsis who offered us all a cheery good morning. I could account for the noticeable absence of Candace, Isla, and Boyd Alexander, who in all likelihood were enduring their morning after the night before — crapulence by any other name still meant hung over. Also inexplicably missing, Conrad and Kat.

Captain Vander Volk rushed into the dining room with Joost. All in a dither, Joost asked Alexsis where Kat was. Still in her cabin. Joost then motioned Virgil to come over to the lounge. After a few words were exchanged, Virgil called Eleni over and directed her down the stairs. Virgil followed Joost out to the deck. Captain Vander Volk returned to the dining area and whispered in Visser's ear, whereupon they both hustled out. Meanwhile everybody at our table had been rubbernecking.

"Something's up, so it is," Vanessa said, and then called across to Flex and Alexsis, "what's going on?"

"Haven't a clue," Alexsis replied, shrugging her shoulders. "Didn't catch what was said. Looking for my mother, that's all I could make of it."

Flex waggled his head. He didn't know either. At the Visser table, Beppie was signing to Pieter.

"Whatever it is," Veridis said, "I'm certain we'll hear about it before too long."

No more than minute later, a dishevelled Kat emerged from down below, Eleni on her heals. Both rushed out to the deck. Moments later we heard a scream, a wailing that just about raised the hairs on the back of my neck. The screaming increased in volume, echoing throughout the entire interior area. I looked askance at Veridis. Olivia, instantly terrified, clung on to Vanessa's arm.

"I've heard similar cries of lament at Greek funerals at the Athens airport," Veridis declared. "Also in a Greek Orthodox churches. Professional mourners."

Alexsis stood and said in wavering voice, "That sounds like Kat! That sounds like my mother!" Standing next to her and leaning on his cane, Flex offered her quiet assurances.

Lucy was the first to get up and head out, saying "Enough of this table tag. I want to know what gives."

It did not take long before we understood the seriousness of what was happening as we gathered on the sundeck. Joost explained as succinctly as he could before Captain Vander Volk commanded his attention. Conrad Steele was found floating beneath the stern of the *Iphigenia* by Aldert and Sander who had been unloading bikes for the day's cycling. Down on the quay, Kat lay prone in frantic disarray, banging on the flagstones with clenched fists, calling out her husband's name between heightened cries of disbelief and curses directed at the heavens, the fates, any entity or being within earshot, including us looking on from above like a chorus of incredulous gawkers, phone cameras ready to record. Eleni sat by her side, arms around her knees, sobbing and bobbing and consoling at the same time. Virgil stood with Niels Visser, prepared to assist in retrieving the body from the water, which would be, by my estimation, at least half a meter below the edge of the quay. Slowly Veridis and I ventured down from the sundeck to the lower level, willing to be of assistance if called upon.

Under Captain Vander Volk's direction, Aldert lowered the dinghy that hung securely over the rear railing of the barge by means of an articulated swing arm. Once the dinghy was in the water, Joost slid down on to it and manoeuvred it into an appropriate position by the rudder and tugged on the floating mass of a bigger than average human body. The rescue team formed with Joost in the dinghy, and Aldert with a sort of cant hook in one hand and sections of rope in the other hand, and Virgil stepping into the scene to assist Visser. Initial difficulties in lifting a dead weight were overcome and within a few minutes that seemed like an eternity the body of Conrad Steele lay on the quay under the supervision of Niels Visser. By this point, the captain let us know that he had contacted local authorities and reported the incident.

I had not noticed it until this tragic moment when the eye looked for relief from the pathos of the moment, specifically Kat's near hysterical response to her husband's calamitous situation and the surrounding teary-eyed attempts to comfort her, no, I had not noticed the decorative gold scrolling on the stern of the barge and below it the name *Iphigenia* in high profile. The same name in the same lettering on the prow, however, had always seemed like a familiar, welcoming address once the physical demands of the daily cycling had relaxed. You were home.

My curiosity took wing and I hovered over the scene, imagination sprung free from restraint, conjuring up what seemed most likely to have transpired — how Conrad's body got to be where it was, and where it had been before that, and why now in this site and in this state, like a gross embarrassment, totally lacking in human dignity.

Hawser lines securing the barge to the nearest dockside cleat created an intricate web of lines over the scene, oddly reflecting my many disparate thoughts. One cable lay more or less slack across a section of flagstone next to where the body was placed. If Conrad had returned drunk to the *Iphigenia* late last night, he could easily have tripped over the cable, lost his balance, and inadvertently plunged into the canal where he drowned. He'd have to have been blind drunk. Visser dispelled that theory after he inspected the body, his suspicion being that all was not as it might have seen on first impressions, that is to say, an accidental death, by drowning, which was what those of us now gathered around whispered to one another. After further assessment and an exchange of comments with Captain Vander Volk, Visser raised his hands. A hushed, pseudo-sacrosanct silence befell us.

Visser intimated that the body should not have been moved, but given the fact of its floating about and possibly sinking, it was perhaps advisable. He admitted being on unsure ground in that regard. With great respect he related what Captain Vander Volk wanted all to understand, that this was not a spectacle for picture taking, that the local police would be arriving shortly to deal with the situation. To please be respectful. To please back away and allow those most connected to Conrad Steele to come to grips with their loss and the grief it brought. Those of us not connected to Conrad Steele complied with the captain's wishes and repaired to the upper deck. I found it difficult to pull away from so unexpected a scene as was evolving that morning, and so could do nothing but look on from a distance in the company of my table companions, including those missing earlier, Monk, Aimée, and Melinda. Munching on a croissant,

Melinda informed us that she'd had a phone call from Cambridge that took up to a quarter of an hour of her valuable time. As to Hash and Kash, we learned later that they had been called back post-haste to their embassy in Brussels.

Down on the quay, Kat attempted to caress Conrad's prostrate body but when Visser held her back in a gentle manner, her sobs of despair increased in volume. When Boyd Alexander finally moved in closer, she made every effort to clutch his hands. When he held back, she began wailing again. Flex, Alexsis, Isla, and Candace had by this juncture joined in the semi-circle of the bewildered members of the Conrad Corps, Kat the most visibly bereaved. There was no consoling her. To add to the absurdity of what was happening, the coral cawing of a local murder of crows struck me as absolutely de trop.

Why the suspicion on Visser's part of something other than an accidental drowning? What was it about Conrad's lying there like a bloated hunk of humanity that raised a red flag? I wondered. In reply to my unvoiced questions, Lucy in her usual timeliness and acuity voiced a question of her own.

"Did any of you notice Steele's left hand? That ghastly, meretricious ring was gone. And so was the finger it rested on."

An effusion of disbelief followed. No one was prepared to credit such an act of brutal malice, insignificant in terms of the whole, now-defunct body though it might have seemed at first glance. I heard an echo of Vanessa's observation that first evening at dinner about how Conrad's big ring would land him in a canal. The irony made me grimace.

"I dare say, Mister Visser believes it's not an accidental drowning at all then," Olivia said.

"He's our local prod, yeah?" Melinda stated in her matter-of-fact way of making a point that was not always obvious to everyone.

"Visser suspects foul play, so he does," Vanessa said. Her conclusion met with general agreement.

"Bingo," Monk said with emphasis. He was in the act of taking a selfie with the ghastly scene on the quay as background. I gave my head a shake. I wanted to give his head a shake.

"A bit ghoulish," Vanessa said directly to Monk. No doubt she had been tempted to photo shoot everything but had restrained herself.

Before getting out of the dinghy, Joost paddled out towards the rudder and deftly picked up something that had caught Visser's notice. Joost tossed it up to Visser who, upon close inspection, nodded his head — definitely what he suspected it to be. No random piece of floating debris, it was the cork top of the jug that had been the centre of so much attention, the one Kat so detested and Aimée so admired.

"Fascinating turn of events," I heard Veridis say.

"Very curious," I said in agreement.

While speculation continued around me, I kept an eye on Visser as he walked about the body, stopping and starting, evidently musing, the wheels of calculation metaphorically clicking in his brain. From where I stood, I did not have a clear view of Conrad's left hand because his hairy arms lay by his sides. What I did see was like a huge lump of putty wrapped in paisley splattered on the quay, a shoeless parody of the human form with the flesh of exposed limbs bluish grey. It looked like fright had been etched into the face, an image Caravaggio would have been at pains to register on canvas. I had no idea of how a body looked after being in water for several hours and came to no conclusions about elapsed time. This I did conclude: in all likelihood Conrad had not made his way back to the *Iphigenia* the previous night. And so, after his meeting with Kinlaw, had he been seeking the kind of diversion he'd had that night in Antwerp? I also concluded that he had not "dressed up" for his business meeting with Calvin Kinlaw. Dark dress shorts had supplanted garish cycling shorts and an Hawaiian short sleeve shirt had pre-empted anything loosely defined as formal wear. Veridis was studying the scene as intently as I was. I asked him if he thought Conrad had donned a waist trimmer, partially revealed now under the dishevelled shirt. Veridis answered, "A girdle? Absolutely. Like something out of *The Green Knight.*"

The odour of death had not permeated the scene as yet and I suspected it would not if the authorities, once they arrived, promptly got on with the requisite procedures. I had some understanding of protocols, not from first-hand police work, but from dialogues in the plots I last worked on. The British crime series that Penny favoured also added to my vocabulary of crime investigation and the ensuing analysis of evidence. Putrefaction, corpse gas, and all the signs of decomposition were some time off, literally, although rigor mortis had probably set in by this point. And yet I wondered, had the stink of canal waters overpowered the rose-based scent that Conrad favoured?

A sudden sense of alienation came over me and, try as I might, I found it difficult to fit the scene before me into anything like logical perspective. No way to establish separation, something I craved. What I was viewing was an actual murder scene that threatened absolute chaos in my little world of purpose and expectation. No film here for network consumption, no editing possible to render comprehensible what was indeed incomprehensible. Clarity was absolutely beyond me at this point. I had no control whatsoever over the brutal intrusion of reality in a very ugly and disturbing manner. I'd worked in the abstract with dead bodies, corpses created for dramatic effect in line with plot, sound effects operating with just the right emphasis, and so on, but this was the first time the vile fact of murder superseded the stereotypical.

Incongruity dominated my perception: the loveliness of the early morning, the surroundings and the birdsong it engendered, anticipation of the excursion through beautiful countryside in the company of new-found friends, all disjointed, out of kilter, misaligned with the perfect ordering I had imagined for the last day of the Triple B adventure.

The incontrovertible fact: the wreckage of an individual life strewn on the quay like so much stuff, like a broken crate of cheap plastic knock-offs. What vile specimens of decrepitude had begun to incubate in that dead flesh? I saw myself in the guise of Steele lying prostrate there — some as yet unknown version of myself, a persona projecting an existential endgame conjured up from the deep subconscious. I dismissed the image as fatuous, a simulacrum produced by guilt or guilt by association. In truth, I had wanted to like the man, but circumstances had not favoured such an outcome. I regretted not having been more generous. Kat's wailing relocated me in the here and now of the present moment as I stood shoulder to shoulder with equally miffed observers.

There followed a series of questions that betrayed both our collective concerns and our curiosity, relevant but disjointed in the way they were posed and responded to, verging on absurdity as they were. Initial interest would by the end of the day evolve into macabre drollery once we got over the initial shock, gained a little more perspective with fact-based info, and let opinions fly unadulterated by sentiment.

"Who could have done this?" Olivia asked.

"Anyone with motive and opportunity." Lucy replied, "Isn't that how it goes?"

"Bingo. I hated the bastard right from the get-go but I'd have to have been out of my mind to do that," Monk said, pointing with phone in hand.

"Imagine, in the canal, right under the *Iphigenia*," Olivia went on, her voice full of disappointment.

"Fitting access to the banks of Styx," Lucy said, drawing a strange look from Veridis.

"When was Conrad last seen alive?" Vanessa wondered. "And by whom?"

"The murderer," Melinda said. "We are looking at a murder scene, are we not?"

"We are, indeed," Veridis said.

"So, as far as we know, Calvin Kinlaw was the last person to have seen him alive," Monk said.

"That's making an untenable assumption," Veridis countered.

"I saw him going to his meeting at the hotel. Before dinner. Nearly tripped on the gangplank. His lovely sandals, yeah? Doesn't make me the last person to have seen him."

"Was he incapacitated by some poison," I wondered aloud, "some injection rendering him powerless, a drink spiked with a drug?"

"A whack on his head?" Monk added.

"What do you think happened to the finger?" Aimée asked.

"I'm sure it's in the canal," Monk said.

"How can you be sure about that?" I asked.

"If it's in the canal," Lucy said, "it'll be hard to retrieve."

"Do fingers float?" Aimée asked.

"And where are the sandals?" Olivia wanted to know.

"What about the cycling today? Got to get away from this until it's over."

"Likely be delayed or cancelled."

"Likely."

"What about Kinlaw, shouldn't he be called in?"

"Business rival, the culprit?"

"Is there possibly a Russian connection?"

And as the group of us looked on the murder scene from afar, more questions piled up on those already unanswered. Was Conrad Steele attacked, then dumped? Beaten up? Were there unnoticed contusions? Abrasions? Did he struggle? Did he suffer? Was there much blood? Why here? Why anywhere? Was the family responsible? If so, how so? Who hated him the most? What about the crew? What about Hash and Kash? What about any of us? If and when asked by the authorities, could we all account for our whereabouts last night? And so it went until random inquisitiveness succumbed to verbal exhaustion.

Regardless, I gave into questioning in the far corner of my mind whether Conrad Steele had reached the apogee of his accomplishments, understood his limitations — unwilling though he might have been to admit publicly he had any — and accepted his inability to get beyond what he had already achieved. Did he know at that crucial moment that a great life-sucking vacancy awaited him? Having worked privately through these considerations without satisfaction, I asked Veridis what he thought. His response: "You assume too much intellect on Conrad's behalf."

I turned my attention to Kat still burbling between howls of regret, stalwart Virgil and the rest standing around her like caricatures of themselves, immovable and unmoved, like figures about to emerge out of a tableau vivant, only it wasn't so vivant. In Alexsis' face I read contemptuous disgust; behind her, Flex looked on dispassionately. With Isla it was a troubling frown, a melange of pity and regret. Candace seemed to have withdrawn into a cataleptic state, so stiff was her pose, so definite her grip on Eleni's arm, her face a mask of obscene beauty much like that of her mother. Boyd Alexander, virtually a head above the rest, the personification of unabashed ambivalence.

From the harried entrance of Captain Vander Volk into the breakfast setting and the alarm he and Joost set off, to Kat's first anguished caterwaul, to our questioning from above of what exactly befell Conrad

226

Steele, no more than twenty minutes had passed, but the sequence of events seemed to have occurred in a warped stretch of time. Dreamlike and unnerving, and yet set to carry on in real time.

Now in the guise of *Inspector* Visser, self-employed as such in a temporary role, Niels Visser continued to oversee the situation. He was intense, constantly considering features of the body lying at his feet, aware also of those watching his every move. My impression was that all along he was loathe to interfere with the corpse, but with brows knit and mouth twisted into a speculative curl, once moved by some instinctual urge to pluck the forbidden fruit, he could not stop his hand from reaching into the side pocket of Conrad Steele's shorts. What he first pulled out were two coins. When next with great care he extracted the severed finger, an arpeggio of horror-stricken shrieks arose.

Kat and the remnants of the Conrad Corps began to withdraw when a patrol car marked with curved blue stripes appeared and two uniformed officers emerged, "Police Municipale" stamped on the back of their vests. Visser held a short conversation with them, gesturing here and there over the body, and then pointing to the stern of the *Iphigenia*. One officer returned to the vehicle to communicate, I assumed, with what had to be headquarters. Shorty thereafter, another vehicle arrived and behind it, a few minutes later, a van. The Belgian authorities in full regalia, two plainclothes detectives, by the looks of it, with whom Visser shook hands, and a forensics team decked out in white coveralls, blue gloves, and blue booties, work satchels in hand, a medical examiner, no doubt, among them. After a word or two with the presumed lead cop who actually took notes and indicating the finger now lying with the coins on Steele's chest along with the cork top of the infamous jug, Visser retreated.

The investigation would unfold in the usual logical fashion, the medical examiner coming to the conclusion that Visser and the rest of us already had, but with the additional and important knowledge like (probable) time of death and the means (probably) used to bring it about. Official photographs would be taken. Blood splatter was minimal, as far as I was able to determine, but a factor to consider nonetheless. Crime scene techies would set about their business inspecting bits and pieces of material evidence, like single strands of stray hair, epithelial specimens, the cork top, the coins, and indeed the rosy-stubbed finger, bag everything, and send it to the lab for analysis. I had a feeling that the cork, coins and finger had meaning beyond the obvious, something metaphorical or symbolic, but if anyone, like Veridis, were to have asked what I meant, I'd need to shake my head. Perhaps forensics in its search for fingerprints and traces of DNA would come up with a significant reveal that tied everything into the motivation for the murder. They might even enclose Conrad's hands in plastic to preserve any traces of an assailant's DNA trapped under the fingernails. Meanwhile the detectives would want access to Conrad's phone and computer and then, as the circle goes, they'd get around to asking us questions as to what, when, and where, and in the process try not to be offensive about it.

In the mode of an Agatha Christie plot, Inspector Niels Visser had us all assemble in the dining area and take our usual seats, his focus being information, not accusation. He was asked to liaise on behalf of the local authorities with the crew of the *Iphigenia* and its guests. He talked briefly about the Belgian police structure, and about the integrated system where federal and local officials cooperated in solving crime. There was also the directorate of maritime and river police as yet not involved in procedures. In stating that each of us would be interviewed, he made every attempt to ease our concerns. He went overboard in placating Kat, assuring her, and the rest of the us, that the crime would be solved quickly. We were to bring passports and phones with us to the interviews. CCTV would have been of assistance in determining exactly what happened to Conrad Steele but unfortunately none was available in the immediate area of the *Iphigenia*. He would keep us abreast of developments as much as possible. A modified cycling event with Joost might possibly be on for the afternoon, depending on police findings.

By the time Visser concluded his remarks, Kat had calmed herself sufficiently to accept the many condolences expressed.

"So sorry to hear of your loss" was a standard utterance.

"Our poor family. Such inconceivable treachery" was typical of Kat's reply. At least that's what she said to me. No doubt about it, she was traumatized. She'd need counselling, some form of professional psychiatric assistance. Holding Eleni's hand was just not going to suffice.

Like most *Iphigenia* guests affected by events — not to forget Captain Vander Volk and crew members — I felt the need to sympathize not only with Kat but also with others in the Conrad Corps. Short exchanges resulted all around. I managed two.

"I fear his death was ordained," Boyd Alexander said, pained. I didn't know what to make of what he said, so I just offered him my condolences and moved on.

Alexsis said in a totally unexpected manner: "Flex argues that I'm being too hard on myself, but it's like I have blood on my hands because I'm not unhappy about Conrad's being dead. You see, any past wish of mine to that effect makes me complicit. That's what I feel at least. It's just all so sudden, and so ugly."

Alexsis clung to my arm in an alarming fashion. I did not resist, believing that despite the appearance of control she was distraught, that this was her way of expressing regret and maybe even guilt. Shock had no predictable way of asserting itself. Alexsis worked up a smile for me, a sort of silent communication acknowledging gratitude for all that had passed between us starting with that first night in the lounge and encompassing all that had evolved since.

"They'll get to the bottom of it," I assured her. "They'll soon find the culprit. Or culprits, whoever they are."

"It can't be soon enough for me."

I turned my attention momentarily to young Pieter Visser, all trembling curiosity, signing madly with Oma Beppie. I wondered how sign language rendered the notion of *murder*. There'd be few, if any, high fives for the boy today. He then watched intently as his grandfather took the floor again and introduced Chief Inspector Jules Maartens and adjutant Basile Janssens.

"We hope not to detain you for too long," Jules Maartens began in his address. He was a large, imposing man, seemingly all business, although a full head of flaxen hair somehow lessened the austerity of his otherwise stern appearance. "All is procedure, yes? We will talk with each of you."

"How long will it be?" Mitchell Monk asked, brushing a hand across his tonsured scalp.

Maartens' forehead creased with lines of perturbation. He lifted his chin and drew back his lips in an expression of disbelief. It struck me immediately that he was a man not to be messed with. "As long as required, monsieur. You recognize, I am certain, the seriousness of the situation." His answer to Monk, penetrating in its direction and intention, like his initial remarks came across with a French accent.

Adjutant Basile Janssens stood by, arms folded on his chest, scanning faces. He was all forehead above faint brows and had a craggy face with filigree veins on his nose. The disparaging snort he let go when

Monk asked his question prompted me to assess him, prematurely maybe, as a focused cop who'd get to the bottom of things, no matter what. I did not want to deal with him.

It was like a couple of officials (sans feathers, drums, and high-heeled boots) had with definite resolve exited Rembrandt's *The Night Watch* to lead us out of the darkness of our fears and uncertainty, these two before us now equipped with nothing but pen and pad and a lot of modern knowhow.

Two areas of the *Iphigenia* were designated for the interviews. One was at the far end of the lounge, set up with a small table and two chairs. Chief Inspector Jules Maartens conducted his interviews there. The other was on the forward deck with Basile Janssens. Both areas provided sufficient privacy. Members of the crew were questioned first and that included chef Dirk Anders and assistant Anna. Kat and her entourage followed next, their number divided equally between the two interrogators. I had no difficulty conceiving of the two cops as interrogators especially after my session with Basile Janssens out on the forward deck, a comfortable setting where I had previously participated in so many casual and friendly discussions. I was the last to be called to account for myself.

Janssens pointed at the chair he wanted me to take, and I took it. Too bad I hadn't put on my ball cap as I had to sit facing the sun. With a snap of the fingers, he said: "Passport!" He checked it over and, having come to certain conclusion about who I was and where I came from, he handed it back to me. I responded to all his questions succinctly. Occupation, place of business, that kind of thing. Janssens was well aware of the nature of the bike and boat adventure we'd all signed on for and that led logically to his asking what my plans were as of the next morning. I was booked on an early train out of Bruges and had reservations at the Hôtel Séjour Latin in

Paris. After that I'd fly to Greece to meet up with my son. As requested, I gave Janssens my email address and cell phone number and those of my son. Selfishly, I was concerned that this whole murder mess would curtail my travel plans. As for the remaining Conrad Corps, their plans would definitely be interrupted.

My presumption about being above suspicion took a turn when Janssen asked me where I was between nine PM last night and two AM this morning. I told him exactly where I was and I gave him the names of those able to confirm what I claimed, Melinda Mancipal foremost among them. What was my impression of what happened? Very disturbing. It looked like Janssens expected me to elaborate, but I refrained from doing so in any significant way. I simply added that all on the *Iphigenia,* from Captain Vander Volk to Young Pieter Visser, will have been disturbed in any number of negative ways — who could not be? He then asked what my relationship with Conrad Steele had been. Quite superficial, actually. We had little in common other than the cycling. What did I think of the man? What could I say, that he was not entirely popular with the guests, Mitchell Monk in particular, that he was given to sartorial extravagance and could act superior no matter the setting, that he had unresolved issues not only with his wife but also with other family members, that he evinced drunken behaviour on more than one occasion? In mulling over a possible answer, I recalled the words spoken by one of the lead characters from the series I had worked on that, in being questioned, witnesses were prone to keep something vital back. Was I keeping anything back? If so, what? My less than friendly chit-chat with Conrad? I wasn't going to get into that or the notion of interpersonal chemistry. I did not mention wanting to be more openly friendly with Conrad. I did not want to get into why I found it difficult to do so. When I did say that Conrad Steele was reviled to some extent by a few of the guests,

Janssens shook his head. You couldn't help but notice his rugged, pitted face. I rephrased as subtly as I could, refusing to say that Conrad Steele was hated.

Janssens then asked about Boyd Alexander, leaning on the old trope, I figured, that the perpetrator was someone from close to home. When I said that Boyd Alexander was not quite the apple of his father's eye, Janssens asked me to clarify and when I explained that their relationship did not strike me as ideal, that Conrad bullied his son mercilessly, he drew a long breath and then blew it out, cheeks deflating in the process. He noted the point, proceeding next to inquire about any unusual comings and goings I might have seen, anything out of the ordinary. I mentioned the late arrival of Candace, Isla, and Boyd Alexander. Was there anything else that might shed light on the situation? I confessed that the cork top found floating under the stern intrigued me. Why? Because last evening at dinner, the jug it fitted was no longer where it had been on the bar. Aimée Reeves, one of the guests, had expressed great interest in it and pursued the possibility of acquiring it. Judging by Janssen's reaction, the point I was making about the jug lacked relevance.

At this juncture, a subordinate in uniform approached and informed Janssens of some development. I did not understand what was said, but relished the fact that whatever it was brought a sort of smile to Janssens' face. The interview concluded with Janssens shaking my hand and patting me on the back. He told me to enjoy the rest of my travels.

By two o'clock, Visser let it be known that Chief Inspector Maartens had cleared the deck, so to say, and regular activities such as they might be on such a fractured day could continue. Not all the guests had reassembled in the dining room. Virgil, Flex, and Alexsis were there; Kat and the rest of the Conrad Corps were not. Beppie and Pieter were elsewhere. Mitchell Monk arrived shortly after Visser began, with the rest of our table already in attendance eager to hear the news.

True to his word, Visser attempted as best he could to keep us abreast of developments. His information, based on the findings of the pathologist, was limited. Conrad Steele did not drown. His death resulted from blunt force trauma. The back of his head had been — Visser searched for the right word but came out with "mangled." The weapon would likely have been a rock, a brick, a length of metal pipe, or indeed the solid pavement, any of which causing intradermal hematoma.

Authorities speculated that the attack occurred elsewhere and that the body was moved to the vicinity of the *Iphigenia* where it ended up in the canal, either by intention or by clumsy accident. Visser did not have access to any really telling forensic details, but he did mention that no ring, no wallet, no phone, and no sandals were found with the body or in the crime scene area. Steele's brutalized remains were being delivered to the lab for further analysis. Toxicology, for example, would factor into the whole picture of such a tragic death. Visser threw other forensic terms around for a bit before concluding that an autopsy would likely be required before the body ended up in the morgue readied for the next turn in his life's journey. I now pictured the corpse of Conrad Steele, once head honcho of a big electronics concern, covered over and prepared for the morgue, identified now by a toe tag. Where would all this ugly mess end up? Media interest in the murder of a high-flying executive could intrude into what remained of our time in Bruges. I was content knowing I was cleared to be away from it all early next morning.

Calvin Kinlaw had come aboard the *Iphigenia* accompanied by Archie Gallant, the one-time fiancé of Victor Troyes' daughter, Jenny. Not surprisingly, there would be much for the lawyer to sort out with Kat and Virgil and rest of the family. Crucial decisions would need to be taken, some touching on the immediate and others far-reaching in import. Surprisingly, Flex and Alexis opted to join the Joost-led cycling excursion to the North Sea, abridged though it would be. Melinda claimed such a choice on Alexsis' part pointed to her being in denial. No one argued the point. Eleni and Candace, Monk and Aimée, Beppie and Pieter would also ride with Joost.

Veridis and I decided to do a modified bike tour of Medieval Bruges. Lucy, Vanessa, Olivia, and Melinda decided to accompany us.

Our little group of six cycled randomly for the better part of an hour around the ancient core of Bruges, stopping where interest or impulse decided. Lucy led, the rest followed, and I for a last time played sweep. The cycling was casual because we were in no rush to get anywhere, just intent on enjoying the Gothic merry-go-round. Biking in this manner allowed us to experience a kind of exorcism, a temporary release from the built-up apprehension the day had delivered us. At least I could claim as much for myself. At Olivia's request, we stopped to visit the Basilica of the Holy Blood. Melinda watched the bikes. We'd then pedaled around the central Market Square a couple of times, gawking and pointing and admiring, occasionally stopping to wait for Vanessa to perfect her shots. After that we pulled into the courtyard of the medieval Belfry of Bruges. Vanessa volunteered to accompany Veridis to the top of the tower.

When the touring around had been declared over, we had no trouble finding a café. Very accommodating. Good variety of drinks. Quick and friendly service. Comfortable seating in view of our bikes bunched together, it struck me oddly, like a piece of modern sculpture about to be collected for display in the Grote Markt. Since much earlier in the day, none of us had touched on the subject of Conrad Steele's murder and the subsequent actions of the local authorities, but the time had definitely come.

Quizzical frowns evolved into comments. We started with impressions of Chief Inspector Maartens and adjutant Basile Janssens and what we knew of their findings.

"During my interview with Maartens," Veridis confessed, "I felt as though I were rendering the incident anecdotal, like what you answer when asked where you were and what you were doing on 9-11. I'd wanted to say agreeable things about Steele but could not. I was intentionally vague, but Maartens saw through me."

"Basile Janssens," Melinda began, "face like a ski boot, all buckles of flesh and blotches of discoloration, but he didn't intimidate me, did he?"

"He was a lovely gentleman," Olivia said, "and I dare say, very solicitous."

"He interviewed me as well," I said. "The man might have looked awesome, but he wasn't intimidating in the usual sense of the word."

"A question of perception, innit?"

"You could put it that way," Lucy said. "I reckon he, like Maartens, just asked pertinent questions."

"Questions, oh yeah. He wanted to know about Conrad Steele, what I thought of him. Not much, yeah? I was prompted to answer that he was the kind of guy who got high on his own farts, but I didn't, did I? Just said I couldn't give a toss about him. That said, but left unexplained, Janssens asked about Kat. A little too totty for my liking. This highbrow deportment didn't do it for me."

"Mel, did you go into the fact you had history with Steele?" Olivia asked. "The convention at Cambridge, like?"

"Never crossed my mind to do so."

"Oh, I did," Olivia said, "but I gave no details. Janssens then asked me specific questions about some of the guests, Virgil Troyes, for example, and Mitchell Monk."

"The presumption being," Veridis suggested, "that the perpetrators, if more than one, are local, very local, family, crew, you or me. That isn't necessarily the case. Just a line of inquiry. It was the same pattern for all of us, surely. I answered similar questions with Maartens. He asked specifically about Mitchell Monk. Why? Probably because of what someone said to the Chief Inspector about him before he got to me."

It crossed my mind at this point that in all our interviews we could have been giving out all kinds of information about everyone of us, not all of it contradictory but some of it quite possibly useful in helping authorities in their determinations.

Vanessa contributed the following. "I told my guy that it was hard not to see Conrad Steele for what he was. It's not like I was ever going to Photoshop my impression of the man, was I? That was especially the case with Mitchell Monk. Held nothing back. I thought him capable of doing Conrad considerable harm and said so."

"That may be so," Lucy said, "but didn't Visser say the attack likely occurred elsewhere. So how could any of our lot do the dirty deed?"

Melinda responded: "I suppose there lurks a killer in all of us who, given the right circumstances, will act violently. Motive and opportunity, yeah?"

I wondered at that point if maybe Melinda herself had motive and opportunity. Banishing the thought as quickly as it popped up, I offered the following for consideration. "I can only surmise that an enemy willing to do you harm, serious harm, might not always be visible or be known to you, but in this case Steele had antagonists within in his own circle, vociferous in their objections to his being there lording it over them, loathing him and not hiding it."

"True," Lucy said. "It's possible that a murderous criminal can hide in plain sight or operate in the shadows beyond our ability even to speculate."

"It seems likely," Olivia said, "that more than one bad actor was involved in getting the body to the *Iphigenia*."

"Not necessarily," Veridis said. "Two assailants would not likely have let the body plunge into the canal."

"Unless that was the intention," I speculated, "to make a splash in the metaphorical sense, no less."

"Point taken, Geoff," Veridis conceded.

That hovering spirit of accusation continued to circle about our table, alighting on one of us for a moment of conjecture and then fluttering speculatively before another.

"Assuming the murderous attack was not the work of some local criminal," Lucy proposed, "then *cui bono*? Who stands to gain from Conrad Steele's death?"

"None of us, surely," I said. "At least not financially. Besides, we all go our separate ways tomorrow morning."

"As you suggested, Melinda," Vanessa said, "it comes down to motive and opportunity."

"Motives for murder are many, yeah?" Melinda added. "Greed, jealousy,
revenge, hatred, and so on."

We continued bandying about various crime solving tropes and boilerplate expectations until Olivia indulging in a little self-deprecating humour asked, "What would Vera do?"

"Vera?"

"Vera Stanhope, from the telly, yeah? She'd focus on the Conrad Corps, that's what she'd do, love. Their reactions with the body lying there in front of them. Or after, when the reality of the situation was accepted for what it was, namely, that Conrad Steele had been murdered. That should indicate something relevant."

"I was struck by Boyd Alexander's reaction," I said, picking up on Melinda's point, "to seeing his father lying there. The young guy seemed euphoric with terror and horrid shock when I first caught a view of him. Then I thought, was it a wild kind of hope I was reading on that troubled face?"

Veridis pointed out what was generally known about Conrad's son. "Boyd Alexander is a remittance man of sorts with little or no ambition to carry on the family business. On the other hand, he stands to inherit a fortune. That's the information I have."

"Motive enough," Vanessa said.

"Motive, yes," I responded. "But as to complicity, he is physical clumsiness personified. Besides, he got back to the *Iphigenia* last night with Candace and Isla, all of them in high spirits and quite inebriated. I talked with them at that time. I don't think him capable of treachery."

Then Vanessa turned our attention from Boyd Alexander to Alexsis. "I heard Alexsis, just before setting out cycling in the Joost group, explain to an inquisitive Aimée: 'You can't give what you ain't got.' I imagine she meant not showing overwhelming sorrow."

True to form, Veridis expanded on Vanessa's observation. "It is conceivable that prior to the murder, Alexsis was simply hiding behind her outward grievances against Conrad Steele and her mother, Kat, with her rejected daughter discontent verbalized in sighs and impatient looks and sardonic rebuttals. That changed somewhat with the arrival of Flex. And now, no need at all for any manifestation of genuine grief."

"Any idea of how her interview with Chief Inspector Maartens went?"

"I asked her about that," Lucy said. "It went extremely well, apparently. Then it was as if she couldn't hold back saying, 'All her grief and lamentation, right, now she knows what I've been going through since my father died.'"

"Kat, then?"

"Despite the high dramatics," Veridis said, "I believe her reaction as a grieving widow is genuine. She has suffered a great loss. None can doubt that."

"Do you think karma played a part in what happened to Conrad?" Vanessa asked.

"We can't assume that one way or the other without knowing every detail about their lives. Impossible." None disagreed with Veridis on that point.

From leaving the notion of what goes around comes around (how Olivia clarified her understanding of karma), we looked at other individuals within the Conrad Corps and without. We excluded ourselves, of course. It had become a bit of a game, accusing then dismissing possible bad actors, "murder mystery 0.2" as Veridis phrased it. Isla in her serene incoherence got an immediate pass. Flex? An outsider, introduced to distract, an antidote to Alexsis' outbursts, yet very aware of family discord. Interesting possibility. Connected to Forrest Troyes, the exiled son, I added, operating as hired gun, so to speak, which was an idea too fantastical to be real, granted, but too insistent in my mind to be dismissed out of hand. Lucy wanted proof. I had none. Virgil Troyes, a subtle rival to Conrad's position as head of the table and AEP might have had the necessary motivation. Yes, a possible suspect. Eleni and Candace? Not in the cards. Archie Gallant? Too gilded and self-sufficient, Vanessa argued, out of the loop since before Victor Troyes' demise. Only conjecture. Calvin Kinlaw? Such a tiny man. Mitchell Monk? Too stupid. Too obvious. Aimée and her fascination with the jug? Whimsical. Totally irrelevant in terms of murdering Conrad. Some agent acting on behalf of rival business interests seeking retribution for dirty dealings in the past? Industrial espionage, always a possibility, but so hard to nail down without extensive research. Enigmatic Oshi Hashimoto, assassin at large? That was a good one. But a possibility, nonetheless. Among the crew, only

Aldert gave us real pause. Though snarly at times, a guy so into karaoke couldn't possibly fit the role of murderer and hatchet man. Sander, possibly. But what motivation? He'd been suborned. A stretch. When Olivia asked about Beppie Visser, we knew it was time to let go. Veridis said he'd get the cheque.

Before saddling up, Lucy slapped the side of her helmet, then indicated a young woman pedaling by on an Urban Dart with two toddlers secured in the cargo area. "Almost forgot to tell you. Alexsis informed Maartens that when she and Flex were returning to the *Iphigenia* late last night, they saw someone on a cargo bike racing away like mad. For his part, Flex corroborated the fact, and provided a partial description, a guy wearing a hoodie."

"That's interesting," I said, wondering just where seeing a guy in a hoodie on a bike late at night might lead.

"Circumstantial, yeah?" from Melinda.

"Well," Veridis said, "Chief Inspector Maartens would certainly have followed up on that kind of information. I'd bet on it."

And off we pedaled back to the barge, single file, through the streets and park, leaving all that speculative tittle-tattle behind us in the Grote Markt. As though coordinated by the fates, Joost's group arrived at the *Iphigenia* the same time as our group. Vanessa observed rather interestingly, as she led us toward the gangplank, how inanimate objects could be conceived of as reflecting one's state of mind, posts, for instance, stanchions, or bikes in a line like a file of accusations. Call it, she added, the body-language of the world at large. I saw what she meant when, for the first time, the black paint of the *Iphigenia* took on a sinister hue.

Breakfast that morning had been grossly interrupted, lunch had amounted to catch as catch can, dinner was to be served at the usual time following the usual procedures. As it turned out, our table would be served first. Under normal circumstances, the final meal on the final night would have been an up-beat, laughter-filled affair, enhanced by a toast to the captain and all his crew and charming little speeches expressing gratitude and satisfaction, culminating in cheers, friendly cajoling, embraces, and the exchange of email addresses. At least that is what I had envisaged, but such a highlight was not to be. "The last supper," as Veridis wryly put it, would be sombre, subdued, and low-key.

Before the first course was served, Visser entered and announced that police authorities had arrested a very likely suspect. Agents of the directorate of maritime and river police had picked the culprit up outside Ghent. A great deal of evidence pointed to his being the perpetrator of the crime. In passing on this information, Chief Inspector Maartens hoped to alleviate any lingering anxieties *Iphigenia* guests might be harbouring. That was all Visser had for us. He sat down in his usual spot next to Beppie.

The places Hash and Kash normally occupied at the Visser table were taken by Flex and Alexsis, an easy enough arrangement to accommodate Archie Gallant and Calvin Kinlaw at the Steele table where *dark* seemed to be the tone of the evening, in aspect and attitude, if not in actual attire. For who brings anything like mourning clothes to wear on a holiday? Ironically, Alexsis did, but this evening she was wearing the *just do it* sweatshirt I'd seen her in previously.

At our table, initial conversation centered on the arrest of a suspect and how that kind of news went over with Kat and the rest of her entourage. Despite the sombre circumstances, she was decked out in a black evening dress, looking elegant in her grand distress, regal even. Kinlaw held her hand and her attention. I supposed he was being sympathetic and professional at the same time. When not victimized by shaking shoulders and other manifestations of emotional upheaval, Kat nodded at what he was saying to her. From all appearances, she was still simmering with anger and betrayal, grief and its cognate grievance the obvious links.

"Still richly ringed and magnificently arrayed, so she is," Vanessa observed at one point when our talk about the arrested suspect petered out for lack of significant detail.

"Not at all likely that she'd show up for dinner in bombazine," Veridis said in that way he had of being serious and facetious all at once.

"Translation, please, Frank," Lucy said.

"Fancy mourning dress."

Varied comments followed as we progressed through the dinner hour. No one was being supercilious, just curious, intellectually and emotionally, about the circumstances that defined our last common meal. After Anna removed the dessert dishes from our table — naturally enough, she was less than her usual exuberant self — and those at the other two tables had pretty much dispersed, some like Virgil and Boyd Alexander offering cursory goodbyes in passing, I grew aware that a kind of savagery of sadness had descended on a setting that normally effused good cheer. Kat's having wandered off enduring her paroxysms of regret did nothing to dispel the sensation. She put me in mind of a wounded mother duck, her waddling brood behind her, scattered and ordered at the same time.

Before retreating with Flex, Alexsis stopped to offer thanks to all at our table for our sympathetic understanding and for having patiently put up with her disturbing antics. After a prolonged moment of consideration, she said, "Conrad wasn't ferried to the other side in a manner commensurate with his station in life. Fate and premeditation often work hand in hand. But it's mostly all beyond our control, is that not the case?" It was as if she had prepared these words well ahead of time, and directed them to me in particular, in an effort to finalize notions about vicissitudes of life expressed in our earlier conversations. I nodded recognition before she moved off, but I really could not unravel the logic of her thought. Being bemused was a condition of my day.

A few of us remained at the table, still puzzled about everything that had gone down. The need to work things out if only in the abstract still commanded our attention. Mitchell Monk and Aimée Reeves bid us all farewell and headed out to the deck leaving us to our supposition and conjecture.

"So what, that a suspect has been arrested," Lucy began. "Proof that he's really the culprit will mean he has the obnoxious ring and maybe even the sandals. Leave all that to the authorities to work out. What about the two coins? What's that all about? And more confusing, the cork top of the jug found floating in the canal? How did that get to where it was found?"

No one, not even Frank Veridis, could provided suitable answers to these questions, and eventually our attention returned once again to the character of Conrad Steele.

"Conrad may have given the appearance of control, but I think he had his head constantly on a swivel," Melinda said authoritatively. "Like a Shakespearean villain, yeah?"

"Noting in his life became him like the leaving it," Veridis said. "Or am I getting beyond what we can actually know and misinterpreting the facts?"

"Possibly," Lucy said, rubbing finger and thumb together, "but it's not like Conrad Steele is perambulating through Elysian Fields, is he?"

"We just never got to see the good side of Conrad Stele," Veridis said, "the human side. I'm sure he had one."

"Speak no evil of the dead," Olivia advised us. "You know, I can still see Conrad's features so different out there from what they had been. I dare say, he'll haunt my dreams."

Olivia's comments conjured up in my mind's eye the rictus of regret etched indelibly into Conrad Steele's shut-down face. And again, imagination provided the shock of seeing his corpse in a heap on the quay, nothing very heroic about him at the time, just a lifeless impersonation of the man he had been, good, bad, indifferent, a bloated bootlegged version of a former self, a refugee landed now on some unknown shore.

At this juncture Melinda declared, "Whoever it was that did the deed, made a bullocks of the job." She then graced us with a frown of comical disgust, and added before hauling herself off towards the stairs, "Sod it, yeah? If I don't see you in the morning, all the best to all of you."

Olivia followed on, having wished those of us remaining at the table a sincere good night. She hoped our travel plans would be less "eventful." I knew I'd be off early in the morning so picking up on the lead of the women from Cambridge, I decided to call it a night. I tried to be as inclusive with my adieus as circumstances allowed, a heart-felt handshake and two prolonged hugs, equally heart-felt.

Before getting into my report to Penny, I Goggled the latest results from the Tour de France. Another form of procrastination once I actually started the email was mentioning the plans other guests had starting the next day. She had by the night of day seven of my Triple B adventure at least a vague familiarity with most of them, Frank Veridis, for instance, who would be returning to Amsterdam for his flight home. He was the only one with whom I managed to exchange an email address. No, also Vanessa, earlier, for the photos.

All I could muster regarding the unfortunate demise of Conrad Steele — I refrained from using the word *murder,* preferring Veridis' term, death by misadventure — was that by a brutal turn of events, his life had been forfeited. Conrad's future would prove to be nothing but a reflection of his past, a past pulled into stark relief in collective memories swimming around in the heads of those that knew him, friend and foe alike. And I wondered what would have been his last mortal thought, his last word shouted out to the world he was departing.

I described briefly the cloudiness that hovers after a bad dream which was upon me still. Another useful analogy: it was like being focused on a television or computer screen where the speaker and the speech were off, where the audio and video were out of sync. These additional two thoughts came to me out of the willowy light of my cabin, that you see a little of yourself in everyone you meet, that you see a little of yourself when looking upon the dead. The second thought did not get typed into what was to be my last message to Penny from the *Iphigenia.* In closing, I wrote that the next email would be sent from Paris, be a little more informative, and a little more up-beat.

Paris

Saturday, July 22, Le Séjour Latin —

Kat Steele found dead. Suspected suicide. Minor delays for guests departing *Iphigenia*. Quick determination pre-empted interviews. Much lamentation. Presently at Schiphol awaiting flight home.

Thus, a totally astonishing email from Frank Veridis that read like a telegram of old. It left me gobsmacked, absolutely befuddled, and more than a little out of sorts with how a well-planned day could deliver you a totally surprising shock to the system, a blast right out of the blue of cyberspace. What a legacy of misery for Alexsis, Isla, and Boyd Alexander.

Rather than thinking through the ramifications of such a drastic turn of events, I opted to respond to what Penny in her latest communication wanted to know about my plans for Paris after the conclusion of the Tour de France. Carry through with things we had decided to do together, like visit the Louvre and the Quai d'Orsay — a facile answer, but far simpler than getting into Kat Steele's demise about which, really, I knew virtually nothing.

My thoughts took an ironic turn as they drifted back from Veridis' newsflash to my early departure from Bruges. I'd bought a coffee and breakfast bun at the train station, and while munching away I looked over the newspapers in the stand at the adjacent kiosk. No headlines yet regarding the murder of a tourist to Bruges, Conrad Steele to be precise, and no photographs of the crime scene at the stern of the *Iphigenia* splashed across a front page, none as yet, but it was still early and headlines and photos marking that gruesome occurrence would no doubt appear sooner rather than later. I would be long gone before news of the event in any form appeared, whether local or regional. I could just imagine the media coverage now with a second death.

Accommodation in Le Séjour Latin, a small boutique hotel in the fifth arrondissement, and the comfortable distance it put me at from the travails of the Conrad Corps suited me just fine. Paris at this juncture meant viewing in person the conclusion to the Tour de France on the Champs Élysees. I intended to focus on that, not murder and suicide. And though tempted, I did not plan to email Veridis for details about how Kat Steele's life ended. Besides, at this hour in the late afternoon, he'd be halfway across the Atlantic.

Penny had organized our stay at Le Séjour Latin, which was situated just off rue Mouffetard, the original plan being that she'd be here with me. Les Deux Soeurs, a stone's throw from the Guy Lartigue fountain, was a small, funky bistro with outdoor tables. It would become for me during my stay in Paris the go-to place of refuge, a short walk from both the hotel and the closest métro station. Over a long draft beer there, I composed another email to Penny describing how accurate her research regarding accommodation had been; also, rue Mouffetard and its intimate, neighbourhood attractions was, as she had predicted, wonderful. That done, I turned my attention to the Tour de France.

On the *Iphigenia* I'd been following the progress of Tadel Pogacar from UAE Team Emirates, who had been favoured to repeat as winner of the *maillot jaune*, the yellow jersey. However, according to the latest report I had access to, he had been bested in the mountains by Jonas Vingegarrd from team Jumbo-Visma, effecting a crucial turning point in the overall standings. There had been fierce competition between the two over the course of the tour. The subsequent ride into Paris would be a casual one for Vingegarrd and his team, leading to his ultimate victory as overall winner. I was looking forward to the conclusion of the race when all competing teams hit the cobbles on the Champs Élysees where the mad dash around the circuit would produce the winner of the last stage. I planned to get positioned near the finish line.

The Tour was tomorrow. Fine. The drama of the last days on the *Iphigenia* was far, far away, although my mind would periodically slip back across the miles to assess the oddness of things that had occurred there and which, for the most part, remained unresolved in my mind.

Though surrounded by many enjoying the ambiance of the locale and adding to it in their own right, I sat alone at a table for the first time in a long time, sufficiently at ease with where I was and why I was there taking in the sights and sounds of the evening as it folded gradually into night. A savoury *plat de jour* and a carafe of local *vin rouge* saw me smiling to myself and licking my lips with gusto. The experience contrasted greatly with what had been typical of meals on the *Iphigenia*, and remembering brought me a kind of nostalgic joy — the banter, the wit, the quips, the give and take over the week, and latterly the probing of our collective efforts to determine just exactly how Conrad Steele bought it and why, each of us at the table giving life to our inner sleuth, reflecting the favourite detective inspector from our entertainment viewing constantly proving he had the right stuff. Well, sort of. Of course, I'd been working a television series involving a husband and wife team of crime investigators. Had Penny been with me on the *Iphigenia*, would she and I have followed suit? We'd often discussed plotting and the difference in general between British and American productions, the former relying on nuance, subtlety of character, and ironic twists in the narrative, the latter largely a showcase for gunplay, explosions, car chases and spectacular crashes, and, worst of all, banal exchanges between stereotypical characters.

Penny's chief criticism of serial detective shows was that the focus cop continued to solve the most arcane of cases, usually involving murder, all despite the obstruction of a superior officer, the police head honcho with higher-ups pressing him, or the mayor's office, or the chief constable in typical British scenarios, a short-sighted, strictly by the book boss who weekly challenged the clever, determined protagonist. Penny mimicking: "I'm going out on a limb for you on this one, so you better get it right." Got it right every time. Weekly. So why didn't the boss just let the plodding gumshoe get on with it without the dumb warnings and dumber restrictions?

What happened to Conrad Steele and subsequently Kat, I had to remind myself, was not intended for prime time viewing. No need for manufactured conflict to increase audience interest. Seeing the floating body of a person you knew in a canal aroused enough interest and, to be blunt about it, not only horror but also genuine concern for your own safety. For me, suicide was as much a source of consternation as murder. And having come to that conclusion, I left Les Deux Soeurs bistro and headed back up rue Mouffetard to the hotel.

* * *

Sunday, July 23 —

The cheering was over. The crowds had dispersed. The ceremonies marking the final day of the Tour de France were concluded in a crescendo of extensive celebration. The final sprint had delivered the winner of the *maillot vert* in typical break-neck, wheel-careening, white-knuckle fashion. Winners in all classification had been declared and feted accordingly. No surprise regarding the champion of the gruelling race, Jonas Vingegarrd. Happy that I'd been a witness to it all.

By late afternoon I was sitting at Les Deux Soeurs again enjoying another long amber one, having wandered back at a leisurely pace to the rue Mouffetard. I took the Pont de l'Alma across the Seine, stopping halfway to take in the panoramic view. The river below was a mirror and in it I saw reflected Conrad Steele's dead body bobbing like a hunk of cork, and I heard an echo of Boyd Alexander's comment, "I fear his death was ordained." Predetermined or premeditated? I turned to carry on across the bridge, frustrated that no satisfactory answer popped up out of the water to latch on to. And I failed at figuring out why Alexsis shortly after the discovery said she felt complicit.

I followed along the left bank of the Seine into the Latin quarter. Going from Boulevard Saint-Michel and the Sorbonne to the hotel took no more than fifteen minutes. At times I wished Penny had been accompanying me. She loved walking and exploring. At other times I wished Frank Veridis were leading me across Paris. In truth, I missed his instructive blah, blah, blah, his erudite palaver. He might even have been able to postulate reasonable theories about what lingered in my questioning mind.

"Well, look at you, Geoff Canter, all toffed up, quite at home sitting there licking his lips."

There was no mistaking the voice nor the accent. Lucy Hunter.

Looking immediately up from my tablet where I was planning my route for the next day's excursions, her smiling face somehow filled me instantly with an increased sense of belonging.

"Lucy Hunter, from the *Iphigenia,* here in Paris," I blurted out happily.

"The same," she said, and pulled her sunglasses off in a comic gesture of declaration. There was no mistaking the brown eyes nor the rosy cheeks. Nor was there any mistaking the cluster of silver rings that adorned her right ear.

"A pleasant surprise indeed," I said taking her in. A contrast to her high visibility sports gear that I remembered so well from the *Iphigenia*, this day she wore a sleeveless flowery blouse, a grey skirt, and the same sensible athletic shoes she'd worn when cycling or sauntering about Bruges and elsewhere. She had a day pack on her back with a small Union Jack badge on the flap.

"Arrived this morning," she said. "I'm into wandering about, enjoying the ambiance. Got a couple of free hours to kill. Love this area of the city, this street. It's a cornucopia of attractions where all one's needs can be met, whether you're local or visitor."

"So I've come to realize. The market is superb. Sunday festivities, very stimulating."

Lucy smiled, then pointed about the immediate area and then over to the Square Saint-Médard, her arms extended, hands open with wiggling fingers, all as much as to say precisely what she meant about enjoying the ambiance. They were the same rough hands that Melinda Manciple mocked to her chagrin.

Across the way on the cobbles, a *galerie* of dining activity and its gregarious chatter rose from tables situated under shade umbrellas, aproned waiters from Le Deux Soeurs toing and froing in frenzied collusion. Street entertainment at its best. Lucy shook her head appreciatively.

"You're in the area, then?" I asked.

"Hotel de France, just around the corner. Virtually. Closest métro station is literally two minutes away. Have an account at the hotel through the Bureau of Investigative Journalism. I'm back on assignment. Got unexpectedly redirected from the International Conference on Human Rights in Brussels to the Global Conference in Climate Change and Environmental Engineering that starts here tomorrow. The memes are advancing."

"Sounds involved. Vanessa with you?"

"She's in Bruges for another day, then back to London. And where are you?"

"My wife, Penny, booked me, well, both of us originally, into Le Séjour Latin just off Place de la Contrascarpe. Convenient."

"Tell me, Geoff, did you get to the Champs Élysees? That was your plan, if I remember correctly, to see the last stage of the Tour."

"I did. Wait, wait. Lucy, why are you still standing? Have a seat here." I pulled out a chair with my foot. It wobbled into place.

"Can I order you anything? A drink? Tea? Some coffee?"

"Proper tea's impossible," she said, hooking her pack on the back of the chair and sitting down, "except along rue Mouffetard at the Tea Room. Geoff, I'll have what you're you having. Cheers, mate."

"Right on," I said and called for a waiter. "Deux bières blondes, s'il vous plait, garçon. Merci."

"Okay, the Tour. Been a fan for ages. Absolutely worth the effort to be there. Exciting in the extreme. No surprises. A couple of Canadian competitors I was following had respectable finishes."

"Brilliant."

"By the way, Lucy, I heard about Kat Steele. Yesterday I received an email from Frank Veridis. He wanted to keep me au courant, I suppose. Surprising as well as mystifying. I mean her dying on the *Iphigenia*, not the email. Suicide, was it?"

"That's what Chief Inspector Maartens (him again) and the medical examiner concluded within fifteen minutes of seeing the body. Suicide seemed a logical enough determination given the evidence in the cabin and the fact that a very distraught Kat had just lost her husband. Hysterical with grief, right?"

"Extremely."

"From all reports, despair seemed her closest ally."

"Right, right. So, Conrad died and Kat died of a broken heart?"

"I wonder. 'Did some villain spike the Belgian bonbons?' Veridis asked at breakfast. Facetious to the very end, old Frank Veridis, but he may have had a point about suicide being too facile an explanation for Kat's death."

"So, maybe not suicide?"

"As I said, I wonder. Virgil, Alexsis, Isla, and all the others in the Conrad Corps were in complete disarray, as you might expect. The rest of us mulled about wondering just what the hell happened before Maartens gave those of us not immediately connected to the Steeles permission to disembark. Characteristically, I did an inventory, so to speak, of those with a reason to hate and eliminate Kat, from Boyd Alexander to Olivia Nunn and Melinda Mancipal. Nothing tangible, of course, nothing to take to Chief Inspector Maartens. Doubt still lingered."

"I follow."

"Meanwhile, Niels Visser sent Beppie and Pieter home while he stayed on to help clarify matters with the local authorities. He booked into our hotel. I was glad he did because he proved to be a useful source of information. He did indulge my need to dig into the facts."

"Like with Conrad's case."

"More so. We had that extra time in Bruges, Vanessa and I. She distracted herself taking innumerable photos in the ancient city while I followed up on the bloody mess that so interfered with the smooth turn-around for Joost and the rest of the *Iphigenia* crew preparing for the return trip to Amsterdam. They were set back half a day, no more. Fortunately, inconvenience was minimal for us who were leaving. As for the Conrad Corps dealing with an unsightly murder and a perceived suicide, getting it all sorted would be complicated. Good thing Calvin Kinlaw was still about."

The waiter arrived with two tall glasses on his shiny tray. With quick flicks of his wrist, both glasses were on the table, one before me and one before Lucy. "Madame, Monsieur," he said and backed away.

"That was interesting," Lucy said, reaching for her glass. "Cheers."

"It deserves a good tip. Canadian, eh."

"Righto."

"The scene you were describing, I can readily visualize it. Much like the day before with Conrad but without the wailing."

"There was wailing aplenty. Isla shrieked when she found a lifeless Kat in her bed, and then Eleni. Virgil sounded the alarm. In no time at all Maartens was there doing what he does best."

"So, suicide then, officially."

"So it would seem. Visser described the scenario as one typical of suicide — pills, alcohol, medications, and such like. Excessive sedation and a drug overdose was a good possibility. Toxicology would determine all that."

"A suicide note?"

"Nothing on paper," Lucy said, shaking her head. "They were looking at her phone for any declaration of intent."

"Anything?"

"Visser had nothing to give me on that account."

"What about an autopsy?"

"Isla told me she and Alexsis had no objections. They both wanted to get to the bottom of it. Not to be outdone by Veridis, Melinda contributed this little jewel of an aside: 'Lady Kat now Lady Cadaver.' Sad."

"What a turnaround. I can see Kat meticulously groomed and turned out each evening, those glossed lips of hers shimmering with reflected light."

"I picture her relaxing on the deck taking the sun, or later at the bar, legs crossed, in her right hand a cocktail, her glorious ring holding down the left hand like an emblazoned anchor."

"Right, right."

"And her aspirated enthusiasm at *Kunst Woestijn,* the atelier we visited en route to Dendermonde. When she was competing with Eleni. I remember what Melinda came out with when we were waiting around, 'Totty women like Kat vanish into a cloud of superlatives.'"

"Prophetic, I guess you could say. Too bad we did not get to appreciate the good in that fascinating woman."

"We'd have to get beyond appearances for that, Geoff."

"True enough. So what was Alexsis' reaction like, in general?"

"Extremely hard to read initially. Later, when things settled down a little, and Kat's body was removed, and the rest of the Conrad Corps repaired to their various accommodations in Bruges, I got to talk at length with Alexsis. As you may know, we'd developed quite a relationship. She said rather philosophically, 'Mother begot me but never really got me, not even from infancy.' Perhaps Kat's death was an anodyne for the misery Alexsis experienced much of her life."

"A reasonable assumption, I'd say."

"Alexsis is a very complex young woman. She appeared quite saddened by Kat's suicide, naturally enough, but I don't think she's capable of your typical sentimental tosh. She found it quite amusing that the ugly jug with the phoenix impression on it was found strategically positioned on the top of Kat's valise. She asked me what I thought about that, and did I think there was any connection to the cork top being found where it was in the canal next to Conrad's body."

"What *do* you think about all that?"

"I think this," Lucy said decidedly after taking a sip of her brew, "there's more going on in the *why* of these two deaths than in the time and place of their occurring. More going on than meets the eye.

Consider the two coins. And Conrad's rosy-stubbed finger. For me, it's been quite absorbing analytically, if you see what I mean. Somehow all that goes beyond the physical evidence. I think that's what Alexsis meant about there being any connection, cork and jug and coins."

"In one of our conversations, Alexsis referred to ferrying across the Styx and the tradition of placing two coins on the eyes of the departed to ensure passage to the afterlife. Or in the mouth of the departed. We were engaging in wordplay at the time, on one of the water taxis. Now it's like a cryptic crossword puzzle, a kind of unintended entertainment. But as you just suggested, maybe it was intended as a commentary, a subtext to the story writ large. But do go on, Lucy."

"Let's go back to the arrest of one Dolf Van Handelaar that the police, acting on a tip, arrested and found no difficulty charging with the murder of Conrad Steele. A very convenient arrest far enough from the scene of the crime."

"What or who was the source of the tip?"

"That info, sadly, was not available to me. At any rate, said culprit was approaching Ghent on the cycle path along the Kanaal Gent-Brugge when he was picked up. His description matched the so-called "hoodie guy" on a cargo bike Flex and Alexsis reported seeing fleeing the area late Friday night. The same individual believed to be who Isla and Candace encountered and referred to as Mr. Van Hoodie — scar on his cheek, tattoos on his arms, death's head ring on a finger of both hands."

"Didn't they say at the time of their revelations it was almost as if the guy had info as to who they were and where they needed to be? No more than just an impression?"

"Possibly, but possibly not. Now, Dutch and Belgian authorities were familiar with Van Handelaar, a known drug dealer and petty criminal but not the sharpest knife in the drawer, apparently. He had form, however. Incriminating evidence was found in his possession, namely, Conrad's glitzy ring, his wallet and charge cards, his smart phone, and even the fancy sandals. Also in his possession, copious cash in euros and a wad of American dollars. And, as might be expected, a supply of drugs including heroin."

"Pretty incriminating."

"From the information that Niels Visser was able to glean and pass on to me, Van Handelaar claimed during his interrogation that he murdered no one, that he had been stitched up, conned into taking the rap, and that he had been conscripted by a guy he met in Antwerp, a young American called Richard Boone, and that the cops should be looking for him. He even sold him some heroin. At one time during the investigation, brief though it was, authorities let suspicion fall on crew members, specifically Aldert and Sander, even Joost, but all that went nowhere."

"Right, right. I remember Aimée saying she'd seen this hoodie guy a couple of times when we were in Ghent. She persisted against Mitch's non-committal, claiming she'd briefly observed him down in the bike parkade talking with Joost. Flex was in the vicinity as well."

"Waiting in line for the loo likely. Circumstantial at best."

I acknowledged with a series of nods what Lucy reported about Van Handelaar's predicament, took a long drink, then thought to ask, "What about fingerprints on the cork top and the two coins? Traces of DNA?"

"Unfortunately, I received no info on any of that because Visser had none."

"Well, how about Conrad's phone? Do you think it revealed anything relevant as to why he was murdered? You know, recent calls, contacts?"

"Visser had limited information," Lucy said, tilting her head slightly, an indication that she was disappointed she could not reveal more on that point. Then she added, "Or he limited what he could pass on to me. Understandably."

"Okay. What else?"

"Eventually the story got sorted. Van Handelaar said his co-conspirator, to use that term, this Richard Boone character, paid him good money. Cash payment, a portion when he agreed to get involved and the major hunk of it after the deed was done. He merely had to help move the body and deliver it to the canal near the *Iphigenia*."

"So, a patsy, and his argued innocence. If what he claimed is true, how does it all shake down?"

"It shakes down to the identity of a young American. One Richard Boone."

"I've wondered about Flex. Could he have been involved?"

"Perfectly alibied. Alexsis."

"Right. Eliminate Boyd Alexander as well. Too pissed. What about Archie Gallant, who just happened to show up at the wrong time? Or was it the right time?"

"If Van Handelaar is to be believed about a young American hiring him, then there's no fit there. Archie Gallant probably did not match the description Van Handelaar gave the police. I did get to talk with him at the Magnifique. He's but a distant part of the whole story. Sad, in many ways. He said the loss of Jennifer Troyes destroyed him and that his love for her was his Achilles' heal."

"Who then?"

"Who knows? In touristy Bruges, there were innumerable individuals who could be described as young Americans."

"Right. So, if not Van Handelaar, who did in Conrad Steele? Richard Boone?"

"Difficult to say, actually. But I can say this. After a hard day's scrutiny of the so-called facts, talking with Visser, talking with all the Conrad Corps at different times when convenient, even with Virgil about Forrest Troyes, believe it or not, and with Calvin Kinlaw, I came to the conclusion that this whole bloody business we were witness to reflected something far deeper. The demise of Conrad and Kat Steele was merely the top layer in a many-layered narrative of family conflict and dysfunction. But who murdered Conrad? No idea. Who might have seen Kat off to her posh beauty salon in the great beyond? I'm really clueless about that as well."

"Right. You know, in hearing of Kat's death, right on the heels of Conrad's, I could not help wondering about the how and why of it. The result? A net of indeterminate conclusions. I even considered possibilities, vague, mind you, that went beyond suicide, like spiked drinks, drugs, poisons, and also who would benefit most by her death."

"Brilliant."

"So, *you* really think it may not have been suicide in Kat's case?"

"Precisely. It's theory, remember, speculation, not proven fact."

"Still."

"Right, then. Given my intuitive drive to outdistance mere extrapolation, I asked a lot of questions once at liberty to do so. There was whatever info I could get from Visser, as I said. Virgil and Eleni were particularly forthcoming and very much in need of a sympathetic ear. Same with Isla and Candace. And Boyd Alexander. You were no longer available, Geoff, having done a runner! You'd fled the scene, which aroused suspicion, especially on Maartens' part."

"What?"

"I'm just taking the piss, mate."

"Good one, Lucy Hunter. Good one." I had to laugh about how easily she'd sucked me in. And given the opening, I'd return the compliment.

"Okay, going on. The conclusion that the Belgian authorities reached definitely had merit. Despite what seemed evidential proof, my inquisitiveness led me way beyond the official pronouncement. You're in no hurry to be anywhere, are you, Geoff?"

"I have until Wednesday. So tell me, then, what was the Russian connection?"

"Meaning what?"

"If it wasn't suicide and if poison was involved in her murder — a good possibility, right? — there must have been a Russian connection."

"As in heartbreak grass?"

"You are very knowledgeable about such means of eliminating someone, are you not?"

"I am but what's — "

"Did Maartens query you about that, your familiarity with poisons?"

"He did not. No, not at all."

"Excellent," I said, then let an exaggerated, well-meaning smile inform her I was just pulling her leg.

"Brilliant, Geoff. Tit for tat."

"Lucy, I couldn't resist. What else have you considered likely?"

"Quite a bit, actually. But given what I do for a living, I'm tempted to believe I'm just indulging in my own version of seeing patterns where they don't really exist. And yet it's imperative I follow my instincts. If you think a story has legs, you run with it."

"As in the many-layered saga of familial conflict and dysfunction associated with Conrad Steele."

"Precisely. It goes beyond Conrad Steele but I like to start there. And work back and then forward."

And swallowing some beer before launching, that's where Lucy Hunter, investigator par excellence, picked up again, the history and character of Conrad Steele. She'd been compelled to get beyond material gleaned from family members met on the *Iphigenia*, compelled to delve into all sources available on the internet, all the serviceable dot com sites, even drawing on the files in the archives of her Bureau of Investigative Journalism.

Conrad Steele was a cousin of Victor and Virgil Troyes. The Steele family having relocated to the UK when he was young, his early education was largely English Public school. Relative success at university gave over to relative success in marketing computer software. He strove to attain oligarchic status vis à vis shady politicians whose lifestyles and behind-the-door dealings led him eventually to the fringes of illegality. He entertained political ambitions but abandoned them when news broke that during his rise from lower middle class ranks, he had been involved in estate fraud schemes and inheritance scams, and though never criminally indicted, his probity was definitely called into question. As one who had worked with him put it, Conrad Steele invited potential partners into his hall of mirrors, into the smoke and glass world of his dubious enterprises. His dealings, whether business or personal, were defined by associates that had been interviewed in various contexts as transactional, as practical rather then principled — read self-serving.

Conrad met Kat when Victor Troyes and his family were visiting London. Jenny, the eldest daughter, was not with them on that trip. Interpersonal connections readily formed. Isla and Alexsis were quite young at the time as was their brother, Forrest. Kat encouraged them to call Conrad uncle. A business relationship with Troyes' company developed and continued well into the succeeding decades. With Victor Troyes' death, Conrad Steele took control of Advanced Electronic Processing, Inc.

In her brief sketch, Lucy referenced a conversation she'd had with Conrad on the *Iphigenia* where he made every effort to convince her he was a nice guy and a loving father when Alexsis' repeated public display of resentment had threatened the equanimity of all the guests. He was echoing the equivocal rational of decent Americans who, after a mass shooting or the murder of an innocent black man at the hands of the police, declared, "That's not us, that's not who we are." But that's exactly who they were because such violent behaviour was continuous. And the take-away truth of the matter? What was observed of the Conrad Corps was exactly who they were, a strife riven set of relationships headed by him. At bottom, the man, if not despicable, was not at all likeable. Indeed, his behaviour at the company conference in Cambridge that Melinda and Olivia mentioned gave evidence of that. He went on about chemistry between individuals then turned his attention to what he called mole conspiracy theory, that moles can make mountains out of insignificant mounds of earth, but were prohibited from doing so by government decree, and then he gave himself over to a laugh, half growl, half heartfelt delight at his own cleverness. True wit, right? A marked difference existed between being diplomatic and being cagey. Lucy concluded her profile by intimating that Conrad Steele might have won a few battles, but he definitely lost the war.

At this point in her narrative, I asked, "Are you implying Alexsis won the war?"

"You know enough about what troubled Alexsis regarding her lot in life."

"I learned about it in some detail the first couple of days out on the bikes. Allusion at times defined our conversations."

"Alexsis is clever and resourceful despite all the encumbrances she was at pains to describe. A fata morgana, given to deceptive appearances. The bike–barge adventure allowed her a greater degree of leeway than she'd had. I suspect she decided to confide in someone like you as a means of antagonizing Conrad and she attained some success in doing so. Right?"

"She did get him to react. So did Boyd Alexander get him to react."

"The surprise arrival of Flex after Antwerp increased Conrad's aggravation but lessened hers. Yesterday, after Chief Inspector Maartens gave us clearance, and allowed us all to carry on with our plans, Alexsis kissed Flex goodbye. All well and good. Here's the thing I find both interesting and puzzling. Back a day or so before Conrad was found murdered, I heard Alexsis say to Flex: 'This tide is not for turning.' Vanessa heard it too."

"When exactly?"

"After *Kunst Woestijn,* the atelier."

"Any explanation forthcoming?"

"Wanting to escape the endless and painful analysis going on in the family suite at the Magnifique hotel last night — the whys and the wherefores and the tearful embraces, Alexis sought us out at our hotel and sat up with Vanessa and me until late into the night. I asked her about the turning tide thing, but she didn't remember anything about it. With two deaths in the family, she was dealing with her own inner turmoil, so remembering something so specific would be difficult. Time finds you out, she said, and I took her to mean Conrad and Kat. She had strung Kat's diamond studded rings on a silver chain and wore them around her neck."

"The spoils of war, to extend the metaphor."

"We asked about Flex. He had to return to the USA immediately, some nebulous athletic undertaking. She was vague about it."

"Slash dashing would be a good bet."

"Not bloody likely," Lucy said with absolute certainty, then drained what remained of her glass of bière blonde. She checked the time.

She had to go. She'd arranged to have dinner with an associate investigative journalist, one Didier Dubois, who had written controversial articles on political corruption in France for Le Monde. He'd be addressing the conference tomorrow. Didier was really big into environmental engineering. Lucy thought to catch up, maybe compare expectations, enjoy a glass of wine with an old compatriot.

"Well, let's get together here at Les Deux Soeurs tomorrow."

"Righto. Sevenish, then. Before I head off, Geoff, a pertinent question. Did Alexsis ever get into how she and Isla were victimized by gaslighting when they were growing up?"

"I have no clear memory of her saying anything like that. Wait. Maybe she did. It would have fit thematically into the personal story she was telling, the restrictions and so on. She did say she thought the world was two faced."

"Regardless of all the various distractions among the great and the good of our little assembly on the *Iphigenia*, our focus was always on Alexsis, wasn't it? Her story was what grabbed our attention."

"True. Absolutely true. And she trusted you implicitly, didn't she?"

"Yes, she did. Now give me your email address and I'll send you the file I got from her last night before she headed back to her room at the Magnifique. Very revealing. From when she was younger. Sketchy research, but indicative of her determination to resist oppression. I had a look at it on the train from Brussels. It reads in part like excerpts from a diary or journal, a short essay, let's say, suitable for presentation in a psychology seminar."

"I look forward to reading it."

"We'll compare notes. Cheerio, mate. *A demain.*" And off Lucy Hunter trotted up rue Mouffetard, her back pack measuring the rhythm of her progress.

True to her word, she forwarded Alexsis' file. I opened it on my tablet as soon as I settled for the night at Le Séjour Latin. *The Creation of a False Narrative* is the title of the piece. It begins with a definition. Gaslighting can be understood as the means, emotional or mental, taken by abusers to manipulate victims by having them question their own reality. Beginning with that fundamental understanding, Alexsis outlines some of the general tactics of the gaslighter, from lying to coercion. She then states what is generally believed to be the source of the term; it originates, she contends, in the 1944 film "Gaslight" that derived from an earlier 1938 dramatization of the same name. The unexplained flickering and dimming of gaslights leads the heroine, who is being manipulated by her conniving, murderous husband, into doubting her sanity. Alexsis next enumerates other productions that feature gaslighting as a ploy for casting doubt on a character's mental state, among them "Rosemary's Baby," "Sleeping with the Enemy," and "Changeling."

Without referencing a source, Alexsis presents what she terms the sad case of Princess Diana. She contends that Diana got gaslighted by the Buckingham Palace crowd in a form of character assassination; the princess was accused of being delusional, a mental case given to egregious lying, a pathetic individual whose tribulations were born of envy and unconventional associations. Alexsis identifies with Diana. These assertions about the royals gave me pause.

What follows next in Alexsis' treatise is a kind of catalogue specifying in detail the ploys of the gaslighter followed up with examples that reflect what has been her reality and that of her sister, Isla. She gets very personal, drawing in Kat and Conrad and how the pair of them attempted through gaslighting to exert absolute control. She proceeds in an orderly and precise manner.

Minimizing the feelings of the victim: "Alexsis, you're exaggerating. Alexsis, must you overreact like that?"

Twisting blame and shifting focus: "Your behaviour, Alexsis, is the reason you feel so bad. Ignorant responses have consequence. That's a lie and you know it! You just faked that for the third time, Alexsis."

When in Conrad's company, I feel threatened, physically, emotionally, and mentally. Always implied is his control over my future and Isla's. He respects no boundaries. He's not the life-size product of a 3-d printer, the work of some evil genius with a hate on for youth, nor a cartoon villain, but a flesh and blood creature of his own design and manufacture. He's a fake. Telling him to fuck off only increases his ire, and then Mother comes along to adjudicate in his favour.

Deny wrongdoing: Disagreement always ends up my fault. I'm being hypersensitive. Am I always to blame? Guilty of defiance?

Spreading rumours while faking concern through compassionate words: "People don't like your designs at all, Alexsis. You're still young. Don't take offence, darling, because no offence is intended. But you know what I feel about your creations, don't you? You know how much I love you."

Answering questions with questions that provoke uncertainty: "What do you mean, that's not what this is about? Isla doesn't feel that way, does she?"

Revamping history: "No, no, no, girls, this is what really happened." They distort my memories of being with Father, our outings in the city and music recitals in Central Park, our family vacations, our trips to Greece. Now Isla remembers incorrectly things that were once so clear. Doubt can colour my own recollections. I hear what Conrad says but focus on what he does and understand it for what it really is. Same applies to Mother.

In a sort of summary statement of ploys and their particular effects on her, Alexsis names the states of being that victims of gaslighting might suffer, most prominent among which are anxiety, depression, self-loathing, addiction, and suicidal impulses. On the upside, if any is really possible, she claims that Isla's diary and poetry provide her with a form of escape. Thank the stars. She continues in that vein: I have my laptop and my periodic accounting of how miserably we are treated and just what the dark place I've inhabited for so long is like. There are may versions of dark, many depths of depression. Subsequent to her dark place reference, which she does not describe in any detail, Alexsis incorporates a series of loosely related statements that continue to define the plight that she is at pains to reveal.

In their view, I'm the unstable one. Meanwhile Isla is alone in her world.

She is totally undervalued as a human being, a young woman, not appreciated for her innate abilities. Her low self-esteem is unwarranted, the ugly creation of control freaks, fabricated on totally false premises.

Staying silent is only so successful in assuaging my feelings of inadequacy, a tactic Isla has perfected. Occasionally I con myself into believing lies, otherwise I tiptoe around troublesome issues.

Isla is constantly apologizing whereas I refuse to believe that Mother thinks my efforts are mediocre at best.

I hear Isla repeating something they've said to her, and I fear she's starting to accept that as real. She is passive while I try to remain strong in my resistance to their manipulations. My poor sister has more or less succumbed to their pressure, but I won't relent in my fight for truth.

Often it seems that Mother is concerned, genuinely concerned, about my welfare and that of Isla's but then she recants and does something totally unsympathetic to our situation. I hate her as much as I hate Conrad, our false father.

Outside help? Friends? They've been manipulated and conned to the point where our "intimate" conversations are merely superficial.

I'm unable to escape. They control, he controls, the assets left to us from our father. A big house with nowhere to hide. Forrest's observation from before he disappeared: The ego charging stations Conrad installed are accessible only to Conrad and Kat.

Mother is merciless where Forrest is concerned. No love lost. They sent him away and he's more or less stayed away out of their grasp. Blessed be the name of Virgil Troyes.

Once Conrad had established himself as master, he suggested rather emphatically that Forrest was a lost cause, that he was not all there because as a child he suffered a fall and seriously injured his brain. Total BS. He insists with a snide grimace that complete madness lies in Forest's future. Truth is, a force-field of conflict had enveloped the two of them; in other words, Conrad suspected that Forrest was on to him. With Kat's acquiescence, Conrad further claimed that Forrest suffered from incipient madness, quoting school reports of distracted and aggressive behaviours that confirmed what doctors determined to be the cause of Forrest's troubles, Post Traumatic Stress Disorder.

Granted, Forrest was significantly aggrieved by the death of his father and resented Conrad replacing him. Alexsis understood that. She also understood all too well Conrad's vindictiveness.

Bipolar disorder eventually supplanted PTSD as the affliction of choice in Conrad's lexicon. Given her limitations at the time, Alexsis did manage to research the concept of manic depression and its varied manifestations. Everything Conrad stated about the disorder was accurate, she concluded, only it did not apply to the Forrest that she knew. No way did he exhibit dramatic mood changes, from gleeful exuberance to drastic depression. Forrest was energetic, climbed trees, played ball, got to engage in all the usual activities a boy can get into regardless of the heavy atmosphere endured in the company of Kat and Conrad. He was never the so–called lost cause, not at all. He was never weirdly jumpy or agitated about the amount of broccoli on his plate. He'd celebrate a victory or difficult accomplishment but was never over confident. He was never too gabby, in fact he was taciturn at times, keeping his thoughts to himself, especially so once he cottoned onto Conrad's lies and insidious intentions. No doubt, he endured and continues to endure his own versions of darkness.

The next perversion of truth, Alexsis pointed out, dealt with genetics. Conrad claimed Forrest inherited the disease (if possible) from his father, who was manic depressive as well. Absolute bullshit. Alexsis declared that her father was always even with them as kids, never extreme in his manifestations of affection for them or, for that matter, his disapproval of their misdeeds. The clincher in the gaslighting of Forrest was that he was illegitimate.

Once sent away to boarding school, Forrest never returned to the home front. His ostracism continued well into his freshman year at college. Blessed be the name of Virgil Troyes. One big deception proposed by Conrad was that Forrest was dead, having been the victim of an avalanche while skiing in Colorado, and that his body would likely not be recovered until summer, if ever. Alexsis suggests that load of malicious crap was concocted to make her and Isla feel more isolated and powerless and have them suffer just a little bit more their sense of having lost a brother.

We're young when Father dies, just kids really, and then Mother marries Conrad shortly after that. Forrest, Isla, and I more or less accept things as they appear, but as we get older and start asking logical questions, that's when deceit and overwhelming parental supervision (tough love bullshit) come on strong denying the three of us freedom of action, of movement, of choice. Like dark shadows and black clouds leaching the colour out of springtime flowers, so has Conrad Steele robbed the spontaneity out of the life our father had promised us.

Alexis concludes her efforts in asserting that not all prisons have bars. She defers to Isla who quotes the Richard Lovelace poem:

> *Stone walls do not a prison make*
> *Nor Iron bars a cage*

* * *

Monday, July 24 —

In my late afternoon email to Penny, I lauded the range and efficiency of the Paris métro service that allowed you to get around a city with little lost in time allotted for various explorations. However, you could achieve only so much in a single day regardless of how well plans were laid down. Patience was absolute de rigeur when sightseeing in a metropolis as seductive as Paris. I'd managed two icons. First, the Eiffel Tower — three-sixty view of everything, amazing, even the sensation of the tower itself moving in the wind and you with it. Second, Notre Dame, where I could do no more than note from afar the progress in the reconstruction of the roof and steeple. Equally amazing what architects and structural engineers had already wrought. From Notre Dame I hoofed it to the Louvre and managed to gain entrance without undue shoving or delay.

You'd need a week in order to get the most out of a visit to the Louvre. I had a few hours before my focus and stamina gave out. Two essential viewings: one, the Mona Lisa — so captivating a presence to so many and yet so small and distant an exhibit; and two, the Venus de Milo, white marbled queen of the *Galerie des Antiques*. There she stood in all her glory, framed by a dark pillared arch, surrounded by other classical statements of ideal beauty and form. The

Salle de Cariatides housed more Greek statuary and their Roman copies, bringing to life half-remembered characters out of the myths and legends, how Venus-Aphrodite, for instance, played her part in causing the Trojan War. Of course, my thoughts turned to David and his work and that I would be sharing a beer with him in a couple of days.

Yet to be visited: the Quay D'Orsay for the impressionists; the Rodin museum, possibly, I'd have to think about it; Montmartre and the Sacré Coeur Basilica; Cliché and the Moulin Rouge. The Père Lachaise cemetery had been high on Penny's list of places to visit so I vowed to get there. I closed off the email saying what a terrific job she'd done in arranging our stay in Paris. She would have a laugh over that. Finding a reasonably priced hotel in the Latin Quarter with access to rue Mouffetard, reputed to be the oldest street in Paris, was no less than a coup of travel planning shrewdness. She would have loved the bohemian, multicultural, artsy fartsy area she'd researched so well. Next time. I mentioned running into Lucy Hunter from the *Iphigenia* here in Paris to attend a conference on rescuing the planet out of the clutches of oligarchs. Small world.

Lucy Hunter appeared at Les deux Soeurs just after seven. I caught a glimpse of her in a patterned, high hemmed dress passing Saint-Médard church. She couldn't be described as diminutive although she was on the short side. Well developed muscular legs carried her forward on a solid frame, the shoes and the backpack striking an incongruous note with the more stylish outfit. The thought occurred that having the opportunity to converse with her one to one was nothing less than absolutely rewarding for me. On the *Iphigenia* her comments and insights had been shared with the other guests, particularly those at our table. Connecting with her here in Paris offered me a chance to study and appreciate more fully a gutsy, determined woman who had been subject to death threats in the service of truth. She sidled in opposite me, hooking her pack on the back of her chair.

After deciding on drinks, we engaged in some chatter about our activities that day. I went on a bit too enthusiastically about the wonders of the Louvre. I quit when Lucy rolled her eyes as if to say why not tell her about something she didn't know. She briefly mentioned how well received Didier's presentation on sustainability was, salient points of which she'd be including in her write-up. She'd received a note from Vanessa who reported that media coverage of the "*Iphigenia* deaths" was well on its way in Bruges. After her first swig, Lucy leaned forward and asked what I thought of Alexsis' effort at describing the *False Narrative* that so restricted the lives of the two sisters and their lost brother, Forrest.

"Alexsis makes every effort, it seems to me, to be objective but her anger seethes below the surface. It's a kind of existential rage. Isla manages to supress through sublimation what Alexsis could not."

"Quite. When Victor died, something in Alexis died and was reborn in a species of tempered hate, fury the midwife. Forrest too, from what she's confided to me. The mother and son bond was severed permanently."

"What might Freud have made of that?"

"Another theory to confuse us," she said, raising a sceptical eyebrow.

"Or some classical Greek dramatist?"

"Blood splatter to entertain us while we contemplate life's many twisted ironies."

"Plenty to consider there," I said philosophically and took a good long philosophical draught of the amber lager.

"Understood from early on," Lucy then said, "was Kat's hypocrisy. Alexsis loathed her mother for jumping so readily into Conrad's bed in the aftermath of Victor's death. As she put it the other night, what happened to the family amounted to an evil that had metastasized. Her 'beloved' mother was an ogress, capable of devouring her own children."

"Strong language."

"Strong feelings. She's educated, well-read, informed despite the restrictions. She followed up that comment with the notion of usurpation. Conrad was like Macbeth, only he killed her father or rather attempted to kill the memory of her father, not the king, though she continued to regard her father as kingly. The sly bastard stole Kat's heart and soul, turning her into a bloody accomplice, Lady Macbeth 0.2. The heartless queen with blood on her hands, remember, went mad and topped herself."

"Right, suicide. But she'd be more like Hamlet's mother Gertrude, no?"

"Brilliant," Lucy said, then as though reaching back deep into her memory bank she came out with 'The funeral baked meats did coldly furnish forth the marriage tables.' That how it goes?"

"I imagine your recall is accurate, Lucy."

"Let me go on. Using figurative language that really didn't surprise me much, Alexsis talked about the situation Isla and she as teens found themselves in. They were choking on the smoldering embers of concealment and suppression. Her resistance was a slow burn to begin with but out of the smoke and confusion of emotional and mental blackmail a raging blaze of animosity emerged."

"The phoenix effect."

"Precisely. As far as she knew, Forrest shared the sentiments although at the time he was suffering his own hell elsewhere."

"On one occasion out on the bikes, Alexsis told me that they'd been deprived of their inheritance."

"Quite so, if all her confidences are true. Steele invested it for them and lost it all, or maintained that's what happened. They were virtually reduced to penury and therefore completely dependent on their manipulative step-father. Small jobs pay very little. No job pays nothing at all."

"Yeah, on the *Iphigenia* I had a sense that all merely endured each other because of some unfathomable bond not to everyone's liking, some narrative that included so much more than the immediate present and its petty disagreements. Boyd Alexander rode precariously along on the periphery."

"Interesting way of phrasing it, Geoff."

"Inspired, right? I tried to piece together how relationships worked, who was respectful of whom, who was sanctioned and who disparaged. My curiosity was fed by bits of conversation overheard here and there, along the bike ways, in the lounge, by the hot tub. Deck chairs became musical chairs in the merry-go-round of my efforts to match voice and gesture to presumed states of mind. That was the technician in me, the synthesizer, wanting to get the sound just right, to fit all components of the scene into perfect understanding. Good luck with that, eh?

"And when Conrad bit it, I visualized each mouth chomping away at some concocted alibi, true, false, or absolutely fanciful, for the police interrogations. All I needed was blackboard and chalk and an audience of interested and concerned local dicks. Integrated into all this is what you and the others at our table contributed. Veridis and I called our observations the wry sanction file."

"We were all so perceptive, weren't we?"

A touch of irony on Lucy's part. She looked off and then invited me with a lift of her chin to regard a family of four that had stopped to take photos in front of the Guy Lartigue fountain. The larger child got around to dousing the smaller one and in the process got herself soaked. Risible. I resettled in my chair and took a quick drink before saying, "What we witnessed on the *Iphigenia* was not exactly the clash of BattleBots. But animosity, acrimony, yes."

"Agreed," Lucy said. "I also asked Alexsis about Forrest and how news of the two deaths would affect him, but she was not too forthcoming on that point. She seemed as though unwilling to tread on sacred ground. However, she showed me a photograph of Forrest."

"Probably the one she showed me. Also one of her father, Victor."

"She did say that Calvin Kinlaw, Mister Fix It, had the inside story on Forrest. And so did Virgil, who mostly kept mum about what he knew. At one time she wanted to go out to the west to visit Forrest on the coast but was prohibited from doing so by Kat and Conrad. All changed now, of course."

"So, she and Isla are free to connect with Forrest."

"Appears so. I also asked about her older sister, Jennifer. She had little to say about her because she remembered little. All she knew was her story was a very sad one, cloaked in mystery. Kat would practically tear up at the mention of Jenny's name."

"Shows some maternal instinct on Kat's part."

"True enough. But get this, Geoff, quite surprisingly, I got a rather lengthy email from Alexsis last night that covered a lot of territory. She's still in Bruges, as are most of the others, waiting clearance to leave. Official paperwork. Death warrants. Transport of bodily remains. Kinlaw is seeing to the details. There are many."

"I suppose she feels really connected to you."

"She does, interestingly enough. Was the case right from the first day on the *Iphigenia*. Said what she was doing in emailing me was 'killing time, pun intended.' Beyond me, any pun there. Just being coy, I couldn't decide. At any rate, she delved in much greater detail than previously into what led to her being alienated, attempting at the same time to explain the reasons for her recalcitrance while doing the bike-barge thing. She admitted quite readily to letting supposition play a role in what she had to say to me."

"Supposition in terms of what?"

"The notion of retribution and justifiable homicide."

"Stretching it a bit, no?"

"Maybe. She admitted often theorizing about certain troubling events in the life of the family that raised suspicion but could garner no reasonable proof. Gut feeling, simply."

"Right, intuition. But no proof."

Here Lucy leaned back and then forward again. She lifted her hands and wiggled her fingers (as I'd seen her do before), then studied them disapprovingly. She winced and then offered this self-deprecating observation. "Wouldn't do on a magazine page advertising engagement rings, right?"

"Lucy, you're a better judge of these things than I."

"Righto," she said, extending the word and giving it a touch of ironic humour. "I did some fact checking just to assure myself of the accuracy in a few of Alexsis more speculative assertions. Pulled up some info on Jenny but not as much as I would have liked. Actually, Geoff, I did a lot of digging, dates, newspapers (once I got past the paywalls), media reports, police statements, podcasts, the whole gamut, even archived interviews with Victor Troyes himself."

"And all this time I was thinking you were clairvoyant."

"Taking the piss, are you? Believe me, Geoff, it was well after midnight before I managed to get any sleep. Plus, I have my report on the conference to finish."

At this juncture we decided to order a meal. With the evening cooling down somewhat and a slight breeze picking up, I thought to grab a table within the bistro but Lucy was all for dining al fresco, "en plein-air" as she put it. It came down to a jug of red house wine, *steak frites* which was a local favourite, and a Greek salad we would share. In less time than we'd anticipated, our acrobatic waiter delivered our order with the kind of flare we'd come to expect of him. We dug in, murmuring approval with each bite. We sipped the wine with appreciation and eventually got back to the content of Alexsis' lengthy email with Lucy picking her way slowly through the *frites.*

Intriguing, how Lucy Hunter curled the pages back to earlier chapters in how Alexsis Troyes' *Creation of a False Narrative* came into being and why all its implications continued to hold our interest in much the same way that a nasty comment made at the Steele table on the *Iphigenia* could rivet our attention. Lucy gave me the edited version, the fast facts account. She said that each episodic slice off the old family block presented in the email had a heading.

Affections and Antipathies.

Doubt was raised in young Alexsis' mind as to how her father died and that early doubt continued to increase in volume. Victor Troyes, initially described in loving detail, was then acknowledged as not being perfect. Who could be? He was fully committed to his business interests and to his family. His oldest daughter had been lost to him, an on-going source of sadness, regret, and contention; the blame game broke out and intensified over time to the dismay of the children. Business activity accounted for his many absences. He had his briefcase full of stress, his late night arrivals, his luxury sedan, his charitable foundations, and his assorted distractions, the most attractive one being his long-standing personal secretary, Cassandra Fortune. Alexsis knew her as Cassie and liked her a great deal unlike Kat who liked her not at all. But then again, Conrad Steele, who showed up for dinner periodically, liked Kat and showed it in less than subtle ways. Victor was indifferent to the potential liaison between the two but Forrest and Alexsis were not. Their antipathy towards Conrad began early in the relationship when they saw their generally unwelcome pseudo-uncle grab and then massage in rather familiar fashion their mother's shapely ass.

Painful Ministrations.

Victor Troyes was murdered in a hit and run crash. Progressing with the lights through an intersection, Troyes' Mercedes was rammed full on, forcefully swept over a distance of a hundred feet, and crushed against a concrete ramp. CCTV footage and that of the dashcam in an approaching delivery van provided evidence that the attack vehicle, a black Hummer, stolen from a rental park the day before, made no attempt to halt. Rather, it appeared to accelerate. Damage done, it burned rubber in its escape and was found later in a secluded area, completely incinerated. Media reports echoed police findings that this was no accidental collision but a targeted homicide. Innumerable conspiracy theories arose as to who was behind the murder of business tycoon Victor Troyes. No suspects were immediately arrested and charged. Investigations would be on-going. The case has yet to be solved.

Memorial services for Victor Troyes were well attended, hundreds in number. Virgil Troyes' eulogy moved many to tears. Forrest, Alexsis, and Isla were inconsolable. A grieving Kat sought and received sympathetic understanding from Conrad Steele.

A week after the remains of Victor Troyes were laid to rest, Cassandra Fortune was found dead in her apartment. A co-worker at AEP, inquiring as to her continued absence and failure to pick up, made the discovery. The coroner established the cause of death to be an overdose of heroin. Suicide was eliminated as motivation. Details of the follow-up by police authorities remained in files inaccessible to reporters despite headlines splashing across front pages the connection between the dead woman and Victor Troyes. He had been driving away from her apartment the night he was murdered. Spicy detail, not to be overlooked in the gossip columns.

Funeral services for Cassandra Fortune were modest, family and friends. Forrest and Alexsis were denied attendance despite protests. They remembered fondly how Cassie at company picnics would tell them what the future held by reading their palms or laying out and interpreting Tarot cards for them. Nonsense! In no way, despite their limited understanding of the world at that stage in their lives, could they be convinced that Cassie was a junkie. Arguing the point, they were again told that they were talking nonsense. When Alexsis informed Virgil of what they thought about both deaths, the first being a murder, and the second being so confusing and yet connected to the first in ways they could not adequately explain, he assured them that in the end the truth would out. Their convictions never faltered. They remained strong to this day.

Lucy interrupted her delivery of the abridged version of Alexsis' lengthy email and cut directly to the chase. "Alexsis," she said decidedly, "is absolutely certain that Conrad Steele and her mother Kat arranged for the elimination of both her father and his paramour, Cassandra Fortune. Forrest is of the same mind. And Virgil Troyes has always had his suspicions."

"What evidence does she offer?"

"None. Well, nothing absolute. Everything just fell too perfectly into place for Conrad and Kat, the quick marriage, his assuming control of AEP, the ensuing gaslighting, Forrest's abandonment, the loss of their inheritance."

"Right, right, her intuition."

"Pretty much. But then she attempts in her email to take me deeper into the web of shifting allegiances, providing a very plausible basis for the rift that opened between her mother and her father, a breach in marital unity, she says, both Virgil and Eleni could attest to. Thus, Jennifer Troyes. Jenny."

Predication.

Existing family conflict intensified with the abduction of Jennifer Troyes when she was twenty and a student at university. At the time she was engaged to Archie Gallant, an agent from Victor Troyes' inner circle who advocated for high-profile athletes, many professional boxers. Gallant was an archer of some repute. Jennifer was nabbed at night while returning to her dorm from the library. A ransom demand for millions ensued. Local police were baffled as to who the perpetrators might be and so was the FBI, called in immediately to oversee the case. Troyes was encouraged to follow established procedures. Extremely slow progress for an outraged father impatient for the safe return of his daughter proved too much. Victor Troyes, decision-maker par excellence, opted to handle matters his way, employing Calvin Kinlaw to conduct negotiations with the kidnappers in a manner he himself prescribed, which in the last analysis was defined by authorities as too devious and too dangerous. Kinlaw failed to achieve positive results, leaving Victor Troyes not only thwarted in his scheme to outsmart the kidnappers but also subjected to ignominious condemnation by his wife, Kat, who told him point-blank and often that he'd fucked up royally. Jennifer was lost. The case remains unresolved. Alexsis remembers Kat in heated moments of conflict when casting aspersions on her husband seemed like the easiest way to relieve frustration and stress: "It's filicide, Bucko, the sacrifice of a beloved daughter to your vast ego."

Media coverage at the time included both fact and fantasy. One rumour had it that the underworld gang behind her abduction sold her into the white slave trade having Saudi connections; another version had it as Libyan connections. There was even speculation that Archie Gallant and Jennifer Troyes herself connived in a plan to somehow bilk the AEP corporation out of untold sums of cash. Victor Troyes swiftly and authoritatively put the kibosh on that piece of hack reporting, calling it, when interviewed on cable news, no more than malicious gossip, an egregious misrepresentation of both characters. An additional piece of provocative surmise posed the question of Jennifer's legitimacy. The tabloid's contention was unsubstantiated, if not totally nebulous: that Jennifer was a by-blow, an indiscretion on a youthful Eleni's part in Paris when quite susceptible to flattery and amorous adventuring, the upshot being that Kat, in accord with Victor who was most receptive to the idea, adopted the infant Jennifer, raised her, and loved her as their own.

"I verified the facts on Jenny's abduction," Lucy commented, "but drew a big blank on the issue of maternity." She attempted to supress a yawn but failed to do so. "Apocryphal, no doubt."

"That's it, then? Alexsis' spontaneous tell-all?"

"Not quite, Geoff, not quite."

What If and Retribution.

Alexsis' so-called mad brother, in reality the young American in Dolf Van Handelaar's story, was in Belgium during the later part of her Triple B adventure. He and Flex arrived in Antwerp at the same time and had reservations on the same flight home from Brussels. Forrest entered and left the country under a false identity, Richard Boone. His passport was fake, a very good fake. As pre-arranged, he met Van Handelaar in Antwerp and set about effecting a plan of action. Forrest followed the route of the *Iphigenia* surreptitiously, communicating with Flex and Alexsis only when necessary. For his part, Van Handelaar followed the route more openly.

What if all of the foregoing were in fact true? What if events involving Forrest and his hired hand led to the elimination of Conrad Steele? What if Dolf Van Handelaar was telling the truth about being set up? What if phone messages provided evidence of a conspiracy between brother and sister to commit serious crimes?

On the night he was murdered, Conrad Steele was inebriated after his business dinner with Calvin Kinlaw in Bruges. Weaving his way back to the barge through the Minnewaterpark in the wee hours of the morning, he was accosted by someone that he recognized and then saluted. In his drunken state, the big man offered inadequate and extremely awkward resistance to being assailed before receiving a lethal smack to the back of his head with a metal pipe. The blow felled him. Permanently. A severed finger of the left hand rendered up the prized ring. Two coins were inserted into a pocket expeditiously. His body was then hefted into the cargo bin of bike that was quickly pedaled across the red bridge and on to the Bargeweg. Conrad Steele's carcass was slid forthwith into the canal at the rear of the *Iphigenia*. A cork top was flung over the scene to indicate finality.

What if the assailant were Forrest Troyes seeking retribution? What if Flex and Alexis witnessed the dumping of the body but only reported seeing a hoodie on a cargo bike rushing away from the scene of the crime? What if Forrest procured heroin from Van Handelaar with a very specific reason in mind? What if Kat never forgave Victor for sacrificing their daughter, Jennifer, and believed he deserved to die. What if a distressed Kat were sedated by a daughter and then administered a lethal dose of heroin? What if that daughter was not Isla?

When Lucy asked the last question posed in Alexsis' email, she appeared to be drawing her narrative to a conclusion — she drew a long breath at last, indicating she'd finished with the content just as she had finished with the *frites* — I was moved to ask a series of questions myself.

"What if all that you presented as coming directly from Alexsis is an accurate portrayal of what actually happened? An accurate account of who was involved? It raises more and more questions, doesn't it? Like why did Forrest and Alexis (with Flex helping) take so long to do in Conrad, if indeed they did? Why on a cycling adventure in Holland and Belgium? And did Alexsis murder her mother? And is this a confession on Alexsis' part? I could go on."

"As to when and where, opportunity is the answer, and convenience," Lucy said. "Family circumstance outside of the ordinary where control of Alexsis was much looser."

"Right."

"As to her email being a confession? I doubt the pique of conscience prompted Alexsis to reveal so much in order to unburden herself of feelings of guilt. The email is rather a playful demonstration of her resolve and that of her brother. I think of it more as an apologia, a justification and a symbolic sentencing."

"So bogus?"

"Possibly. Possibly not."

"One way or the other, how could she trust you not to go to the cops?"

"If queried, she could claim total fabrication, call what she sent me nothing but imagined wish-fulfilment, a what-if fantasy concocted up out of having too much time on her hands before flying back to America. Besides, she did trust me implicitly, didn't she?"

"Right. But then again, she could just do a runner, no?"

"That would imply guilt. This way she just has to play along with official conclusions. Assuming, as you say, it's an accurate account of who, what, when, and where. By now, you and I are both very familiar with the why."

"So, if accurate, Dolf Van Handelaar was a cut-out for Forrest Troyes and cleverly set up to take the fall because of an anonymous tip to the cops that they acted on."

"If what we have is an accurate account, yes."

"Right. What about Kat?"

"In a pseudo postscript, Alexsis briefly describes how, when viewing at close range Conrad's heaped-up corpse after it was pulled from the canal, the fury that lay hidden within for so long burst forth and she willingly embraced the cruel act she knew she, in theory, was capable of. She said I could fill in the details with the understanding that blood will have blood. I can only surmise that once Forrest did his part, Alexsis the shape-shifter would not neglect to do hers."

"Isla told me that Alexsis is quite capable of lying. As did Conrad. You have to ask yourself: is she lying about this?"

"Possibly. Possibly not."

"When it all shakes down, you and I and someone like Frank Veridis, playing detectives from a distance, suspected all along that Alexsis was simply hiding behind her outward grievances, her rejected daughter discontent, her sardonic jabs. She was just waiting for the propitious moment. Matricide. Sedation and lethal injection, antidotes to years of grievance."

"That about sums it up. But there's an interesting piece of the puzzle we've not looked at yet, the jug that Kat so despised. When called into the scene of her mother's (presumed) suicide, Alexsis noted the jug standing on Kat's valise 'like a miniature statue of liberty signifying freedom.' She thought it significant, perhaps symbolic, but ironic and somewhat amusing, and told me so shortly after. I was lurking about the passageway then, at the bottom of the stairs. Visser indicated that the jug would be dusted for fingerprints. Logical, of course, but potentially revealing nothing of significance. Remember, Conrad called the jug a funeral urn. Alexsis might well have placed the jug on the valise herself — presuming her intimations reveal the truth about retribution. Its emblazoned phoenix, symbolic of transformation, augurs well for Alexsis and her siblings."

"For Boyd Alexander as well."

"I've come to believe the acrimony we witnessed in the Conrad Corps started a long time ago, long before the dissolution of Kat and Victor's marriage, ages ago, in fact, long before we settled on the superiority of a single deity. For my money, we're dealing with *lex talionis,* an eye for an eye and a tooth for a tooth, retributive justice, revenge in the raw and in the not so raw, dramatizing that treachery can be evident even in a sophisticated circle of contemporary society."

"So, nothing new there."

"Precisely. I've said it before, Geoff, and I'll say it again here. If the story has legs, run with it."

Nafplion

July 27, Hotel Orestes —
Hot and dry, so it was, but with a soothing wind cutting in and out of the scene before me rattling the awnings with whimsical insistence. I had a preferred spot on the hotel patio with a view though the palm trees of Bourtzi Castle. It was constructed by the Venetians centuries ago in the middle of Nafplion Harbour. Beyond the castle, the Argolic Gulf opened up to betray across the atmospheric distancing hills and mountains that revealed themselves in shades of blue, purple, and mauve. Within reach on my table, a bottle of Fix. Blond, smooth, and full said the waiter when I enquired as to why it was deemed a premium Geek Lager. I took him at his word and was glad that I did. Why was the hotel called Orestes? The name of a legendary hero like Agamemnon, the waiter further explained, from Mycenae. He also informed me and seemed delighted to do so that CNN had designed Nafplion as one of Europe's most beautiful towns. From what I had seen since arriving, I had to agree.

Late model vehicles, sleek yachts moored along the quay, and other indications of modernity like beautifully appointed accommodations assured me that I was in the twenty-first century; and yet I had the sensation of having fallen back into a world where the passage of time and the activities it engendered were measured differently. Such a contrast to the crush, day and night, of the northern cities I'd recently visited. Here, past and present had a distinctively Greek arrangement. Here, the new was attempting to supplant the old and was discovering how much of a struggle it could be. You just had to slow down and pace yourself. And then there was the light, the immense light.

My latest email to Penny kept me focused on where I was and how I got here, not to omit connecting with our son. I wrote that my last day in Paris was eventful — the Quay D'Orsay for the impressionists, the Rodin museum, and I was able to get out to the Pierre Lachaise Cemetery. I made every effort to be as informative as possible, providing details where most appropriate. The flight from Charles de Gaulle across the Alps to Athens went smoothly. Athens airport to Corinth on the train, bus to Nafplion, and now I had in my pocket the key to a perfectly suitable room in the Hotel Orestes that David reserved for me once he got the message that I'd altered original plans regarding length of stay. Penny had planned a more extensive tour, but I decided to save all that for the future, when David could play guide to his mother and father. Thus, I limited my time in the Nafplion area to three days and changed my flight home. I closed off stating that David would be joining me here on the patio at five after he returned from the field.

David had informed me that he and some of his archaeological cronies resided in the Hotel Orestes as well while others in his student group had equally reasonable accommodation elsewhere as organized by course managers. At ten to five, David showed. He wrapped his hands tightly around my shoulders and then let go. At his age (he turned twenty-one before leaving home), he'd better have developed some strength. It was evident he had. He came around and gave me as convincing bear hug as I was giving him. I got winded in the embrace. His right hand was rougher than I remembered. I supposed the left was the same. Manual work. He held up my bottle for the waiter to see and raised two fingers.

"*Endaxi,*" the waiter said. "Okay, you got it."

I'd been told that my son David resembled me physically. That was one way to describe him, average height but taller than his old man, and just as interested in athletic endeavours. Under the aegis of genetic diversity that determines what you see is not necessarily what you get, Penny and I didn't do too badly with David because he inherited his brainy head from her. He was studious from an early age, a determined achiever, and focused to the point of being stubborn (like his mother). His intellectual interests ranged widely which kept him out of typical teenage trouble. He was thoughtful and considerate when it came to others. Among his failings — yes, he did have them, like not always responding as quickly as he might when required to do so — sartorial indifference, even when it came to dressing up for graduation, rated high.

And there he was standing before me on a patio in Nafplion in Greece wearing cut-off denim shorts and a t-shirt I'd not seen before with MYCENAE stamped across the front and "I really dig it" written below. Around his neck a soiled kerchief hung loosely. On his feet, ragged sandals. He'd had his long hair cut so his ball cap fit strangely. The eager eyes and toothy smile. I was expecting more of an Indiana Jones look but this was fine. I hugged him again.

"Settled in?"

"Great room, son, terrific view of the sea."

"So how was your bike-barge adventure?"

"Very adventurous," I said. What Lucy Hunter and I dissected, parsed, and served up to each other as the likely truth about what befell Conrad and Kat Steele, I refrained from getting into. I did mention some of the highlights, Ghent, Bruges, for instance, and described some of the individuals I engaged with, like Frank Veridis, Melinda Mancipal, and the younger ones like Alexsis, Isla, and Boyd Alexander. I finished up with the two deaths that occurred on the last days.

"Food poisoning?"

"Neither that nor heart attack from overexertion," I said and before I could elaborate on the many features of the *Iphigenia*, my joker of a son cut in.

"Lucky you survived then, Dad," he said. "Mom did express some concern when she knew you'd be own your own."

"She need not have worried, son. I survived. I kept her apprised in my emails. I explained that in Holland, a speed bump in a drive-in equates to a hill climb."

"I get it, Dad. What about FaceTime? I use it with Mom."

"I don't have it. I've always preferred to email. Make it personal. Besides I like the narrative mode. It gives me chance to sort through the things I want to say in a measured, sequential way."

David listed other alternatives, other platforms that were serviceable but were of little interest to me. I nodded patiently thinking back to the elaborate email Lucy received from Alexsis. The adieux she and I exchanged in Paris were very Gallic, a nudge on both cheeks.

"Why email with so much else available? I rarely check for emails anymore. You are the exception, Dad. We communicate mostly with WhatsApp now."

I was grateful for being the exception. Otherwise I might still be sitting in airport limbo. After describing my experiences in Paris and going on about how much I enjoyed seeing the conclusion to the Tour de France, I asked David about his studies and how the whole archaeological endeavour was coming along.

I had a general idea what was involved when he applied and was accepted for the programme; it provided certificates, transcripts, academic accreditation, accommodation, local transportation. The real benefit of the experience was that it would add credits to his degree from York University. There were costs, of course. But to be fair, David's scholarship and weekend jobs cut expenditures down considerably. For David specifically, the programme combined his interest in archaeology with anthropology. He'd always had a thing for Greek myths and heroes like Odysseus, Achilles, Hercules and so on. At one time his high school buddies nicknamed him Homer.

So when I asked what he was actually doing, he launched exuberantly. Mycenae was probably the most important archaeological site in all of Greece. He was fortunate to be part of the work being done on the lower town site which was situated below the citadel. There were thirty students under the supervision of instructors experienced in many areas, from traditional trench excavations to the use of ground penetrating radar and aerial photography. He listed and described a host of activities and concluded his panegyric of the whole operation by stating that what he found most enjoyable were the excursions to cultural sites like the ancient theatre at Epidaurus.

David left to clean up and returned a little later with plans for a simple meal and we headed off to what he called restaurant row. We both ordered gyro plates and a jug of house wine that proved to be excellent for house wine. No claims on my part to being a sommelier. I was impressed that he'd picked up some basic Greek, enough to be socially polite: hello, good afternoon, please, and thank you. While consuming our meal, he waxed poetic about the history of Mycenae and the archaeological excavation begun there with the arrival in 1874 of Heinrich Schliemann, who was renowned for unearthing the ancient city of Troy. One of the greatest finds, if not the greatest, was the gold death mask of King Agamemnon. David had a picture of it on his phone and passed the phone over to me. An incredible find indeed. An incredible archaeological treasure. To be honest, it was absolutely mesmerizing. The height of Mycenaean civilization, David continued, was from

1400 to 1200 BCE. Natural disaster in the twelfth century likely brought on its collapse.

When we had finished our meal, the waiter placed a carafe of local raki and two shot glasses on our table. "From the house," he said and smiled.

David poured for both of us, sipped his, and then changed direction, leaving Mycenae and all its attractions for later discussion. He mentioned informing his mother that he kept particular company with a student from Trent University who definitely shared his enthusiasm, Margo Sylvester. The information apparently got Penny's interest up and she insisted he bring "this perfect companion" around when they returned home. I would meet her tomorrow.

"Dad, are you up for a stroll around the town?" David asked when talk of Margo Sylvester faded out and the last drop of raki had burned our throats for thc last time.

"Been a long day of travelling for this old man," I said. "Early retirement. Sleep like a log."

David wanted to pay the waiter, but I knew he expected me to pick up the tab. I did not want to disappoint the expectations that a son has for his father. It was great being with him. A wisp of unsettling memory dangled before me at that moment, Boyd Alexander and his father Conrad at the big table on the *Iphigenia*.

David and I sauntered down to the harbour and fell into beatific appreciation of the setting sun and its chromatic extravagance.

"A nacreous sky," David opined.

"A what?"

"The colours in the sky are like mother of pearl. The same in their watery reflections."

"Right, right. Bourtzi Castle out there is all lit up. Spectacular."

"We students are up early and off to the field. Sleep in, Dad. Take a bus or better a taxi to the citadel,

292

explore around, then drop down to where we're working in the old town site. Bring water."

"Will do, son."

Before hitting the sack, I allowed myself a view from the balcony of my room.

Bourtzi Castle was now like a floating mirage. David's nacreous sky had evolved into an impressionist's palette of aqua greens and mauves and reddish yellows. Penny would have loved being here.

* * *

July 28, Nafplion —
I woke out of a disorienting dream: the gold death mask of King Agamemnon was seeping blood profusely. From the corner of the eyes. Startling but totally inexplicable imagery, I decided, other than maybe the brain's imperative to get me up and make for the WC. Too much raki the night before?

Though late arising and having seen to perfunctory morning rituals, before long I was riding in a taxi heading out to Mycenae. Coffee and a sweet bun to hand and I was well on my way, cutting through olive groves and shimmering landscapes where cicadas sang, admiring simple homes where bougainvillea and grape vines hung like national adornments and oleander bushes seemed to set the day on fire.

The taxi deposited me in the parking lot where numerous tourist busses were parked. Apparently, I would not be alone here. Following others along the path leading up to the Lion Gate, I was struck by the ruggedness of the terrain on which the citadel had been constructed all those centuries ago. Massive blocks of stone demarked the enclosing walls. Formidable, given where they stood. Equally impressive was the entrance itself, the lionesses emblematic, it struck me as I stood in speculative awe, of power, authority, and solid defence. I overheard a guide explain to a group of tourists that these so-called Cyclopean walls dated from 1350 BCE and the Lion Gate from 1250 BCE.

I wandered over the site, examining the various areas where excavations had been conducted. Layer upon layer of civilization uncovered in pursuit of knowledge and understanding. Time, ancient and modern. I though back to something Alexsis Troyes said about dwelling too much in the past, that memory could produce mirages. She may have had a point. On second thought, it was probably Frank Veridis who came up with that quip. At any rate, the ubiquitous song of the cicadas, rising and falling, rising and falling, was like a choral commentary on what once was and why it was no more. And for someone like Alexsis Troyes, what would time make of her legacy?

Down from the Lion Gate, cut into the slope of a knoll, was the Tomb of Aegisthus, a dome shaped, bee-hive grave (called a tholos) similar in design and construction to the Tomb of Clytemnestra and the Treasury of Atreus aka the Tomb of Agamemnon. Inside that of Clytemnestra, I heard the guide from earlier say to her group, "Though these tombs were looted in the iron age, much was uncovered when archaeologist began serious work. Many artifacts can be viewed in the museum here. The mask of Agamemnon is on display in Athens, at the National Archaeological Museum." Bloodless, I surmised, and brilliant.

A waiting line of shoulder-to-shoulder tourists dissuaded me from seeking entrance to the museum. The day was heating up and I was beginning to feel it. Serenaded by the cicadas, I headed down the slope, grateful I'd brought sufficient bottled water in my convenient daypack.

I skirted the perimeter of what David had referred to as the Lower Town. Extensive excavation had been carried out over recent years revealing quite an elaborate complex of stone walls and building foundations that the passing centuries had buried. Gradually I worked my way over to where a series of awnings and blue tarps protected a dynamic fusion of enthusiastic chatter and business-like physical activity. David was on the look out for me and introduced me to the instructor he was working with over some electronic instrument fixed on a tripod.

"What once was is being known again," the instructor said and pointed all around the site. "Go, show your father what happens in this place."

David indicated what each student was doing at the different tables: recording, mapping, data collecting, cataloguing, even museum research on laptops. Then he got into the actual excavating. Some workers were digging methodically with handheld tools in designated areas or along stone walls. Others were working within frames marked out by lined quadrants or at tables sorting through shards. All so methodical, systematic, precise. A young woman was doing a kind of finder's dance shaking and sifting excavated material through a screen hanging from an overhead support, smiling all the while.

"Margo Sylvester?" I asked.

"Yes," David said, wiping his brow and then mine, "we'll get together later."

From the Lower Town archaeological site, I walked at a reasonable pace down to the modern town of Mykines where at the Electra, a restaurant operated by an affable couple, I slowly gorged myself on musaka and custard pie. Before bidding each other adieu, Lucy Hunter, knowing that I'd be travelling to Greece, informed me that time here, like sand in an hour glass, moved exceedingly slow. She was right, I decided, as I remained on the Electra terrasse for an extended period trying to discern any irony inherent in the buzz of the cicadas. A local bus got me back to Nafplion and some further downtime. I had at least three hours to pull myself together before David and Margo joined me, as planned, on the hotel patio.

"Yiassas," Margo Sylvester said and introduced herself. I took in bright blue eyes and a wide smile. Margo's tan was as deep as David's. He stood beside her, grinning for a moment, then pulled a couple of chairs out from the table. I saw immediately why he enjoyed her company. I would get to know her that evening as an intelligent, articulate, savvy young woman with an engaging personality. She had an obvious sense of humour and a laugh that tickled your funny bone. Admittedly, she put me in mind of Alexsis Troyes in her ability to readily engage with someone just met.

Margo adjusted the back of her denim dress and sat down on one of the chairs David had pulled out. I was impressed seeing that she did not produce a phone and place it out of dire necessity on the table in front of her and then fiddle with it.

"What will you have, Margo? Glass of wine?"

"Ouzo on ice," she said and called out to the waiter in Greek.

David would have what I was having and let the waiter know. Fix, of course. He paid up front for all the drinks. Additional glasses of water appeared on the table along with the drinks and a plate of olives and a bowl of pistachios.

"*Mezethes*," Margo explained, "snacks."

"Margo knows Greek."

"From a night course at home. Enough to communicate basic needs."

After a bit of small talk about the Greek alphabet, ouzo, the weather, and how I was getting on in the heat, David said, "Margo, tell my father about your previous experience in Greece."

"Sure," Margo said, sliding an olive pit to the side. "An 'excursion of discovery' was what Barb Carter and I called it. Barb was a fellow student."

"When was it?"

"Summertime, a year or two back. A total blast. The idea was to familiarize ourselves with the geographical areas of archaeological interest without the academic pressure. Delphi, for example. The upshot? The trip confirmed our love of the subject we hoped to take to professional levels."

At this point, Margo gave into a hearty laugh which made me smile. She sipped some ouzo, then continued her tale.

"The trip had its adventures, you know, two young females not totally familiar with local practices, especially when it came to nightlife. I suppose we were a little naïve. In Crete, we got conned into staying a night in a kind of bordello organized for the seduction and abuse of young women. Called Playpen of Paradise. It was owned by Silas Flower, the nefarious business tycoon from Bay Street who shot himself."

"I remember that," I said, nodding. "Yes, big news story at the time."

"Once Barb and I caught on, we played it cool. Kept awake all night. Early next morning we grabbed some yogurt from the kitchen and dashed out to the big entrance gate. Locked, naturally. We couldn't climb over it so we slid under it, barely. We stretched our arms through the bars to retrieve our packs and the yogurt, then hustled away. Hitchhiked back to safety."

"All's well that ends well. Isn't that how it goes?"

"One hundred percent," Margo said, and reached for another olive.

"No worries here," David said, organizing a handful of pistachios into a designed pile on the table, "all very structured and supervised."

"But mostly it's about sifting dirt and extracting treasures now, right?"

"Pretty much," Margo agreed. "But we do have our free time and our laughs, don't we, David?"

"We do. Remember, dad, it's not just about finding spearheads and jugs and cataloguing them although that *is* what's done a lot of the time."

"What we're involved in," Margo explained, "is very much about bridging archaeologically related social sciences with the humanities such as art, history and classical literature. Ancient religions and the myths have their place. Also, the sagas and the exploits of legendary characters like Agamemnon and Odysseus."

"Interesting," I said, reaching for more pistachios, the shells from which I passed across the table to David. I was very interested in what Margo had to say. She was coming across as well-informed and articulate. Her expression was energetic — when enthused about a subject and compelled to go on about it as she definitely was, she reminded me of Penny. She held your attention.

"The corrclation and integration of disciplines is very much a theme in the present project here at Mycenae and suits me perfectly. Having access to the *Centro* and all it offers is a real benefit."

When I asked what exactly the Centro was, she explained it was the summer base of field operations and research. Facilities included everything from labs and computer room to an extensive library. Then David, who was listening contentedly, said interdisciplinary collaboration was of paramount importance. It combined archaeology and ancient history.

"Right, right."

"You may have passed the Centro today," David said, "after leaving the excavation site."

"You see, Mister Canter," Margo continued, "I'm working to complete a split degree, one half being Mediterrean archaeology, the other half being Ancient Greek and Roman Studies."

"So you would be dealing with Homer's *Iliad*. What I remember most about the Trojan War was the wooden horse and breaching the wall and the soothsayer, or whatever she was, whose warnings always went unheeded."

"Cassandra." David said. "Victorious Agamemnon brought her back to Mycenae as a concubine."

"Many scholarly works have been published connecting Homeric literature and the world of Mycenae under its most famous king. Fascinating stuff. There's so much more to the literature, so much to delve into. Imaginary worlds, if you will, with roots in reality."

"I also remember Achilles, the great warrior. As a kid, David here was forever playacting Achilles with a long stick for a spear."

"I can believe that. As far as I can tell he still has imagination."

"Like father, like son," David piped in.

"Homer's *Iliad*," Margo went on, "was initially oral in its social function, you know. It is a work of the imagination largely, but it provides us with snap shots of what life was like on the Argolid plain and elsewhere during the bronze age. Playwrights of the classical period drew on the sagas and myths and legendary figures that Homer mentions. They dramatized in the great tragedies the disport of the gods and goddesses and their influence on human affairs."

"More often than not the spilling of blood resulted," David said.

"And the working out of family curses," Margo added. "A very significant theme in the old literature."

"We got to attend a production of one of the tragedies," David said, "on an excursion to Epidaurus. At night, under the stars."

"You can tell me about it over dinner. What'll it be? Something Greek."

"Anyone for fish? I know a place," David said, ready to please. "I'm up for platter of *marithia*."

"Which is what?"

"Small fish, sort of sardines. They're deep fried, like French fries. You eat every bit, head to tail. Very Greek, very tasty."

"Made to order," I said.

Margo appeared non-committal. She knitted her brow momentarily, pursed her lips, then said, "Alright. Anything once."

"Right on, Margo," David said, fitting one palm into the other. "We're off then."

Margo had shimmering, dark hair twisted in a long cascade at the back of her neck. And as we sauntered along towards this place David knew, she pulled the hair forward and with long unadorned fingers gave it a little twist. She did this a couple of times. And again, I understood perfectly David's keenness to be in her company.

Taverna Aeolus was a two-minute walk from the patio at the Hotel Orestes. Outdoor tables under colourful awnings, kitchen aromas, bouzouki music. It was early in the evening so we had the place pretty much to ourselves.

The waiter said something that sounded like Orestes and angled his head slightly. He led us to a corner table and then disappeared inside the taverna, returning shortly after with a basket of bread, a jug of cold water and three glasses that he placed in the middle of the table.

"That's the second time I heard a waiter say that. At first, I thought it had something to do with the hotel I'm staying in."

Margo said, "I think it means something like 'How can I help you?'"

In addition to the *marithia,* we ordered salad, dolmades, and a jug of house wine. Service was quick and before we could get back to Homer and company, we were digging in. David had been right, the small, deep-fried fish were like French fries: you grabbed one by the tail, and chomped away with crunchy crepitation resonating in the ears, and then grabbed another, devouring it in the same way. Well, David and I did. Margo was more restrained. She was very meticulous in stripping the head away from the body of the *marithia*. Her very studied efforts reminded me of how an archaeologist worked over a dig, carefully extracting a shard of pottery from the earth.

When the second platter of *marithia* that we ordered was finished, David looked over at the neat mound of rejected parts that Margo had accumulated in a side dish.

"Margo —"

"Yes, David?"

"Margo, can I please have your heads?"

Margo broke out laughing. She had a quick swig of wine and then slid her little dish of fish heads over to David. We all cracked up. David ate all the severed fish heads with gusto and after licking his lips he ordered another jug of house wine.

"You were going to tell me about the theatre at Epidaurus," I said. Hearing the name of the theatre made me think of Alexsis and her memories of attending plays there with her father and family.

"It's ancient," Margo said, "built into the side of a hill. A marvel."

"You have another day, Dad. Take a short side trip to see it. You won't be disappointed."

"Right. Maybe I'll do that."

"When we were there with all our group," Margo explained, "we saw a production of Sophocles' *Electra*. He based his tragedy about matricide on material from the epic cycle, the *Nostoi*. He wrote it in about 400 BCE."

"Didn't catch too much of the classical Greek that was spoken," David said, "but no matter, we knew the basic story and its themes. Justice, honour, revenge and its consequence. Time-honoured motifs. How Clytemnestra, who betrayed and murdered Agamemnon, met her fate at the hands of Orestes. I have an English translation of Sophocles' play. You'd enjoy reading it, Dad. I'll bring it to your room along with a very good reference anthology of all the myths and associated material."

"Sophocles focuses on Electra's dilemma," Margo went on to say, "whereas the earlier tragedies of Aeschylus or Euripides treat the subject in a broader way, giving play to how Orestes, knowing matricide was damnable, endured madness until he was purified."

Matricide.

It seemed relevant at this time to reveal to both David and Margo what happened the last days on the *Iphigenia*, how two murders in a family were allegedly the result of two previous murders in the same family, all the result of a tragic loss of a daughter a decade or so earlier.

A sceptical David suggested that maybe I was likely drawing on a bit of plot from one of the episodes I'd been working on that involved the husband and wife detective team. He told Margo I was a sound editor in film and television productions. He can cajole as well as the next guy, the next guy often being his father.

"Au contraire!"

I delved into all the detail, all the different personalities on the *Iphigenia* and how they clashed from time to time, all the conflicts, minor and major, Mitchell Monk versus Conrad Steele or Virgil Troyes, for instance, Boyd Alexander and his resistance to the pressure of being other than what he was, Alexsis versus the world Kat, her mother, dominated and from which her brother Forrest was banned. Unsettling for guests, I emphasized, the tension a single individual could introduce into a setting of shared expectancy, that individual being no other than Alexsis with whom I sympathized.

I stopped to take a breath. For a moment or two David and Margo registered little more than surprise, then their awe-filled expressions of incredulity filled the void that their silence had left.

Going on, I described Conrad Steele's corpse lying in a heap on the quay in all its appalling insinuation, and my impression at the time of the absolute zero of being. Did I recognize then a reflection of my own reality? I definitely did and there was nothing I could do to edit out anything extraneous to the hard, cold fact a man I was acquainted with had been brutally murdered. Patricide. The next day revealed a case of matricide. I added what Lucy Hunter and I in Paris concluded after coming to a clearer understanding of the facts. If all the material we had to consider was accurate, then Forrest and Alexsis Troyes literally got away with murder.

On the way back to the Hotel Orestes, David promised that he would get in touch with his mother and give her the lowdown on how well things had gone for us here in Nafplion. I had some reading to do before calling it a night. I perused all material in David's reference book touching on both the lead-up to the Trojan War and its aftermath, with particular emphasis on the fate of Agamemnon and his royal family. The author drew on all available sources to tell as complete a story as possible and those included variations. By two o'clock I'd gained sufficient insight into the curse of the House of Atreus. The story unfolded as follows.

In the sphere of the immortals, Eris, goddess of discord, threw a golden apple into the festivities of a wedding she was excluded from attending, the gift designed "for the fairest" of all. The selection narrowed down to three goddesses: Aphrodite, Hera, and Athena. The decision fell to Paris, prince of Troy, who judged in favour of Aphrodite having succumbed to the promise that he would possess the most beautiful woman on earth.

Enter Helen. The renowned beauty was married to Menelaus, Agamemnon's brother, under the protective assurance of the vow of Tyndareus, a one-for-all and all-for-one agreement. When a guest in the house of Menelaus, Paris broke the laws of hospitality, seduced Helen, and absconded with her back to Troy, whereupon Agamemnon called on all the lords to battle and to take back what rightfully belonged to Menelaus. A fleet of a thousand ships set out to take Troy. Winds and strong tides held the armed force back until the soothsayer Calchas concocted a plan whereby the angered goddess Artemis would be placated and allow the fleet to proceed. Agamemnon eventually gave into Calchas' scheme and sanctioned the sacrifice of his daughter Iphigenia. The evil deed caused Clytemnestra great suffering. She decried the loss of Iphigenia in such a gruesome ritual as much as she resented having been taken in by the deception that the great warrior Achilles, innocent of the machinations, would be marrying Iphigenia, the royal princess.

With Agamemnon at Troy, Mycenae was ruled by a disenchanted Clytemnestra who in the long absence of her husband had consorted with Aegisthus, cousin of Agamemnon. Princess Electra was reduced to penury and servitude, suffered indignity, and held a virtual prisoner in her own home. Her life was filled with misery and abandoned hope. Prince Orestes lived in exile, harbouring the desire to wreak revenge on a faithless mother Clytemnestra and adulterous usurper Aegisthus.

Queen Clytemnestra's resentment was boundless and lasted for ten years, the length of the Trojan War from which a triumphant Agamemnon eventually returned home, Cassandra in tow. Clytemnestra welcomed Agamemnon into the palace and murdered him, motivated by her implacable need for justice, her rationale being that he was guilty of killing their daughter, Iphigenia, and deserved to die. It was a sordid execution, Cassandra's bloodied corpse thrown upon the murdered Agamemnon. Evil begat evil.

A long suffering Electra, given to explosions of anger and resentment, prayed for the return of Orestes who, duty bound, would kill his father's killer. Following Apollo's injunction to destroy both his mother and her lover, Orestes in the company of faithful friend Pylades advanced disguised on Mycenae. Electra was onboard with plans to avenge the death of her father; the younger princess Chrysothemis was not.

The ruse employed: Orestes and Pylades offered to show the queen an urn containing Orestes' ashes — she was most willing to have proof that any threat from Orestes was eliminated. They gained access to the palace. Obeying Apollo's ruling, Orestes slaughtered Aegisthus and, despite the bite of conscience, dispatched his mother, Queen Clytemnestra. Matricide was an abhorrent act for which Orestes would be punished and he knew it; he was plagued by the Erinyes, the Furies, but after years of mad wonderings achieved purification and was released from guilt.

It was as though the events of the last days of the Triple B adventure on the *Iphigenia* guided me in pulling together a coherent, relevant, and serviceable narrative about Agamemnon's death and those that followed. The plot in a nutshell: father killed child, wife killed husband, children killed mother.

But then there was the added fact that prior to being ousted, Aegisthus murdered Atreus, Agamemnon's father, in order restore his own father Thyestes to the throne. This info left me with my head spinning. I'd gleaned sufficient background, however, to fully appreciate what Sophocles in his play *Electra* had to say.

* * *

July 29, Epidaurus —

In the morning I explored the streets and back alleys of a very engaging and historically significant Nafplion. Eventually I got around to huffing it up the nine hundred and ninety-nine steps to the Venetian-built fortress of Palamidi. Stunning panorama view of the town, the sea, the mountains beyond the distant shores, and in the foreground a sea of red poppies. I had an excellent vantage point for musing. I imagined ancient vessels pulling their way up the Argolid gulf. I visualized the return of Agamemnon after his victory in the Trojan War, riding his chariot up to and then through the Lion Gate to claim all that was his. I fantasized about warning him of the fate that lay ahead for him, but he pushed on regardless. He had, ironically, Cassandra to depend on.

In the afternoon, after munching a quick souvlaki and downing a bottle of Fix, I boarded a local bus bound for Epidaurus. For a brief while and the first in a long time, my thoughts focused on returning home. I'd get back to the Athens airport following in reverse the way I got to Nafplion. No problem. Pizza later with David was a likely bet, followed up with a summary of our day's activities. I hoped he'd bring Margo and her infectious laughter along. A week remained in their very active and productive archaeological endeavour among the ruins of Mycenae. Penny and I would welcome them both home.

From the brochure picked up at the entrance to the Sanctuary of Asclepius at Epidaurus, I read that the theatre, dedicated to the god of healing, was built in the fourth century BCE and could accommodate fourteen hundred spectators and do so in an aesthetically pleasing, beautifully symmetrical alignment of seats. A wonder of classical architectural engineering, the theatre was reputed to have both perfect viewing and perfect acoustics. Thousands visited the site annually. I was just one of hundreds scrambling about, exploring different areas of the theatre. I was up, I was down, and then I was up again sitting strategically on the uppermost tier, hearing distinctly the words a young woman down in the circular area of the orchestra was directing to her companion sitting a few metres along from me. "Out damned spot, out I say..." The companion raised a thumb, then went down to join his mate.

And again, I thought of Alexsis and her recollection of sitting here under the star-filled sky, not understanding the language spoken and yet fulfilled somehow, knowing the meaning of the story that was unfolding in rather dramatic fashion.

I pulled from my daypack a bottle of water and David's English translation of Sophocles' *Electra*. The rest of the afternoon at my discretion, I began to read, vowing to finish the play before leaving the theatre. I kept my vow, challenged in the reading to determine what kind of woman would want to murder her mother. Sophocles paints Electra as a mess of morals and motivations. Her complaints are many, her dirges endless. Above all, she is motivated by the power of hate, absolute in her need to avenge the death of her father Agamemnon. She dismisses the Choral warning that her destruction will be self-inflicted. The rhythm of the play's poetic lines swept me along to the inevitable conclusion, the bloody execution of Clytemnestra and Aegisthus by the hand of Orestes and the impassioned will of Electra. The Chorus calls it the way it is: blood will have blood.

Although Sophocles does not reach beyond the execution of a faithless mother and her scheming paramour, would Electra, I pondered, like Orestes, go mad? Would she need to seek absolution and be healed by divine decree? Or would bloody revenge be healing enough?

I closed the book and began my descent back to the world of bus rides and other practical considerations.

Epilogue

My flight home is nine hours long. The movie I've been watching concludes with the culprit being cuffed by his worthy nemesis. So inspired, the mid-Atlantic reverie continues as I contemplate the varied roles professional actors assume, comic, tragic, anything in between. They enter your life through the silver screen or via contemporary digital outlets with the simplest of finger controls. Their notoriety will eventually fade into the curated cans of past successful productions but the characters they made famous will not. Indeed, they may have aged, but you see them in some film from a decade ago or from back in the years before the Y2K paranoia or the 9/11 catastrophe, and you say, right, right, I remember. Superb editing. Totally satisfactory resolution. Great acting.

On the tail of that recollection, questions arise in the private head space that imagination in flight leaves open to interpretation. How much acting was involved in the events that we on the *Iphigenia* bore witness to? Real people, real conflicts, real deaths viewed, at least in my case, against an epic backdrop. Of paramount consideration in understanding the absolute meaning of events is what the perspicacious Lucy Hunter alluded to as the many-layered story of family strife and dysfunction. Prompted once again by what she was inclined to read symbolically, I move what were connected real time actions into the realm of allegory to make better sense of them. There lies a thematic nugget of meaning in the heart of the narrative that ties all the factors into a unified whole. Establishing truth requires decoding the various enigmatic elements. Therefore again, why dump Conrad's corpse into the canal? How does that relate to the two pennies found on his body? Do the pennies have a bearing on what Alexsis said about how fate and premeditation played into Conrad's not being ferried to the other side in a manner commensurate with his station in life? Was she being ironic? What is the significance of the jug at the scene of Kat's death? Its cork top floating next to the dead and deeply departed Conrad? Two parts of a single meaning? How revealing was the phoenix effect in that regard? Was cutting off the finger to get the ring an ironic and symbolic severing of their hated marriage? Was what was done therefore undone? Lucy's insight again: paradoxically, knowing the story of Alexsis and her designs was like attending to tragic events uncovered from the ashes of time, from long before we settled on the superiority of a single deity.

What if Alexsis' mad brother Forrest, like legendary Orestes, really were mad? What if, when all the sifting was done, Alexsis Troyes, like Electra the obsessed daughter of Agamemnon, were to suffer a similar fate? Or was her active involvement in the execution of *lex talionis* that saw to the demise of her insufferable mother sufficient to release her from a lifetime of suffering and lament? Was it enough for her to conclude that finally blood did have blood? Time, I decided, would be the final arbiter. Time beyond my need, or indeed my ability, to influence in any way.

And a little further across the Atlantic, I visualize a frieze dramatizing the doings of the Troyes family, carved with precision and aesthetic understanding, a frieze worthy of a place, if not on the Parthenon or in the Louvre's *Galerie des Antiques,* then in the collective imagination.

The End

Reed Stirling lives in Cowichan Bay, BC, and writes fiction when not painting landscapes, or travelling, or taking coffee at The Drumroaster, a local café where physics and metaphysics clash daily.

Shades Of Persephone, published in 2019, is a literary mystery set in Greece.

Lighting The Lamp, a fictional memoir, was published in March 2020.

Set in Montreal, *Séjour Saint-Louis (2021)*, dramatizes family conflicts, specifically father-son.

Reed Stirling's shorter work has appeared over the years in a variety of publications.

www.ingramcontent.com/pod-product-compliance
Lightning Source LLC
Chambersburg PA
CBHW070107120726
47909CB00002B/523